TRIUMPH OF THE NIGHT

BOOKS BY ROBERT PHILLIPS

Poetry
Inner Weather
The Pregnant Man
Running on Empty
Personal Accounts: New & Selected Poems
The Wounded Angel

Fiction
The Land of Lost Content

Criticism & Biography
Denton Welch
William Goyen
The Confessional Poets

Anthologies
Aspects of Alice: Lewis Carroll's Dreamchild
Moonstruck: An Anthology of Lunar Poetry
Triumph of the Night: Tales of Terror and the
Supernatural by 20th century literary masters.

Editions
Letters of Delmore Schwartz
Last & Lost Poems of Delmore Schwartz
The Ego Is Always at the Wheel: Bagatelles by
Delmore Schwartz
The Stories of Denton Welch
Collected Stories of Noel Coward

TRIUMPH OF THE NIGHT

TALES OF TERROR AND THE SUPERNATURAL BY 20TH CENTURY MASTERS

EDITED BY ROBERT PHILLIPS

Carroll & Graf Publishers, Inc.
New York

First Carroll & Graf edition 1989

Carroll & Graf Publishers, Inc.
260 Fifth Avenue
New York, NY 10001

Triumph of the night : Tales of terror and the supernatural by 20th
century literary masters / edited by Robert Phillips.
    p.   cm.
  ISBN 0–88184–517–5 : $18.95
  1. Ghost stories, English. 2. Ghost stories, American. 3. English
fiction—20th century. 4. American fiction—20th century. I. Phillips,
Robert S.
PR1308.G5T75   1989
823'.0873308—dc20   89–30469
                                                               CIP

Text Design: Terry McCabe

Manufactured in the United States of America

Contents

Acknowledgments

Every effort has been made to contact copyright holders. In the event of inadvertent omissions or errors, the editor should be notified at Wieser & Wieser, Inc., 118 East 25th Street, New York, NY 10010.

For permission to reprint the stories in this anthology, grateful acknowledgment is made to:

Alfred A. Knopf, Inc., for *The Celestial Omnibus* by E. M. Forster, from *The Collected Tales of E. M. Forster,* © 1947; and *The Demon Lover* by Elizabeth Bowen, from *The Collected Stories of Elizabeth Bowen,* © 1981; and *The Indian* by John Updike from *The Music School,* © 1966.

Clarkson N Potter, Inc., for *Ghost and Flesh, Water and Dirt* by William Goyen from *Had I a Hundred Mouths,* © 1985.

Doubleday & Company for *First Dark* by Elizabeth Spencer, from *The Stories of Elizabeth Spencer,* © 1981.

E. P. Dutton for *Full Circle* by Denton Welch, from *The Stories of Denton Welch,* © 1986; and *The Portobello Road* by Muriel Spark, from *The Stories of Muriel Spark,* © 1985.

The Ecco Press for *The Others* from *The Assignation and Other Stories* by Joyce Carol Oates, © 1988.

Farrar, Straus & Giroux, for *The Daemon Lover* by Shirley Jackson from *The Lottery,* © 1949.

The Triumph of the Night

Harcourt, Brace, Jovanovich for *A Haunted House* by Virginia Woolf, from *A Haunted House and Other Short Stories,* © 1949 by Leonard Woolf.

Harper & Row Publishers, Inc., for *I Used to Live Here Once* by Jean Rhys, from *Sleep it Off, Lady,* © 1976; and *Sound is Second Sight* by Lynne Sharon Schwartz from *Acquainted With The Night* © 1984.

Houghton Mifflin Company for *The Prison Window* by Louis Auchincloss from *Second Chance,* © 1970. Reprinted by permission of the author; and *Missing Person* by Peter Taylor, from *Presences,* © 1973. Reprinted by permission of the author.

The Hogarth Press Ltd., for *Andrina* by George MacKay Brown, from *Andrina and Other Stories,* © 1983.

Malzberg, Barry N, for *Away* © by the author.

New Directions Publishing Corp., for *The Followers* by Dylan Thomas, from *The Collected Stories of Dylan Thomas,* © 1984; and *The Mysteries of the Joy Rio* by Tennessee Williams, from *Collected Stories,* © 1985.

Random House, Inc., for *Miriam* by Truman Capote, from *A Tree of Night,* © 1949; and *Up North* by Mavis Gallant, from *Home Truths,* © 1981.

Russell, Howard Lewis, for *The Wedding Cake Couple,* © 1986 by the author.

Charles Scribner's Sons, for *The Jolly Corner* by Henry James, from Vol XVII of *The New York Edition of Henry James,* 1909; and *Afterward* by Edith Wharton, from *The Short Stories of Edith Wharton,* © 1931, by permission of Watkins/Loomis Agency.

Society of Authors Representatives for the Literary Trustees of Walter de la Mare for *Seaton's Aunt.*

Viking Press, for *A Little Place off the Edgware Road* by Graham Greene from *The Collected Stories of Graham Greene,* © 1972.

The Yellow Wallpaper by Charlotte Perkins Gilman first appeared in *The New England Magazine,* 1892.

The Bell in the Fog by Gertrude Atherton is from *The Bell in the Fog and Other Stories,* 1905.

The title of this anthology is taken from a story by Edith Wharton.

FOR LOUISA BAUR
AND TO THE MEMORY OF
JOHN I.H. BAUR

We ask only to be reassured
About the noises in the cellar
And the window that should not have been open.
      T.S. Eliot, THE FAMILY REUNION

INTRODUCTION

First, a word about what this book is not. It is not a collection of the best 20th-century ghost stories, and for several reasons.

There already have been scores of anthologies of ghost stories, some of which include 20th-century writing. But invariably, many of the same names and even the same stories crop up. I deliberately have excluded from this book those many would expect to find. You will look in vain for Wilkie Collins, Algernon Blackwood, H. P. Lovecraft, Ambrose Bierce, M.R. James, H. G. Wells, E. F. Benson, Cynthia Asquith, Rosemary Timperley, August Derleth, Sir Arthur Conan Doyle, Marjorie Bowen, Oliver Onions, J. Sheridan le Fanu, and their ilk. They are, or were, professional ghost story writers, and devoted themselves almost exclusively to the genre. Their best works have by now become war-horses.

Rather, I have chosen ghost stories by writers that many readers probably did not know wrote ghost stories. I hope that even devotees of the genre will encounter some surprises here. Who would have thought, for instance, that Truman Capote wrote them? Or Graham Greene? Or Tennessee Williams? (Williams even wrote ghost plays. At least, his late production, *Clothes for a Summer Hotel*, was a ghost play, and part of the audience's confusion and lack of sympathy with it was because they failed to comprehend that the characters onstage were intended as the ghosts of F. Scott and Zelda Fitzgerald and Ernest Hemingway.)

1

Secondly, I have restricted myself to stories written in the English language. I regret omitting favorites by Thomas Mann, Ilse Achinger, Jorge Luis Broges and others, but the result would have been too large a volume. United Kingdom spelling and punctuation have been left as in the original.

In making my selection, my criterion was excellence first, and subject second. Far too many stories or poems are anthologized because they happen to be on the right subject for a themed anthology. With certain writers, selection was difficult—because they wrote a number of first-rate ghost stories. The reader may be surprised not to find Henry James' *The Turn of the Screw*. To be sure, it is one of James' consummate ghostly tales, if not the consummate. But it is readily available in many editions and most people interested in the ghost story already know it by heart. I have chosen instead my favorite of James' numerous ghost stories, *The Jolly Corner*, in which the protagonist encounters the ghost of the self he himself might have become. (It is a theme explored by Peter Taylor as well. For some reason, whenever story-teller Taylor writes a ghost story, it is cast into play form.) Other fine James ghost tales I might have included are *The Friends of the Friends* and *Sir Edmund Orme*.

Edith Wharton poses a similar problem. I have included *Afterward*, but Mrs. Wharton's *The Eyes*, and *All Souls* and *Pomegranate Seed*, may well be equally fine.

That splendid Anglo-Irish writer, Elizabeth Bowen, caused me loss of sleep, and not just because of the terrifying nature of her stores, especially *The Demon Lover*. For some time I was unable to choose between this and at least six others: *The Cat Jumps, Sunday Afternoon, The Cheery Soul, The Happy Autumn Fields, Pink May,* and *Green Holly*.

I'm quite certain I selected the correct Muriel Spark story. But readers should also become acquainted with her *The Leaf Sweeper* and *The Executor*. The late William Goyen, one of this country's most underrated writers, populated many of his stories with ghosts. In addition to the one included here, two of my favorites are *A Shape of Light* and *Bridge of Music, River of Sand*.

In all, I have included twenty-seven stories, with the aim of promoting a balanced spectrum of male and female writers.

The majority are by Americans and English writers, though Canadian, Welsh, Irish, and Scottish writers also are represented. Some were born in the last century; the majority were not. They range from the Master (Henry James) to a young writer still in his mid-twenties (Howard Lewis Russell). What they all have in common, almost without exception, is a vision of ghosts as projections of a protagonist's anxious state—ghosts of the mind. In the 20th-century ghost tale there are no clanking chains and howling demons. The horror comes from what James called "the terror of the usual." By and large these ghosts walk in daylight, and appear in places where ghosts are not expected, such as behind the wheel of a car or at a flea market. The writers achieve their effects by introducing the otherworldly in worldly settings.

There are certain recurring themes in 20th-century ghost stories—haunted houses and rooms (Woolf and Gilman), demon lovers (Bowen and Jackson) demon animals (Schwartz), special children (Atherton, Capote, and Spencer), children's visions (Forster and Gallant), ghosts of the self (James and Taylor), first wives (Wharton, and Ellen Glasgow, in *The Past*, a story far too long to include here), special missions (Greene and Welch), revenge (Auchincloss and Wharton), guilt (Updike), and love from beyond (Goyen and George Mackay Brown).

Originally I thought to arrange the book in sections by theme. But ultimately I realized this tipped the authors' hands in several cases, ruining surprise and impact. Instead, they are presented in an order the logic of which is known only by me. There are stories that will make your flesh creep. But they will also enlarge your horizon and introduce you to a few writers you had not previously read.

ROBERT PHILLIPS
Katonah, New York
September, 1989

THE

DEMON

LOVER

Elizabeth Bowen

Towards the end of her day in London Mrs Drover went round to her shut-up house to look for several things she wanted to take away. Some belonged to herself, some to her family, who were by now used to their country life. It was late August; it had been a steamy, showery day: at the moment the trees down the pavement glittered in an escape of humid yellow afternoon sun. Against the next batch of clouds, already piling up ink-dark, broken chimneys and parapets stood out. In her once familiar street, as in any unused channel, an unfamiliar queerness had silted up; a cat wove itself in and out of railings, but no human eye watched Mrs Drover's return. Shifting some parcels under her arm, she slowly forced round her latchkey in an unwilling lock, then gave the door, which had warped, a push with her knee. Dead air came out to meet her as she went in.

The suitcase window having been boarded up, no light came down into the hall. But one door, she could just see, stood ajar, so she went quickly through into the room and unshuttered the big window in there. Now the prosaic woman, looking about her, was more perplexed than she knew by everything that she saw, by traces of her long former habit of life—the yellow smoke-stain up the white marble mantelpiece, the ring left by a vase on the top of the escritoire; the bruise in the wallpaper where, on the door being thrown open widely, the china handle had always hit the wall. The piano, having gone away to be stored, had left what looked like claw-marks on its part of

4

the parquet. Though not much dust had seeped in, each object wore a film of another kind; and, the only ventilation being the chimney, the whole drawing-room smelled of the cold hearth. Mrs Drover put down her parcels on the escritoire and left the room to proceed upstairs; the things she wanted were in a bedroom chest.

She had been anxious to see how the house was—the part-time caretaker she shared with some neighbours was away this week on his holiday, known to be not yet back. At the best of times he did not look in often, and she was never sure that she trusted him. There were some cracks in the structure, left by the last bombing on which she was anxious to keep an eye. Not that one could do anything—

A shaft of refracted daylight now lay across the hall. She stopped dead and stared at the hall table—on this lay a letter addressed to her.

She thought first—then the caretaker *must* be back. All the same, who, seeing the house shuttered, would have dropped a letter in at the box? It was not a circular, it was not a bill. And the post office redirected, to the address in the country, everything for her that came through the post. The caretaker (even if he *were* back) did not know she was due in London today—her call here had been planned to be a surprise—so his negligence in the manner of this letter, leaving it to wait in the dusk and the dust, annoyed her. Annoyed, she picked up the letter which bore no stamp. But it cannot be important, or they would know . . . She took the letter rapidly upstairs with her, without a stop to look at the writing till she reached what had been her bedroom, where she let in light. The room looked over the garden and other gardens: the sun had gone in; as the clouds sharpened and lowered, the trees and rank lawns seemed already to smoke with dark. Her reluctance to look again at the letter came from the fact that she felt intruded upon—and by someone contemptuous of her ways. However, in the tense-ness preceding the fall of rain she read it: it was a few lines.

Dear Kathleen: You will not have forgotten that today is our anniversary, and the day we said. The years have gone by at once slowly and fast. In view of the fact that nothing has changed, I shall rely upon you to keep your promise. I was sorry to see you leave London, but was satisfied that you

would be back in time. You may expect me, therefore, at the
hour arranged. Until then . . .

K.

Mrs Drover looked for the date: it was today's. She dropped
the letter on to the bed-springs, then picked it up to see the
writing again—her lips, beneath the remains of lipstick, beginning to go white. She felt so much the change in her own face
that she went to the mirror, polished a clear patch in it and
looked at once urgently and stealthily in. She was confronted
by a woman of forty-four, with eyes staring out under a hat-
brim that had been rather carelessly pulled down. She had not
put on any more powder since she left the shop where she ate
her solitary tea. The pearls her husband had given her on their
marriage hung loose round her now rather thinner throat,
slipping in the V of the pink wool jumper her sister knitted last
autumn as they sat round the fire. Mrs Drover's most normal
expression was one of controlled worry, but of assent. Since the
birth of the third of her little boys, attended by a quite serious
illness, she had had an intermittent muscular flicker to the left
of her mouth, but in spite of this she could always sustain a
manner that was at once energetic and calm.

Turning from her own face as precipitately as she had gone
to meet it, she went to the chest where the things were,
unlocked it, threw up the lid and knelt to search. But as rain
began to come crashing down she could not keep from looking
over her shoulder at the stripped bed on which the letter lay.
Behind the blanket of rain the clock of the church that still
stood struck six—with rapidly heightening apprehension she
counted each of the slow strokes. 'The hour arranged . . . My
God,' she said, '*what* hour? How should I . . . ? After twenty-
five years . . .'

The young girl talking to the soldier in the garden had not ever
completely seen his face. It was dark; they were saying goodbye under a tree. Now and then—for it felt, from not seeing
him at this intense moment, as though she had never seen him
at all—she verified his presence for these few moments longer
by putting out a hand, which he each time pressed, without
very much kindness, and painfully, on to one of the breast
buttons of his uniform. That cut of the button on the palm of

her hand was, principally, what she was to carry away. This was so near the end of a leave from France that she could only wish him already gone. It was August 1916. Being not kissed, being drawn away from and looked at intimidated Kathleen till she imagined spectral glitters in the place of his eyes. Turning away and looking back up the lawn she saw, through branches of trees, the drawing-room window alight: she caught a breath for the moment when she could go running back there into the safe arms of her mother and sister, and cry: 'What shall I do, what shall I do? He has gone.'

Hearing her catch her breath, her fiancé said, without feeling: 'Cold?'

'You're going away such a long way.'

'Not so far as you think.'

'I don't understand?'

'You don't have to,' he said. 'You will. You know what we said.'

'But that was—suppose you—I mean, suppose.'

'I shall be with you,' he said, 'sooner or later. You won't forget that. You need do nothing but wait.'

Only a little more than a minute later she was free to run up the silent lawn. Looking in through the window at her mother and sister, who did not for the moment perceive her, she already felt that unnatural promise drive down between her and the rest of all human kind. No other way of having given herself could have made her feel so apart, lost and foresworn. She could not have plighted a more sinister troth.

Kathleen behaved well when, some months later, her fiancé was reported missing, presumed killed. Her family not only supported her but were able to praise her courage without stint because they could not regret, as a husband for her, the man they knew almost nothing about. They hoped she would, in a year or two, console herself—and had it been only a question of consolation things might have gone much straighter ahead. But her trouble, behind just a little grief, was a complete dislocation from everything. She did not reject other lovers, for these failed to appear: for years she failed to attract men—and with the approach of her 'thirties she became natural enough to share her family's anxiousness on this score. She began to put herself out, to wonder; and at thirty-two she was very greatly relieved to find herself being courted by William Drover. She married him, and the two of them settled down in this quiet, aboreal part of Kensington: in this house the years piled up, her children were born and they all lived till they were driven out by the bombs of the next war. Her movements as Mrs Drover were circumscribed, and she dismissed any idea that they were still watched.

As things were—dead or living—the letter-writer sent her only a threat. Unable, for some minutes, to go on kneeling with her back exposed to the empty room, Mrs Drover rose from the chest to sit on an upright chair whose back was firmly against the wall. The desuetude of her former bedroom, her married London home's whole air of being a cracked cup from which memory, with its reassuring power, had either evaporated or leaked away, made a crisis—and at just this crisis the letter-writer had, knowledgeably, struck. The hollowness of the house this evening cancelled years on years of voices, habits, and steps. Through the shut windows she only heard rain fall on the roofs around. To rally herself, she said she was in a mood—and for two or three seconds shutting her eyes, told herself that she had imagined the letter. But she opened them—there it lay on the bed.

On the supernatural side of the letter's entrance she was not permitting her mind to dwell. Who, in London, knew she meant to call at the house today? Evidently, however, this had been known. The caretaker, *had* he come back, had had no cause to expect her: he would have taken the letter in his pocket, to forward it, at his own time, through the post. There was no other sign that the caretaker had been in—but, if not? Letters dropped in at doors of deserted houses do not fly or walk to tables in halls. They do not sit on the dust of empty tables with the air of certainty that they will be found. There is needed some human hand—but nobody but the caretaker had a key. Under circumstances she did not care to consider, a house can be entered without a key. It was possible that she was not alone now. She might be being waited for, downstairs. Waited for—until when? Until 'the hour arranged.' At least that was not six o'clock: six has struck.

She rose from the chair and went over and locked the door.

The thing was, to get out. To fly? No, not that: she had to catch her train. As a woman whose utter dependability was the keystone of her family life she was not willing to return to the country, to her husband, her little boys and her sister, without the objects she had come up to fetch. Resuming work at the chest she set about making up a number of parcels in a rapid, fumbling-decisive way. These, with her shopping parcels, would be too much to carry; these meant a taxi—at the thought of the taxi her heart went up and her normal breathing resumed. I will ring up the taxi now; the taxi cannot come too soon: I shall hear the taxi out there running its engine, till I walk calmly down to it through the hall. I'll ring up—But no: the telephone is cut off . . . She tugged at a knot she had tied wrong.

The idea of flight . . . He was never kind to me, not really. I don't remember him kind at all. Mother said he never considered me. He was set on me, that was what it was—not love. Not love, not meaning a person well. What did he do, to make me promise like that? I can't remember—But she found that she could.

She remembered with such dreadful acuteness that the twenty-five years since then dissolved like smoke and she instinctively looked for the weal left by the button on the palm of her hand. She remembered not only all that he said and did but the complete suspension of *her* existence during that August week. I was not myself—they all told me so at the time. She remembered—but with one white burning blank as where acid has dropped on a photograph: *under no conditions* could she remember his face.

So, wherever he may be waiting, I shall not know him. You have no time to run from a face you do not expect.

The thing was to get to the taxi before any clock struck what could be the hour. She would slip down the street and round the side of the square to where the square gave on the main road. She would return in the taxi, safe, to her own door, and bring the solid driver into the house with her to pick up the parcels from room to room. The idea of the taxi driver made her decisive, bold: she unlocked her door, went to the top of the staircase and listened down.

She heard nothing—but while she was hearing nothing the *passé* air of the staircase was disturbed by a draught that travelled up to her face. It emanated from the basement: down there a door or window was being opened by someone who chose this moment to leave the house.

The rain had stopped; the pavements steamily shone as Mrs

Drover let herself out by inches from her own front door into the empty street. The unoccupied houses opposite continued to meet her look with their damaged stare. Making towards the thoroughfare and the taxi, she tried not to keep looking behind. Indeed, the silence was so intense—one of those creeks of London silence exaggerated this summer by the damage of war—that no tread could have gained on hers unheard. Where her street debouched on the square where people went on living, she grew conscious of, and checked, her unnatural pace. Across the open end of the square two buses impassively passed each other: women, a perambulator, cyclists, a man wheeling a barrow signalized, once again, the ordinary flow of life. At the square's most populous corner should be—and was—the short taxi rank. This evening, only one taxi—but this, although it presented its blank rump, appeared already to be alertly waiting for her. Indeed, without looking round the driver started his engine as she panted up from behind and put her hand on the door. As she did so, the clock struck seven. The taxi faced the main road: to make the trip back to her house it would have to turn—she had settled back on the seat and the taxi *had* turned before she, surprised by its knowing movement, recollected that she had not 'said where.' She leaned forward to scratch at the glass panel that divided the driver's head from her own.

The driver braked to what was almost a stop, turned round and slid the glass panel back: the jolt of this flung Mrs Drover forward till her face was almost into the glass. Through the aperture driver and passenger, not six inches between them, remained for an eternity eye to eye. Mrs Drover's mouth hung open for some seconds before she could issue her first scream. After that she continued to scream freely and to beat with her gloved hands on the glass all round as the taxi, accelerating without mercy, made off with her into the hinterland of deserted streets.

A LITTLE PLACE
OFF THE
EDGWARE ROAD

Graham Greene

Craven came up past the Achilles statue in the thin summer rain. It was only just after lighting-up time, but already the cars were lined up all the way to the Marble Arch, and the sharp acquisitive faces peered out ready for a good time with anything possible which came along. Craven went bitterly by with the collar of his mackintosh tight round his throat: it was one of his bad days.

All the way up the Park he was reminded of passion, but you needed money for love. All that a poor man could get was lust. Love needed a good suit, a car, a flat somewhere, or a good hotel. It needed to be wrapped in cellophane. He was aware all the time of the stringy tie beneath the mackintosh, and the frayed sleeves: he carried his body about with him like something he hated. (There were moments of happiness in the British Museum reading-room, but the body called him back.) He bore, as his only sentiment, the memory of ugly deeds committed on park chairs. People talked as if the body died too soon—that wasn't the trouble, to Craven, at all. The body kept alive—and through the glittering tinselly rain, on his way to a rostrum, passed a little man in a black suit carrying a banner, 'The Body shall rise again.' He remembered a dream he had three times woken trembling from: he had been alone in the huge dark cavernous burying ground of all the world. Every grave was connected to another under the ground: the globe was honeycombed for the sake of the dead, and on each occasion of dreaming he had discovered anew the horrifying fact

11

that the body doesn't decay. There are no worms and dissolution. Under the ground the world was littered with masses of dead flesh ready to rise again with their warts and boils and eruptions. He had lain in bed and remembered—as 'tidings of great joy'—that the body after all was corrupt.

He came up into the Edgware Road walking fast—the Guardsmen were out in couples, great languid elongated beasts—the bodies like worms in their tight trousers. He hated them, and hated his hatred because he knew what it was, envy. He was aware that every one of them had a better body than himself: indigestion creased his stomach: he felt sure that his breath was foul—but who could he ask? Sometimes he secretly touched himself here and there with scent: it was one of his ugliest secrets. Why should he be asked to believe in the resurrection of this body he wanted to forget? Sometimes he prayed at night (a hint of religious belief was lodged in his breast like a worm in a nut) that *his* body at any rate should never rise again.

He knew all the side streets round the Edgware Road only too well: when a mood was on, he simply walked until he tired, squinting at his own image in the windows of Salmon & Gluckstein and the ABCs. So he noticed at once the posters outside the disused theatre in Culpar Road. They were not unusual, for sometimes Barclays Bank Dramatic Society would hire the place for an evening—or an obscure film would be trade-shown there. The theatre had been built in 1920 by an optimist who thought the cheapness of the site would more than counter-balance its disadvantages of lying a mile outside the conventional theatre zone. But no play had ever succeeded, and it was soon left to gather rat-holes and spider-webs. The covering of the seats was never renewed, and all that ever happened to the place was the temporary false life of an amateur play or a trade show.

Craven stopped and read—there were still optimists it appeared, even in 1939, for nobody but the blindest optimist could hope to make money out of the place as 'The Home of the Silent Film.' The first season of 'primitives' was announced (a high-brow phrase): there would never be a second. Well, the seats were cheap, and it was perhaps worth a shilling to him, now that he was tired, to get in somewhere out of the rain. Craven bought a ticket and went in to the darkness of the stalls.

In the dead darkness a piano tinkled something monotonously recalling Mendelssohn: he sat down in a gangway seat,
and could immediately feel the emptiness all round him. No,
there would never be another season. On the screen a large
woman in a kind of toga wrung her hands, then wobbled with
curious jerky movements towards a couch. There she sat and
stared out like a sheep-dog distractedly through her loose and
black and stringy hair. Sometimes she seemed to dissolve
altogether into dots and flashes and wiggly lines. A sub-title
said, 'Pompilia betrayed by her beloved Augustus seeks an end
to her troubles.'

Craven began at last to see—a dim waste of stalls. There
were not twenty people in the place—a few couples whispering
with their heads touching, and a number of lonely men like
himself wearing the same uniform of the cheap mackintosh.
They lay about at intervals like corpses—and again Craven's
obsession returned: the tooth-ache of horror. He thought
miserably—I am going mad: other people don't feel like this.
Even a disused theatre reminded him of those interminable
caverns where the bodies were waiting for resurrection.

'A slave to his passion Augustus calls for yet more wine.'

A gross middle-aged Teutonic actor lay on an elbow with his
arm round a large woman in a shift. The Spring Song tinkled
ineptly on, and the screen flickered like indigestion. Somebody
felt his way through the darkness, scrabbling past Craven's
knees—a small man: Craven experienced the unpleasant feeling of a large beard brushing his mouth. Then there was a long
sigh as the newcomer found the next chair, and on the screen
events had moved with such rapidity that Pompilia had already
stabbed herself—or so Craven supposed—and lay still and
buxom among her weeping slaves.

A low breathless voice sighed out close to Craven's ear:
'What's happened? Is she asleep?'

'No. Dead.'

'Murdered?' the voice asked with a keen interest.

'I don't think so. Stabbed herself.'

Nobody said 'Hush': nobody was enough interested to object
to a voice: they drooped among the empty chairs in attitudes of
weary inattention.

The film wasn't nearly over yet: there were children somehow to be considered: was it all going on to a second genera-

tion? But the small bearded man in the next seat seemed to be interested only in Pompilia's death. The fact that he had come in at that moment apparently fascinated him. Craven heard the word 'coincidence' twice, and he went on talking to himself about it in low out-of-breath tones. 'Absurd when you come to think of it,' and then 'no blood at all.' Craven didn't listen: he sat with his hands clasped between his knees, facing the fact as he had faced it so often before, that he was in danger of going mad. He had to pull himself up, take a holiday, see a doctor (God knew what infection moved in his veins). He became aware that his bearded neighbour had addressed him directly. 'What?' he asked impatiently, 'what did you say?'

'There would be more blood than you can imagine.'

'What are you talking about?'

When the man spoke to him, he sprayed him with damp breath. There was a little bubble in his speech like an impediment. He said, 'When you murder a man . . .'

'This was a woman,' Craven said impatiently.

'That wouldn't make any difference.'

'And it's got nothing to do with murder anyway.'

'That doesn't signify.' They seemed to have got into an absurd and meaningless wrangle in the dark.

'I know, you see,' the little bearded man said in a tone of enormous conceit.

'Know what?'

'About such things,' he said with guarded ambiguity.

Craven turned and tried to see him clearly. Was he mad? Was this a warning of what he might become—babbling incomprehensibly to strangers in cinemas? He thought, By God, no, trying to see: I'll be sane yet. I *will* be sane. He could make out nothing but a small black hump of body. The man was talking to himself again. He said, 'Talk. Such talk. They'll say it was all for fifty pounds. But that's a lie. Reasons and reasons. They always take the first reason. Never look behind. Thirty years of reasons. Such simpletons,' he added again in that tone of breathless and unbounded conceit. So this was madness. So long as he could realize that, he must be sane himself—relatively speaking. Not so sane perhaps as the seekers in the park or the Guardsmen in the Edgware Road, but saner than this. It was like a message of encouragement as the piano tinkled on.

Then again the little man turned and sprayed him. 'Killed herself, you say? But who's to know that? It's not a mere question of what hand holds the knife.' He laid a hand suddenly and confidingly on Craven's: it was damp and sticky. Craven said with horror as a possible meaning came to him: 'What are you talking about?'

'I know,' the little man said. 'A man in my position gets to know almost everything.'

'What is your position?' Craven said, feeling the sticky hand on his, trying to make up his mind whether he was being hysterical or not—after all, there were a dozen explanations—it might be treacle.

'A pretty desperate one *you'd* say.' Sometimes the voice almost died in the throat altogether. Something incomprehensible had happened on the screen—take your eyes from these early pictures for a moment and the plot had proceeded on at such a pace . . . Only the actors moved slowly and jerkily. A young woman in a nightdress seemed to be weeping in the arms of a Roman centurion: Craven hadn't seen either of them before. '*I am not afraid of death, Lucius—in your arms.*'

The little man began to titter—knowingly. He was talking to himself again. It would have been easy to ignore him altogether if it had not been for those sticky hands which he now removed: he seemed to be fumbling at the seat in front of him. His head had a habit of lolling suddenly sideways—like an idiot child's. He said distinctly and irrelevantly: 'Bayswater Tragedy.'

'What was that?' Craven said sharply. He had seen those words on a poster before he entered the park.

'What?'

'About the tragedy.'

'To think they call Cullen Mews Bayswater.' Suddenly the little man began to cough—turning his face towards Craven and coughing right at him: it was like vindictiveness. The voice said brokenly, 'Let me see. My umbrella.' He was getting up.

'You didn't have an umbrella.'

'My umbrella,' he repeated. 'My—' and seemed to lose the word altogether. He went scrabbling out past Craven's knees.

Craven let him go, but before he had reached the billowy dusty curtains of the Exit the screen went blank and bright—the film had broken, and somebody immediately turned up one dirt-choked chandelier above the circle. It shone down just enough for Craven to see the smear on his hands. This wasn't hysteria: this was a fact. He wasn't mad: he had sat next a madman who in some mews—what was the name Colon, Collin . . . Craven jumped up and made his own way out: the black curtain flapped in his mouth. But he was too late: the man had gone and there were three turnings to choose from. He chose instead a telephone-box and dialled with an odd sense for him of sanity and decision 999.

It didn't take two minutes to get the right department. They were interested and very kind. Yes, there had been a murder in a mews—Cullen Mews. A man's neck had been cut from ear to ear with a bread knife—a horrid crime. He began to tell them how he had sat next the murderer in a cinema: it couldn't be anyone else: there was blood now on his hands—and he remembered with repulsion as he spoke the damp beard. There must have been a terrible lot of blood. But the voice from the Yard interrupted him. 'Oh no,' it was saying, 'we have the murderer—no doubt of it at all. It's the body that's disappeared.'

Craven put down the receiver. He said to himself aloud, 'Why should this happen to *me?* Why to *me?*' He was back in the horror of his dream—the squalid darkening street outside was only one of the innumerable tunnels connecting grave to grave where the imperishable bodies lay. He said, 'It was a dream, a dream,' and leaning forward he saw in the mirror above the telephone his own face sprinkled by tiny drops of blood like dew from a scent-spray. He began to scream, 'I won't go mad. I won't go mad. I'm sane. I won't go mad.' Presently a little crowd began to collect, and soon a policeman came.

THE

OTHERS

Joyce Carol Oates

Early one evening in a crowd of people, most of them commuters, he happened to see, quite by accident—he'd taken a slightly different route that day, having left the building in which he worked by an entrance he rarely used—and this, as he'd recall afterward, with the fussy precision which had characterized him since childhood, and helped to account for his success in his profession, because there was renovation being done in the main lobby—a man he had not seen in years, or was it decades: a face teasingly familiar, yet made strange by time, like an old photograph about to disintegrate into its elements.

Spence followed the man into the street, into a blowsy damp dusk, but did not catch up to him and introduce himself: that wasn't his way. He was certain he knew the man, and that the man knew him, but how, or why, or from what period in his life the man dated, he could not have said. Spence was forty-two years old and the other seemed to be about that age, yet, oddly, older: his skin liverish, his profile vague as if seen through an element transparent yet dense, like water; his clothing—handsome tweed overcoat, sharply creased gray trousers—hanging slack on him, as if several sizes too large.

Outside, Spence soon lost sight of the man in a swarm of pedestrians crossing the street; and made no effort to locate him again. But for most of the ride home on the train he thought of nothing else: who was that man, why was he certain the man would have known him, what were they to each other, resembling each other only very slightly, yet close as twins? He felt stabs of excitement that left him weak and breathless but it wasn't until that night, when he and his wife were undressing for bed, that he said, or heard himself say, in a voice of bemused wonder, and dread: "I saw someone today who looked just like my cousin Sandy—"

"Did I know Sandy?" his wife asked.

"—my cousin Sandy who died, who drowned, when we were both in college."

"But did I know him?" his wife asked. She cast him an impatient sidelong glance and smiled her sweet-derisive smile. "It's difficult to envision him if I've never seen him, and if he's been dead for so long, why should it matter so much to you?"

Spence had begun to perspire. His heart beat hard and steady as if in the presence of danger. "I don't understand what you're saying," he said.

"The actual words, or their meaning?"

"The words."

She laughed as if he had said something witty, and did not answer him. As he fell asleep he tried not to think of his cousin Sandy whom he had not seen in twenty years and whom he'd last seen in an open casket in a funeral home in Damascus, Minnesota.

The second episode occurred a few weeks later when Spence was in line at a post office, not the post office he usually frequented but another, larger, busier, in a suburban township adjacent to his own, and the elderly woman in front of him drew his attention: wasn't she, too, someone he knew? or had known, many years ago? He stared, fascinated, at her stitched-looking skin, soft and puckered as a glove of some exquisite material, and unnaturally white; her eyes that were small, sunken, yet shining; her astonishing hands—delicate, even skel-etal, discolored by liver spots like coins, yet with rings on several fingers, and in a way rather beautiful. The woman appeared to be in her mid-nineties, if not older: fussy, anxious, very possibly addled: complaining ceaselessly to herself, or to others by way of herself. Yet her manner was mirthful; nervous bustling energy crackled about her like invisible bees.

He believed he knew who she was: Miss Reuter, a teacher of his in elementary school. Whom he had not seen in more years than he wanted to calculate.

Miss Reuter, though enormously aged, was able, it seemed, to get around by herself. She carried a large rather glitzy shopping bag made of a silvery material, and in this bag, and in another at her feet, she was rummaging for her change purse, as she called it, which she could not seem to find. The post office clerk waited with a show of strained patience; the line now consisted of a half-dozen people.

Spence asked Miss Reuter—for surely it was she: while virtually unrecognizable she was at the same time unmistakable —if she needed some assistance. He did not call her by name and as she turned to him, in exasperation, and gratitude—as if she knew that he, or someone, would come shortly to her aid—she did not seem to recognize him. Spence paid for her postage and a roll of stamps and Miss Reuter, still rummaging in her bag, vexed, cheerful, befuddled, thanked him without looking up at him. She insisted it must be a loan, and not a gift, for she was, she said, "not yet an object of public charity."

Afterward Spence put the incident out of his mind, knowing the woman was dead. It was purposeless to think of it, and would only upset him.

After that he began to see them more frequently. The Others—as he thought of them. On the street, in restaurants, at church; in the building in which he worked; on the very floor, in the very department, in which his office was located. (He was a tax lawyer for one of the largest of American "conglomerates"—yes and very well paid.) One morning his wife saw him standing at a bedroom window looking out toward the street. She poked him playfully in the ribs. "What's wrong?" she said. "None of this behavior suits you."

"There's someone out there, at the curb."

"No one's there."

"I have the idea he's waiting for me."

"Oh yes, I do see someone," his wife said carelessly. "He's often there. But I doubt that he's waiting for you."

She laughed, as at a private joke. She was a pretty freckled snub-nosed woman given to moments of mysterious amusement. Spence had married her long ago in a trance of love from which he had yet to awaken.

Spence said, his voice shaking, "I think—I'm afraid I think I might be having a nervous breakdown. I'm so very, very afraid."

"No," said his wife, "—you're the sanest person I know. All surface and no cracks, fissures, potholes."

Spence turned to her. His eyes were filling with tears. "Don't joke. Have pity."

She made no reply; seemed about to drift away; then slipped an arm around his waist and nudged her head against his shoulder in a gesture of camaraderie. Whether mocking, or altogether genuine, Spence could not have said.

"It's just that I'm so afraid."

"Yes, you've said."

"—of losing my mind. Going mad."

She stood for a moment, peering out toward the street. The elderly gentleman standing at the curb glanced back but could not have seen them, or anyone, behind the lacy bedroom curtains. He was well dressed, and carried an umbrella. An umbrella? Perhaps it was a cane.

Spence said, "I seem to be seeing, more and more, these people—people I don't think are truly there."

"*He's* there."

"I think they're dead. Dead people."

His wife drew back and cast him a sidelong glance, smiling mysteriously. "It does seem to have upset you," she said.

"Since I know they're not there—"

"*He's* there,"

"—so I must be losing my mind. A kind of schizophrenia, waking dreams, hallucinations—"

Spence was speaking excitedly, and did not know exactly what he was saying. His wife drew away from him in alarm, or distaste.

"You take everything so personally," she said.

One morning shortly after the New Year, when the air was sharp as a knife and the sky so blue it brought tears of pain to one's eyes, Spence set off on the underground route from his train station to his building. Beneath the city's paved surface was a honeycomb of tunnels, some of them damp and befouled but most of them in good condition, with, occasionally, a corridor of gleaming white tiles that looked as if it had been lovingly polished by hand. Spence preferred aboveground, or believed he should prefer aboveground, for reasons vague and puritanical, but in fierce weather he made his way underground, and worried only that he might get lost, as he some-times did. (Yet, even lost, he had only to find an escalator or steps leading to the street—and he was no longer lost.)

This morning, however, the tunnels were far more crowded than usual. Spence saw a preponderance of elderly men and women, with here and there a young face, startling, and seem-ingly unnatural. Here and there, yet more startling, a child's face. Very few of the faces had that air, so disconcerting to him in the past, of the eerily familiar laid upon the utterly unfamil-iar; and these he resolutely ignored.

He soon fell into step with the crowd, keeping to their pace—which was erratic, surging, faster along straight stretches of tunnel and slower at curves; he found it agreeable to be borne along by the flow, as of a tide. A tunnel of familiar tear-stained mosaics yielded to one of the smart gleaming tun-nels and that in turn to a tunnel badly in need of repair—and, indeed, being noisily repaired, by one of those crews of work-men that labor at all hours of the day and night beneath the surface of the city—and as Spence hurried past the deafening vibrations of the air hammer he found himself descending stairs into a tunnel unknown to him: a place of warm, humming, droning sound, like conversation, though none of his fellow pedestrians seemed to be talking. Where were they going, so many people? And in the same direction?—with only, here and there, a lone, clearly lost individual bucking the tide, white-faced, eyes snatching at his as if in desperate recognition.

Might as well accompany them, Spence thought, and see.

THE

FOLLOWERS

Dylan Thomas

It was six o'clock on a winter's evening. Thin, dingy rain spat and drizzled past the lighted street lamps. The pavements shone long and yellow. In squeaking goloshes, with mackintosh collars up and bowlers and trilbies weeping, youngish men from the offices bundled home against the thistly wind—

'Night, Mr Macey.'

'Going my way, Charlie?'

'Ooh, there's a pig of a night!'

'Good night, Mr Swan.'—

and older men, clinging on to the big, black circular birds of their umbrellas, were wafted back, up the gaslit hills, to safe, hot, slippered, weatherproof hearths, and wives called Mother, and old, fond, fleabag dogs, and the wireless babbling.

Young women from the offices, who smelt of scent and powder and wet pixie hoods and hair, scuttled, giggling, arm-in-arm, after the hissing trams, and screeched as they splashed their stockings in the puddles rainbowed with oil between the slippery lines.

In a shop window, two girls undressed the dummies:

'Where you going to-night?'

'Depends on Arthur. Up she comes.'

'Mind her cami-knicks, Edna . . .'

The blinds came down over another window.

A newsboy stood in a doorway, calling the news to nobody, very softly:

'Earthquake. Earthquake in Japan.'

Water from a chute dripped on to his sacking. He waited in his own pool of rain.

A flat, long girl drifted, snivelling into her hanky, out of a jeweller's shop, and slowly pulled the steel shutters down with a hooked pole. She looked, in the grey rain, as though she were crying from top to toe.

A silent man and woman, dressed in black, carried the wreaths away from the front of their flower shop into the scented deadly darkness behind the window lights. Then the lights went out.

A man with a balloon tied to his cap pushed a shrouded barrow up a dead end.

A baby with an ancient face sat in its pram outside the wine vaults, quiet, very wet, peering cautiously all round it.

It was the saddest evening I had ever known.

A young man, with his arm round his girl, passed by me, laughing; and she laughed back, right into his handsome, nasty face. That made the evening sadder still.

I met Leslie at the corner of Crimea Street. We were both about the same age: too young and too old. Leslie carried a rolled umbrella, which he never used, though sometimes he pressed doorbells with it. He was trying to grow a moustache. I wore a check, ratting cap at a Saturday angle. We greeted each other formally:

'Good evening, old man.'

'Evening, Leslie.'

'Right on the dot, boy.'

'That's right,' I said. 'Right on the dot.'

A plump, blonde girl, smelling of wet rabbits, self-conscious even in that dirty night, minced past on high-heeled shoes. The heels clicked, the soles squelched.

Leslie whistled after her, low and admiring.

'Business first,' I said.

'Oh, boy!' Leslie said.

'And she's too fat as well.'

'I like them corpulent,' Leslie said. 'Remember Penelope Bogan? a Mrs too.'

'Oh, come *on*. That old bird of Paradise Alley! How's the exchequer, Les?'

'One and a penny. How you fixed?'

'Tanner.'

'What'll it be, then? The Compasses?'

'Free cheese at the Marlborough.'

We walked towards the Marlborough, dodging umbrella spokes, smacked by our windy macs, stained by steaming lamplight, seeing the sodden, blown scourings and street-wash of the town, papers, rags, dregs, rinds, fag-ends, balls of fur, flap, float, and cringe along the gutters, hearing the sneeze and rattle of the bony trams and a ship hoot like a fog-ditched owl in the bay, and Leslie said:

'What'll we do after?'

'We'll follow someone,' I said.

'Remember following that old girl up Kitchner Street? The one who dropped her handbag?'

'You should have given it back.'

'There wasn't anything in it, only a piece of bread-and-jam.'

'Here we are,' I said.

The Marlborough saloon was cold and empty. There were notices on the damp walls: No Singing. No Dancing. No Gambling. No Peddlers.

'You sing,' I said to Leslie, 'and I'll dance, then we'll have a game of nap and I'll peddle my braces.'

The barmaid, with gold hair and two gold teeth in front, like a well-off rabbit's, was blowing on her nails and polishing them on her black marocain. She looked up as we came in, then blew on her nails again and polished them without hope.

'You can tell it isn't Saturday night,' I said. 'Evening, Miss. Two pints.'

'And a pound from the till,' Leslie said.

'Give us your one-and-a-penny, Les,' I whispered and then said aloud. 'Anybody can tell it isn't Saturday night. Nobody sick.'

'Nobody here to *be* sick,' Leslie said.

The peeling, liver-coloured room might never have been drunk in at all. Here, commercials told jokes and had Scotches and sodas with happy, dyed, port-and-lemon women; dejected regulars grew grand and muzzy in the corners, inventing their pasts, being rich, important, and loved; reprobate grannies in dustbin black cackled and nipped; influential nobodies revised the earth; a party, with earrings, called 'Frilly Willy' played the crippled piano, which sounded like a hurdy-gurdy playing under water, until the publican's nosy wife said, 'No.' Strangers came and went, but mostly went. Men from the valleys dropped in for nine or ten; sometimes there were fights; and always there was something doing, some argie-bargie, giggle and bluster, horror or folly, affection, explosion, nonsense, peace, some wild goose flying in the boozy air of that comfortless, humdrum nowhere in the dizzy, ditchwater town at the end of the railway lines. But that evening it was the saddest room I had ever known.

Leslie said, in a low voice: 'Think she'll let us have one on tick?'

'Wait a bit, boy,' I murmured. 'Wait for her to thaw.'

But the barmaid heard me, and looked up. She looked clean through me, back through my small history to the bed I was born in, then shook her gold head.

'I don't know what it is,' said Leslie as we walked up Crimea Street in the rain, 'but I feel kind of depressed to-night.'

'It's the saddest night in the world,' I said.

We stopped, soaked and alone, to look at the stills outside the cinema we called the Itch-pit. Week after week, for years and years, we had sat on the edges of the springless seats there, in the dank but snug, flickering dark, first with toffees and monkey-nuts that crackled for the dumb guns, and then with cigarettes: a cheap special kind that would make a fire-swallower cough up the cinders of his heart. 'Let's go in and see Lon Chaney,' I said, 'and Richard Talmadge and Milton Sills and . . . and Noah Berry,' I said, 'and Richard Dix . . . and Slim Summerville and Hoot Gibson.'

We both sighed.

'Oh, for our vanished youth,' I said.

We walked on heavily, with wilful feet, splashing the passers-by.

'Why don't you open your brolly?' I said.

'It won't open. You try.'

We both tried and the umbrella suddenly bellied out, the spokes tore through the soaking cover; the wind danced its tatters; it wrangled above us in the wind like a ruined mathematical bird. We tried to tug it down: an unseen, new spoke sprang through its ragged ribs. Leslie dragged it behind him, along the pavement, as though he had shot it.

A girl called Dulcie, scurrying to the Itch-pit, sniggered 'Hallo,' and we stopped her.

'A rather terrible thing has happened,' I said to her. She was so silly that, even when she was fifteen, we had told her to eat soap to make her straw hair crinkle, and Les took a piece from the bathroom, and she did.

'I know,' she said, 'you broke your gamp.'

'No, you're wrong there,' Leslie said. 'It isn't *our* umbrella at all. It fell off the roof. *You* feel,' he said. 'You can feel it fell off the roof.' She took the umbrella gingerly by its handle.

'There's someone up there throwing umbrellas down,' I said. 'It may be serious.'

She began to titter, and then grew silent and anxious as Leslie said: 'You never know. It might be walking-sticks next.'

'Or sewing-machines,' I said.

'You wait here, Dulcie, and we'll investigate,' Leslie said.

We hurried on down the street, turned a blowing corner and then ran.

Outside Rabiotti's café, Leslie said: 'It isn't fair on Dulcie.' We never mentioned it again.

A wet girl brushed by. Without a word, we followed her. She cantered, long-legged, down Inkerman Street and through Paradise Passage, and we were at her heels.

'I wonder what's the point in following people,' Leslie said, 'it's kind of daft. It never gets you anywhere. All you do is follow them home and then try to look through the window and see what they're doing and mostly there's curtains anyway. I bet nobody else does things like that.'

'You never know,' I said. The girl turned into St Augustus Crescent, which was a wide lamplit mist. 'People are always following people. What shall we call her?'

'Hermione Weatherby,' Leslie said. He was never wrong about names. Hermione was fey and stringy, and walked like a long gym-mistress, full of love, through the stinging rain.

'You never know. You never know what you'll find out. Perhaps she lives in a huge house with all her sisters—'

'How many?'

'Seven. All full of love. And when she gets home they all change into kimonos and lie on divans with music and whisper to each other and all they're doing is waiting for somebody like us to walk in, lost, and then they'll all chatter round us like starlings and put us in kimonos too, and we'll never leave the house until we die. Perhaps it's so beautiful and soft and noisy—like a warm bath full of birds . . .'

'I don't want birds in my bath,' said Leslie. 'Perhaps she'll slit her throat if they don't draw the blinds. I don't care what happens so long as it's interesting.'

She slip-slopped round a corner into an avenue where the neat trees were sighing and the cosy windows shone.

'I don't want old feathers in the tub,' Leslie said.

Hermione turned in at number thirteen, Beach-view.

'You can see the beach all right,' Leslie said, 'if you got a periscope.'

We waited on the pavement opposite, under a bubbling lamp, as Hermione opened her door, and then we tiptoed across and down the gravel path and were at the back of the house, outside an uncurtained window.

Hermione's mother, a round, friendly, owlish woman in a pinafore, was shaking a chip-pan on the kitchen stove.

'I'm hungry,' I said.

'Ssh!'

We edged to the side of the window as Hermione came into the kitchen. She was old, nearly thirty, with a mouse-brown shingle and big earnest eyes. She wore horn-rimmed spectacles and a sensible, tweed costume, and a white shirt with a trim bow-tie. She looked as though she tried to look like a secretary in domestic films, who had only to remove her spectacles and have her hair cherished, and be dressed like a silk dog's dinner, to turn into a dazzler and make her employer Warner Baxter, gasp, woo, and marry her; but if Hermione took off her glasses, she wouldn't be able to tell if he was Warner Baxter or the man who read the meters.

We stood so near the window, we could hear the chips spitting.

'Have a nice day in the office, dear? There's weather,' Hermione's mother said, worrying the chip-pan.

'What's *her* name, Les?'

'Hetty.'

Everything there in the warm kitchen, from the tea-caddy and the grandmother clock, to the tabby that purred like a kettle, was good, dull, and sufficient.

'Mr Truscott was something awful,' Hermione said as she put on her slippers.

'Where's her kimono?' Leslie said.

'Here's a nice cup of tea,' said Hetty.

'Everything's nice in that old hole,' said Leslie, grumbling. 'Where's the seven sisters like starlings?'

It began to rain much more heavily. It bucketed down on the black back yard, and the little comfy kennel of a house, and us, and the hidden, hushed town, where, even now, in the haven of the Marlborough, the submarine piano would be tinning 'Daisy,' and the happy henna'd women squealing into their port.

Hetty and Hermione had their supper. Two drowned boys watched them enviously.

'Put a drop of Worcester on the chips,' Leslie whispered; and by God she did.

'Doesn't anything happen anywhere?' I said, 'in the whole wide world? I think the *News of the World* is all made up. Nobody murders no one. There isn't any sin any more, or love, or death, or pearls and divorces and mink-coats or anything, or putting arsenic in the cocoa . . .'

'Why don't they put on some music for us,' Leslie said, 'and do a dance? It isn't every night they got two fellows watching them in the rain. Not *every* night, anyway!'

All over the dripping town, small lost people with nowhere to go and nothing to spend were gooseberrying in the rain outside wet windows, but nothing happened.

'I'm getting penumonia,' Leslie said.

The cat and the fire were purring, grandmother time tick-tocked our lives away. The supper was cleared, and Hetty and Hermione, who had not spoken for many minutes, they were so confident and close in their little lighted box, looked at one another and slowly smiled.

They stood still in the decent, purring kitchen, facing one another.

'There's something funny going to happen,' I whispered very softly.

'It's going to begin,' Leslie said.

We did not notice the sour, racing rain any more.

The smiles stayed on the faces of the two still, silent women.

'It's going to begin.'

And we heard Hetty say in a small secret voice: 'Bring out the album, dear.'

Hermione opened a cupboard and brought out a big, stiff-coloured photograph album, and put it in the middle of the table. Then she and Hetty sat down at the table, side by side, and Hermione opened the album.

'That's Uncle Eliot who died in Porthcawl, the one who had the cramp,' said Hetty.

They looked with affection at Uncle Eliot, but we could not see him.

'That's Martha-the-woolshop, you wouldn't remember her, dear, it was wool, wool, wool, with her all the time; she wanted to be buried in her jumper, the mauve one, but her husband put his foot down. He'd been in India. That's your Uncle Morgan,' Hetty said, 'one of the Kidwelly Morgans, remember him in the snow?'

Hermione turned a page. 'And that's Myfanwy, she got queer all of a sudden, remember. It was when she was milking. That's your cousin Jim, the Minister, until they found out. And that's our Beryl,' Hetty said.

But she spoke all the time like somebody repeating a lesson: a well-loved lesson she knew by heart.

We knew that she and Hermione were only waiting.

Then Hermione turned another page. And we knew, by their secret smiles, that this was what they had been waiting for.

'My sister Katinka,' Hetty said.

'Auntie Katinka,' Hermione said. They bent over the photo-graph.

'Remember that day in Aberystwyth, Katinka?' Hetty said softly. 'The day we went on the choir outing.'

'I wore my new white dress,' a new voice said.

Leslie clutched at my hand.

'And a straw hat with birds,' said the clear, new voice.

Hermione and Hetty were not moving their lips.

'I was always a one for birds on my hat. Just the plumes of course. It was August the third, and I was twenty-three.'

'Twenty-three come October, Katinka,' Hetty said.

'That's right, love,' the voice said. 'Scorpio I was. And we met Douglas Pugh on the Prom and he said: "You look like a queen to-day, Katinka," he said, "You look like a queen, Katinka," he said. Why are those two boys looking in that window?'

We ran up the gravel drive, and around the corner of the house, and into the avenue and out on to St Augustus Crescent. The rain roared down to drown the town. There we stopped for breath. We did not speak or look at each other. Then we walked on through the rain. At Victoria corner, we stopped again.

'Good night, old man,' Leslie said.

'Good night,' I said.

And we went our different ways.

THE

YELLOW

WALLPAPER

Charlotte Perkins Gilman

It is very seldom that mere ordinary people like John and myself secure ancestral halls for the summer.

A colonial mansion, a hereditary estate, I would say a haunted house and reach the height of romantic felicity—but that would be asking too much of fate!

Still I will proudly declare that there is something queer about it.

Else, why should it be let so cheaply? And why have stood so long untenanted?

John laughs at me, of course, but one expects that.

John is practical in the extreme. He has no patience with faith, an intense horror of superstition, and he scoffs openly at any talk of things not to be felt and seen and put down in figures.

John is a physician, and *perhaps*—(I would not say it to a living soul, of course, but this is dead paper and a great relief to my mind)—*perhaps* that is one reason I do not get well faster.

You see, he does not believe I am sick! And what can one do?

If a physician of high standing, and one's own husband assures friends and relatives that there is really nothing the matter with one but temporary nervous depression—a slight hysterical tendency—what is one to do?

My brother is also a physician, and also of high standing, and he says the same thing.

So I take phosphates or phosphites—whichever it is—and tonics, and air and exercise, and journeys, and am absolutely forbidden to "work" until I am well again.

Personally, I disagree with their ideas.

Personally, I believe that congenial work, with excitement and change, would do me good.

But what is one to do?

I did write for a while in spite of them; but it *does* exhaust me a good deal—having to be so sly about it, or else meet with heavy opposition.

I sometimes fancy that in my condition, if I had less opposition and more society and stimulus—but John says the very worst thing I can do is to think about my condition, and I confess it always makes me feel bad.

So I will let it alone and talk about the house.

The most beautiful place! It is quite alone, standing well back from the road, quite three miles from the village. It makes me think of English places that you read about, for there are hedges and walls and gates that lock, and lots of separate little houses for the gardeners and people.

There is a *delicious* garden! I never saw such a garden—large and shady, full of box-bordered paths, and lined with long grape-covered arbors with seats under them.

There were greenhouses, but they are all broken now.

There was some legal trouble, I believe, something about the heirs and co-heirs; anyhow, the place has been empty for years.

That spoils my ghostliness, I am afraid, but I don't care—there is something strange about the house—I can feel it.

I even said so to John one moonlight evening, but he said what I felt was a draught, and shut the window.

I get unreasonably angry with John sometimes. I'm sure I never used to be so sensitive. I think it is due to this nervous condition.

But John says if I feel so I shall neglect proper self-control; so I take pains to control myself—before him, at least, and that makes me very tired.

I don't like our room a bit. I wanted one downstairs that opened onto the piazza and had roses all over the window, and such pretty old-fashioned chintz hangings! But John would not hear of it.

He said there was only one window and not room for two beds, and no near room for him if he took another.

He is very careful and loving, and hardly lets me stir without special direction.

I have a schedule prescription for each hour in the day; he takes all care from me, and so I feel basely ungrateful not to value it more.

He said he came here solely on my account, that I was to have perfect rest and all the air I could get. "Your exercise depends on your strength, my dear," said he, "and your food somewhat on your appetite; but air you can absorb all the time." So we took the nursery at the top of the house.

It is a big, airy room, the whole floor nearly, with windows that look all ways, and air and sunshine galore. It was nursery first, and then playroom and gymnasium, I should judge, for the windows are barred for little children, and there are rings and things in the walls.

The paint and paper look as if a boys' school had used it. It is stripped off—the paper—in great patches all around the head of my bed, about as far as I can reach, and in great places on the other side of the room low down. I never saw a worse paper in my life. One of those sprawling, flamboyant patterns commiting every artistic sin.

It is dull enough to confuse the eye in following, pronounced enough constantly to irritate and provoke study, and when you follow the lame uncertain curves for a little distance they suddenly commit suicide—plunge off at outrageous angles, destroy themselves in unheard-of contradictions.

The color is repellent, almost revolting: a smouldering unclean yellow, strangely faded by the slow-turning sunlight. It is a dull yet lurid orange in some places, a sickly sulphur tint in others.

No wonder the children hated it! I should hate it myself if I had to live in this room long.

There comes John, and I must put this away—he hates to have me write a word.

We have been here two weeks, and I haven't felt like writing before, since that first day.

I am sitting by the window now, up in this atrocious nursery, and there is nothing to hinder my writing as much as I please, save lack of strength.

John is away all day, and even some nights when his cases are serious.

I am glad my case is not serious!

But these nervous troubles are dreadfully depressing.

John does not know how much I really suffer. He knows there is no *reason* to suffer, and that satisfies him.

Of course it is only nervousness. It does weigh on me so not to do my duty in any way!

I meant to be such a help to John, such a real rest and comfort, and here I am a comparative burden already!

Nobody would believe what an effort it is to do what little I am able—to dress and entertain, and order things.

It is fortunate Mary is so good with the baby. Such a dear baby!

And yet I *cannot* be with him, it makes me so nervous.

I suppose John never was nervous in his life. He laughs at me so about this wallpaper!

At first he meant to repaper the room, but afterward he said that I was letting it get the better of me, and that nothing was worse for a nervous patient than to give way to such fancies.

He said that after the wallpaper was changed it would be the heavy bedstead, and then the barred windows, and then that gate at the head of the stairs, and so on.

"You know the place is doing you good," he said, "and really, dear, I don't care to renovate the house just for a three months' rental."

"Then do let us go downstairs," I said. "There are such pretty rooms there."

Then he took me in his arms and called me a blessed little goose, and said he would go down cellar, if I wished, and have it whitewashed into the bargain.

But he is right enough about the beds and windows and things.

It is as airy and comfortable a room as anyone need wish, and, of course, I would not be so silly as to make him uncomfortable just for a whim.

I'm really getting quite fond of the big room, all but that horrid paper.

Out of one window I can see the garden—those mysterious deep-shaded arbors, the riotous old-fashioned flowers, and bushes and gnarly trees.

Out of another I get a lovely view of the bay and a little private wharf belonging to the estate. There is a beautiful shaded lane that runs down there from the house. I always fancy I see people walking in these numerous paths and arbors, but John has cautioned me not to give way to fancy in the least. He says that with my imaginative power and habit of story-making, a nervous weakness like mine is sure to lead to all manner of excited fancies, and that I ought to use my will and good sense to check the tendency. So I try.

I think sometimes that if I were only well enough to write a little it would relieve the press of ideas and rest me.

But I find I get pretty tired when I try.

It is so discouraging not to have any advice and companionship about my work. When I get really well, John says we will ask Cousin Henry and Julia down for a long visit; but he says he would as soon put fireworks in my pillow-case as to let me have those stimulating people about now.

I wish I could get well faster.

But I must not think about that. This paper looks to me as if it *knew* what a vicious influence it had!

There is a recurrent spot where the pattern lolls like a broken neck and two bulbous eyes stare at you upside down.

I get postively angry with the impertinence of it and the everlastingness. Up and down and sideways they crawl, and those absurd unblinking eyes are everywhere. There is one place where two breadths didn't match, and the eyes go all up and down the line, one a little higher than the other.

I never saw so much expression in an inanimate thing before, and we all know how much expression they have! I used to lie awake as a child and get more entertainment and terror out of blank walls and plain furniture than most children could find in a toy-store.

I remember what a kindly wink the knobs of our big old bureau used to have, and there was one chair that always seemed like a strong friend.

I used to feel that if any of the other things looked too fierce I could always hop into that chair and be safe.

The furniture in this room is no worse than inharmonious, however, for we had to bring it all from downstairs. I suppose when this was used as a playroom they had to take the nursery things out, and no wonder! I never saw such ravages as the children have made here.

The wallpaper, as I said before, is torn off in spots, and it sticketh closer than a brother—they must have had perseverance as well as hatred.

Then the floor is scratched and gouged and splintered, the plaster itself is dug out here and there, and this great heavy bed, which is all we found in the room, looks as if it had been through the wars.

But I don't mind it a bit—only the paper.

There comes John's sister. Such a dear girl as she is, and so careful of me! I must not let her find me writing.

She is a perfect and enthusiastic housekeeper, and hopes for no better profession. I verily believe she thinks it is the writing which made me sick!

But I can write when she is out, and see her a long way off from these windows.

There is one that commands the road, a lovely shaded winding road, and one that just looks off over the country. A lovely country, too, full of great elms and velvet meadows.

This wallpaper has a kind of sub-pattern in a different shade, a particularly irritating one, for you can only see it in certain lights, and not clearly then.

But in the places where it isn't faded and where the sun is just so—I can see a strange, provoking, formless sort of figure that seems to skulk about behind that silly and conspicuous front design.

There's sister on the stairs!

Well, the Fourth of July is over! The people are all gone, and I am tired out. John thought it might do me good to see a little company, so we just had Mother and Nellie and the children down for a week.

Of course I didn't do a thing. Jennie sees to everything now.

But it tired me all the same.

John says if I don't pick up faster he shall send me to Weir Mitchell in the fall.

But I don't want to go there at all. I had a friend who was in his hands once, and she says he is just like John and my brother, only more so!

Besides, it is such an undertaking to go so far.

I don't feel as if it was worthwhile to turn my hand over for anything, and I'm getting dreadfully fretful and querulous.

I cry at nothing, and cry most of the time.

Of course, I don't when John is here, or anybody else, but when I am alone.

And I am alone a good deal just now. John is kept in town very often by serious cases, and Jennie is good and lets me alone when I want her to.

So I walk a little in the garden or down that lovely lane, sit on the porch under the roses, and lie down up here a good deal.

I'm getting really fond of the room in spite of the wallpaper. Perhaps *because* of the wallpaper.

It dwells in my mind so!

I lie on this great immovable bed—it is nailed down, I believe—and follow that pattern about by the hour. It is as good as gymnastics, I assure you. I start, we'll say, at the bottom, down in the corner over there where it has not been touched, and I determine for the thousandth time that I *will* follow that pointless pattern to some sort of a conclusion.

I know a little of the principle of design, and I know this thing was not arranged on any laws of radiation, or alternation, or repetition, or symmetry, or anything else that I ever heard of.

It is repeated, of course, by the breadths, but not otherwise.

Looked at in one way, each breadth stands alone; the bloated curves and flourishes—a kind of "debased Romanesque" with *delirium tremens*—go waddling up and down in isolated columns of fatuity.

But, on the other hand, they connect diagonally, and the sprawling outlines run off in great slanting waves of optic horror, like a lot of wallowing sea-weeds in full chase.

The whole thing goes horizontally, too, at least it seems so, and I exhaust myself trying to distinguish the order of its going in that direction.

They have used a horizontal breadth for a frieze, and that adds wonderfully to the confusion.

There is one end of the room where it is almost intact, and there, when the crosslights fade and the low sun shines directly upon it, I can almost fancy radiation after all—the interminable grotesque seems to form around a common center and rush off in headlong plunges of equal distraction.

It makes me tired to follow it. I will take a nap, I guess.

I don't know why I should write this.

I don't want to.

I don't feel able.

And I think John would think it absurd. But I *must* say what I feel and think in some way—it is such a relief!

But the effort is getting to be greater than the relief.

Half the time now I am awfully lazy, and lie down ever so much.

John says I mustn't lose my strength, and has me take cod liver oil and lots of tonics and things, to say nothing of ale and wine and rare meat.

Dear John! He loves me very dearly, and hates to have me sick. I tried to have a real earnest reasonable talk with him the other day, and tell him how I wish he would let me go and make a visit to Cousin Henry and Julia.

But he said I wasn't able to go, nor able to stand it after I got there, and I did not make out a very good case for myself, for I was crying before I had finished.

It is getting to be a great effort for me to think straight. Just this nervous weakness, I suppose.

And dear John gathered me up in his arms, and just carried me upstairs and laid me on the bed, and sat by me and read to me till it tired my head.

He said I was his darling and his comfort and all he had, and that I must take care of myself for his sake, and keep well.

He says no one but myself can help me out of it, that I must use my will and self-control and not let any silly fancies run away with me.

There's one comfort—the baby is well and happy, and does not have to occupy this nursery with the horrid wallpaper.

If we had not used it, that blessed child would have! What a fortunate escape! Why, I wouldn't have a child of mine, an impressionable little thing, live in such a room for worlds.

I never thought of it before, but it is lucky that John kept me here after all; I can stand it so much easier than a baby, you see.

Of course I never mention it to them any more—I am too wise—but I keep watch of it all the same.

There are things in that paper that nobody knows about but me, or ever will.

Behind that outside pattern the dim shapes get clearer every day.

It is always the same shape, only very numerous.

And it is like a woman stooping down and creeping about

behind that pattern. I don't like it a bit. I wonder—I begin to think—I wish John would take me away from here!

It is so hard to talk with John about my case, because he is so wise, and because he loves me so.

But I tried it last night.

It was moonlight. The moon shines in all around just as the sun does.

I hate to see it sometimes, it creeps so slowly, and always comes in by one window or another.

John was asleep and I hated to waken him, so I kept still and watched the moonlight on that undulating wallpaper till I felt creepy.

The faint figure behind seemed to shake the pattern, just as if she wanted to get out.

I got up softly and went to feel and see if the paper *did* move, and when I came back John was awake.

"What is it, little girl?" he said. "Don't go walking about like that—you'll get cold."

I thought it was a good time to talk, so I told him that I really was not gaining here, and that I wished he would take me away.

"Why, darling!" said he. "Our lease will be up in three weeks, and I can't see how to leave before.

"The repairs are not done at home, and I cannot possibly leave town just now. Of course, if you were in any danger, I could and would, but you really are better, dear, whether you can see it or not. I am a doctor, dear, and I know. You are gaining flesh and color, your appetite is better, I feel really much easier about you."

"I don't weigh a bit more," said I, "nor as much; and my appetite may be better in the evening when you are here but it is worse in the morning when you are away!"

"Bless her little heart!" said he with a big hug. "She shall be as sick as she pleases! But now let's improve the shining hours by going to sleep, and talk about it in the morning!"

"And you won't go away?" I asked gloomily.

"Why, how can I, dear? It is only three weeks more and then we will take a nice little trip of a few days while Jennie is getting the house ready. Really, dear, you are better!"

"Better in body perhaps—" I began, and stopped short, for

he sat up straight and looked at me with such a stern, re-proachful look that I could not say another word.

"My darling," said he, "I beg of you, for my sake and for our child's sake, as well as for your own, that you will never for one instant let that idea enter your mind! There is nothing so dangerous, so fascinating, to a temperament like yours. It is a false and foolish fancy. Can you not trust me as a physician when I tell you so?"

So of course I said no more on that score, and we went to sleep before long. He thought I was asleep first, but I wasn't and lay there for hours trying to decide whether that front pattern and the back pattern really did move together or separately.

On a pattern like this, by daylight, there is a lack of sequence, a defiance of law, that is a constant irritant to a normal mind.

The color is hideous enough, and unreliable enough, and infuriating enough, but the pattern is torturing.

You think you have mastered it, but just as you get well under way in following, it turns a back-somersault and there you are. It slaps you in the face, knocks you down, and tramples upon you. It is like a bad dream.

The outside pattern is a florid arabesque, reminding one of a fungus. If you can imagine a toadstool in joints, an interminable string of toadstools, budding and sprouting in endless convolutions—why, that is something like it.

That is sometimes!

There is one marked peculiarity about this paper, a thing nobody seems to notice but myself, and that is that it changes as the light changes.

When the sun shoots in through the east window—I always watch for that first long, straight ray—it changes so quickly that I never can quite believe it.

That is why I watch it always.

By moonlight—the moon shines in all night when there is a moon—I wouldn't know it was the same paper.

At night in any kind of light, in twilight, candlelight, camp-light, and worst of all by moonlight, it becomes bars! The outside pattern, I mean, and the woman behind it is as plain as can be.

I didn't realize for a long time what the thing was that

showed behind, that dim sub-pattern, but now I am quite sure it is a woman.

By daylight she is subdued, quiet. I fancy it is the pattern that keeps her so still. It is so puzzling. It keeps me quiet by the hour.

I lie down ever so much now. John says it is good for me, and to sleep all I can.

Indeed he started the habit by making me lie down for an hour after each meal.

It is a very bad habit, I am convinced, for you see, I don't sleep.

And that cultivates deceit, for I don't tell them I'm awake—oh, no!

The fact is I am getting a little afraid of John.

He seems very queer sometimes, and even Jennie has an inexplicable look.

It strikes me occasionally, just as a scientific hypothesis, that perhaps it is the paper!

I have watched John when he did not know I was looking, and come into the room suddenly on the most innocent excuses, and I've caught him several times *looking at the paper!* And Jennie too. I caught Jennie with her hand on it once.

She didn't know I was in the room, and when I asked her in a quiet, a very quiet voice, with the most restrained manner possible, what she was doing with the paper, she turned around as if she had been caught stealing, and looked quite angry— asked me why I should frighten her so!

Then she said that the paper stained everything it touched, that she had found yellow smooches on all my clothes and John's and she wished we would be more careful!

Did not that sound innocent? But I know she was studying that pattern, and I am determined that nobody shall find it out but myself!

Life is very much more exciting now than it used to be. You see, I have something more to expect, to look forward to, to watch, I really do eat better, and am more quiet than I was.

John is so pleased to see me improve! He laughed a little the other day, and said I seemed to be flourishing in spite of my wallpaper.

I turned it off with a laugh. I had no intention of telling him it was *because* of the wallpaper—he would make fun of me. He might even want to take me away.

I don't want to leave now until I have found it out. There is a week more, and I think that will be enough.

I'm feeling ever so much better! I don't sleep much at night, for it is so interesting to watch developments; but I sleep a good deal during the daytime.

In the daytime it is tiresome and perplexing.

There are always new shoots on the fungus, and new shades of yellow all over it. I cannot keep count of them, though I have tried conscientiously.

It is the strangest yellow, that wallpaper! It makes me think of all the yellow things I ever saw—not beautiful ones like buttercups, but old, foul, bad yellow things.

But there is something else about that paper—the smell! I noticed it the moment we came into the room, but with so much air and sun it was not bad. Now we have had a week of fog and rain, and whether the windows are open or not, the smell is here.

It creeps all over the house.

I find it hovering in the dining-room, skulking in the parlor, hiding in the hall, lying in wait for me on the stairs.

It gets into my hair.

Even when I go to ride, if I turn my head suddenly and surprise it—there is that smell!

Such a peculiar odor, too! I have spent hours in trying to analyze it, to find what it smelled like.

It is not bad—at first—and very gentle, but quite the subtlest, most enduring odor I ever met.

In this damp weather it is awful. I wake up in the night and find it hanging over me.

It used to disturb me at first. I thought seriously of burning the house—to reach the smell.

But now I am used to it. The only thing I can think of that it is like is the *color* of the paper! A yellow smell!

There is a very funny mark on this wall, low down, near the mopboard. A streak that runs round the room. It goes behind every piece of furniture, except the bed, a long, straight, even *smooch*, as if it had been rubbed over and over.

I wonder how it was done and who did it, and what they did

it for. Round and round and round—round and round and round—it makes me dizzy!

I really have discovered something at last.

Through watching so much at night, when it changes so, I have finally found out.

The front pattern *does* move—and no wonder! The woman behind shakes it!

Sometimes I think there are a great many women behind, and sometimes only one, and she crawls around fast, and her crawling shakes it all over.

Then in the very bright spots she keeps still, and in the very shady spots she just takes hold of the bars and shakes them hard.

And she is all the time trying to climb through. But nobody could climb through that pattern—it strangles so; I think that is why it has so many heads.

They get through, and then the pattern strangles them off and turns them upside down, and makes their eyes white!

If those heads were covered or taken off it would not be half so bad.

I think that woman gets out in the daytime!

And I'll tell you why—privately—I've seen her!

I can see her out of every one of my windows!

It is the same woman, I know, for she is always creeping, and most women do not creep by daylight.

I see her in that long shaded lane, creeping up and down. I see her in those dark grape arbors, creeping all around the garden.

I see her on that long road under the trees, creeping along, and when a carriage comes she hides under the blackberry vines.

I don't blame her a bit. It must be very humiliating to be caught creeping by daylight!

I always lock the door when I creep by daylight. I can't do it at night, for I know John would suspect something at once.

And John is so queer now that I don't want to irritate him. I wish he would take another room! Besides, I don't want anybody to get that woman out at night but myself.

I often wonder if I could see her out of all the windows at once.

But, turn as fast as I can, I can only see out of one at one time.

And though I always see her, she may be able to creep faster than I can turn! I have watched her sometimes away off in the open country, creeping as fast as a cloud shadow in a high wind.

If only that top pattern could be gotten off from the under one! I mean to try it, little by little.

I have found out another funny thing, but I shan't tell it this time! It does not do to trust people too much.

There are only two more days to get this paper off, and I believe John is beginning to notice. I don't like the look in his eyes.

And I heard him ask Jennie a lot of professional questions about me. She had a very good report to give.

She said I slept a good deal in the daytime.

John knows I don't sleep very well at night, for all I'm so quiet!

He asked me all sorts of questions, too, and pretended to be very loving and kind.

As if I couldn't see through him!

Still, I don't wonder he acts so, sleeping under this paper for three months.

It only interests me, but I feel sure John and Jennie are affected by it.

Hurrah! This is the last day, but it is enough. John is to stay in town over night, and won't be out until this evening.

Jennie wanted to sleep with me—the sly thing; but I told her I should undoubtedly rest better for a night all alone.

That was clever, for really I wasn't alone a bit. As soon as it was moonlight and that poor thing began to crawl and shake the pattern, I got up and ran to help her.

I pulled and she shook. I shook and she pulled, and before morning we had peeled off yards of that paper.

A strip about as high as my head and half around the room.

And then when the sun came and that awful pattern began to laugh at me, I declared I would finish it today!

We go away tomorrow, and they are moving all my furniture down again to leave things as they were before.

Jennie looked at the wall in amazement, but I told her merrily that I did it out of pure spite at the vicious thing.

She laughed and said she wouldn't mind doing it herself, but I must not get tired.

How she betrayed herself that time!

But I am here, and no person touches this paper but Me— not *alive!*

She tried to get me out of the room—it was too patent! But I said it was so quiet and empty and clean now that I believed I would lie down again and sleep all I could, and not to wake me even for dinner—I would call when I woke.

So now she is gone, and the servants are gone, and the things are gone, and there is nothing left but that great bedstead nailed down, with the canvas mattress we found on it.

We shall sleep downstairs tonight, and take the boat home tomorrow.

I quite enjoy the room, now it is bare again.

How those children did tear about here!

This bedstead is fairly gnawed!

But I must get to work.

I have locked the door and thrown the key down into the front path.

I don't want to go out, and I don't want to have anybody come in, till John comes.

I want to astonish him.

I've got a rope up here that even Jennie did not find. If that woman does get out, and tries to get away, I can tie her!

But I forgot I could not reach far without anything to stand on!

This bed will *not* move!

I tried to lift and push it until I was lame, and then I got so angry I bit off a little piece at one corner—but it hurt my teeth.

Then I peeled off all the paper I could reach standing on the floor. It sticks horribly and the pattern just enjoys it. All those strangled heads and bulbous eyes and waddling fungus growths just shriek with derision!

I was getting angry enough to do something desperate. To jump out of the window would be admirable exercise, but the bars are too strong even to try.

Besides I wouldn't do it. Of course not. I know well enough that a step like that is improper and might be misconstrued.

I don't like to *look* out of the windows even—there are so many of those creeping women, and they creep so fast.

I wonder if they all come out of that wallpaper as I did!

But I am securely fastened now by my well-hidden rope—you don't get *me* out in the road there!

I suppose I shall have to get back behind the pattern when it comes night, and that is hard!

It is so pleasant to be out in this great room and creep around as I please!

I don't want to go outside. I won't even if Jennie asks me to.

For outside you have to creep on the ground, and everything is green instead of yellow.

But here I can creep smoothly on the floor, and my shoulder just fits in that long smooch around the wall, so I cannot lose my way.

Why, there's John at the door!

It is no use, young man, you can't open it!

How he does call and pound!

Now he's crying to Jennie for an axe.

It would be a shame to break down that beautiful door!

"John, dear!" said I in the gentlest voice. "The key is down by the front steps, under a plantain leaf!"

That silenced him for a few moments.

Then he said, very quietly indeed, "Open the door, my darling!"

"I can't," said I. "The key is down by the front door under a plantain leaf!" And then I said it again, several times, very gently and slowly, and said it so often that he had to go and see, and he got it of course, and came in. He stopped short by the door.

"What is the matter?" he cried. "For God's sake, what are you doing!"

I kept on creeping just the same, but I looked at him over my shoulder.

"I've got out at last," said I, "in spite of you and Jane. And I've pulled off most of the paper, so you can't put me back!"

Now why should that man have fainted? But he did, and right across my path by the wall, so that I had to creep over him every time!

THE

PRISON

WINDOW

Louis Auchincloss

"You always forget, Aileen, that we're not an art institute. Perhaps it would be more fun if we were, but we're not. The Museum of Colonial America, as its name implies, exists for a very specific purpose. We're a history museum. That doesn't mean, of course, that there aren't a great many ways of accomplishing that purpose, such as awakening the young to a proper sense of their heritage and revitalizing the old forms of communication . . ."

"I know, I know," Aileen Post interrupted. It was not the thing to do for a curator to interrupt the director, but when the curator was middle-aged and female and the director male and very young, exceptions had to be admitted. "I know all the jargon. I realize that we have to be 'relevant' and 'swinging' and 'up to the minute.' I understand very clearly that we have to be everything on God's earth but simply beautiful!"

"History is not always beautiful, Aileen."

"Oh, Tony! Don't be sententious. Save it for the trustees. You know what I mean. The *illustrations* of history should be beautiful! We can read about the horrors. We don't have to look at them. Why should there be any but lovely things in my gallery? Why should I have to put *that* in the same room with the Bogardus tankard and the Copley portrait of Lilian van Rensselaer?"

Here she pointed a scornful finger at an ancient rusted piece of iron grillwork that might have fitted into a small window space, two feet by two, which lay on a pillow of yellow velvet on the table by Tony Side's desk.

47

"Because it's a sacred relic," Tony replied, with the half-mocking smile that, as a modern director, he was careful to assume in discussing serious topics. "Because tradition has it that it covered a window on the ground floor of the Ludlow House in Barclay Street. During the Revolution it was the sole outlet to a large, dark storage room in which Yankee prisoners were miserably and sometimes fatally confined."

If the distressed virgin curator of beautiful things suggested too much the past, her superior was almost too redolent of the present and future. He had long chestnut locks—as long as his trustees would tolerate, perhaps half an inch longer—that fell oddly about a pale, hawklike face and greenish eyes that fixed his interlocutor with the expression of being able to take in any enormity. Tony twisted his long arms in a curious ravel and nodded his head repeatedly as if to say, "Ah, yes, keep on, keep going. I'm way ahead of you, *way* ahead!" It might have been the point of his act to be both emperor and clown.

"It's not that I haven't any feeling for those poor wretches," Aileen protested, her face clouding as it always did at the thought of pain. "God knows, it isn't that. But must their agony be commemorated in *my* gallery? It isn't as if there weren't memorials enough everywhere to dead patriots."

Aileen herself might have been an academic painting of a martyr. One could imagine viewing the long, gray, osseous face and those large, gray, desperately staring eyes raised heavenward, through the smoke of a heretic's pyre. It seemed a wasteful fate that had cast her, tall and bony, with neatly set hair and black dresses, in the role of priestess of antiques.

"Your concept of history is too limited, too snobbish," Tony warned her. "It's odd, for you're completely unsnobbish yourself. But be objective for once and take a new look at your eighteenth century. Aileen Post's eighteenth century. Isn't it all tankards and silverware and splendid portraits and mahogany furniture? Doesn't it boil down to the interior decoration of the rich? Where are your butchers and grocers? Where are your beggars? Where are your slaves?"

"But you shouldn't judge beautiful artifacts by their owners!" Aileen exclaimed with passion. "They represent the aspirations of the age! The way the spire of a gothic cathedral represents the thrust of man's soul toward heaven! What is history but the story of his reaching? Do you want a museum to show the whips and manacles, the starvation, the failure? Leave that to Madame Tussaud and the printed record. I want the person who comes into my gallery to breathe in the inspiration of the past!"

"Tut, tut, Aileen," Tony warned her, wagging a finger. "You're playing with nemesis. In your books the rich and mighty enjoy not only the delights of this world but the respect of posterity. What is left for the wretched but that pie in the sky they no longer believe in? Watch out! Those wretched can be very determined. They want their bit of the here and now."

"Who? The dead? The dead poor?"

"Why not?" Tony smiled broadly. "Aren't I helping them right now? By setting up the prison window in the very center of your gallery?" He got up and made her a little bow. "Those are orders, my dear."

Aileen left the room without another word. She knew that, mock bow or no, his orders were to be obeyed. Tony Side, under his perpetual smile, was a very serious young man who had no idea of staying in the Colonial Museum for more than a few years. It was too obvious that he was headed for greater things. He would keep his name before the eyes of other institutes—and particularly before the eyes of their trustees—by arranging shows that need have only slender ties to the colonial era. Already he had achieved a considerable success with a gaudy display of eighteenth-century balloons and primitive flying machines against a background of blown-up photographs of Cape Canaveral. It had even been written up in *Life*.

Traversing the Ludlow Gallery of decorative arts on her way back to her office, Aileen noted bitterly that there were only two people in it. Two visitors on a Saturday morning in the middle of the biggest city of the nation! It spoke little for the much touted "cultural revival." Aileen scorned the huge, mute, unthinking crowds that pushed by the high-priced master-pieces of the Metropolitan and the shaggy youths and pert-eyed, trousered girls who gawked at abstracts in the Whitney and the Modern. She told her friends at the Cosmopolitan Club that beauty was obsolete and fashion despot. She nodded grimly when they laughed at her. They would live to see their idols perish as hers was perishing.

When she had first come to the Colonial Museum, twenty-five years before, it had seemed a symbol of permanence in an

ever-changing city. The great memorial plaques in the front
hall, the names of benefactors carved in stone, the portraits of
former presidents and directors had heralded one into the
glittering collection as a released soul might be heralded into
perpetual bliss. The institution had seemed to rise above its
paucity of visitors; its dignity had waxed with its noble and
solemn emptiness. The solitary wanderer was rewarded by the
rich sustaining silence in which he found himself embraced. It
was as if the museum, with its high task of preserving beauty
for eternity, could afford the luxury of being capriciously choosy
as its votaries.

But now all that was over. Modern New York had repudiated
the concept of permanence. No grave, no shrine, no cache of
riches was any longer safe. No quantity of carved names on
marble, no number of "irrevocable" trust instruments drawn
up by long dead legal luminaries, no assemblage of conditions,
prayers, engraved stipulations or printed supplications could
arrest the erosion of endowments or the increase of costs. The
"dead hand" of the past became as light as dust when the
money it once represented had slipped away. Aileen found
herself faced with the probability that she might survive on her
own selected tomb.

It was unthinkable. The treasures of the Ludlow Gallery
were like so many members of her family. At least a third of
them had come to the museum as a direct result of her own
detective work and solicitations. The great Beekman breakfront
she had discovered in a storage house; the tea service of
Governor Winthrop had been redeemed at a sheriff's sale; the
Benjamin Wests of the Jarvis family had come as one man's
tribute to the "ardor and faith" of Aileen Post. She could
smell out eighteenth-century artifacts through stone walls; she
could track them down in the dreariest and most massive
accumulations of Victorians. How she pitied people who spoke
of her misguided adoration of the inanimate! As if a Copley
portrait could be dead! As if a coffee urn from Westover could
be without life! Only ugliness was dead, and it was Aileen's
passionate faith that it should never be resurrected.

Certainly nothing seemed deader than the iron window.
Tony, who for all his vulgarisms was a gentleman at heart, had
allowed her to choose its site in the gallery, but she knew that

he would correct her if she tried to hide it. She had placed it finally, framed in dark polished mahogany, upright, in a glass case, in front of the Wollaston portrait of Valerian Ludlow, the owner of the house from which it had come. Certainly it was conspicuous enough there, in the very center of the gallery. Peering through it, on his first inspection, Tony was pleased.

"It makes it look as if old Ludlow were behind bars," he pointed out with a chuckle. "Very likely he deserved to be."

Aileen at first tried not to see the window when she passed through the gallery. She would keep her eyes averted and quicken her pace as she approached the hated object. But she found that this made it worse. What good was it to banish it from her vision if she only succeeded in summoning it to fill her mind? Somehow she would have to make her peace with it, before it became an obsession.

She then adopted the practice, each time that she had to pass it, of making herself pause to look at it, or really to look through it, for there was nothing to see but its rusted blackness. She observed that one side was slightly more rugged than the other and had probably been the external side, facing on Barclay Street. Gazing through it, as if from inside the Ludlow house, she tried to imagine that thoroughfare as it must have appeared to an incarcerated patriot. Then she would walk around the grille and peer in, as if from the street, to visualize, with a shudder, the dark, fetid hole where the prisoners might have been penned. Sometimes visitors in the gallery would stop to watch her, and, when she had finished, taken her place to stare through the window to see what she had been noting. Aileen, amused, became almost reconciled to her new "artifact."

One morning, however, when she was alone in the gallery and looking through the grille from the "prison cell" side she had a curious and rather frightening experience. Ordinarily, she had not looked through the bars *at* anything in particular, but rather at her imagined reconstruciton of an eighteenth-century street. That day when she happened to glance at the portrait of Valerian Ludlow, it struck her that he would have often passed that barred cellar window, in his own house, on the way to his own front door, and she attempted to picture him as he might have appeared striding by, viewed at knee height. The portrait helped her by showing him full length, standing by an open window, looking out to a sea on which floated two little vessels, presumably his own, with wind-puffed sails. The expression on his round face (the cheeks seemed to repeat the puffed sails) was one of mercantile complacency. Mr. Ludlow had obviously been one of the blessed of earth.

But now Aileen seemed to see something in his countenance that she had not noticed before. The eyes, instead of being merely opaque, either because of the artist's inadequacy or the subject's lack of expression, had a hard, black glitter. They changed the whole aspect of the portrait from one of seemingly harmless self-satisfaction to one of almost sinister acquisitiveness. At the same time the quality of the past seemed to have lost its richness and glow. Mr. Ludlow's red velvet coat now had a shabby look, and the sea on which his vessels bobbed was brown rather than a lustrous green. Yet these changes, instead of making the whole picture more trenchant, more interesting, as they might have, seemed instead to push it back into an earlier era of clumsy primitives. Ludlow was now not only disagreeable; he was badly painted. Was his new degradation of character simply the artist's error? Had he come out mean, in the way of a clown drawn by a child? Or was Aileen seeing the real Ludlow for the first time?

Walking now quickly around the grilled window, with a conscious effort of will—for she was distinctly frightened—she turned suddenly and looked through it from the other side. She gave a little cry and then stopped her own mouth, for the sensation that had abruptly appalled her had as abruptly ceased. She had, for two seconds, stared into an absolute blackness, and at the same time her nostrils had been filled with a suffocating stench. Now she smelled nothing, and she was looking once more through the window toward the great glass case that housed the tankard collection.

Badly shaken, she returned to her office to go back to work on her article for the museum magazine on Dutch silver. But she was clear now that she would have to deal strongly with this preoccupation. In future she would walk by the window, not with consciously averted eye, not with undue attention, but simply taking it in casually, as she might take in any other exhibit. She would not flatter it with her fear or with her disdain. She would treat it, if its emanations compelled her to pause, with an icy disapproval, as she might treat a snoopy guard, set there by a jealous director to catch her out in something wrong.

By staying away from the window, she avoided any repetition of the shock of the sinister Ludlow and the black pit (figments, she assured herself, of her overcharged imagination), but she was not sure that she had eliminated all of the window's influence. She still had a sense, whenever she passed it, of some small, crouching, indistinguishable creature, some huge insect or tiny rodent, humped there by its base. And whenever she had to work near it, in the center of the gallery, she was conscious of something in the air, an aroma or maybe just a thickening of the atmosphere, that at once depressed her. If she looked about at the treasures of the gallery from any spot in the immediate circumference of the window, they appeared unaccountably drab. The silver seemed to thicken and tarnish and to lose the special elegance of its century. Bowls, plates, urns suddenly resembled the kind of ugly testimonials given to railroad presidents in the era following the Civil War. The beautiful carved wooden lady of victory that had once adorned the prow of a clipper ship might have been a widening, middle-aging nursemaid in Central Park. And the portraits, all the portraits, not only Valerian Ludlow's, seemed to have hardened into so many dusty merchants and merchants' wives as might have choked the wall of the Chamber of Commerce.

Sometimes she would watch visitors furtively from the door of her office to see, when they were standing near the prison window, if they noticed what she had noticed, but if they did, they showed no sign of it. Yet how could she be sure, if the things actually had changed, that they would notice it? Perhaps what she saw, under the malign influence of whatever the squatting creature was, was simply *their* vision of beautiful things. Perhaps that was the mystic significance of the window: that, peering through it, one saw art as it appeared to the Philistine! Aileen's mind had become a sea of hateful speculations.

One afternoon, at her desk, she looked up and gave a start to see an old lady standing before her. She had not heard anyone come in. It took her two or three seconds before she realized that she knew who it was. It was Mrs. Ada Ludlow Sherry, one of those "old New Yorkers" who made life for the curators both difficult and possible. She gave money and she gave things, but her gifts were hardly a *quid pro quo* for her almost daily interference. She was small and bent but very strong, and her skin, enamellike, and her hair, falsely red, gave the impression of having been preserved by a dipping in some hardening unguent. Her agate eyes snapped at Aileen.

"Are you aware, Miss Post, that an atrocious act of vandalism has been committed in your gallery?"

"Oh, no!"

"Some villain has poked a hole in my great-great-grandfather. Don't you ever check up on your portraits? There's a ghastly, gaping rip where his left eye was!"

"In Valerian Ludlow!" Aileen jumped up and ran into the gallery to the Wollaston painting. Sure enough, old Ludlow blinked at her with one black eye and one blue, the latter being the color of the wall on which he was hung. Aileen gave a little scream of panic.

"This was done within the hour!" she cried. "He had both eyes when I last went by!"

Tony Side was summoned, the alarm was rung and all guards were questioned. Nothing was discovered, and after an hour of futile excitement Aileen was back again at her desk, depleted and scared, with the irate Mrs. Sherry, who refused now to depart. Aileen felt nothing but antipathy as she listened to the old lady's animadversions. Obviously, Mrs. Sherry cared far more for the grudge than for the grievance. She had none of Aileen's nausea at the damage to a beautiful object or her despair for the soul of the perpetrator.

"Some black boy, of course," Mrs. Sherry was grumbling. "Unless it was a Puerto Rican. They're always prating about the hard times they've had, always griping about how they've been deprived of education and opportunities. Is *this* what they want opportunities for? I'd like to see the cat-o'-nine-tails brought back. I'd like to see these boys lashed before the public in Times Square! What do they exist for but to tear our world apart? They don't care that they have nothing to put in its place! It's revenge, pure and simple!"

"Revenge," Aileen murmured thoughtfully, glancing apprehensively through the doorway toward the iron grille. Could it be the revenge of a Yankee prisoner of war? But why? Revenge against whom?

"Everybody's too soft and sentimental with them," Mrs. Sherry continued. "If it *is* softness. If it isn't just cowardice, as I suspect it is. Where have our guts gone to, Miss Post? Where are our men, that we are exposed to all this? I tell you one thing, young lady. Nobody would have poked an eye out of Valerian Ludlow's portrait in his day!"

"What would he have done?"

"Don't you know what he would have done? Haven't you read his journal? *He* knew how to handle insubordinates!"

As Aileen watched the terrible old woman, she had just for a second the same eerie sense of blackness that she had experienced in peering through the iron grille. Then, as it passed, she felt a sudden, odd detachment from the immediate scene. She found herself observing Mrs. Sherry as if the latter had been a monologist performing at a private party. She noted the protuberance of the front molars and the drops of saliva at the corners of the thin lips. She marked how the almost transparent, onion-skin eyelids snapped up and down and how hatefully dark were the merciless eyes. Except for the teeth Mrs. Sherry might have been a bird, a big, dark bird of rich, subdued colors whose feathers only made more horrible its dark face and beak, a condor tearing at a carcass. Both of Aileen's hands went to her lips in horror as she saw her world in a sudden new light. The feathers, the feathers alone, were art. The head, the beak, the glazed eyes, the talons were—man!

"Oh, be quiet! Be quiet, please!"

Mrs. Sherry stared down at Aileen incredulously. "I beg your pardon?"

When Aileen, stunned, gathered that she must have actually uttered her reproach aloud, she desperately summoned up the courage to go on. "You're saying the most dreadful things, and you have no business to. You don't know who damaged that portrait! You have no idea. It might have been a guard. It might have been me. It might have been you, yourself!" Aileen rose as if propelled by two strong hands clutching her elbows, and she spoke with a passionate urgency, a wondering, bemused prisoner of her own new flow of eloquence. "How do I know that you're not just trying to get someone in trouble? Or a whole race of people in trouble? How do I know what mad, twisted motives you may have? Look at your umbrella. You might have done it with *that!* But, my God, there's something sticking to it!" She seized the umbrella and rushed out into the gallery crying, "Guard! Guard!" When the bewildered man hurried up to her she shouted, "I've got her. The vandal! She did it with this! Look!"

Here she held the umbrella up to the portrait, the tip toward the hole. Then she lowered it slowly, dumbly, apologetically, looking shamefaced at the shamefaced guard. For the round tip of the umbrella had a thick rubber cover. Mrs. Sherry must have made it do double duty as a walking stick. Pushed into a canvas, it would have made a much bigger hole than the one in Valerian Ludlow's left eye.

"And now, Miss Post, will you be so good as to return my property? And let me ask this gentleman to conduct me to the director of this institution that I may complain of your insane behavior?"

Mrs. Sherry was so carried away that, turning from the stricken Aileen after she had snatched back her umbrella, she made the mistake of taking the guard's arm. Her exit was comic rather than magnificent. But nothing could console Aileen.

Tony, when he came, was very kind. He said that the vandalism had obviously unnerved her. He regretted that so important a member of the museum as Mrs. Sherry should have been insulted, but he hoped that she could be placated. He suggested that Aileen would do well to take a few days off and get a good rest.

"No, I'm all right, I really am," she insisted in a stony voice. "I promise, you won't have to worry about me."

When Tony had left, obviously much concerned about her, Aileen sat for ten minutes, absolutely still. Then she rose and strode with a new resolution to the middle of the gallery. As she leaned slowly down and stared into the hated window, she whispered hoarsely:

"Who are you, in there? Why have you come back to haunt us? Are you the spirit of some poor boy who died in that black chamber?" As she listened, she felt her first impulse of sympathy for whatever might be behind those bars. She had a vision of a thin, undernourished face, that of some nineteen-year-old Yankee boy, with long light hair and eyes liquid with homesickness, pressed up against the bars. "Were you left behind in General Washington's retreat? Was that how the British caught you? But why do you hate the Ludlows? Wasn't their house requisitioned by the governor? Was that their fault?" In the silence, as she listened intently, she had again that eerie sense of a close malevolence. "Or do you know something about them that we don't know? Was Valerian Ludlow a secret Tory? Was he a traitor?"

The blackness that she imagined behind the bars seemed now to lift, and her eyes fell upon the great portrait in the corner of the gallery of General Cornwallis, his hand on a globe on which the eastern shoreline of the thirteen colonies was clearly visible. Aileen straightened up and returned to her office. There would be no further revelations that day.

The following morning she was greeted by the doorman with the news: "There's been another of them vandals in your gallery, Miss Post." When she arrived at her floor, breathless, after running up two flights, she found Tony and three guards standing before the glass case of the silver tankards. He silently pointed to something as she hurried to his side. On the top tray one of the tankards lay toppled over. Its cover had been wrenched off the hinges and had fallen to the bottom of the case. The coat of arms had been gashed several times by a heavy instrument, possibly a stone. She did not have to look twice to recognize the Ludlow crest.

"Nobody's to touch it until the detective from the police department comes," Tony explained. "This is a weird one. The glass, you see, has not been removed." He put his arm around Aileen's shoulders and led her out of earshot of the guards. "It had to be an inside job," he told her. "Whoever did it must have got the key to the case from your office. But we've checked, and your key case is locked. He may have slipped into your office one day when it was open, taken the key, had it duplicated and put it back. It might have been the same guy who used your umbrella to poke the hole in the Ludlow portrait while you were out to lunch."

"*My* umbrella!"

"Well, I didn't want to upset you, but we found a smitch of canvas by the rack in your office where you keep your pink umbrella. It has to be some nut, of course, with some fantastic grudge against the Ludlow family."

"Oh, you've put that together, have you?" she murmured. "You've recognized the Ludlow tankard?"

"My dear Aileen. Even though I'm a museum director, I'm not a complete nincompoop."

Aileen was seized with a fit of violent trembling. She felt the same fierce prosecuting excitement that she had experienced when she had denounced Mrs. Sherry to the guard. Pulling Tony further away down the gallery, she whispered desperately, "Maybe *I* did it! Maybe I poked the hole in the portrait and then tried to throw the blame on Mrs. Sherry! Maybe I came here last night and let myself into the gallery and scraped the tankard!"

Tony's little smile never failed him, but she could tell by the way it seemed just to flicker that he did not wholly dismiss the theory. "But assuming all this, my dear, what on earth would be your motive?"

"I had no motive."

"Then why would you do it?"

"Because I'm the instrument of a fiend! The fiend that you brought in when you made me take *that!*"

Tony took in the little barred window, and at last even his smile ceased. "I said before that you needed a rest," he replied in his kindest tone. "This time I insist upon it. I want you to take three weeks off, and I want you to see a doctor."

Aileen was surprised and heartened by her own reaction to this disaster. Instead of crumpling before circumstance, she discovered that her spirit was strong and her emotional state serene. When Tony told her that the police detective had said that the force used in rubbing the stone or other substance against the crest of the Ludlow tankard had been greater than that of a woman, she had merely nodded and taken her dignified leave of him. She had recovered faith in her own sanity and did not need the confirmation of a cop. She had promised that she would consult a psychiatrist, but she was already resolved that she would not. There was no use in a confrontation between the world of medicine and the occult. It could result only in her commitment to a lunatic asylum.

She was grateful for the solitude of her enforced vacation and of the time that it afforded her to deal with her ghostly opponent. For she knew now that she had one. No human being could help her. It was her grim and lonely task to track down and outwit the sinister spirit that was seeking to destroy her gallery.

She spent her days in the library of the New York Historical Society, reading everything that there was to read on the history of the Ludlow family. The material was rich. She found considerable evidence of a curious effeminate streak in the Ludlow males of the eighteenth century. The first Ludlow in New York, a royal governor, had insisted on wearing woman's robes while presiding at the council, on the theory that he thus more appropriately represented his sovereign, Queen Anne. A generation later, his son had been criticized for making his more muscular African slaves wait on table half-naked, and this son's son, in turn, incurred the resentment of society by keeping exotic birds, expensively imported from Rio, loose in the house where they pecked his guests. The wives of all these gentlemen, on the other hand, had been big, blocky, plainly dressed women, such as one might expect in a community that was still, after all, almost the frontier.

Aileen, like many old-maid scholars, was as sophisticated about the past as she was timid about the present, and she perfectly understood that there might have been a streak of cruelty, or even sadism, in such eccentrics as the male Ludlows. But nowhere could she find the slightest evidence that any of them had been guilty of any public or private injustice, and the record of Valerian Ludlow in the Revolution seemed to repudiate the least imputation of Toryism. She had come almost to the end of her documents when a librarian asked her if she would like to see the microfilm of the manuscript of Valerian Ludlow's journal.

"I should like to look at it, of course," she replied. "I've read it so often in print, I know it almost by heart."

"You mean the DeLancey Tyler edition."

"Well, yes. Isn't that the only one? It's supposed to be complete."

"*Supposed* to be."

Aileen looked more closely at the young man. "You mean it isn't?"

He shrugged. "Tyler was a great-grandson of the journalist. He published his book in 1900. You know how prudish people were in those days."

Aileen knew by the bound of her heart that her search was over. She spent the next two days tensely reading the diary of Valerian Ludlow on the microfilm machine. The librarian had been quite right. There were substantial sections omitted in the Tyler edition. Ludlow had been a vain and easily offended gentleman of exquisite tastes and domineering manner. He had entered in the journal every slight that he had imagined himself to have received, and he had carefully recorded every punishment meted out to a servant. His descendant and editor had left in all his purchases of artifacts, all his recorded dealings with architects and decorators, all his conversations with the great, but he had carefully suppressed the invidious details of the correction of his staff and family. Aileen read breathlessly as she cranked the machine, turning the pages of the neat, flowing, somehow merciless handwriting. The realization that she was on the threshold of her revelation was actually painful.

She found at last this entry, dated July 30, 1747:

I have neglected my journal for a week because of a disturbing episode which, through God's grace, has now ended happily for most but not all. A group of slaves last Tuesday seized a farm on Lydecker Street and held it against the bailiff and his men for twenty-four hours. What the purpose of these ignorant fellows was we do not know, and they all fled. One constable, however, was killed when his own rifle blew up in his face. Public feeling has been very passionate, and on Thursday morning a large mob called here to demand my Rolfe. I met the leaders at the doorstep, and, I must say, they were very civil. They explained their reasons for believing that Rolfe had been the leading insurrectionist. I found these reasons convincing, the more so as I had had to confine Rolfe to the storeroom only that morning for insubordination. I delivered him up for what I understood was to be a trial, but I doubt that he had one. What is sure is that the mob burnt him alive in Bowling Green. It was a slow fire, and they say the poor fellow's bellows could be heard for six hours. I have discussed this unfortunate matter with Attorney Reynolds, and he advises me that if no trial occurred, I may be able to demand the price of Rolfe from the City Council, as he was taken under a show of authority.

Aileen turned from the machine with a gasp and rocked to and fro in her agony. For minutes she writhed as if she had been that wretched creature on the fire. How could flesh endure it? Six *hours?* The tears came at last to her eyes as she gave herself up to the relief of hating mankind. Mankind? Could she hate Rolfe, too, bellowing hour after hour, bound over a small flame like a sausage? Could she hate the man who must have listened, agonized, at that storeroom window while his master negotiated with the mob? Oh, God, God! But there was no God. There was only beauty, and whatever commiseration she felt for Rolfe she had to prevent him from destroying that. She jumped up as she came out of her daze. If she were only in time!

When her taxi arrived at the museum she fled up the steps and jammed her way through the revolving door.

"Is everything all right, Tom?" she asked the doorman.

"Never a dull moment these days, Miss Post. We had quite a scare an hour ago in your gallery. There was some defective wiring in the broom closet that started a small fire. We've had the chief and hook and ladder and all. Some excitement! But it's all out now."

She bounded up the two flights to her office and fumbled crazily among her keys until she found the one for the prison window's case. Then she sped down the gallery and opened it. She paused for just a moment as she faced the hated bars, and murmuring, "Forgive me, Rolfe," she picked them up and bore them to the window over the courtyard. Looking down to be sure there was no one beneath, she shoved them out, closing her eyes as she heard the clangor of the smashing to a hundred pieces.

For a moment she felt as if someone were pulling her over the sill, dragging her after it. With a violent effort she bounded back and stared about her. She was alone, perfectly alone, although below she could hear the shouts of the alarmed guards. In a moment they would come up, and all would be over. She would lose the job that was simply her whole life. As the inky depression began to surge and bubble about her, like rising water in a filthy tub, she saw at last what it was that the squatting spirit had been after.

"Why me?" she could only groan. "Why, in God's name, me? Was it such a crime to think that even their possessions were beautiful?"

SEATON'S

AUNT

Walter de la Mare

I had heard rumors of Seaton's aunt long before I actually
encountered her. Seaton, in the hush of confidence, or at any
little show of toleration on our part, would remark, 'My aunt,'
or 'My old aunt, you know,' as if his relative might be a kind of
cement to an *entente cordiale*.

He had an unusual quantity of pocket-money; or, at any rate,
it was bestowed on him in unusually large amounts; and he
spent it freely, though none of us would have described him as
an 'awfully generous chap.' 'Hullo, Seaton,' we would say,
'the old Begum?' At the beginning of term, too, he used to
bring back surprising and exotic dainties in a box with a trick
padlock that accompanied him from his first appearance at
Gummidge's in a billycock hat to the rather abrupt conclusion
of his schooldays.

From a boy's point of view he looked distastefully foreign
with his yellowish skin, slow chocolate-coloured eyes, and lean
weak figure. Merely for his looks he was treated by most of us
true-blue Englishmen with condescension, hostility, or contempt. We used to call him 'Pongo,' but without any much
better excuse for the nickname than his skin. He was, that is,
in one sense of the term what he assuredly was not in the other
sense, a sport.

Seaton and I, as I may say, were never in any sense intimate
at school; our orbits only intersected in class. I kept deliberately aloof from him. I felt vaguely he was a sneak, and remained quite unmollified by advances on his side, which, in a

boy's barbarous fashion, unless it suited me to be magnanimous, I haughtily ignored.

We were both of us quick-footed, and at Prisoner's Base used occasionally to hide together. And so I best remember Seaton—his narrow watchful face in the dusk of a summer evening; his peculiar crouch, and his inarticulate whisperings and mumblings. Otherwise he played all games slackly and limply; used to stand and feed at his locker with a crony or two until his 'tuck' gave out; or waste his money on some outlandish fancy or other. He bought, for instance, a silver bangle, which he wore above his left elbow, until some of the fellows showed their masterly contempt of the practice by dropping it nearly red-hot down his neck.

It needed, therefore, a rather peculiar taste, and a rather rare kind of schoolboy courage and indifference to criticism, to be much associated with him. And I had neither the taste nor, probably, the courage. None the less, he did make advances, and on one memorable occasion went to the length of bestowing on me a whole pot of some outlandish mulberry-coloured jelly that had been duplicated in his term's supplies. In the exuberance of my gratitude I promised to spend the next half-term holiday with him at his aunt's house.

I had clean forgotten my promise when, two or three days before the holiday, he came up and triumphantly reminded me of it.

'Well, to tell you the honest truth, Seaton, old chap—' I began graciously: but he cut me short.

'My aunt expects you,' he said; 'she is very glad you are coming. She's sure to be quite decent to *you*, Withers.'

I looked at him in sheer astonishment; the emphasis was so uncalled for. It seemed to suggest an aunt not hitherto hinted at, and a friendly feeling on Seaton's side that was far more disconcerting than welcome.

We reached his aunt's house partly by train, partly by a lift in an empty farm-cart, and partly by walking. It was a whole-day holiday, and we were to sleep the night; he lent me extraordinary night-gear, I remember. The village street was unusually wide, and was fed from a green by two converging roads, with an inn, and a high green sign at the corner. About a hundred yards down the street was a chemist's shop—a Mr Tanner's.

We descended the two steps into his dusky and odorous interior to buy, I remember, some rat poison. A little beyond the chemist's was the forge. You then walked along a very narrow path, under a fairly high wall, nodding here and there with weeds and tufts of grass, and so came to the iron garden-gates, and saw the high flat house behind its huge sycamore. A coach-house stood on the left of the house, and on the right a gate led into a kind of rambling orchard. The lawn lay away over to the left again, and at the bottom (for the whole garden sloped gently to a sluggish and rushy pond-like stream) was a meadow.

We arrived at noon, and entered the gates out of the hot dust beneath the glitter of the dark-curtained windows. Seaton led me at once through the little garden-gate to show me his tadpole pond, swarming with what (being myself not in the least interested in low life) seemed to me the most horrible creatures—of all shapes, consistencies, and sizes, but with which Seaton was obviously on the most intimate of terms. I can see his absorbed face now as, squatting on his heels he fished the slimy things out in his sallow palms. Wearying at last of these pets, we loitered about awhile in an aimless fashion. Seaton seemed to be listening, or at any rate waiting, for something to happen or for someone to come. But nothing did happen and no one came.

That was just like Seaton. Anyhow, the first view I got of his aunt was when, at the summons of a distant gong, we turned from the garden, very hungry and thirsty, to go into luncheon. We were approaching the house when Seaton suddenly came to a standstill. Indeed, I have always had the impression that he plucked at my sleeve. Something, at least, seemed to catch me back, as it were, as he cried, 'Look out, there she is!'

She was standing at an upper window which opened wide on a hinge, and at first sight she looked an excessively tall and overwhelming figure. This, however, was mainly because the window reached all but to the floor of her bedroom. She was in reality rather an undersized woman, in spite of her long face and big head. She must have stood, I think, unusually still, with eyes fixed on us, though this impression may be due to Seaton's sudden warning and to my consciousness of the cautious and subdued air that had fallen on him at sight of her. I know that without the least reason in the world I felt a kind of

guiltiness, as if I had been 'caught.' There was a silvery star
pattern sprinkled on her black silk dress, and even from the
ground I could see the immense coils of her hair and the rings
on her left hand which was held fingering the small jet buttons
of her bodice. She watched our united advance without stirring, until, imperceptibly, her eyes raised and lost themselves
in the distance, so that it was out of an assumed reverie that
she appeared suddenly to awaken to our presence beneath her
when we drew close to the house.

'So this is your friend, Mr Smithers, I suppose?' she said,
bobbing to me.

'Withers, Aunt,' said Seaton.

'It's much the same,' she said, with eyes fixed on me. 'Come
in, Mr Withers, and bring him along with you.'

She continued to gaze at me—at least, I think she did so. I
know that the fixity of her scrutiny and her ironical 'Mr' made
me feel peculiarly uncomfortable. None the less she was extremely kind and attentive to me, though, no doubt, her kindness and attention showed up more vividly against her complete
neglect of Seaton. Only one remark that I have any recollection
of she made to him: 'When I look on my nephew, Mr Smithers,
I realize that dust we are, and dust shall become. You are hot,
dirty, and incorrigible, Arthur.'

She sat at the head of the table, Seaton at the foot, and I,
before a wide waste of damask tablecloth, between them. It
was an old and rather close dining-room, with windows thrown
wide to the green garden and a wonderful cascade of fading
roses. Miss Seaton's great chair faced this window, so that its
rose-reflected light shone full on her yellowish face, and on just
such chocolate eyes as my schoolfellow's, except that hers were
more than half-covered by unusually long and heavy lids.

There she sat, steadily eating, with those sluggish eyes fixed
for the most part on my face; above them stood the deep-lined
fork between her eyebrows; and above that the wide expanse of
a remarkable brow beneath its strange steep bank of hair. The
lunch was copious, and consisted, I remember, of all such
dishes as are generally considered too rich and too good for the
schoolboy digestion—lobster mayonnaise, cold game sausages,
an immense veal and ham pie farced with eggs, truffles, and
numberless delicious flavours; besides kickshaws, creams, and

sweetmeats. We even had a wine, a half-glass of old darkish sherry each.

Miss Seaton enjoyed and indulged an enormous appetite. Her example and a natural schoolboy voracity soon overcame my nervousness of her, even to the extent of allowing me to enjoy to the best of my bent so rare a spread. Seaton was singularly modest; the greater part of his meal consisted of almonds and raisins, which he nibbled surreptitiously and as if he found difficulty in swallowing them.

I don't mean that Miss Seaton 'conversed' with me. She merely scattered trenchant remarks and now and then twinkled a baited question over my head. But her face was like a dense and involved accompaniment to her talk. She presently dropped the 'Mr,' to my intense relief, and called me now Withers, or Wither, now Smithers, and even once towards the close of the meal distinctly Johnson, though how on earth my name suggested it, or whose face mine had reanimated in memory, I cannot conceive.

'And is Arthur a good boy at school, Mr Wither?' was one of her many questions. 'Does he please his masters? Is he first in his class? What does the reverend Dr Gummidge think of him, eh?'

I knew she was jeering at him, but her face was adamant against the least flicker of sarcasm or facetiousness. I gazed fixedly at a blushing crescent of lobster.

'I think you're eighth, aren't you, Seaton?'

Seaton moved his small pupils towards his aunt. But she continued to gaze with a kind of concentrated detachment at me.

'Arthur will never make a brilliant scholar, I fear,' she said, lifting a dexterousy burdened fork to her wide mouth . . .

After luncheon she preceded me up to my bedroom. It was a jolly little bedroom, with a brass fender and rugs and a polished floor, on which it was possible, I afterwards found, to play 'snow-shoes.' Over the washstand was a little black-framed water-colour drawing, depicting a large eye with an extremely fishlike intensity in the spark of light on the dark pupil; and in 'illuminated' lettering beneath was printed very minutely, 'Thou God Seest ME,' followed by a long looped monogram, 'S.S.,' in the corner. The other pictures were all of the sea: brigs on blue water; a schooner overtopping chalk cliffs; a rocky island of prodigious steepness, with two tiny sailors dragging a monstrous boat up a shelf of beach.

'This is the room, Withers, my poor dear brother William died in when a boy. Admire the view!'

I looked out of the window across the tree-tops. It was a day hot with sunshine over the green fields, and the cattle were standing swishing their tails in the shallow water. But the view at the moment was no doubt made more vividly impressive by the apprehension that she would presently enquire after my luggage, and I had brought not even a toothbrush. I need have had no fear. Hers was not that highly civilized type of mind that is stuffed with sharp, material details. Nor could her ample presence be described as in the least motherly.

'I would never consent to question a schoolfellow behind my nephew's back,' she said, standing in the middle of the room, 'but tell me, Smithers, why is Arthur so unpopular? You, I understand, are his only close friend.' She stood in a dazzle of sun, and out of it her eyes regarded me with such leaden penetration beneath their thick lids that I doubt if my face concealed the least thought from her. 'But there, there,' she added very suavely, stooping her head a little, 'don't trouble to answer me. I never extort an answer. Boys are queer fish. Brains might perhaps have suggested his washing his hands before luncheon; but—not my choice, Smithers. God forbid! And now, perhaps, you would like to go into the garden again. I cannot actually see from here, but I should not be surprised if Arthur is now skulking behind that hedge.'

He was. I saw his head come out and take a rapid glance at the windows.

'Join him, Mr Smithers; we shall meet again, I hope, at the teatable. The afternoon I spend in retirement.'

Whether or not, Seaton and I had not been long engaged with the aid of two green switches in riding round and round a lumbering old grey horse we found in the meadow, before a rather bunched-up figure appeared, walking along the fieldpath on the other side of the water, with a magenta parasol studiously lowered in our direction throughout her slow progress, as if that were the magnetic needle and we the fixed Pole. Seaton at once lost all nerve and interest. At the next lurch of the old mare's heels he toppled over into the grass, and I slid off the sleek broad back to join him where he stood, rubbing his

shoulder and sourly watching the rather pompous figure till it
was out of sight.

'Was that your aunt, Seaton?' I enquired; but not till then.
He nodded.

'Why didn't she take any notice of us, then?'

'She never does.'

'Why not?'

'Oh, she knows all right, without; that's the damn awful part
of it.' Seaton was one of the very few fellows at Gummidge's
who had the ostentation to use bad language. He had suffered
for it too. But it wasn't, I think, bravado. I believe he really felt
certain things more intensely than most of the other fellows,
and they were generally things that fortunate and average
people do not feel at all—the peculiar quality, for instance, of
the British schoolboy's imagination.

'I tell you, Withers,' he went on moodily, slinking across the
meadow with his hands covered up in his pockets, 'she sees
everything. And what she doesn't see she knows without.'

'But how?' I said, not because I was much interested, but
because the afternoon was so hot and tiresome and purposeless, and it seemed more of a bore to remain silent. Seaton
turned gloomily and spoke in a very low voice.

'Don't appear to be talking of her, if you wouldn't mind.
It's—because she's in league with the Devil.' He nodded his
head and stooped to pick up a round flat pebble. 'I tell you,' he
said, still stooping, 'you fellows don't realize what it is. I know
I'm a bit close and all that. But so would you be if you had that
old hag listening to every thought you think.'

I looked at him, then turned and surveyed one by one the
windows of the house.

'Where's your *pater*?' I said awkwardly.

'Dead, ages and ages ago, and my mother too. She's not my
aunt even by rights.'

'What is she, then?'

'I mean she's not my mother's sister, because my grandmother married twice; and she's one of the first lot. I don't
know what you call her, but anyhow she's not my real aunt.'

'She gives you plenty of pocket-money.'

Seaton looked steadfastly at me out of his flat eyes. 'She can't
give me what's mine. When I come of age half of the whole lot
will be mine; and what's more'—he turned his back on the

house—'I'll make her hand over every blessed shilling of it.'

I put my hands in my pockets and stared at Seaton. 'Is it much?'

He nodded.

'Who told you?' He got suddenly very angry; a darkish red came into his cheeks, his eyes glistened, but he made no answer, and we loitered listlessly about the garden until it was time for tea . . .

Seaton's aunt was wearing an extraordinary kind of lace jacket when we sidled sheepishly into the drawing-room together. She greeted me with a heavy and protracted smile, and bade me bring a chair close to the little table.

'I hope Arthur has made you feel at home,' she said as she handed me my cup in her crooked hand. 'He don't talk much to me; but then I'm an old woman. You must come again, Wither, and draw him out of his shell. You old snail!' She wagged her head at Seaton, who sat munching cake and watching her intently.

'And we must correspond, perhaps.' She nearly shut her eyes at me. 'You must write and tell me everything behind the creature's back.' I confess I found her rather disquieting company. The evening drew on. Lamps were brought in by a man with a nondescript face and very quiet footsteps. Seaton was told to bring out the chessmen. And we played a game, she and I, with her big chin thrust over the board at every move as she gloated over the pieces and occasionally croaked 'Check!'—after which she would sit back inscrutably staring at me. But the game was never finished. She simply hemmed me in with a gathering cloud of pieces that held me impotent, and yet one and all refused to administer to my poor flustered old king a merciful *coup de grâce*.

'There,' she said, as the clock struck ten—'a drawn game, Withers. We are very evenly matched. A very creditable defence, Withers. You know your room. There's supper on a tray in the dining-room. Don't let the creature over-eat himself. The gong will sound three-quarters of an hour *before* a punctual breakfast.' She held out her cheek to Seaton, and he kissed it with obvious perfunctoriness. With me she shook hands.

'An excellent game,' she said cordially, 'but my memory is poor, and'—she swept the pieces helter-skelter into the box—

'the result will never be known.' She raised her great head far back. 'Eh?'

It was a kind of challenge, and I could only murmur: 'Oh, I was absolutely in a hole, you know!' when she burst out laughing and waved us both out of the room.

Seaton and I stood and ate our supper, with one candlestick to light us, in a corner of the dining-room. 'Well, and how would you like it?' he said very softly, after cautiously poking his head round the doorway.

'Like what?'

'Being spied on—every blessed thing you do and think?'

'I shouldn't like it at all,' I said, 'if she does.'

'And yet you let her smash you up at chess!'

'I didn't let her!' I said indignantly.

'Well, you funked it, then.'

'And I didn't funk it either,' I said, 'she's so jolly clever with her knights.'

Seaton stared at the candle. 'Knights,' he said slowly. 'You wait, that's all.' And we went upstairs to bed.

I had not been long in bed, I think, when I was cautiously awakened by a touch on my shoulder. And there was Seaton's face in the candlelight—and his eyes looking into mine.

'What's up?' I said, lurching on to my elbow.

'*Ssh!* Don't scurry,' he whispered. 'She'll hear. I'm sorry for waking you, but I didn't think you'd be asleep so soon.'

'Why, what's the time, then?' Seaton wore, what was then rather unusual, a night-suit, and he hauled his big silver watch out of the pocket in his jacket.

'It's a quarter to twelve. I never get to sleep before twelve—not here.'

'What do you do, then?'

'Oh, I read: and listen.'

'Listen?'

Seaton stared into his candle-flame as if he were listening even then. 'You can't guess what it is. All you read in ghost stories, that's all rot. You can't see much, Withers, but you know all the same.'

'Know what?'

'Why, that they're there.'

'Who's there?' I asked fretfully, glancing at the door.

'Why, in the house. It swarms with 'em. Just you stand still and listen outside my bedroom door in the middle of the night. I have, dozens of times; they're all over the place.'

'Look here, Seaton,' I said, 'you asked me to come here, and I didn't mind chucking up a leave just to oblige you and because I'd promised; but don't get talking a lot of rot, that's all, or you'll know the difference when we get back.'

'Don't fret,' he said coldly, turning away. 'I shan't be at school long. And what's more, you're here now, and there isn't anybody else to talk to. I'll chance the other.'

'Look here, Seaton,' I said, 'you may think you're going to scare me with a lot of stuff about voices and all that. But I'll just thank you to clear out; and you may please yourself about pottering about all night.'

He made no answer; he was standing by the dressing-table looking across his candle into the looking-glass; he turned and stared slowly round the walls.

'Even this room's nothing more than a coffin. I suppose she told you—"It's all exactly the same as when my brother William died"—trust her for that! And good luck to him, say I. Look at that.' He raised his candle close to the little water-colour I have mentioned. 'There's hundreds of eyes like that in this house; and even if God does see you, He takes precious good care you don't see Him. And it's just the same with them. I tell you what, Withers, I'm getting sick of all this. I shan't stand it much longer.'

The house was silent within and without, and even in the yellowish radiance of the candle a faint silver showed through the open window on my blind. I slipped off the bedclothes, wide awake, and sat irresolute on the bedside.

'I know you're only guying me,' I said angrily, 'but why is the house full of—what you say? Why do you hear—what you do hear? Tell me that, you silly fool!'

Seaton sat down on a chair and rested his candlestick on his knee. He blinked at me calmly. 'She brings them,' he said, with lifted eyebrows.

'Who? Your aunt?'

He nodded.

'How?'

'I told you,' he answered pettishly. 'She's in league. You don't know. She as good as killed my mother; I know that. But it's not only her by a long chalk. She just sucks you dry, I know.

And that's what she'll do for me; because I'm like her—like my
mother, I mean. She simply hates to see me alive. I wouldn't
be like that old she-wolf for a million pounds. And so'—he
broke off, with a comprehensive wave of his candlestick—
'they're always here. Ah, my boy, wait till she's dead! She'll
hear something then, I can tell you. It's all very well now, but
wait till then! I wouldn't be in her shoes when she has to clear
out—for something. Don't you go and believe I care for ghosts,
or whatever you like to call them. We're all in the same box.
We're all under her thumb.'

He was looking almost nonchalantly at the ceiling at the
moment, when I saw his face change, saw his eyes suddenly
drop like shot birds and fix themselves on the cranny of the
door he had left just ajar. Even from where I sat I could see his
cheek change colour; it went greenish. He crouched without
stirring, like an animal. And I, scarcely daring to breathe, sat
with creeping skin, sourly watching him. His hands relaxed,
and he gave a kind of sigh.

'Was *that* one?' I whispered, with a timid show of jaunti-
ness. He looked round, opened his mouth, and nodded. 'What?'
I said. He jerked his thumb with meaningful eyes, and I knew
that he meant that his aunt had been there listening at our
door cranny.

'Look here, Seaton,' I said once more, wriggling to my feet.
'You may think I'm a jolly noodle; just as you please. But your
aunt has been civil to me and all that, and I don't believe a
word you say about her, that's all, and never did. Every
fellow's a bit off his pluck at night, and you may think it a fine
sport to try your rubbish on me. I heard your aunt come
upstairs before I fell asleep. And I'll bet you a level tanner
she's in bed now. What's more, you can keep your blessed
ghosts to yourself. It's a guilty conscience, I should think.'

Seaton looked at me intently, without answering for a moment. 'I'm not a liar, Withers; but I'm not going to quarrel
either. You're the only chap I care a button for; or, at any
rate, you're the only chap that's ever come here; and it's
something to tell a fellow what you feel. I don't care a fig for
fifty thousand ghosts; although I swear on my solemn oath that
I know they're here. But she'—he turned deliberately—'you
laid a tanner she's in bed, Withers; well, I know different.
She's never in bed much of the night, and I'll prove it, too, just

to show you I'm not such a nolly as you think I am. Come on!'

'Come on where?'

'Why, to see.'

I hesitated. He opened a large cupboard and took out a small dark dressing-gown and a kind of shawl-jacket. He threw the jacket on the bed and put on the gown. His dusky face was colourless, and I could see by the way he fumbled at the sleeves he was shivering. But it was no good showing the white feather now. So I threw the tasselled shawl over my shoulders and, leaving our candle brightly burning on the chair, we went out together and stood in the corridor.

'Now then, listen!' Seaton whispered.

We stood leaning over the staircase. It was like leaning over a well, so still and chill the air was all around us. But presently, as I suppose happens in most old houses, began to echo and answer in my ears a medley of infinite small stirrings and whisperings. Now out of the distance an old timber would relax its fibres, or a scurry die away behind the perishing wainscot. But amid and behind such sounds as these I seemed to begin to be conscious, as it were, of the lightest of footfalls, sounds as faint as the vanishing remembrance of voices in a dream. Seaton was all in obscurity except his face; out of that his eyes gleamed darkly, watching me.

'You'd hear, too, in time, my fine soldier," he muttered. 'Come on!'

He descended the stairs, slipping his lean fingers lightly along the balusters. He turned to the right at the loop, and I followed him barefooted along a thickly carpeted corridor. At the end stood a door ajar. And from here we very stealthily and in complete blackness ascended five narrow stairs. Seaton, with immense caution, slowly pushed open a door, and we stood together, looking into a great pool of duskiness, out of which, lit by the feeble clearness of a night-light, rose a vast bed. A heap of clothes lay on the floor; beside them two slippers dozed, with noses each to each, a foot or two apart. Somewhere a little clock ticked huskily. There was a close smell; lavender and eau de Cologne, mingled with the fragrance of ancient sachets, soap, and drugs. Yet it was a scent even more peculiarly compounded than that.

And the bed! I stared warily in; it was mounded gigantically, and it was empty.

Seaton turned a vague, pale face, all shadows: 'What did I say?' he uttered. 'Who's—who's the fool now, I say? How are we going to get back without meeting her, I say? Answer me Oh, I wish to God you hadn't come here, Withers.'

He stood audibly shivering in his skimpy gown, and could hardly speak for his teeth chattering. And very distinctly, in the hush that followed his whisper, I heard approaching a faint unhurried voluminous rustle. Seaton clutched my arm, dragged me to the right across the room to a large cupboard, and drew the door close to on us. And, presently, as with bursting lungs I peeped out into the long, low, curtained bedroom, waddled in that wonderful great head and body. I can see her now, all patched and lined with shadow, her tied-up hair (she must have had enormous quantities of it for so old a woman), her heavy lids above those flat, slow, vigilant eyes. She just passed across my ken in the vague dusk; but the bed was out of sight.

We waited on and on, listening to the clock's muffled ticking. Not the ghost of a sound rose up from the great bed. Either she lay archly listening or slept a sleep serener than an infant's. And when, it seemed, we had been hours in hiding and were cramped, chilled, and half suffocated, we crept out on all fours, with terror knocking at our ribs, and so down the five narrow stairs and back to the little candle-lit blue-and-gold bedroom.

Once there, Seaton gave in. He sat livid on a chair with closed eyes.

'Here,' I said, shaking his arm, 'I'm going to bed; I've had enough of this foolery; I'm going to bed.' His lips quivered, but he made no answer. I poured out some water into my basin and, with that cold pictured azure eye fixed on us, bespattered Seaton's sallow face and forehead and dabbled his hair. He presently sighed and opened fish-like eyes.

'Come on!' I said. 'Don't get shamming, there's a good chap. Get on my back, if you like, and I'll carry you into your bedroom.'

He waved me away and stood up. So, with my candle in one hand, I took him under the arm and walked him along according to his direction down the corridor. His was a much dingier room than mine, and littered with boxes, paper, cages, and clothes. I huddled him into bed and turned to go. And suddenly, I can hardly explain it now, a kind of cold and deadly terror swept over me. I almost ran out of the room, with eyes fixed rigidly in front of me, blew out my candle, and buried my head under the bedclothes.

When I awoke, roused not by a gong, but by a long-continued tapping at my door, sunlight was raying in on cornice and bedpost, and birds were singing in the garden. I got up, ashamed of the night's folly, dressed quickly, and went downstairs. The breakfast room was sweet with flowers and fruit and honey. Seaton's aunt was standing in the garden beside the open French window, feeding a great flutter of birds. I watched her for a moment, unseen. Her face was set in a deep reverie beneath the shadow of a big loose sun-hat. It was deeply lined, crooked, and, in a way I can't describe, fixedly vacant and strange. I coughed politely, and she turned with a prodigious smiling grimace to ask how I had slept. And in that mysterious fashion by which we learn each other's secret thoughts without a syllable said, I knew that she had followed every word and movement of the night before, and was triumphing over my affected innocence and ridiculing my friendly and too easy advances.

We returned to school, Seaton and I, lavishly laden, and by rail all the way. I made no reference to the obscure talk we had had, and resolutely refused to meet his eyes or to take up the hints he let fall. I was relieved—and yet I was sorry—to be going back, and strode on as fast as I could from the station, with Seaton almost trotting at my heels. But he insisted on buying more fruit and sweets—my share of which I accepted with a very bad grace. It was uncomfortably like a bribe, and, after all, I had no quarrel with his rum old aunt, and hadn't really believed half the stuff he had told me.

I saw as little of him as I could after that. He never referred to our visit or resumed his confidences, though in class I would sometimes catch his eye fixed on mine, full of a mute understanding, which I easily affected not to understand. He left Gummidge's, as I have said, rather abruptly, though I never heard of anything to his discredit. And I did not see him or have any news of him again till by chance we met one summer afternoon in the Strand.

He was dressed rather oddly in a coat too large for him and a bright silky tie. But we instantly recognized one another under the awning of a cheap jeweller's shop. He immediately attached himself to me and dragged me off, not too cheerfully, to lunch with him at an Italian restaurant near by. He chattered about our old school, which he remembered only with dislike and disgust; told me coldbloodedly of the disastrous fate of one or two of the older fellows who had been among his chief tormentors; insisted on an expensive wine and the whole gamut of the foreign menu; and finally informed me, with a good deal of niggling, that he had come up to town to buy an engagement-ring.

And of course: 'How is your aunt?' I enquired at last.

He seemed to have been awaiting the question. It fell like a stone into a deep pool, so many expressions flitted across his long, sad, sallow, un-English face.

'She's aged a good deal,' he said softly, and broke off.

'She's been very decent,' he continued presently after, and paused again. 'In a way.' He eyed me fleetingly. 'I dare say you heard that—she—that is, that we—had lost a good deal of money.'

'No,' I said.

'Oh, yes!' said Seaton, and paused again.

And somehow, poor fellow, I knew in the clink and clatter of glass and voices that he had lied to me; that he did not possess, and never had possessed, a penny beyond what his aunt had squandered on his too ample allowance of pocket-money.

'And the ghosts?' I enquired quizzically.

He grew instantly solemn, and, though it may have been my fancy, slightly yellowed. But 'You are making game of me, Withers,' was all he said.

He asked for my address, and I rather reluctantly gave him my card.

'Look here, Withers,' he said, as we stood together in the sunlight on the kerb, saying goodbye, 'here I am, and—and it's all very well. I'm not perhaps as fanciful as I was. But you are practically the only friend I have on earth—except Alice. . . . And there—to make a clean breast of it, I'm not sure that my aunt cares much about my getting married. She doesn't say so, of course. You know her well enough for that.' He looked sidelong at the rattling gaudy traffic.

'What I was going to say is this: Would you mind coming down? You needn't stay the night unless you please, though, of course, you know you would be awfully welcome. But I should like you to meet my—to meet Alice; and then, perhaps, you might tell me your honest opinion of—of the other too.'

I vaguely demurred. He pressed me. And we parted with a half promise that I would come. He waved his ball-topped cane at me and ran off in his long jacket after a bus.

A letter arrived soon after, in his small weak handwriting, giving me full particulars regarding route and trains. And without the least curiosity, even perhaps with some little annoyance that chance should have thrown us together again, I accepted his invitation and arrived one hazy midday at his out-of-the-way station to find him sitting on a low seat under a clump of 'double' hollyhocks, awaiting me.

He looked preoccupied and singularly listless but seemed, none the less, to be pleased to see me.

We walked up the village street, past the little dingy apothecary's and the empty forge, and, as on my first visit, skirted the house together, and, instead of entering by the front door, made our way down the green path into the garden at the back. A pale haze of cloud muffled the sun; the garden lay in a grey shimmer—its old trees, its snap-dragoned faintly glittering walls. But now there was an air of slovenliness where before all had been neat and methodical. In a patch of shallowy dug soil stood a worn-down spade leaning against a tree. There was an old decayed wheelbarrow. The roses had run to leaf and briar; the fruit-trees were unpruned. The goddess of neglect had made it her secret resort.

'You ain't much of a gardener, Seaton,' I said at last, with a sigh of relief.

'I think, do you know, I like it best like this,' said Seaton. 'We haven't any man now, of course. Can't afford it.' He stood staring at his little dark oblong of freshly turned earth. 'And it always seems to me,' he went on ruminatingly, 'that, after all, we are all nothing better than interlopers on the earth, disfiguring and staining wherever we go. It may sound shocking blasphemy to say so; but then it's different here, you see. We are further away.'

'To tell you the truth, Seaton, I *don't* quite see,' I said; 'but it isn't a new philosophy, is it? Anyhow, it's a precious beastly one.'

'It's only what I think,' he replied, with all his odd old stubborn meekness. 'And one thinks as one *is*.'

We wandered on together, talking little, and still with that expression of uneasy vigilance on Seaton's face. He pulled out his watch as we stood gazing idly over the green meadows and the dark motionless bulrushes.

'I think, perhaps, it's nearly time for lunch,' he said. 'Would you like to come in?'

We turned and walked slowly towards the house, across whose windows I confess my own eyes, too, went restlessly meandering in search of its rather disconcerting inmate. There was a pathetic look of bedraggledness, of want of means and care, rust and overgrowth and faded paint. Seaton's aunt, a little to my relief, did not share our meal. So he carved the cold meat, and dispatched a heaped-up plate by an elderly servant for his aunt's private consumption. We talked little and in half-suppressed tones, and sipped some Madeira which Seaton after listening for a moment or two fetched out of the great mahogany sideboard.

I played him a dull and effortless game of chess, yawning between the moves he himself made almost at haphazard, and with attention elsewhere engaged. Towards five o'clock came the sound of a distant ring, and Seaton jumped up, overturning the board, and so ended a game that else might have fatuously continued to this day. He effusively excused himself, and after some little while returned with a slim, dark, pale-faced girl of about nineteen, in a white gown and hat, to whom I was presented with some little nervousness as his 'dear old friend and schoolfellow.'

We talked on in the golden afternoon light, still, as it seemed to me, and even in spite of our efforts to be lively and gay, in a half-suppressed, lack-lustre fashion. We all seemed, if it were not my fancy, to be expectant, to be almost anxiously awaiting an arrival, the appearance of someone whose image filled our collective consciousness. Seaton talked least of all, and in a restless interjectory way, as he continually fidgeted from chair to chair. At last he proposed a stroll in the garden before the sun should have quite gone down.

Alice walked between us. Her hair and eyes were conspicuously dark against the whiteness of her gown. She carried herself not ungracefully, and yet with peculiarly little movement of her arms and body, and answered us both without turning her head. There was a curious provocative reserve in that impassive melancholy face. It seemed to be haunted by some tragic influence of which she herself was unaware.

And yet somehow I knew—I believe we all knew—that this walk, this discussion of their future plans was a futility. I had nothing to base such scepticism on, except only a vague sense of oppression, a foreboding consciousness of some inert invincible power in the background, to whom optimistic plans and love-making and youth are as chaff and thistledown. We came back, silent, in the last light. Seaton's aunt was there—under an old brass lamp. Her hair was as barbarously massed and curled as ever. Her eyelids, I think, hung even a little heavier in age over their slow-moving inscrutable pupils. We filed in softly out of the evening, and I made my bow.

'In this short interval, Mr Withers,' she remarked amiably, 'you have put off youth, put on the man. Dear me, how sad it is to see the young days vanishing! Sit down. My nephew tells me you met by chance—or act of Providence, shall we call it?—and in my beloved Strand! You, I understand, are to be best man—yes, best man! Or am I divulging secrets?' She surveyed Arthur and Alice with overwhelming graciousness. They sat apart on two low chairs and smiled in return.

'And Arthur—how do you think Arthur is looking?'

'I think he looks very much in need of a change,' I said.

'A change! Indeed?' She all but shut her eyes at me and with an exaggerated sentimentality shook her head. 'My dear Mr Withers! Are we not *all* in need of a change in this fleeting, fleeting world?' She mused over the remark like a connoisseur. 'And you,' she continued, turning abruptly to Alice, 'I hope you pointed out to Mr Withers all my pretty bits?'

'We only walked round the garden,' the girl replied; then, glancing at Seaton, added almost inaudibly, 'it's a very beautiful evening.'

'*Is* it?' said the old lady, starting up violently. 'Then on this very beautiful evening we will go in to supper. Mr Withers, your arm; Arthur, bring your bride.'

We were a queer quarter, I thought to myself, as I solemnly led the way into the faded, chilly dining-room, with this indefinable old creature leaning wooingly on my arm—the large flat bracelet on the yellow-laced wrist. She fumed a little, breathing heavily, but as if with an effort of the mind rather than of the body; for she had grown much stouter and yet little more proportionate. And to talk into that great white face, so close to mine, was a queer experience in the dim light of the corridor, and even in the twinkling crystal of the candles. She was naïve—appallingly naïve; she was crafty and challenging; she was even arch; and all these in the brief, rather puffy passage from one room to the other, with these two tongue-tied children bringing up the rear. The meal was tremendous. I have never seen such a monstrous salad. But the dishes were greasy and over-spiced, and were indifferently cooked. One thing only was quite unchanged—my hostess's appetite was as gargantuan as ever. The heavy silver candelabra that lighted us stood before her high-backed chair. Seaton sat a little removed, his plate almost in darkness.

And throughout this prodigious meal his aunt talked, mainly to me, mainly *at* him, but with an occasional satirical sally at Alice and muttered explosions of reprimand to the servant. She had aged, and yet, if it be not nonsense to say so, seemed no older. I suppose to the Pyramids a decade is but as the rustling down of a handful of dust. And she reminded me of some such unshakeable prehistoricism. She certainly was an amazing talker—rapid, egregious, with a delivery that was perfectly overwhelming. As for Seaton—her flashes of silence were for him. On her enormous volubility would suddenly fall a hush; acid sarcasm would be left implied; and she would sit softly moving her great head, with eyes fixed full in a dreamy smile but with her whole attention, one could see, slowly, joyously absorbing his mute discomfiture.

She confided in us her views on a theme vaguely occupying at the moment, I suppose, all our minds. 'We have barbarous institutions, and so must put up, I suppose, with a never-ending procession of fools—of fools *ad infinitum*. Marriage, Mr Withers, was instituted in the privacy of a garden; *sub rosa*, as it were. Civilization flaunts it in the glare of day. The dull marry the poor; the rich the effete; and so our New Jerusalem is peopled with naturals, plain and coloured, at either end. I detest folly; I detest still more (if I must be frank, dear Arthur) mere cleverness. Mankind has simply become a tailless host of uninstinctive animals. We should never have taken to Evolution, Mr Withers. "Natural Selection!"—little gods and fishes! —the deaf for the dumb. We should have used our brains— intellectual pride, the ecclesiastics call it. And by brains I mean—what do I mean, Alice?—I mean, my dear child,' and she laid two gross fingers on Alice's narrow sleeve, 'I mean courage. Consider it, Arthur. I read that the scientific world is once more beginning to be afraid of spiritual agencies. Spiritual agencies that tap, and actually float, bless their hearts! I think just one more of those mulberries—thank you.

'They talk about "blind Love," ' she ran on derisively as she helped herself, her eyes roving over the dish, 'but why blind? I think, Mr Withers, from weeping over its rickets. After all, it is we plain women that triumph, is it not so—beyond the mockery of time. Alice, now! Fleeting, fleeting is youth, my child. What's that you were confiding to your plate, Arthur? Satirical boy. He laughs at his old aunt: nay, but thou didst laugh. He detests all sentiment. He whispers the most acid asides. Come, my love, we will leave these cynics; we will go and commiserate with each other on our sex. The choice of two evils, Mr Smithers!' I opened the door, and she swept out as if borne on a torrent of unintelligible indignation; and Arthur and I were left in the clear four-flamed light alone.

For a while we sat in silence. He shook his head at my cigarette-case, and I lit a cigarette. Presently he fidgeted in his chair and poked his head forward into the light. He paused to rise, and shut again the shut door.

'How long will you be?' he asked me.

I laughed.

'Oh, it's not that!' he said, in some confusion. 'Of course, I like to be with her. But it's not that. The truth is, Withers, I don't care about leaving her too long with my aunt.'

I hesitated. He looked at me questioningly.

'Look here, Seaton,' I said, 'you know well enough that I don't want to interfere in your affairs, or to offer advice where it is not wanted. But don't you think perhaps you may not treat your aunt quite in the right way? As one gets old, you know, a little give and take. I have an old godmother, or something of the kind. She's a bit queer, too . . . A little allowance; it does no harm. But hang it all, I'm no preacher.'

He sat down with his hands in his pockets and still with his eyes fixed almost incredulously on mine. 'How?' he said.

'Well, my dear fellow, if I'm any judge—mind, I don't say that I am—but I can't help thinking she thinks you don't care

for her; and perhaps takes your silence for—for bad temper.
She has been very decent to you, hasn't she?'
     ' "Decent"? My God!' said Seaton.
     I smoked on in silence; but he continued to look at me with
that peculiar concentration I remembered of old.
     'I don't think, perhaps, Withers,' he began presently, 'I
don't think you quite understand. Perhaps you are not quite
our kind. You always did, just like the other fellows, guy me at
school. You laughed at me that night you came to stay here—
about the voices and all that. But I don't mind being laughed
at—because I know.'
     'Know what?' It was the same old system of dull question
and evasive answer.
     'I mean I know that what we see and hear is only the
smallest fraction of what is. I know she lives quite out of this.
She *talks* to you; but it's all make-believe. It's all a "parlour
game." She's not really with you; only pitting her outside wits
against yours and enjoying the fooling. She's living on inside on
what you're rotten without. That's what it is—a cannibal feast.
She's a spider. It doesn't much matter what you call it. It
means the same kind of thing. I tell you, Withers, she hates
me; and you can scarcely dream what that hatred means. I
used to think I had an inkling of the reasons. It's oceans deeper
than that. It just lies behind: herself against myself. Why, after
all, how much do we really understand of anything? We don't
even know our own histories, and not a tenth, not a tenth of
the reasons. What has life been to me?—nothing but a trap.
And when one sets oneself free for a while, it only begins
again. I thought you might understand; but you are on a
different level: that's all.'
     'What on earth are you talking about?' I said contemptu-
ously, in spite of myself.
     'I mean what I say,' he said gutturally. 'All this outside's only
make-believe—but there! what's the good of talking? So far as
this is concerned I'm as good as done. You wait.'
     Seaton blew out three of the candles and, leaving the vacant
room in semi-darkness, we groped our way along the corridor
to the drawing-room. There a full moon stood shining in at the
long garden windows. Alice sat stooping at the door, with her
hands clasped in her lap, looking out, alone.
     'Where is she?' Seaton asked in a low tone.

She looked up, and their eyes met in a glance of instantaneous understanding, and the door immediatley afterwards opened behind us.

'*Such* a moon!' said a voice, that once heard, remained unforgettably on the ear. 'A night for lovers, Mr Withers, if ever there was one. Get a shawl, my dear Arthur, and take Alice for a little promenade. I dare say we old cronies will manage to keep awake. Hasten, hasten, Romeo! My poor, poor Alice, how laggard a lover!'

Seaton returned with a shawl. They drifted out into the moonlight. My companion gazed after them till they were out of hearing, turned to me gravely, and suddenly twisted her white face into such a convulsion of contemptuous amusement that I could only stare blankly in reply.

'Dear innocent children!' she said, with inimitable unctuousness. 'Well, well, Mr Withers, we poor seasoned old creatures must move with the times. Do you sing?'

I scouted the idea.

'Then you must listen to my playing. Chess'—she clasped her forehead with both cramped hands—'chess is now completely beyond my poor wits.'

She sat down at the piano and ran her fingers in a flourish over the keys. 'What shall it be? How shall we capture them, those passionate hearts? That first fine careless rapture? Poetry itself.' She gazed softly into the garden a moment and presently, with a shake of her body, began to play the opening bars of Beethoven's 'Moonlight' Sonata. The piano was old and woolly. She played without music. The lamplight was rather dim. The moonbeams from the window lay across the keys. Her head was in shadow. And whether it was simply due to her personality or to some really occult skill in her playing I cannot say; I only know that she gravely and deliberately set herself to satirize the beautiful music. It brooded on the air, disillusioned, charged with mockery and bitterness. I stood at the window; far down the path I could see the white figure glimmering in that pool of colourless light. A few faint stars shone, and still that amazing woman behind me dragged out of the unwilling keys her wonderful grotesquerie of youth and love and beauty. It came to an end. I knew the player was watching me. 'Please, please, go on!' I murmured, without turning. '*Please* go on playing, Miss Seaton.'

No answer was returned to this honeyed sarcasm, but I realized in some vague fashion that I was being acutely scrutinized, when suddenly there followed a procession of quiet, plaintive chords which broke at last softly into the hymn, 'A Few More Years Shall Roll.'

I confess it held me spellbound. There is a wistful, strained plangent pathos in the tune; but beneath those masterly old hands it cried softly and bitterly the solitude and desperate estrangement of the world. Arthur and his lady-love vanished from my thoughts. No one could put into so hackneyed an old hymn tune such an appeal who had never known the meaning of the words. Their meaning, anyhow, isn't commonplace.

I turned a fraction of an inch to glance at the musician. She was leaning forward a little over the keys, so that at the approach of my silent scrutiny she had but to turn her face into the thin flood of moonlight for every feature to become distinctly visible. And so, with the tune abruptly terminated, we steadfastly regarded one another; and she broke into a prolonged chuckle of laughter.

'Not quite so seasoned as I supposed, Mr Withers. I see you are a real lover of music. To me it is too painful. It evokes too much thought . . .'

I could scarcely see her little glittering eyes under their penthouse lids.

'And now,' she broke off crisply, 'tell me, as a man of the world, what do you think of my new niece?'

I was not a man of the world, nor was I much flattered in my stiff and dullish way of looking at things by being called one; and I could answer her without the least hesitation.

'I don't think, Miss Seaton, I'm much of a judge of character. She's very charming.'

'A brunette?'

'I think I prefer dark women.'

'And why? Consider, Mr Withers; dark hair, dark eyes, dark cloud, dark night, dark vision, dark death, dark grave, dark DARK!'

Perhaps the climax would have rather thrilled Seaton, but I was too thick-skinned. 'I don't know much about all that,' I answered rather pompously. 'Broad daylight's difficult enough for most of us.'

'Ah,' she said, with a sly inward burst of satirical laughter.

'And I suppose,' I went on, perhaps a little nettled, 'it isn't the actual darkness one admires, it's the contrast of the skin, and the colour of the eyes, and—and their shining. Just as,' I went blundering on, too late to turn back, 'just as you only see the stars in the dark. It would be a long day without any evening. As for death and the grave, I don't suppose we shall much notice that.' Arthur and his sweetheart were slowly returning along the dewy path. 'I believe in making the best of things.'

'How very interesting!' came the smooth answer. 'I see you are a philosopher, Mr Withers. H'm! "As for death and the grave, I don't suppose we shall much notice that." Very interesting . . . And I'm sure,' she added in a particularly suave voice, 'I profoundly hope so.' She rose slowly from her stool. 'You will take pity on me again, I hope. You and I would get on famously—kindred spirits—elective affinities. And, of course, now that my nephew's going to leave me, now that his affections are centred on another, I shall be a very lonely old woman . . . Shall I not, Arthur?'

Seaton blinked stupidly. 'I didn't hear what you said, Aunt.'

'I was telling our old friend, Arthur, that when you are gone I shall be a very lonely old woman.'

'Oh, I don't think so,' he said in a strange voice.

'He means, Mr Withers, he means, my dear child,' she said, sweeping her eyes over Alice, 'he means that I shall have memory for company—heavenly memory—the ghosts of other days. Sentimental boy! And did you enjoy our music, Alice? Did I really stir that youthful heart? . . . O, O, O,' continued the horrible old creature, 'you billers and cooers, I have been listening to such flatteries, such confessions! Beware, beware, Arthur, there's many a slip.' She rolled her little eyes at me, she shrugged her shoulders at Alice, and gazed an instant stonily into her nephew's face.

I held out my hand. 'Good night, good night!' she cried. 'He that fights and runs away. Ah, good night, Mr Withers; come again soon!' She thrust out her cheek at Alice, and we all three filed slowly out of the room.

Black shadow darkened the porch and half the spreading sycamore. We walked without speaking up the dusty village street. Here and there a crimson window glowed. At the fork of the high-road I said goodbye. But I had taken hardly more than a dozen paces when a sudden impulse seized me.

'Seaton!' I called.

He turned in the cool stealth of the moonlight.

'You have my address; if by any chance, you know, you should care to spend a week or two in town between this and the—the Day, we should be delighted to see you.'

'Thank you, Withers, thank you,' he said in a low voice.

'I dare say'—I waved my stick gallantly at Alice—'I dare say you will be doing some shopping; we could all meet,' I added, laughing.

'Thank you, thank you, Withers—immensely,' he repeated.

And so we parted.

But they were out of the jog-trot of my prosaic life. And being of a stolid and incurious nature, I left Seaton and his marriage, and even his aunt, to themselves in my memory, and scarcely gave a thought to them until one day I was walking up the Strand again, and passed the flashing gloaming of the second-rate jeweller's shop where I had accidentally encountered my old schoolfellow in the summer. It was one of those stagnant autumnal days after a night of rain. I cannot say why, but a vivid recollection returned to my mind of our meeting and of how suppressed Seaton had seemed, and of how vainly he had endeavoured to appear assured and eager. He must be married by now, and had doubtless returned from his honeymoon. And I had clean forgotten my manners, had sent not a word of congratulation, nor—as I might very well have done, and as I knew he would have been pleased at my doing—even the ghost of a wedding present. It was just as of old.

On the other hand, I pleaded with myself, I had had no invitation. I paused at the corner of Trafalgar Square, and at the bidding of one of those caprices that seize occasionally on even an unimaginative mind, I found myself pelting after a green bus, and actually bound on a visit I had not in the least intended or foreseen.

The colours of autumn were over the village when I arrived. A beautiful late afternoon sunlight bathed thatch and meadow. But it was close and hot. A child, two dogs, a very old woman with a heavy basket I encountered. One or two incurious tradesmen looked idly up as I passed by. It was all so rural and remote, my whimsical impulse had so much flagged, that for a while I hesitated to venture under the shadow of the sycamore-tree to enquire after the happy pair. Indeed I first passed by the faint-blue gates and continued my walk under the high, green, and tufted wall. Hollyhocks had attained their topmost bud and seeded in the little cottage gardens beyond; the Michaelmas daisies were in flower; a sweet warm aromatic smell of fading leaves was in the air. Beyond the cottages lay a field where cattle were grazing, and beyond that I came to a little churchyard. Then the road wound on, pathless and house-less, among gorse and bracken. I turned impatiently and walked quickly back to the house and rang the bell.

The rather colourless elderly woman who answered my en-quiry informed me that Miss Seaton was at home, as if only taciturnity forbade her adding, 'But she doesn't want to see *you*.'

'Might I, do you think, have Mr Arthur's address?' I said.

She looked at me with quiet astonishment as if waiting for an explanation. Not the faintest of smiles came into her thin face.

'I will tell Miss Seaton,' she said after a pause. 'Please walk in.'

She showed me into the dingy undusted drawing-room, filled with evening sunshine and with the green-dyed light that penetrated the leaves overhanging the long French windows. I sat down and waited on and on, occasionally aware of a creak-ing footfall overhead. At last the door opened a little, and the great face I had once known peered round at me. For it was enormously changed; mainly, I think, because the aged eyes had rather suddenly failed, and so a kind of stillness and darkness lay over its calm and wrinkled pallor.

'Who is it?' she asked.

I explained myself and told her the occasion of my visit.

She came in, shut the door carefully after her, and, though the fumbling was scarcely perceptible, groped her way to a chair. She had on an old dressing-gown, like a cassock, of a patterned cinnamon colour.

'What is it you want?' she said, seating herself and lifting her blank face to mine.

'Might I just have Arthur's address?' I said deferentially. 'I am so sorry to have disturbed you.'

'H'm. You have come to see my nephew?'

'Not necessarily to see him, only to hear how he is, and, of course, Mrs Seaton, too. I am afraid my silence must have appeared . . .'

'He hasn't noticed your silence,' croaked the old voice out of the great mask; 'besides, there isn't any Mrs Seaton.'

'Ah, then,' I answered, after a momentary pause, 'I have not seemed so black as I painted myself! And how is Miss Outram?'

'She's gone into Yorkshire,' answered Seaton's aunt.

'And Arthur too?'

She did not reply, but simply sat blinking at me with lifted chin, as if listening, but certainly not for what I might have to say. I began to feel rather at a loss.

'You were no close friend of my nephew's, Mr Smithers?' she said presently.

'No,' I answered, welcoming the cue, 'and yet, do you know, Miss Seaton, he is one of the very few of my old schoolfellows I have come across in the last few years, and I suppose as one gets older one begins to value old associations . . .' My voice seemed to trail off into a vacuum. 'I thought Miss Outram,' I hastily began again, 'a particularly charming girl. I hope they are both quite well.'

Still the old face solemnly blinked at me in silence.

'You must find it very lonely, Miss Seaton, with Arthur away?'

'I was never lonely in my life,' she said sourly. 'I don't look to flesh and blood for my company. When you've got to be my age, Mr Smithers (which God forbid), you'll find life a very different affair from what you seem to think it is now. You won't seek company then, I'll be bound. It's thrust on you.' Her face edged round to the clear green light, and her eyes groped, as it were, over my vacant, disconcerted face. 'I dare say, now,' she said, composing her mouth, 'I dare say my nephew told you a good many tarradiddles in his time. Oh, yes, a good many, eh? He was always a liar. What, now, did he say of me? Tell me, now.' She leant forward as far as she could, trembling, with an ingratiating smile.

'I think he is rather superstitious,' I said coldly, 'but, honestly, I have a very poor memory, Miss Seaton.'

'Why?' she said. '*I* haven't.'

'The engagement hasn't been broken off, I hope.'

'Well, between you and me,' she said, shrinking up and with an immensely confidential glance, 'it has.'

'I'm sure I'm very sorry to hear it. And where is Arthur?'

'Eh?'

'Where is Arthur?'

We faced each other mutely among the dead old bygone furniture. Past all my analysis was that large, flat, grey, cryptic countenance. And then, suddenly, our eyes for the first time really met. In some indescribable way out of that thick-lidded obscurity a far small something stooped and looked out at me for a mere instant of time that seemed of almost intolerable protraction. Involuntarily I blinked and shook my head. She muttered something with great rapidity, but quite inarticulately; rose and hobbled to the door. I thought I heard, mingled in broken mutterings, something about tea.

'Please, please, don't trouble,' I began, but could say no more, for the door was already shut between us. I stood and looked out on the long-neglected garden. I could just see the bright weedy greenness of Seaton's tadpole pond. I wandered about the room. Dusk began to gather, the last birds in that dense shadowiness of trees had ceased to sing. And not a sound was to be heard in the house. I waited on and on, vainly speculating. I even attempted to ring the bell; but the wire was broken, and only jangled loosely at my efforts.

I hesitated, unwilling to call or to venture out, and yet more unwilling to linger on, waiting for a tea that promised to be an exceedingly comfortless supper. And as darkness drew down, a feeling of the utmost unease and disquietude came over me. All my talks with Seaton returned on me with a suddenly enriched meaning. I recalled again his face as we had stood hanging over the staircase, listening in the small hours to the inexplicable stirrings of the night. There were no candles in the room; every minute the autumnal darkness deepened. I cautiously opened the door and listened, and with some little dismay withdrew, for I was uncertain of my way out. I even tried the garden, but was confronted under a veritable thicket of foliage by a padlocked gate. It would be a little too ignominious to be caught scaling a friend's garden fence!

Cautiously returning into the still and musty drawing-room, I took out my watch, and gave the incredible old woman ten minutes in which to reappear. And when that tedious ten minutes had ticked by I could scarcely distinguish its hands. I determined to wait no longer, drew open the door and, trusting to my sense of direction, groped my way through the corridor that I vaguely remembered led to the front of the house.

I mounted three or four stairs and, lifting a heavy curtain, found myself facing the starry fanlight of the porch. From here I glanced into the gloom of the dining-room. My fingers were on the latch of the outer door when I heard a faint stirring in the darkness above the hall. I looked up and became conscious of, rather than saw, the huddled old figure looking down on me.

There was an immense hushed pause. Then, 'Arthur, Arthur,' whispered an inexpressibly peevish rasping voice, 'is that you? Is that you, Arthur?'

I can scarcely say why, but the question startled me. No conceivable answer occurred to me. With head craned back, hand clenched on my umbrella, I continued to stare up into the gloom, in this fatuous confrontation.

'Oh, oh,' the voice croaked. 'It is *you*, is it? *That* disgusting man! . . . Go away out. Go away out.'

At this dismissal, I wrenched open the door and, rudely slamming it behind me, ran out into the garden, under the gigantic old sycamore, and so out at the open gate.

I found myself half up the village street before I stopped running. The local butcher was sitting in his shop reading a piece of newspaper by the light of a small oil-lamp. I crossed the road and enquired the way to the station. And after he had with minute and needless care directed me, I asked casually if Mr Arthur Seaton still lived with his aunt at the big house just beyond the village. He poked his head in at the little parlour door.

'Here's a gentleman enquiring after young Mr Seaton, Millie,' he said. 'He's dead, ain't he?'

'Why, yes, bless you,' replied a cheerful voice from within. 'Dead and buried these three months or more—young Mr Seaton. And just before he was to be married, don't you remember, Bob?'

I saw a fair young woman's face peer over the muslin of the little door at me.

'Thank you,' I replied, 'then I go straight on?'

'That's it, sir; past the pond, bear up the hill a bit to the left, and there's the station lights before your eyes.'

We looked intelligently into each other's faces in the beam of the smoky lamp. But not one of the many questions in my mind could I put into words.

And again I paused irresolutely a few paces further on. It

was not, I fancy, merely a foolish apprehension of what the raw-boned butcher might 'think' that prevented my going back to see if I could find Seaton's grave in the benighted church-yard. There was precious little use in pottering about in the muddy dark merely to discover where he was buried. And yet I felt a little uneasy. My rather horrible thought was that, so far as I was concerned—one of his extremely few friends—he had never been much better than 'buried' in my mind.

ANDRINA

George Mackay Brown

Andrina comes to see me every afternoon in winter, just before it gets dark. She lights my lamp, sets the peat fire in a blaze, sees that there is enough water in my bucket that stands on the wall niche. If I have a cold (which isn't often, I'm a tough old seaman) she fusses a little, puts an extra peat or two on the fire, fills a stone hot-water bottle, puts an old thick jersey about my shoulders.

That good Andrina—as soon as she has gone, after her occasional ministrations to keep pleurisy or penumonia away—I throw the jersey from my shoulders and mix myself a toddy, whisky and hot water and sugar. The hot water bottle in the bed will be cold long before I climb into it, round about midnight: having read my few chapters of Conrad.

Towards the end of February last year I did get a very bad cold, the worst for years. I woke up, shuddering, one morning, and crawled between fire and cupboard, gasping like a fish out of water, to get a breakfast ready. (Not that I had an appetite.) There was a stone lodged somewhere in my right lung, that blocked my breath.

I forced down a few tasteless mouthfuls, and drank hot ugly tea. There was nothing to do after that but get back to bed with my book. Reading was no pleasure either—my head was a block of pulsing wood.

'Well,' I thought, 'Andrina'll be here in five or six hours' time. She won't be able to do much for me. This cold, or flu, or whatever it is, will run its course. Still, it'll cheer me to see the girl.'

*   *   *

Andrina did not come that afternoon. I expected her with the first cluster of shadows: the slow lift of the latch, the low greeting, the 'tut-tut' of sweet disapproval at some of the things she saw as soon as the lamp was burning . . . I was, though, in that strange fatalistic mood that sometimes accompanies a fever, when a man doesn't really care what happens. If the house was to go on fire, he might think, 'What's this, flames?' and try to save himself: but it wouldn't horrify or thrill him.

I accepted that afternoon, when the window was blackness at last with a first salting of stars, that for some reason or another Andrina couldn't come. I fell asleep again.

I woke up. A grey light at the window. My throat was dry—there was a fire in my face—my head was more throbbingly wooden than ever. I got up, my feet flashing with cold pain on the stone floor, drank a cup of water, and climbed back into bed. My teeth actually clacked and chattered in my head for five minutes or more—a thing I had only read about before.

I slept again, and woke up just as the winter sun was making brief stained glass of sea and sky. It was, again, Andrina's time. Today there were things she could do for me: get aspirin from the shop, surround my greyness with three or four very hot bottles, mix the strongest toddy in the world. A few words from her would be like a bell-buoy to a sailor in a hopeless fog. She did not come.

She did not come again on the third afternoon.

I woke, tremblingly, like a ghost in a hollow stone. It was black night. Wind soughed in the chimney. There was, from time to time, spatters of rain against the window. It was the longest night of my life. I experienced, over again, some of the dull and sordid events of my life; one certain episode was repeated again and again like an ancient gramophone record being put on time after time, and a rusty needle scuttling over worn wax. The shameful images broke and melted at last into sleep. Love had been killed but many ghosts had been awakened.

When I woke up I heard, for the first time in four days, the sound of a voice. It was Stanley the postman speaking to the dog of Bighouse. 'There now, isn't that loud big words to say so early? It's just a letter for Minnie, a drapery catalogue. There's

a good boy, go and tell Minnie I have a love letter for her . . .
Is that you, Minnie? I thought old Ben here was going to tear
me in pieces then. Yes, Minnie, a fine morning, it is that . . .'

I have never liked that postman—a servile lickspittle to
anyone he thinks is of consequence in the island—but that
morning he came past my window like a messenger of light.
He opened the door without knocking (I am a person of small
consequence). He said, 'Letter from a long distance, skipper.'
He put the letter on the chair nearest the door. I was shaping
my mouth to say, 'I'm not very well. I wonder . . .' If words
did come out of my mouth, they must have been whispers, a
ghost appeal. He looked at the dead fire and the closed window. He said, 'Phew! It's fuggy in here, skipper. You want to
get some fresh air . . .' Then he went, closing the door behind
him. (He would not, as I had briefly hoped, be taking word to
Andrina, or the doctor down in the village.)

I imagined, until I drowsed again, Captain Scott writing his
few last words in the Antarctic tent.

In a day or two, of course, I was as right as rain; a tough old
salt like me isn't killed off that easily.

But there was a sense of desolation on me. It was as if I had
been betrayed—deliberately kicked when I was down. I came
almost to the verge of self-pity. Why had my friend left me in
my bad time?

Then good sense asserted itself. 'Torvald, you old fraud,' I
said to myself. 'What claim have you got, anyway, on a winsome
twenty-year-old? None at all. Look at it this way, man—you've
had a whole winter of her kindness and consideration. She
brought a lamp into your dark time; ever since the Harvest
Home when (like a fool) you had too much whisky and she
supported you home and rolled you unconscious into bed . . .
Well, for some reasons or another, Andrina hasn't been able to
come these last few days. I'll find out, today, the reason.'

It was high time for me to get to the village. There was not a
crust or scraping of butter or jam in the cupboard. The shop
was also the post office—I had to draw two weeks' pension. I
promised myself a pint or two in the pub, to wash the last of
that sickness out of me.

It struck me, as I trudged those two miles, that I knew
nothing about Andrina at all. I had never asked, and she had

said nothing. What was her father? Had she sisters and brothers? Even the district of the island where she lived had never cropped up in our talks. It was sufficient that she came every evening, soon after sunset, and performed her quiet ministrations and lingered awhile and left a peace behind—a sense that everything in the house was pure, as if it had stood with open doors and windows at the heart of a clean summer wind.

Yet the girl had never done, all last winter, asking me questions about myself—all the good and bad and exciting things that had happened to me. Of course I told her this and that. Old men love to make their past vivid and significant, to stand in relation to a few trivial events in as fair and bold a light as possible. To add spice to those bits of autobiography, I let on to have been a reckless wild daring lad—a known and somewhat feared figure in many a port from Hong Kong to Durban to San Francisco. I presented to her a character somewhere between Captain Cook and Captain Hook.

And the girl loved those pieces of mingled fiction and fact; turning the wick of my lamp down a little to make everything more mysterious, stirring the peats into new flowers of flame . . .

One story I did not tell her completely. It is the episode in my life that hurts me whenever I think of it (which is rarely, for that time is locked up and the key dropped deep in the Atlantic: but it haunted me—as I hinted—during my recent illness).

On her last evening at my fireside I did, I know, let drop a hint or two to Andrina—a few half-ashamed half-boastful fragments. Suddenly, before I had finished—as if she could foresee and suffer the end—she had put a white look and cold kiss on my cheek, and gone out at the door; as it turned out, for the last time.

Hurt or not, I will mention it here and now. You who look and listen are not Andrina—to you it will seem a tale of crude country manners: a mingling of innocence and heartlessness.

In the island, fifty years ago, a young man and a young woman came together. They had known each other all their lives up to then, of course—they had sat in the school room together—but on one particular day in early summer this boy from one croft and this girl from another distant croft looked at each other with new eyes.

After the midsummer dance in the barn of the big house,

they walked together across the hill through the lingering
enchantment of twilight—it is never dark then—and came to
the rocks and the sand and sea just as the sun was rising. For
an hour and more they lingered, tranced creatures indeed,
beside those bright sighings and swirlings. Far in the north-
east the springs of day were beginning to surge up.

It was a tale soaked in the light of a single brief summer. The
boy and the girl lived, it seemed, on each other's heartbeats.
Their parents' crofts were miles apart, but they contrived to
meet, as if by accident, most days; at the crossroads, in the
village shop, on the side of the hill. But really these places
were too earthy and open—there were too many windows—
their feet drew secretly night after night to the beach with its
bird-cries, its cave, its changing waters. There no one disturbed their communings—the shy touches of hand and mouth—
the words that were nonsense but that became in his mouth
sometimes a sweet mysterious music—'Sigrid.'

The boy—his future, once this idyll of a summer was ended,
was to go to the university in Aberdeen and there study to be a
man of security and position and some leisure—an estate his
crofting ancestors had never known.

No such door was to open for Sigrid—she was bound to the
few family acres—the digging of peat—the making of butter
and cheese. But for a short time only. Her place would be
beside the young man with whom she shared her breath and
heartbeats, once he had gained his teacher's certificate. They
walked day after day beside the shining beckoning waters.

But one evening, at the cave, towards the end of that summer, when the corn was taking a first burnish, she had something urgent to tell him—a tremulous perilous secret thing.
And at once the summertime spell was broken. He shook his
head. He looked away. He looked at her again as if she were
some slut who had insulted him. She put out her hand to
him, her mouth trembling. He thrust her away. He turned.
He ran up the beach and along the sand-track to the road
above; and the ripening fields gathered him soon and hid
him from her.

And the girl was left alone at the mouth of the cave, with the
burden of a greater more desolate mystery on her.

The young man did not go to any seat of higher learning.
That same day he was at the emigration agents in Hamnavoe,

asking for an urgent immediate passage to Canada or Australia or South Africa—anywhere.

Thereafter the tale became complicated and more cruel and pathetic still. The girl followed him as best she could to his transatlantic refuge a month or so later; only to discover that the bird had flown. He had signed on a ship bound for furthest ports, as an ordinary seaman: so she was told, and she was more utterly lost than ever.

That rootlessness, for the next half century, was to be his life: making salt circles about the globe, with no secure footage anywhere. To be sure, he studied his navigation manuals, he rose at last to be a ship's officer, and more. The barren years became a burden to him. There is a time, when white hairs come, to turn one's back on long and practised skills and arts, that have long since lost their savours. This the sailor did, and he set his course homeward to his island; hoping that fifty winters might have scabbed over an old wound.

And so it was, or seemed to be. A few remembered him vaguely. The name of a certain vanished woman—who must be elderly, like himself, now—he never mentioned, nor did he ever hear it uttered. Her parents' croft was a ruin, a ruckle of stones on the side of the hill. He climbed up to it one day and looked at it coldly. No sweet ghost lingered at the end of the house, waiting for a twilight summons—'Sigrid . . .'

I got my pension cashed, and a basket full of provisions, in the village shop. Tina Stewart the postmistress knew everybody and everything; all the shifting subtle web of relationship in the island. I tried devious approaches with her. What was new or strange in the island? Had anyone been taken suddenly ill? Had anybody—a young woman, for example—had to leave the island suddenly, for whatever reason? The hawk eye of Miss Stewart regarded me long and hard. No, said she, she had never known the island quieter. Nobody had come or gone. 'Only yourself, Captain Torvald, has been bedridden, I hear. You better take good care of yourself, you all alone up there. There's still a greyness in your face . . .' I said I was sorry to take her time up. Somebody had mentioned a name—Andrina —to me, in a certain connection. It was a matter of no importance. Could Miss Stewart, however, tell me which farm or croft this Andrina came from?

Tina looked at me a long while, then shook her head. There was nobody of that name—woman or girl or child—in the island; and there never had been, to her certain knowledge.

I paid for my messages, with trembling fingers, and left.

I felt the need of a drink. At the bar counter stood Isaac Irving the landlord. Two fishermen stood at the far end, next the fire, drinking their pints and playing dominoes.

I said, after the third whisky, 'Look, Isaac, I suppose the whole island knows that Andrina—that girl—has been coming all winter up to my place, to do a bit of cleaning and washing and cooking for me. She hasn't been for a week now and more. Do you know if there's anything the matter with her?' (What I dreaded to hear was that Andrina had suddenly fallen in love; her little rockpools of charity and kindness drowned in that huge incoming flood; and cloistered herself against the time of her wedding.)

Isaac looked at me as if I was out of my mind. 'A young woman,' said he. 'A young woman up at your house? A home help, is she? I didn't know you had a home help. How many whiskies did you have before you came here, skipper, eh?' And he winked at the two grinning fishermen over by the fire.

I drank down my fourth whisky and prepared to go.

'Sorry, skipper,' Isaac Irving called after me. 'I think you must have imagined that girl, whatever her name is, when the fever was on you. Sometimes that happens. The only women I saw when I had the flue were hags and witches. You're lucky, skipper—a honey like Andrina!'

I was utterly bewildered. Isaac Irving knows the island and its people, if anything, even better than Tina Stewart. And he is a kindly man, not given to making fools of the lost and the delusion-ridden.

Going home, March airs were moving over the island. The sky, almost overnight, was taller and bluer. Daffodils trumpeted, silently the entry of spring from ditches here and there. A young lamb danced, all four feet in the air at once.

I found, lying on the table, unopened, the letter that had been delivered three mornings ago. There was an Australian postmark. It had been posted in late October.

'I followed your young flight from Selskay half round the world, and at last stopped here in Tasmania, knowing that it was useless for me to go any farther. I have kept a silence too, because I had such regard for you that I did not want you to suffer as I had, in many ways, over the years. We are both old, maybe I am writing this in vain, for you might never have returned to Selskay; or you might be dust or salt. I think, if you are still alive and (it may be) lonely, that what I will write might gladden you, though the end of it is sadness, like so much of life. Of your child—our child—I do not say anything, because you did not wish to acknowledge her. But that child had, in her turn, a daughter, and I think I have seen such sweetness but rarely. I thank you that you, in a sense (though unwillingly), gave that light and goodness to my age. She would have been a lamp in your winter, too, for often I spoke to her about you and that long-gone summer we shared, which was, to me at least, such a wonder. I told her nothing of the end of that time, that you and some others thought to be shameful. I told her only things that came sweetly from my mouth. And she would say, often, "I wish I knew that grandfather of mine. Gran, do you think he's lonely? I think he would be glad of somebody to make him a pot of tea and see to his fire. Some day I'm going to Scotland and I'm going to knock on his door, wherever he lives, and I'll do things for him. Did you love him very much, gran? He must be a good person, that old sailor, ever to have been loved by you. I *will* see him. I'll hear the old stories from his own mouth. Most of all, of course, the love story—for you, gran, tell me nothing about that . . ." I am writing this letter, Bill, to tell you that this can never now be. Our granddaughter Andrina died last week, suddenly, in the first stirrings of spring . . .'

Later, over the fire, I thought of the brightness and burgeoning and dew that visitant had brought across the threshold of my latest winter, night after night; and of how she had always come with the first shadows and the first star; but there, where she was dust, a new time was brightening earth and sea.

AWAY

Barry N. Malzberg

My name is Josiah Bushnell Grinnell. In 1853, responding to the invocation of the famous Horace Greeley, publisher of the New York *Tribune*, I take myself to the new state of Iowa and thereupon establish both a town and a college. "Go west young man, go west and grow with the country." Greeley has said, and solemn young fellow that I am, I take him seriously. What a surprise, what a disappointment to learn only after I am established where the tall corn grows that Greeley stole this from an obscure Indiana newspaperman named Soule and has appropriated the statement as his own. If I had known this, I might have gone to Indiana.

Instead, here I am in Iowa. What an unusually solemn man I am! I have always taken the invocations of my elders seriously, which is why the college I establish, the town to be named after me, the entire state itself takes on a somewhat sectarian whiff. A century later it is impossible for citizens to enter upon our interstates without murmuring prayers. In 1857, Sioux Indians massacre men, women, and children at Spirit Lake, the last massacre by Indians in the midwest and the released souls, the violated spirits add their pain and terror to the general chatter. On a hot May afternoon, the dead sun sprawling low in the panels of sky, the sounds of the cattle rising toward the dusk, it is possible to imagine oneself if one were a small man lying in a field, gazing, that one had entered upon the outer regions of the landscape painted by the honorable John Calvin. It is a difficult state, a difficult time.

I, Josiah Bushnell Grinnell, know this; know of all the inter-
stices and difficulties of the sovereign state of Iowa. Cleaved
from the Wisconsin territory, admitted to statehood on December 28, 1846, Iowa sprawls, flatland, on the way to the west.
There are ways around it—there are ways around everything,
the good Lord knows—but once on the interstate, it is hard to
find the way.

Here it is. It is 1954. I have been deceased for many decades, however, my spirit—no less than those massacred at
Spirit Lake—lives on. Iowa is the possessor of its inhabitants,
no one who has ever lived in this state has known true release.
We hang around. This may seem an unlikely statement, a
remarkable condition, but wait your turn, enjoy the common
passage before you act in judgment. Here in 1954 the senior
senator from this great state, the honorable, if that is quite the
term I am seeking, Bourke B. Hickenlooper is inveighing
against the Communists at a Fourth of July picnic. Hickenlooper,
with McCarthy, with Jenner, is the pride of what may be called
the conservative wing. To Hickenlooper it is an insult when the
first Negro set the first Negro foot on the Negro shores of the
first Negro city in this country, uttering incoherent Negro
chants. It is not that Hickenlooper is a racist, you understand.
It is merely that he is still linked to Spirit Lake by ancestry and
blood, still sees the frame of the assassin arched against the
moonlight. "We must expel the Communists from our shores,"
Hickenlooper says. He is on a podium, at some remove from
the crowd, screaming without benefit of microphone. Fourth of
July picnics are still important in the Iowa of this time. Politicians are expected to make speeches, to invoke Americana.
Hickenlooper is merely doing his duty. Of his true thoughts of
the matter we know not. He may or may not have an interior.
Most politicians do not. "McCarran Act!" Hickenlooper screams.
"Joseph McCarthy! Millard Tydings! Eighty-seven hundred
card-carrying Communists!" And so on. The crowd reacts stiffly.
It is very hot. A band plays in the distance, raucous parade
ground arias of the kind soon enough to be popularized by
Meredith Willson (born in Mason City) in *The Music Man*.
"Who promoted Peress?" Hickenlooper asks. The crowd mut-
ters. Their mood is not hostile but they are tired.

My name is Josiah Bushnell Grinnell. It is hard to explain
exactly what I am doing at this picnic or what I expect to come

of it. We Iowans (or transplanted Iowans) as I have said, our
spirits live on. Even after death. Relegated to some limbo we
come in and out, reincarnates or observers, bound to some
flatland of the spirit, replicating our history, moving in and out
of time. Screams of the settlers at Spirit Lake. Bullshit of
Greeley. Moving ever west. From this limbo I emerge at odd
times, strange moments, find myself at Iowa State Events.
Such seems to be the case now. I am jammed in with this
crowd, listening to Bourke B. Hickenlooper. To my left and
right are Iowans of various sexes and ages, most of them young,
in a burst of color, standing at parade rest, listening to the
rantings of the honorable senator. Now and then a baby yowls
or a young woman faints, her parasol preceding her on a
graceless slide to the ground. Men leap to the rescue of the
women, the babies are pacified in other ways. The huge bowl
of the sky presses. It is indecently hot, even for a spirit, even
for the gullible sectarian spirit of a man who would listen to
Horace Greeley (at least I never knew of Horatio Alger; it is
impossible to say to what state he might have sent me).
"Hickenlooper!" I shout. "Hey, Hickenlooper!"

The crowd stares at me. Sometimes I can be heard and
sometimes not; sometimes I am visible and at other times
invisible. Reincarnation, like life itself, is a chancy business. At
this time it would appear that I can be seen. Yards downrange
the senator stares at me, his stride momentarily broken. "Hey,
Senator!" I shout. Hickenlooper removes his enormous hat,
peers at me. I stride forward, closing the ground between us.

"You're all wrong, don't you know that?" I say. "Listen to
me!" I say, turning around, gesturing at the farmers, their
wives, the beaus and beauxettes in their holiday undress who
look at me incuriously. "This man is not telling the truth. We
lived to open frontiers, he is closing them!"

I am stared at incomprehendingly. One could, after all,
envision no other possibility. Politics may be entertainment
but metaphysics is unendurable in the Hawkeye State. "He
speaketh with forked tongue!" I point out.

There are a forest of shrugs around me. I turn back toward
the podium, find Hickenlooper in brisk conference with several
aides who have jumped to the sides of the platform. He cups
an ear, listens intently. They gesture at me. "Answer the
charge!" I yell. "Don't hide behind the others, explain your-

self. Tell why you are breeding fear, why you are seeking to close off that which will be opened."

Hickenlooper points at me. The hand is commanding, enormous. At my side, suddenly, are two earnest, honest Iowa state police; they seize me by the elbows. "If you will, sir," one says, "if you'll just come along."

"Don't arrest me," I say, struggling in their grasp, "arrest that man. That man is the assassin. I am Josiah Bushnell Grinnell, the founder of Grinnell College. I am a man of substance—"

"Card-carrying!" I hear Hickenlooper shout and then, this is the truth, I hear no more; speedily, forcibly, forcefully, I am carried from the grounds. Beaus and beauxettes, farmers and their daughters, little towheaded children and Iowa cattle, they all look at me mournfully. The troopers are insistent. "Don't you understand?" I say to them. "This isn't the end, this is just the passage, it's going to happen again, again, and again—"

Stay calm, sir, one says, "everything will be all right. Just don't struggle, understand the situation—"

I close my eyes. Again and again and it is too late. In the sudden, cool rushing darkness ninety-seven years are taken from me as if by death itself and I am at Spirit Lake once more, oh God, I am at Spirit Lake and in the sudden, clinging, rushing, tumultuous darkness, I hear the sound of the Sioux closing in around us; one high wail coming then, concentrating them, poised—

I scream then, try once more to give the alarm. But I cannot; my throat is dry, my lungs are cut out, my fate is darkness; in the night, eleven years after union, three years before the Civil War, they are coming, they are coming and the stain will leach outward, ever outward—

Go west young man, go west—

I listened, I came, I propagated, and I could not save them. And in the face of the Hickenloopers, through to dissolution itself, I never, never will. Until by something that is, at last, beyond me, I too will be cut off.

THE

PORTOBELLO

ROAD

Muriel Spark

One day in my young youth at high summer, lolling with my lovely companions upon a haystack, I found a needle. Already and privately for some years I had been guessing that I was set apart from the common run, but this of the needle attested the fact to my whole public: George, Kathleen, and Skinny. I sucked my thumb, for when I had thrust my idle hand deep into the hay, the thumb was where the needle had stuck.

When everyone had recovered George said, 'She put in her thumb and pulled out a plum.' Then away we were into our merciless hacking-hecking laughter again.

The needle had gone fairly deep into the thumby cushion and a small red river flowed from this tiny puncture. So that nothing of our joy should lag. George put in quickly.

'Mind your bloody thumb on my shirt.'

Then hac-hec-hoo, we shrieked into the hot Borderland afternoon. Really I should not care to be so young of heart again. That is my thought every time I turn over my old papers and come across the photograph. Skinny, Kathleen, and myself are in the photo atop the haystack. Skinny had just finished analysing the inwards of my find.

'It couldn't have been done by brains. You haven't much brains but you're a lucky wee thing.'

Everyone agreed that the needle betokened extraordinary luck. As it was becoming a serious conversation, George said,

'I'll take a photo.'

I wrapped my hanky round my thumb and got myself

organised. George pointed up from his camera and shouted, 'Look, there's a mouse!'

Kathleen screamed and I screamed although I think we knew there was no mouse. But this gave us an extra session of squalling hee-hoo's. Finally we three composed ourselves for George's picture. We look lovely and it was a great day at the time, but I would not care for it all over again. From that day I was known as Needle.

One Saturday in recent years I was mooching down the Portobello Road, threading among the crowds of marketers on the narrow pavement when I saw a woman. She had a haggard, careworn, wealthy look, thin but for the breasts forced-up high like a pigeon's. I had not seen her for nearly five years. How changed she was! But I recognised Kathleen, my friend; her features had already begun to sink and protrude in the way that mouths and noses do in people destined always to be old for their years. When I had last seen her, nearly five years ago, Kathleen, barely thirty, had said,

'I've lost all my looks, it's in the family. All the women are handsome as girls, but we go off early, we go brown and nosey.'

I stood silently among the people, watching. As you will see, I wasn't in a position to speak to Kathleen. I saw her shoving in her avid manner from stall to stall. She was always fond of antique jewellery and of bargains. I wondered that I had not seen her before in the Portobello Road on my Saturday morning ambles. Her long stiff-crooked fingers pounced to select a jade ring from amongst the jumble of brooches and pendants, onyx, moonstone and gold, set out on the stall.

'What do you think of this?' she said.

I saw then who was with her. I had been half-conscious of the huge man following several paces behind her, and now I noticed him.

'It looks all right,' he said. 'How much is it?'

'How much is it?' Kathleen asked the vendor.

I took a good look at this man accompanying Kathleen. It was her husband. The beard was unfamiliar, but I recognised beneath it his enormous mouth, the bright sensuous lips, the large brown eyes forever brimming with pathos.

It was not for me to speak to Kathleen, but I had a sudden inspiration which caused me to say quietly,

'Hallo, George.'

The giant of a man turned round to face the direction of my face. There were so many people—but at length he saw me.

'Hallo, George,' I said again.

Kathleen had started to haggle with the stall-owner, in her old way, over the price of the jade ring. George continued to stare at me, his big mouth slightly parted so that I could see a wide slit of red lips and white teeth between the fair grassy growths of beard and moustache.

'My God!' he said.

'What's the matter?' said Kathleen.

'Hallo, George!' I said again, quite loud this time, and cheerfully.

'Look!' said George. 'Look who's there, over beside the fruit stall.'

Kathleen looked but didn't see.

'Who is it?' she said impatiently.

'It's Needle,' he said. 'She said "Hallo, George." '

'*Needle*,' said Kathleen. 'Who do you mean? You don't mean our old friend *Needle* who—'

'Yes. There she is. My God!'

He looked very ill, although when I had said 'Hallo, George' I had spoken friendly enough.

'I don't see anyone faintly resembling poor Needle,' said Kathleen looking at him. She was worried.

George pointed straight at me. 'Look *there*. I tell you that is Needle.'

'You're ill, George. Heavens, you must be seeing things. Come on home. Needle isn't there. You know as well as I do, Needle is dead.'

I must explain that I departed this life nearly five years ago. But I did not altogether depart this world. There were those odd things still to be done which one's executors can never do properly. Papers to be looked over, even after the executors have torn them up. Lots of business except, of course, on Sundays and Holidays of Obligation, plenty to take an interest in for the time being. I take my recreation on Saturday mornings. If it is a wet Saturday I wander up and down the substantial lanes of Woolworth's as I did when I was young and visible. There is a pleasurable spread of objects on the counters which

I now perceive and exploit with a certain detachment, since it suits with my condition of life. Creams, toothpastes, combs and hankies, cotton gloves, flimsy flowering scarves, writing-paper and crayons, ice-cream cones and orangeade, screwdrivers, boxes of tacks, tins of paint, of glue, of marmalade; I always liked them but far more now that I have no need of any. When Saturdays are fine I go instead to the Portobello Road where formerly I would jaunt with Kathleen in our grown-up days. The barrow-loads do not change much, of apples and rayon vests in common blues and low-taste mauve, of silver plate, trays and teapots long since changed hands from the bygone citizens to dealers, from shops to the new flats and breakable homes, and then over to the barrow-stalls and the dealers again: Georgian spoons, rings, ear-rings of turquoise and opal set in the butterfly pattern of true-lovers' knot, patch-boxes with miniature paintings of ladies on ivory, snuff-boxes of silver with Scotch pebbles inset.

Sometimes as occasion arises on a Saturday morning, my friend Kathleen, who is a Catholic, has a Mass said for my soul, and then I am in attendance, as it were, at the church. But most Saturdays I take my delight among the solemn crowds with their aimless purposes, their eternal life not far away, who push past the counters and stalls, who handle, buy, steal, touch, desire, and ogle the merchandise. I hear the tinkling tills, I hear the jangle of loose change and tongues and children wanting to hold and have.

That is how I came to be in the Portobello Road that Saturday morning when I saw George and Kathleen. I would not have spoken had I not been inspired to it. Indeed it's one of the things I can't do now—to speak out, unless inspired. And most extraordinary, on that morning as I spoke, a degree of visibility set in. I suppose from poor George's point of view it was like seeing a ghost when he saw me standing by the fruit barrow repeating in so friendly a manner, 'Hallo, George!'

We were bound for the south. When our education, what we could get of it from the north, was thought to be finished, one by one we were sent or sent for to London. John Skinner, whom we called Skinny, went to study more archaeology, George to join his uncle's tobacco farm, Kathleen to stay with her rich connections and to potter intermittently in the Mayfair hat shop which one of them owned. A little later I also went to London to see life, for it was my ambition to write about life, which first I had to see.

'We four must stick together,' George said very often in that yearning way of his. He was always desperately afraid of neglect. We four looked likely to shift off in different directions and George did not trust the other three of us not to forget all about him. More and more as the time came for him to depart for his uncle's tobacco farm in Africa he said,

'We four must keep in touch.'

And before he left he told each of us anxiously,

'I'll write regularly, once a month. We must keep together for the sake of the old times.' He had three prints taken from the negative of that photo on the haystack, wrote on the back of them 'George took this the day that Needle found the needle' and gave us a copy each. I think we all wished he could become a bit more callous.

During my lifetime I was a drifter, nothing organised. It was difficult for my friends to follow the logic of my life. By the normal reckonings I should have come to starvation and ruin, which I never did. Of course, I did not live to write about life as I wanted to do. Possibly that is why I am inspired to do so now in these peculiar circumstances.

I taught in a private school in Kensington for almost three months, very small children. I didn't know what to do with them but I was kept fairly busy escorting incontinent little boys to the lavatory and telling the little girls to use their handkerchiefs. After that I lived a winter holiday in London on my small capital, and when that had run out I found a diamond bracelet in the cinema for which I received a reward of fifty pounds. When it was used up I got a job with a publicity man, writing speeches for absorbed industrialists, in which the dictionary of quotations came in very useful. So it went on. I got engaged to Skinny, but shortly after that I was left a small legacy, enough to keep me for six months. This somehow decided me that I didn't love Skinny so I gave him back the ring.

But it was through Skinny that I went to Africa. He was engaged with a party of researchers to investigate King Solomon's mines, that series of ancient workings ranging from the ancient port of Ophir, now called Beira, across Portuguese East

Africa and Southern Rhodesia to the mighty jungle-city of Zimbabwe whose temple walls still stand by the approach to an ancient and sacred mountain, where the rubble of that civilization scatters itself over the surrounding Rhodesian waste. I accompanied the party as a sort of secretary. Skinny vouched for me, he paid my fare, he sympathised by his action with my inconsequential life although when he spoke of it he disapproved. A life like mine annoys most people; they go to their jobs every day, attend to things, give orders, pummel typewriters, and get two or three weeks off every year, and it vexes them to see someone else not bothering to do these things and yet getting away with it, not starving, being lucky as they call it. Skinny, when I had broken off our engagement, lectured me about this, but still he took me to Africa knowing I should probably leave his unit within a few months.

We were there a few weeks before we began enquiring for George, who was farming about four hundred miles away to the north. We had not told him of our plans.

'If we tell George to expect us in his part of the world he'll come rushing to pester us the first week. After all, we're going on business,' Skinny had said.

Before we left Kathleen told us, 'Give George my love and tell him not to send frantic cables every time I don't answer his letters right away. Tell him I'm busy in the hat shop and being presented. You would think he hadn't another friend in the world the way he carries on.'

We had settled first at Fort Victoria, our nearest place of access to the Zimbabwe ruins. There we made enquiries about George. It was clear he hadn't many friends. The older settlers were the most tolerant about the half-caste woman he was living with, as we found, but they were furious about his methods of raising tobacco which we learned were most unprofessional and in some mysterious way disloyal to the whites. We could never discover how it was that George's style of tobacco farming gave the blacks opinions about themselves, but that's what the older settlers claimed. The newer immigrants thought he was unsociable and, of course, his living with that nig made visiting impossible.

I must say I was myself a bit off-put by this news about the brown woman. I was brought up in a university town to which came Indian, African, and Asiatic students in a variety of tints and hues. I was brought up to avoid them for reasons connected with local reputation and God's ordinances. You cannot easily go against what you were brought up to do unless you are a rebel by nature.

Anyhow, we visited George eventually, taking advantage of the offer to transport from some people bound north in search of game. He had heard of our arrival in Rhodesia and though he was glad, almost relieved, to see us he pursued a policy of sullenness for the first hour.

'We wanted to give you a surprise, George.'

'How were we to know that you'd get to hear of our arrival, George? News here must travel faster than light, George.'

'We did hope to give you a surprise, George.'

At last he said, 'Well, I must say it's good to see you. All we need now is Kathleen. We four simply must stick together. You find when you're in a place like this, there's nothing like old friends.'

He showed us his drying sheds. He showed us a paddock where he was experimenting with a horse and a zebra mare, attempting to mate them. They were frolicking happily, but not together. They passed each other in their private play time and again, but without acknowledgment and without resentment.

'It's been done before,' George said. 'It makes a fine strong beast, more intelligent than a mule and sturdier than a horse. But I'm not having any success with this pair, they won't look at each other.'

After a while, he said, 'Come in for a drink and meet Matilda.'

She was dark brown, with a subservient hollow chest and round shoulders, a gawky woman, very snappy with the houseboys. We said pleasant things as we drank on the stoep before dinner, but we found George difficult. For some reason he began to rail at me for breaking off my engagement to Skinny, saying what a dirty trick it was after all those good times in the old days. I diverted attention to Matilda. I supposed, I said, she knew this part of the country well?

'No,' said she, 'I been a-shellitered my life. I not put out to working. Me nothing to go from place to place is allowed like dirty girls does.' In her speech she gave every syllable equal stress.

George explained, 'Her father was a white magistrate in

Natal. She had a sheltered upbringing, different from the other
coloureds, you realise.'

'Man, me no black-eyed Susan,' said Matilda, 'no, no.'

On the whole, George treated her as a servant. She was
about four months advanced in pregnancy, but he made her
get up and fetch for him, many times. Soap: that was one of the
things Matilda had to fetch. George made his own bath soap,
showed it proudly, gave us the recipe which I did not trouble
to remember; I was fond of nice soaps during my lifetime and
George's smelt of brilliantine and looked likely to soil one's
skin.

'D'yo brahn?' Matilda asked me.

George said, 'She is asking if you go brown in the sun.'

'No, I go freckled.'

'I got sister-in-law go freckles.'

She never spoke another word to Skinny nor to me, and we
never saw her again.

Some months later I said to Skinny,

'I'm fed up with being a camp-follower.'

He was not surprised that I was leaving his unit, but he
hated my way of expressing it. He gave me a Presbyterian
look.

'Don't talk like that. Are you going back to England or
staying?'

'Staying, for a while.'

'Well, don't wander too far off.'

I was able to live on the fee I got for writing a gossip column
in a local weekly, which wasn't my idea of writing about life, of
course. I made friends, more than I could cope with, after I left
Skinny's exclusive little band of archaeologists. I had the attrac-
tions of being newly out from England and of wanting to see
life. Of the countless young men and go-ahead families who
purred me along the Rhodesian roads, hundred after hundred
miles, I only kept up with one family when I returned to my
native land. I think that was because they were the most
representative, they stood for all the rest: people in those parts
are very typical of each other, as one group of standing stones
in that wilderness is like the next.

I met George once more in a hotel in Bulawayo. We drank
highballs and spoke of war. Skinny's party were just then

deciding whether to remain in the country or return home.
They had reached an exciting part of their research, and whenever I got a chance to visit Zimbabwe he would take me for
a moonlight walk in the ruined temple and try to make me see
phantom Phoenicians flitting ahead of us, or along the walls. I
had half a mind to marry Skinny; perhaps, I thought, when his
studies were finished. The impending war was in our bones: so
I remarked to George as we sat drinking highballs on the hotel
stoep in the hard bright sunny July winter of that year.

George was inquisitive about my relations with Skinny. He
tried to pump me for about half an hour and when at last I said,
'You are becoming aggressive, George,' he stopped. He became quite pathetic. He said, 'War or no war I'm clearing out
of this.'

'It's the heat does it,' I said.

'I'm clearing out in any case. I've lost a fortune in tobacco.
My uncle is making a fuss. It's the other bloody planters; once
you get the wrong side of them you're finished in this wide
land.'

'What about Matilda?' I asked.

He said, 'She'll be all right. She's got hundreds of relatives.'

I had already heard about the baby girl. Coal black, by
repute, with George's features. And another on the way, they
said.

'What about the child?'

He didn't say anything to that. He ordered more highballs
and when they arrived he swizzled his for a long time with a
stick. 'Why didn't you ask me to your twenty-first?' he said then.

'I didn't have anything special, no party, George. We had a
quiet drink among ourselves, George, just Skinny and the old
professors and two of the wives and me, George.'

'You didn't ask me to your twenty-first,' he said. 'Kathleen
writes to me regularly.'

This wasn't true. Kathleen sent me letters fairly often in
which she said, 'Don't tell George I wrote to you as he will be
expecting word from me and I can't be bothered actually.'

'But you,' said George, 'don't seem to have any sense of old
friendships, you and Skinny.'

'Oh, George!' I said.

'Remember the times we had,' George said. 'We used to
have times.' His large brown eyes began to water.

'I'll have to be getting along,' I said.

'Please don't go. Don't leave me just yet. I've something to tell you.'

'Something nice?' I laid on an eager smile. All responses to George had to be overdone.

'You don't know how lucky you are,' George said.

'How?' I said. Sometimes I got tired of being called lucky by everybody. There were times when, privately practising my writings about life, I knew the bitter side of my fortune. When I failed again and again to reproduce life in some satisfactory and perfect form, I was the more imprisoned, for all my care-free living, within my craving for this satisfaction. Sometimes, in my impotence and need I secreted a venom which infected all my life for days on end and which spurted out indiscriminately on Skinny or on anyone who crossed my path.

'You aren't bound by anyone,' George said. 'You come and go as you please. Something always turns up for you. You're free, and you don't know your luck.'

'You're a damn sight more free than I am,' I said sharply. 'You've got your rich uncle.'

'He's losing interest in me,' George said. 'He's had enough.'

'Oh well, you're young yet. What was it you wanted to tell me?'

'A secret,' George said. 'Remember we used to have those secrets.'

'Oh, yes we did.'

'Did you ever tell any of mine?'

'Oh no, George.' In reality, I couldn't remember any particular secret out of the dozens we must have exchanged from our schooldays onwards.

'Well, this is a secret, mind. Promise not to tell.'

'Promise.'

'I'm married.'

'Married, George! Oh, who to?'

'Matilda.'

'How dreadful!' I spoke before I could think, but he agreed with me.

'Yes, it's awful, but what could I do?'

'You might have asked my advice,' I said pompously.

'I'm two years older than you are. I don't ask advice from you, Needle, little beast.'

'Don't ask for sympathy then.'

'A nice friend you are,' he said, 'I must say after all these years.'

'Poor George!' I said.

'There are three white men to one white woman in this country,' said George. 'An isolated planter doesn't see a white woman and if he sees one she doesn't see him. What could I do? I needed the woman.'

I was nearly sick. One, because of my Scottish upbringing. Two, because of my horror of corny phrases like 'I needed the woman,' which George repeated twice again.

'And Matilda got tough,' said George, 'after you and Skinny came to visit us. She had some friends at the Mission, and she packed up and went to them.'

'You should have let her go,' I said.

'I went after her,' George said. 'She insisted on being married, so I married her.'

'That's not a proper secret, then,' I said. 'The news of a mixed marriage soon gets about.'

'I took care of that,' George said. 'Crazy as I was, I took her to the Congo and married her there. She promised to keep quiet about it.'

'Well, you can't clear off and leave her now, surely,' I said.

'I'm going to get out of this place. I can't stand the woman and I can't stand the country. I didn't realise what it would be like. Two years of the country and three months of my wife has been enough.'

'Will you get a divorce?'

'No, Matilda's Catholic. She won't divorce.'

George was fairly getting through the highballs, and I wasn't far behind him. His brown eyes floated shiny and liquid as he told me how he had written to tell his uncle of his plight, 'Except, of course, I didn't say we were married, that would have been too much for him. He's a prejudiced hardened old colonial. I only said I'd had a child by a coloured woman and was expecting another, and he perfectly understood. He came at once by plane a few weeks ago. He's made a settlement on her, providing she keeps her mouth shut about her association with me.'

'Will she do that?'

'Oh, yes, or she won't get the money.'

'But as your wife she has a claim on you, in any case.'

'If she claimed as my wife she'd get far less. Matilda knows what she's doing, greedy bitch she is. She'll keep her mouth shut.'

'Only, you won't be able to marry again, will you, George?'

'Not unless she dies,' he said. 'And she's as strong as a trek ox.'

'Well, I'm sorry, George,' I said.

'Good of you to say so,' he said. 'But I can see by your chin that you disapprove of me. Even my old uncle understood.'

'Oh, George, I quite understand. You were lonely, I suppose.'

'You didn't even ask me to your twenty-first. If you and Skinny had been nicer to me, I would never have lost my head and married the woman, never.'

'You didn't ask me to your wedding,' I said.

'You're a catty bissom, Needle, not like what you were in the old times when you used to tell us your wee stories.'

'I'll have to be getting along,' I said.

'Mind you keep the secret,' George said.

'Can't I tell Skinny? He would be very sorry for you, George.'

'You mustn't tell anyone. Keep it a secret. Promise.'

'Promise,' I said. I understood that he wished to enforce some sort of bond between us with this secret, and I thought, 'Oh well, I suppose he's lonely. Keeping his secret won't do any harm.'

I returned to England with Skinny's party just before the war.

I did not see George again till just before my death, five years ago.

After the war Skinny returned to his studies. He had two more exams, over a period of eighteen months, and I thought I might marry him when the exams were over.

'You might do worse than Skinny,' Kathleen used to say to me on our Saturday morning excursions to the antique shops and the junk stalls.

She too was getting on in years. The remainder of our families in Scotland were hinting that it was time we settled down with husbands. Kathleen was a little younger than me, but looked much older. She knew her chances were diminishing but at that time I did not think she cared very much. As for myself, the main attraction of marrying Skinny was his prospective expeditions to Mesopotamia. My desire to marry him had to be stimulated by the continual reading of books about Babylon and Assyria; perhaps Skinny felt this, because he supplied the books and even started instructing me in the art of deciphering cuneiform tablets.

Kathleen was more interested in marriage than I thought. Like me, she had racketed around a good deal during the war; she had actually been engaged to an officer in the U.S. navy, who was killed. Now she kept an antique shop near Lambeth, was doing very nicely, lived in a Chelsea square, but for all that she must have wanted to be married and have children. She would stop and look into all the prams which the mothers had left outside shops or area gates.

'The poet Swinburne used to do that,' I told her once.

'Really? Did he want children of his own?'

'I shouldn't think so. He simply liked babies.'

Before Skinny's final exam he fell ill and was sent to a sanatorium in Switzerland.

'You're fortunate after all not to be married to him,' Kathleen said. 'You might have caught T.B.'

I was fortunate, I was lucky . . . so everyone kept telling me on different occasions. Although it annoyed me to hear, I knew they were right, but in a way that was different from what they meant. It took me very small effort to make a living; book reviews, odd jobs for Kathleen, a few months with the publicity man again, still getting up speeches about literature, art, and life for industrial tycoons. I was waiting to write about life and it seemed to me that the good fortune lay in this, whenever it should be. And until then I was assured of my charmed life, the necessities of existence always coming my way and I with far more leisure than anyone else. I thought of my type of luck after I became a Catholic and was being confirmed. The Bishop touches the candidate on the cheek, a symbolic reminder of the sufferings a Christian is supposed to undertake. I thought, how lucky, what a feathery symbol to stand for the hellish violence of its true meaning.

I visited Skinny twice in the two years that he was in the sanatorium. He was almost cured, and expected to be home within a few months. I told Kathleen after my last visit.

'Maybe I'll marry Skinny when he's well again.'

'Make it definite, Needle, and not so much of the maybe. You don't know when you're well off,' she said.

This was five years ago, in the last year of my life. Kathleen and I had become very close friends. We met several times each week, and after our Saturday morning excursions in the Portobello Road very often I would accompany Kathleen to her aunt's house in Kent for a long week-end.

One day in the June of that year I met Kathleen specially for lunch because she had phoned me to say she had news.

'Guess who came into the shop this afternoon,' she said.

'Who?'

'George.'

We had half imagined George was dead. We had received no letters in the past ten years. Early in the war we had heard rumours of his keeping a night club in Durban, but nothing after that. We could have made enquiries if we had felt moved to do so.

At one time, when we discussed him, Kathleen had said,

'I ought to get in touch with poor George. But then I think he would write back. He would demand a regular correspondence again.'

'We four must stick together,' I mimicked.

'I can visualise his reproachful limpid orbs,' Kathleen said.

Skinny said, 'He's probably gone native. With his coffee concubine and a dozen mahogany kids.'

'Perhaps he's dead,' Kathleen said.

I did not speak of George's marriage, nor of any of his confidences in the hotel at Bulawayo. As the years passed we ceased to mention him except in passing, as someone more or less dead so far as we were concerned.

Kathleen was excited about George's turning up. She had forgotten her impatience with him in former days; she said,

'It was so wonderful to see old George. He seems to need a friend, feels neglected, out of touch with things.'

'He needs mothering, I suppose.'

Kathleen didn't notice the malice. She declared, 'That's exactly the case with George. It always has been, I can see it now.'

She seemed ready to come to any rapid new and happy conclusion about George. In the course of the morning he had told her of his wartime night club in Durban, his game-shooting expeditions since. It was clear he had not mentioned Matilda. He had put on weight, Kathleen told me, but he could carry it.

I was curious to see this version of George, but I was leaving for Scotland next day and did not see him till September of that year, just before my death.

While I was in Scotland I gathered from Kathleen's letters that she was seeing George very frequently, finding enjoyable company in him, looking after him. 'You'll be surprised to see how he has developed.' Apparently he would hang round Kathleen in her shop most days, 'it makes him feel useful' as she maternally expressed it. He had an old relative in Kent whom he visited at week-ends; this old lady lived a few miles from Kathleen's aunt, which made it easy for them to travel down together on Saturdays, and go for long country walks.

'You'll see such a difference in George,' Kathleen said on my return to London in September. I was to meet him that night, a Saturday. Kathleen's aunt was abroad, the maid on holiday, and I was to keep Kathleen company in the empty house.

George had left London for Kent a few days earlier. 'He's actually helping with the harvest down there!' Kathleen told me lovingly.

Kathleen and I planned to travel down together, but on that Saturday she was unexpectedly delayed in London on some business. It was arranged that I should go ahead of her in the early afternoon to see to the provisions for our party; Kathleen had invited George to dinner at her aunt's house that night.

'I should be with you by seven,' she said. 'Sure you won't mind the empty house? I hate arriving at empty houses, myself.'

I said no, I liked an empty house.

So I did, when I got there. I had never found the house more likeable. A large Georgian vicarage in about eight acres, most of the rooms shut and sheeted, there being only one servant. I discovered that I wouldn't need to go shopping, Kathleen's aunt had left many and delicate supplies with notes attached to them: 'Eat this up please do, see also fridge' and 'A treat for three hungry people see also 2 bttles beaune for yr party on back kn table.' It was like a treasure hunt as I followed clue after clue through the cool silent domestic quarters. A house in which there are no people—but with all the signs of tenancy—can be a most tranquil good place. People take up space in a house out of proportion to their size. On my previous visits I had seen the rooms overflowing as it seemed, with Kathleen, her aunt, and the little fat maidservant; they were always on the move. As I wandered through that part of the house which was in use, opening windows to let in the pale yellow air of September, I was not conscious that I, Needle, was taking up any space at all, I might have been a ghost.

The only thing to be fetched was the milk. I waited till after four when the milking should be done, then set off for the farm which lay across two fields at the back of the orchard. There, when the byreman was handing me the bottle, I saw George.

'Hallo, George,' I said.

'Needle! What are you doing here?' he said.

'Fetching milk,' I said.

'So am I. Well, it's good to see you, I must say.'

As we paid the farm-hand, George said, 'I'll walk back with you part of the way. But I mustn't stop, my old cousin's without any milk for her tea. How's Kathleen?'

'She was kept in London. She's coming on later, about seven, she expects.'

We had reached the end of the first field. George's way led to the left and on to the main road.

'We'll see you tonight, then?' I said.

'Yes, and talk about old times.'

'Grand,' I said.

But George got over the stile with me.

'Look here,' he said. 'I'd like to talk to you, Needle.'

'We'll talk tonight, George. Better not keep your cousin waiting for the milk.' I found myself speaking to him almost as if he were a child.

'No, I want to talk to you alone. This is a good opportunity.'

We began to cross the second field. I had been hoping to have the house to myself for a couple more hours and I was rather petulant.

'See,' he said suddenly, 'that haystack.'

'Yes,' I said absently.

'Let's sit there and talk. I'd like to see you up on a haystack again. I still keep that photo. Remember that time when—'

'I found the needle,' I said very quickly, to get it over.

But I was glad to rest. The stack had been broken up, but we managed to find a nest in it. I buried my bottle of milk in the hay for coolness. George placed his carefully at the foot of the stack.

'My old cousin is terribly vague, poor soul. A bit hazy in her head. She hasn't the least sense of time. If I tell her I've only been gone ten minutes she'll believe it.'

I giggled, and looked at him. His face had grown much larger, his lips full, wide and with a ripe colour that is strange in a man. His brown eyes were abounding as before with some inarticulate plea.

'So you're gong to marry Skinny after all these years?'

'I really don't know, George.'

'You played him up properly.'

'It isn't for you to judge. I have my own reasons for what I do.'

'Don't get sharp,' he said, 'I was only funning.' To prove it, he lifted a tuft of hay and brushed my face with it.

'D'you know,' he said next, 'I didn't think you and Skinny treated me very decently in Rhodesia.'

'Well, we were busy, George. And we were younger then, we had a lot to do and see. After all, we could see you any other time, George.'

'A touch of selfishness,' he said.

'I'll have to be getting along, George.' I made to get down from the stack.

He pulled me back. 'Wait, I've got something to tell you.'

'O.K., George, tell me.'

'First promise not to tell Kathleen. She wants it kept a secret so that she can tell you herself.'

'All right. Promise.'

'I'm going to marry Kathleen.'

'But you're already married.'

Sometimes I heard news of Matilda from the one Rhodesian family with whom I still kept up. They referred to her as 'George's Dark Lady' and of course they did not know he was married to her. She had apparently made a good thing out of George, they said, for she minced around all tarted up, never did a stroke of work and was always unsettling the respectable coloured girls in their neighbourhood. According to accounts, she was a living example of the folly of behaving as George did.

'I married Matilda in the Congo,' George was saying.

'It would still be bigamy,' I said.

He was furious when I used that word bigamy. He lifted a handful of hay as if he would throw it in my face, but controlling himself meanwhile he fanned it at me playfully.

'I'm not sure that the Congo marriage was valid,' he continued. 'Anyway, as far as I'm concerned, it isn't.'

'You can't do a thing like that,' I said.

'I need Kathleen. She's been decent to me. I think we were always meant for each other, me and Kathleen.'

'I'll have to be going,' I said.

But he put his knee over my ankles, so that I couldn't move. I sat still and gazed into space.

He tickled my face with a wisp of hay.

'Smile up, Needle,' he said; 'let's talk like old times.'

'Well?'

'No one knows about my marriage to Matilda except you and me.'

'And Matilda,' I said.

'She'll hold her tongue so long as she gets her payments. My uncle left an annuity for the purpose, his lawyers see to it.'

'Let me go, George.'

'You promised to keep it a secret,' he said, 'you promised.'

'Yes, I promised.'

'And now that you're going to marry Skinny, we'll be properly coupled off as we should have been years ago. We should have been—but youth!—our youth got in the way, didn't it?'

'Life got in the way,' I said.

'But everything's going to be all right now. You'll keep my secret, won't you? You promised.' He had released my feet. I edged a little further from him.

I said, 'If Kathleen intends to marry you, I shall tell her that you're already married.'

'You wouldn't do a dirty trick like that, Needle? You're going to be happy with Skinny, you wouldn't stand in the way of my—'

'I must, Kathleen's my best friend,' I said swiftly.

He looked as if he would murder me and he did. He stuffed hay into my mouth until it could hold no more, kneeling on my body to keep it still, holding both my wrists tight in his huge left hand. I saw the red full lines of his mouth and the white slit of his teeth last thing on earth. Not another soul passed by as he pressed my body into the stack, as he made a deep nest for me, tearing up the hay to make a groove the length of my corpse, and finally pulling the warm dry stuff in a mound over this concealment, so natural-looking in a broken haystack. Then George climbed down, took up his bottle of milk and went his way. I suppose that was why he looked so unwell when I stood, nearly five years later, by the barrow in the Portobello Road and said in easy tones, 'Hallo, George!'

The Haystack Murder was one of the notorious crimes of that year.

My friends said, 'A girl who had everything to live for.'

After a search that lasted twenty hours, when my body was found, the evening papers said, ' "Needle" is found: in haystack!'

Kathleen, speaking from that Catholic point of view which takes some getting used to, said, 'She was at Confession only the day before she died—wasn't she lucky?'

The poor byre-hand who sold us the milk was grilled for hour after hour by the local police, and later by Scotland Yard. So was George. He admitted walking as far as the haystack with me, but he denied lingering there.

'You hadn't seen your friend for ten years?' the Inspector asked him.

'That's right,' said George.

'And you didn't stop to have a chat?'

'No. We'd arranged to meet later at dinner. My cousin was waiting for the milk, I couldn't stop.'

The old soul, his cousin, swore that he hadn't been gone more than ten minutes in all, and she believed it to the day of her death a few months later. There was the microscopic evidence of hay on George's jacket, of course, but the same evidence was on every man's jacket in the district that fine harvest year. Unfortunately, the byreman's hands were even brawnier and mightier than George's. The marks on my wrists had been done by such hands, so the laboratory charts indicated when my post-mortem was all completed. But the wrist-marks weren't enough to pin down the crime to either man. If I hadn't been wearing my long-sleeved cardigan, it was said, the bruises might have matched up properly with someone's fingers.

Kathleen, to prove that George had absolutely no motive, told the police that she was engaged to him. George thought this a little foolish. They checked up on his life in Africa, right back to his living with Matilda. But the marriage didn't come out—who would think of looking up registers in the Congo? Not that this would have proved any motive for murder. All the same, George was relieved when the enquiries were over without the marriage to Matilda being disclosed. He was able to have his nervous breakdown at the same time as Kathleen had hers, and they recovered together and got married, long after the police had shifted their enquiries to an Air Force camp five miles from Kathleen's aunt's home. Only a lot of excitement and drinks come of those investigations. The Haystack Murder was one of the unsolved crimes that year.

Shortly afterwards the byre-hand emigrated to Canada to start afresh, with the help of Skinny who felt sorry for him.

After seeing George taken away home by Kathleen that Saturday in the Portobello Road, I thought that perhaps I might be seeing more of him in similar circumstances. The next Saturday I looked out for him, and at last there he was, without Kathleen, half-worried, half-hopeful.

I dashed his hopes. I said, 'Hallo, George!'

He looked in my direction, rooted in the midst of the flowing market-mongers in that convivial street. I thought to myself, 'He looks as if he had a mouthful of hay.' It was the new bristly maize-coloured beard and moustache surrounding his great mouth which suggested the thought, gay and lyrical as life.

'Hallo, George!' I said again.

I might have been inspired to say more on that agreeable morning, but he didn't wait. He was away down a side street and along another street and down one more, zig-zag, as far and as devious as he could take himself from the Portobello Road.

Nevertheless he was back again next week. Poor Kathleen had brought him in her car. She left it at the top of the street, and got out with him, holding him tight by the arm. It grieved me to see Kathleen ignoring the spread of scintillations on the stalls. I had myself seen a charming Battersea box quite to her taste, also a pair of enamelled silver earrings. But she took no notice of these wares, clinging close to George, and, poor Kathleen—I hate to say how she looked.

And George was haggard. His eyes seemed to have got

smaller as if he had been recently in pain. He advanced up the road with Kathleen on his arm, letting himself lurch from side to side with his wife bobbing beside him, as the crowds asserted their rights of way.

'Oh, George!' I said. 'You don't look at all well, George.'

'Look!' said George. 'Over there by the hardware barrow. That's Needle.'

Kathleen was crying. 'Come back home, dear,' she said.

'Oh, you don't look well, George!' I said.

They took him to a nursing home. He was fairly quiet, except on Saturday mornings, when they had a hard time of it to keep him indoors and away from the Portobello Road.

But a couple of months later he did escape. It was a Monday.

They searched for him in the Portobello Road, but actually he had gone off to Kent to the village near the scene of the Haystack Murder. There he went to the police and gave himself up, but they could tell from the way he was talking that there was something wrong with the man.

'I saw Needle in the Portobello Road three Saturdays running,' he explained, 'and they put me in a private ward but I got away while the nurses were seeing to the new patient. You remember the murder of Needle—well, I did it. Now you know the truth, and that will keep bloody Needle's mouth shut.'

Dozens of poor mad fellows confess to every murder. The police obtained an ambulance to take him back to the nursing home. He wasn't there long. Kathleen gave up her shop and devoted herself to looking after him at home. But she found that the Saturday mornings were a strain. He insisted on going to see me in the Portobello Road and would come back to insist that he'd murdered Needle. Once he tried to tell her something about Matilda, but Kathleen was so kind and solicitous, I don't think he had the courage to remember what he had to say.

Skinny had always been rather reserved with George since the murder. But he was kind to Kathleen. It was he who persuaded them to emigrate to Canada so that George should be well out of reach of the Portobello Road.

George has recovered somewhat in Canada but of course he will never be the old George again, as Kathleen writes to Skinny. 'That Haystack tragedy did it for George,' she writes, 'I feel sorrier for George sometimes than I am for poor Needle. But I do often have Masses said for Needle's soul.'

I doubt if George will ever see me again in the Portobello Road. He broods much over the crumpled snapshot he took of us on the haystack. Kathleen does not like the photograph, I don't wonder. For my part, I consider it quite a jolly snap, but I don't think we were any of us so lovely as we look in it, gazing blatantly over the ripe cornfields, Skinny with his humorous expression, I secure in my difference from the rest, Kathleen with her head prettily perched on her hand, each reflecting fearlessly in the face of George's camera the glory of the world, as if it would never pass.

THE

INDIAN

John Updike

The town, in New England, of Tarbox, restrained from embracing the sea by a margin of tawny salt marshes, locates its downtown four miles inland up the Musquenomenee River, which ceases to be tidal at the waterfall of the old hosiery mill, now given over to the manufacture of plastic toys. It was to the mouth of this river, in May of 1634, that the small party of seventeen men, led by the younger son of the governor of the Massachusetts Bay Colony—Jeremiah Tarbox being only his second in command—came in three rough skiffs with the purpose of establishing amid such an unpossessed abundance of salt hay a pastoral plantation. This, with God's forbearance, they did. They furled their sails and slowly rowed, each boat being equipped with four oarlocks, in search of firm land, through marshes that must appear, now that their grass is no longer harvested by men driving horses shod in great wooden discs, much the same today as they did then—though undoubtedly the natural abundance of ducks, cranes, otter, and deer has been somewhat diminished. Tarbox himself, in his invaluable diary, notes that the squealing of the livestock in the third skiff attracted a great cloud of "protestating sea-fowl." The first houses (not one of which still stands, the oldest in town dating, in at least its central timbers and fireplace, from 1642) were strung along the base of the rise of firm land called Near Hill, which, with its companion Far Hill, a mile away, in effect bounds the densely populated section of the present township. In winter the population of Tarbox numbers something less than seven thousand; in summer the figure may be closer to nine thousand. The width of the river mouth and its sheltered advantage within Tarbox Bay seemed to promise the makings of a port to rival Boston; but in spite of repeated dredging operations the river has proved incorrigibly silty, and its shallow winding channels, rendered especially fickle where the fresh water of the river most powerfully clashes with the restless saline influx of the tide, frustrate all but pleasure craft. These Chris-Craft and Kit-Kats, skimming seaward through the exhilarating avenues of wild hay, in the early morning may pass, as the fluttering rust-colored horizon abruptly yields to the steely blue monotone of the open water, a few dour clammers in hip boots patiently harrowing the tidewater floor. The intent posture of their silhouettes distinguishes them from the few bathers who have drifted down from the dying campfires by whose side they have dozed and sung and drunk away a night on the beach—one of the finest and least spoiled, it should be said, on the North Atlantic coast. Picturesque as Millet's gleaners, their torsos doubled like playing cards in the rosy mirror of the dawn-stilled sea, these sparse representatives of the clamming industry, founded in the eighteen-eighties by an immigration of Greeks and continually harassed by the industrial pollution upriver, exploit the sole vein of profit left in the name of old Musquenomenee. This shadowy chief broke the bread of peace with the son of the Governor, and within a year both were dead. The body of the one was returned to Boston to lie in the Kings Chapel graveyard; the body of the other is supposedly buried, presumably upright, somewhere in the woods on the side of Far Hill where even now no houses have intruded, though the tract is rumored to have been sold to a divider. Until the postwar arrival of Boston commuters, still much of a minority, Tarbox lived (discounting the summer people, who came and went in the marshes each year like the migrations of mallards) as a town apart. A kind of curse has kept its peace. The handmade-lace industry, which reached its peak just before the American Revolution, was destroyed by the industrial revolution; the textile mills, never numerous, were finally emptied by the industrialization of the South. They have been succeeded by a scattering of small enterprises, electronic in the main, which have staved off decisive depression.

Viewed from the spur of Near Hill where the fifth edifice, now called Congregationalist, of the religious society incorporated in 1635 on this identical spot thrusts its spire into the sky, and into a hundred colored postcards purchasable at all four local drugstores—viewed from this eminence, the business district makes a neat and prosperous impression. This is especially true at Christmastime, when colored lights are strung from pole to pole, and at the height of summer, when girls in shorts and bathing suits decorate the pavements. A one-hour parking limit is enforced during business hours, but the traffic is congested only during the evening homeward exodus: A stoplight has never been thought quite necessary. A new Woolworth's with a noble façade of corrugated laminated Fiberglas has been erected on the site of a burned-out tenement. If the building which it vacated across the street went begging nearly a year for a tenant, and if some other properties along the street nervously change hands and wares now and then, nevertheless there is not that staring stretch of blank shopwindows which desolates the larger mill towns to the north and west. Two hardware stores confront each other without apparent rancor; three banks vie in promoting solvency; several luncheonettes withstand waves of factory workers and high-school students; and a small proud army of *petit-bourgeois* knights— realtors and lawyers and jewellers—parades up and down in clothes that would not look quaint on Madison Avenue. The explosive thrust of superhighways through the land has sprinkled on the town a cosmopolitan garnish; one resourceful divorcée has made a good thing of selling unabashedly smart women's clothes and Scandinavian kitchen accessories, and, next door, a foolish young matron nostalgic for Vassar has opened a combination paperback bookstore and art gallery, so that now the Tarbox town derelict, in sneaking with his cherry-red face and tot of rye from the liquor store to his home above the shoe-repair nook, must walk a garish gantlet of abstract paintings by a minister's wife from Gloucester. Indeed, the whole street is laid open to an accusatory chorus of brightly packaged titles by Freud, Camus, and those others through whose masterworks our civilization moves toward its dark climax. Strange to say, so virulent is the spread of modern culture, some of these same titles can be had, seventy-five cents cheaper, in the homely old magazine-and-newspaper store in the middle of the block. Here,

sitting stoically on the spines of the radiator behind the large
left-hand window, the Indian can often be seen.

He sits in this window for hours at a time, politely waving to
any passerby who happens to glance his way. It is hard always
to avoid his eye, his form is so unexpected, perched on the
radiator above cards of pipes and pyramids of Prince Albert tins
and fanned copies of *True* and *Male* and *Sport*. He looks,
behind glass, somewhat shadowy and thin, but outdoors he is
solid enough. During other hours he takes up a station by
Leonard's Pharmaceutical on the corner. There is a splintered
telephone pole here that he leans against when he wearies of
leaning against the brick wall. Occasionally he even sits upon
the fire hydrant as if upon a campstool, arms folded, legs
crossed, gazing across at the renovations on the face of Poirier's
Liquor Mart. In cold or wet weather he may sit inside the
drugstore, expertly prolonging a coffee at the counter, running
his tobacco-dyed fingertip around and around the rim of the
cup as he watches the steam fade. There are other spots—
untenanted doorways, the benches halfway up the hill, idle
chairs in the barbershops—where he loiters, and indeed there
cannot be a square foot of the downtown pavement where he
has not at some time or other paused; but these two spots, the
window of the news store and the wall of the drugstore, are his
essential habitat.
    It is difficult to discover anything about him. He wears a
plaid lumberjack shirt with a gray turtleneck sweater underneath, and chino pants olive rather than khaki in color, and
remarkably white tennis sneakers. He smokes and drinks coffee, so he must have some income, but he does not, apparently, work. Inquiry reveals that now and then he is employed
—during the last Christmas rush he was seen carrying baskets
of Hong Kong shirts and Italian crèche elements through the
aisles of the five-and-ten—but he soon is fired or quits, and the
word "lazy," given somehow more than its usual force of disapproval, sticks in the mind, as if this is the clue. Disconcert-
ingly, he knows your name. Even though you are a young
mutual-fund analyst newly bought into a neo-saltbox on the
beach road and downtown on a Saturday morning to rent a
wallpaper steamer, he smiles if he catches your eye, lifts his
hand lightly, and says, "Good morning, Mr.——," supplying

your name. Yet his own name is impossible to learn. The simplest fact about a person, identity's very seed, is in his case utterly hidden. It can be determined, by matching consistencies of hearsay, that he lives in that tall, speckle-shingled, disreputable hotel overlooking the atrophied railroad tracks, just down from the Amvets, where shuffling Polish widowers and one-night-in-town salesmen hang out, and in whose bar, evidently, money can be wagered and women may be approached. But his name, whether it is given to you as Tugwell or Frisbee or Wigglesworth, even if it were always the same name would be in its almost parodic Yankeeness incredible. "But he's an Indian!"

The face of your informant—say, the chunky Irish dictator of the School Building Needs Committee, a dentist—undergoes a faint rapt transformation. His voice assumes its habitual whisper of extravagant discretion. "Don't go around saying that. He doesn't like it. He prides himself on being a typical run-down Yankee."

But he *is* an Indian. This is, alone, certain. Who but a savage would have such an immense capacity for repose? His cheekbones, his never-faded skin, the delicate little jut of his scowl, the drooping triangularity of his eye sockets, the way his vertically lined face takes the light, the lusterless black of his hair are all so profoundly Indian that the imagination, surprised by his silhouette as he sits on the hydrant gazing across at the changing face of the liquor store, effortlessly plants a feather at the back of his head. His air of waiting, of gazing; the softness of his motions; the odd sense of proprietorship and ease that envelops him; the good humor that makes his vigil gently dreadful—all these are totally foreign to the shambling shy-eyes and moist lower lip of the failed Yankee. His age and status are too peculiar. He is surely older than forty and younger than sixty—but *is* this sure? And, though he greets everyone by name with a light wave of his hand, the conversation never passes beyond a greeting, and even in the news store, when the political contention and convivial obscenity literally drive housewives away from the door, he does not seem to participate. He witnesses, and now and then offers in a gravelly voice a debated piece of town history, but he does not participate.

It is caring that makes mysteries. As you grow indifferent,

they lift. You live longer in the town, season follows season, the half-naked urban people arrive on the beach, multiply, and like leaves fall away again, and you have ceased to identify with them. The marshes turn green and withdraw through gold into brown, and their indolent, untouched, enduring existence penetrates your fibre. You find you must drive down toward the beach once a week or it is like a week without love. The ice cakes pile up along the banks of the tidal inlets like the rubble of ruined temples. You begin to meet, without seeking them out, the vestigial people: the unmarried daughters of vanished mill owners, the retired high-school teachers, the senile deacons in their unheated seventeenth-century houses with attics full of old church records in spidery brown ink. You enter, by way of an elderly baby-sitter, a world where at least they speak of him as "the Indian." An appalling snicker materializes in the darkness on the front seat beside you as you drive dear Mrs. Knowlton home to her shuttered house on a back road. "If you knew what they say, Mister, if you knew what they say." And at last, as when in a woods you break through miles of underbrush into a clearing, you stand up surprised, taking a deep breath of the obvious, agreeing with the trees that of course this is the case. Anybody who is anybody knew all along. The mystery lifts, with some impatience, here, in Miss Horne's low-ceilinged front parlor, which smells of warm fireplace ashes and of peppermint balls kept ready in red-tinted knobbed glass goblets for whatever open-mouthed children might dare to come visit such a very old lady, all bent double like a little gripping rose clump, Miss Horne, a fable in her lifetime. Her father had been the sixth minister before the present one (whom she does *not* care for) at the First Church, and *his* father the next but one before him. There had been a Horne among those first seventeen men. Well—where was she? —yes, the Indian. The Indian had been loitering—waiting, if you prefer—in the center of town when she was a tiny girl in gingham. And he is no older now than he was then.

FULL

CIRCLE

Denton Welch

I remember it well, that still night before the war, when I walked up to the entrance of the majestic house. The last glimmer from the dead sun was still hanging in the air. It lighted up the curious twisted chimney shafts and baroque gables, dramatizing them, so that it was difficult to tell whether the houses were Elizabethan or Victorian.

I pulled the long shaft of the hand-bell and heard it echoing down what I imagined to be a stone passage. Soon there were footsteps and the door was opened to me by a footman with striped waistcoat.

For a moment I was surprised and rather taken aback by this uniform, never having seen it in real life before. I had imagined in a cloudy way that if people still had footmen, they dressed them like hotel waiters. Now this nineteenth-century relic delighted me. I looked at his smooth, good-looking, commonplace face and said,

"Can you tell me where I can get a bed for the night near here? I'm walking along the Downs to Winchester and have lost my way."

He looked at my rucksack with a darting, rather furtive look, as if to read my intentions from it; then said in a soft voice,

"There's nowhere, unless you choose to go back to Steyning."

"How far is that?" I asked.

"About three or four miles."

I saw that I would get nothing more from him. He was waiting, not too politely, to shut the door. He wanted to get back to the wireless in the servants' hall or to his book by the fire. I felt, for some reason, that the family was away and that the servants had the house to themselves.

It was on the tip of my tongue to ask if he could not put me up somewhere in the house, but I had not the courage to listen to the weak excuse he would probably make for refusing. So I let him shut the door gently in my face.

Now I was surrounded by the night again, with nowhere to sleep "unless I chose to go back to Steyning." His wording seemed ironical. As if anyone would "choose" to walk back three or four miles after having walked twenty!

I crossed the cobbled court and stood by one of the stone urns which punctuated the balustrade. The coarse park grass on the other side lapped right up to this low wall. I heard the noise of animals chewing in the dark and to the right I thought I caught the glimmer from some crack between the curtains of a window. I wondered if the dark mass could be a cottage. I decided to climb over the balustrade and walk across the park to see. As I passed, sheep coughed, rose jerkily to their feet and ran away to lean against the trees in fright. Sometimes I would see them with their rumps in the air, their front legs still bent under them in an involuntary attitude of prayer. They seemed unable to move; then suddenly their legs would flick straight.

As I drew nearer I saw that the light was moving. A man was carrying a lantern out to his beasts. I felt glad that I would not have to knock again at a strange door.

"May I shelter in one of your outhouses?" I asked, hoping that my voice would not startle him.

He turned round abruptly, then came towards me with the lantern held high.

"Where do you come from?" he asked, shining the lantern on my face.

"I am on a walking tour. I have been up to the big house, the footman said that I'd have to go back to Steyning if I wanted a bed."

"They wouldn't help you there!" he said contemptuously. It was contempt as much for my ignorance as for the inhabitants of the house.

He stood silently for a moment, looking at me. I thought he was going to ask me into the cottage, but when he spoke, it was to say,

"Come along with me, I'll show you where there's some hay."

He took me across the tiny farm-yard and led me to a shed which joined the barn. The smell of hay met me as I stood in the doorway. The man had gone in and was stirring it up in one of the corners.

"You ought to be all right there," he said.

I eased my rucksack off my shoulders as I thanked him. Leaning against the wall I realized how tired I was. I hoped that he would leave me so that I could sink into the hay.

I did not have to wait, for after one further swift glance at my face he said good-night. I watched the lantern swinging across the farm-yard and waited until it had disappeared into the cottage and the door had clicked behind him. Then I undid my belt, kicked off my shoes, and after wrapping myself in my raincoat, lay down to sleep.

I was so tired that the events of the day kept passing before my closed eyes, running and mixing together in that fantastic, restless way. Cows in their stalls nearby shook their chains or knocked against the wooden walls.

Just as I began to wonder if I should ever fall asleep, I felt the delicious sinking and fading of consciousness. I lay like this until something jerked my eyes open. I was not yet fully awake but I knew that the dim light had changed in the shed. It was darker still. Someone was standing in the doorway.

"Who's that?" I cried out in alarm before I realized that it must only be someone from the cottage.

"It's all right, mate," the man said in a soft voice. He came towards me and sat on the edge of the pile of hay. I saw then that he was only a youth, two or three years younger than myself. I thought that he was probably the son of the farmer. He had a pleasant face but his lips and eyes were sullen. He seemed almost on the point of tears.

"What's wrong?" I found myself saying against my will. I did not want him to think me curious.

There was no answer for a moment, and I thought that he had resented my question, until he suddenly burst out,

"Would you let your father still beat you if you were eighteen?"

"Not if I could help it," I said with a laugh, trying to make the atmosphere lighter.

"No more would I, and I haven't!" His voice reached almost

to a shout on the last words. "Just look at that," he went on, turning his back to me for my inspection. In the dimness I could just see dark stains on the white shirt. They might have been oil, mud, or blood. I said nothing, and in his impatience he pulled his shirt over his head. Then I knew what they were. On the white flesh were raw wounds and long bruises.

"He made my brother help him tie my hands to a tree, then he did that with his belt," he said. "But he won't do it again in a hurry; I've treated him the same way!"

"What have you done?" I asked fearfully.

"Kicked him in the belly till he was sick on the floor!" The youth laughed and leaned back till the hay pricked his wounds and he flinched.

If the man with the lantern was his father, I wondered why I had heard nothing. He had certainly not been "kicked in the belly till he was sick on the floor" when he led me to the shed, and if the incident had happened after he left me I surely would have heard some of the inevitable noise through my half-sleep.

However, I determined to ask no more questions. I accepted the fact that a father had beaten a son who was too old to be beaten, and that the son had replied by kicking the father in the stomach.

My companion showed no desire to go back into the house and said that he would stay with me, out in the shed till the morning. He lay on his stomach, trying to ease his back into the most comfortable position. I had ointment for blisters and scratches in my pack. I got it out and rubbed some gently on the less important wounds (I could do nothing about the others). His flesh seemed burning, and I could feel how his whole frame trembled if I hurt him.

When I had finished he groped in the dark, then found my hand and held it firmly, as if to thank me.

Almost immediately after this he fell asleep still touching me. Moving as little as possible I put away the ointment and lay down beside him. His smooth breathing and the warmth from his breath lulled me. Soon I too must have fallen asleep, for I remember waking later at the climax of some violent dream in which my companion or someone like him only rather older, was standing in a doorway watching a woman take a tray of cakes from the oven. She seemed quite unaware of his presence till he sprang at her, pushing her onto the kitchen-range and snatching the cakes with his other hand. I awoke at the terrible scream she gave as her hands and face touched the hotplates of the stove.

I opened my eyes. My companion still lay close to me in the hay with his hand on mine; but his breathing seemed to have grown thicker and I thought that I smelled an unpleasant odor from his body, an unkempt, unwashed smell which had not been there before. I supposed that the warmth had drawn it out from his old clothes. I tried not to think of it and composed myself for sleep again, hoping that I would not dream.

But I did. Scene after scene of squalor and brutality passed before me. The youth was always the chief actor. In each scene he seemed to be heavier and coarser than in the last. I was always the helpless spectator, hidden in some cupboard or spying through some skylight, from the roof.

In my last dream I saw him following a little girl across a Common. She was pretty, she danced gaily as she went along, throwing stones into the air and skipping. I saw him steal up behind her and grasp her round the waist. She screamed but he put his hand over her mouth and dragged her underneath the bushes. I saw him pin her hands down and kneel on her legs, spread-eagling her. Then he tore at her clothes, and I awoke with such horror that I found myself sweating; while my throat was sore with dryness. For a moment I lay there collecting myself, inexpressibly thankful that it had only been a dream. I thought I would tell my companion when he woke of the horrors I had dreamed about him. It would amuse him. I could still feel his body near me and his hand on mine. He was very still, so I did not disturb him.

Although I kept my eyes shut, I knew that it was day, because of the red glow of the light shining through the flesh of my eyelids.

As I became more conscious of my surroundings I noticed the unpleasant smell again, but there was no doubting it now. It was the smell of human dirt, despair, and squalor. His hand on mine seemed strangely rough and horny and there was a coldness pervading his whole body. I thought that he must have been chilled in only his thin shirt and trousers.

I sat up, opened my eyes and looked down on my companion. Then in a moment I had jumped to my feet and lay back against the wall, my legs and arms trembling from shock.

A strange man lay there, and his face was grey and seamed and filthy. A line of dried dirt ran round his open, grey-lipped mouth, and a dribble of saliva was caught in the stubble on his chin. The strong hair on his chest frothed out of the rents in his sweat-blackened shirt. He was utterly still. I could not understand how my convulsive jump had not awakened him.

Then I knew.

I ran to the cottage door just as I was, without my shoes. The thick mud pushed through my woollen socks and lay in little cushions between my toes. I fumbled with the buckle of my belt as I rapped on the door.

The man I had seen the night before slowly opened it. He held a towel in his hands and his arms were dripping.

"What is it?" he asked grudgingly, thinking, I suppose, that I had come to borrow something.

"Quick, there is a man in the shed. He is ill."

I knew that my voice was much too loud, but I could not control it.

The man pushed past me, still carrying his towel. When I caught up with him he was kneeling by the man in the shed. He had torn away what remained of the other's collar and was holding his head between his hands. Then he let it fall back on the hay and stared at it.

"It's our Tom," he said half to himself, half to me. "I haven't seen him for twenty years." And in quite another voice he added, "Go and tell my sister Annie to come quick."

I started to run back to the house, but a woman in a white apron met me. The strings of it were flying in the wind.

"What is it?" she asked in agitation. "What's wrong?"

"Your brother's in the shed, he wants you," was all I could say.

I did not go back. I left them together and waited with my stockinged feet sinking into the mud.

I heard the woman begin to weep and through the dark opening I saw her throw her apron over her face. It seemed a curious, almost stagy gesture. "He has come home to die, he has come home to die," she kept on repeating.

Then I heard the man calling me. "Young man, will you help me?" he asked.

I could not bear to touch it, but I went in and picked up the boots behind my back so that I would be able to walk without looking at it.

We laid the body on the parlor sofa. The man looked at me and said, "He was our brother. He ran away twenty years ago because my father beat him for going out with girls. But before he left he got my father in the cow-stall and kicked him so that when we found him he was half dead. He only lived for six months after that. But Tom didn't know what he'd done!" he added passionately.

I wondered why the man had told me this terrible story, but then I realized that he had again been half talking to himself for his voice changed, as before, when he said,

"Now I suppose I'll have to go for the police."

It was then that I had the unreasoning fear that I might be charged with the murder of their brother.

I thought, while I waited to be questioned, of the youth who had come in the night before, and of how he slept touching me, while I saw in my dreams all the terrible acts which had made him into the tramp who lay beside me when I woke in the morning.

SOUND

IS SECOND

SIGHT

Lynne Sharon Schwartz

A farmer of austere habits lived some ways from town in a ramshackle farmhouse, and he looked as forlorn and ramshackle as his house with its weatherbeaten wooden slats and cracked shingles. Tall, taciturn, dressed in drab, loose-fitting clothes, he would gaze down at the ground as he walked. He carried a gnarled walking stick and let his mud-colored hair droop around his face, and so he appeared older than he was. Actually he was not old at all, nor crabbed as some believed, merely a solitary. Out of habit he kept his distance, and the people of the town thought it best to keep their distance as well.

His only companion was a small greyhound dog, slender, blond, and frolicsome after the manner of her kind. She was fiercely devoted to the farmer and, unlike the townspeople, not frightened off by his gnarled walking stick or his silence or his gaunt, shielded face. Outdoors, in the fields or in town, the farmer and his dog were silent and undemonstrative, yet they had the air of creatures very much attuned and in comfort together. The townspeople were puzzled by the dog. Not a farm dog by any means. Not a dog that could be useful. Her very prettiness and uselessness seemed out of place in that stony countryside, and when she strutted down the main street she drew hostile glances. Rumors sprang up that the dog, for all her prettiness, had sinister powers; possibly even the farmer did. Her origins were mysterious: all anyone knew was that after vanishing for several days the farmer had returned with the dog perched in the front seat of his truck, sniffing in her disdainful way.

In fact he had found her in a nearby and larger market town. The dogcatcher had seemed hesitant to sell her: a well-meaning fellow, he hinted that the dog had brought bad luck to former owners, best leave her to her fate. But the farmer had a sudden craving for the pretty creature, whom he had spied standing in a corner of the yard apart from the pack of other animals; she reminded him of himself, isolated, the butt of nasty tall tales, perhaps even ill-treated when young, as he had been. She had an unearthly howl, the dogcatcher also warned, wild enough to rouse the dead. But she made no sound at all in her corner of the cluttered yard, so the farmer paid no heed and bought her.

Evenings, alone in the house, they romped together in front of the fire, the farmer bellowing and laughing, the dog yelping and snapping playfully. She barked seldom. Her bark was indeed loud and piercing, almost a howl, and it was as if she held it in out of deference to human ears. Despite his carelessness about the outside of the house, the farmer kept the inside pleasant and tidy: the wood floors, with their wide planks, were swept clean, the logs piled near the fireplace had a sweet smoky smell, and the soft cushions on the floor were inviting. Besides all that, the dog got good food to eat; she made a contented, obedient housemate.

And then one day after spending almost at week away at the nearby market town, the farmer and his dog came home with a bright-eyed wife, who also excited curiosity among the townspeople, and a few of the more outspoken wondered slyly whether he had found her in the same mysterious way as he had found the dog. She was small and rounded, with rosy cheeks, milky skin, and black curls. She smiled indulgently at the confusion of the dog, who bristled when she stroked her blond fur. She laughed at the farmer's long shield of hair and brushed it off his really rather handsome face with a tender gesture. Nor was she much bothered by the ramshackle appearance of the house, for she saw that the inside was cheerful and tidy. The vegetable garden behind the house was her delight: under the farmer's care, tomatoes and beans and peas were flourishing in such abundance she could hardly pick them fast enough. The people of the town, who could find nothing to fault her with since she was unfailingly courteous and proper, were astonished that so sprightly a creature could be happy living with the taciturn farmer, yet she appeared quite happy. When the three of them walked down the main street, it was the farmer and his wife, now, who were silent and undemonstrative, yet seemed very much attuned and in comfort together. The dog fretted alongside. Occasionally she gave out her lacerating howl, which made passersby start, and startled even the farmer, who hastened to quiet her. The dog was not neglected—the farmer still stroked her and spoke kindly to her and took her along daily to the fields, but in the nature of things it was not the same.

Evenings, in the broken-down house, the farmer and his wife lay on rugs in front of the fire, while the dog fussed in a cold corner, ignoring their beckonings. The farmer had never been so happy in his life. He had grown up lonely and lived lonely, and, given the awkward shyness that no one till now had found appealing, had never expected to be other than lonely till the day he died. He was no less astonished than the townspeople that this pretty, loving wife welcomed his company and settled so easily into his house. It was a gift he could not fathom, dared not even question, and while it did not change his appearance—he still dressed in drab, nondescript clothing—or the appearance of his house—still forlorn and ramshackle—he felt himself a changed man. For this his heart was full of gratitude to his wife, and in his innocence, he envisioned living with her serenely to the end of his days.

What the farmer loved most about his wife was not her prettiness or her sweet nature, but her voice. It was like music; it could sing out low like a cello or high like a flute, and flit through the whole range in between. When she called to him in the fields, mid-day, her pure long-lasting note cut a path through the air. When she rushed to greet him or tell him news of the garden her voice was full, impelled by energy. And when she lay with him before the fire its timbre was more than deep—dense, as if the sound itself might be grasped and held, caressed. To the farmer her voice expressed all moods and possibilities; living with her after living silent for so long with the dog was like embracing another dimension, having a sixth sense.

The dog clearly did not love the sound of the wife's voice, although it was never anything but gentle and cajoling, in a

futile effort to win her trust. The dog still bristled at her touch
and took food grudgingly from her hands. If the farmer whistled her over while his wife was nearby, she hung back and
needed to be coaxed. And when the two were alone, the dog
would snap at her skirts, or snarl, or set up a howling the wife
could not stop. In the garden she stepped across the wife's path
to trip her up. In the kitchen she knocked over a tureen of
soup—the wife had to jump aside so as not to be scalded. She
reproached the dog softly, in dismay more than anger. The
wife did not mention these incidents to the farmer—they seemed,
after all, so petty. She was a tolerant soul who took what came
along. She too had been lonely and ill-treated as a child, and
also, because of her prettiness, suspected of evils she did not
commit, so she found herself fortunate in her new life; her
thoughts were rooted in its daily pleasures. She was hardly one
to brood over the fussing of a dog: surely the creature would
come round in time.

This happy period in the farmer's life lasted for three years,
and then the wife took sick with a mysterious illness, not
painful but enervating. It had never been seen before in that
region, and there seemed nothing anyone could do to save her.
The farmer fed her with his own hands and pleaded with her to
rally, if only for his sake, but she shook her head gravely, like
one already past the threshold. In despair he wanted to take the
very strength from his own body and feed it to her. But she
was doomed. Stunned with grief, he buried her some distance
from the house. After a time, though his grief remained acute,
there mingled with it a feeling that, just as he had grown up
lonely and lived lonely, so he was to remain lonely till the day
he died, and that the time with his wife was a fleeting interlude
given to him unfathomably. He sought solace in the company
of his dog, who became frolicsome and good-tempered as in
the early days. When they walked together in the town they
once again had the air of creatures very much attuned and in
comfort together. As for the townspeople, after paying their
condolences they kept their distance as before.

One moonlit summer night as he lay awake with the windows wide open, the farmer heard his wife's voice calling his
name far out across the fields. He rushed to the window and
called back into the night. Over and over her voice called, now
closer, now farther off, as if it were drifting about, seeking him

in the dark but powerless to find the way. Then the dog went to the window and began to bark. As the shrill howling persisted, the voice came closer and closer until at last it was there in the room, that voice he used to feel was almost palpable. The farmer was overjoyed. All night long his wife's voice talked with him and kept him company, while the dog crouched silent in a corner. They talked, as always, of small daily things—the farm and the town, the vegetable garden—and of love. The range and timbre of the wondrous voice were unaltered by death. As day broke she left.

She came often after that. Each time, the farmer passed the whole night with her, talking of daily things and feeling joyful, if baffled, at this great gift given back to him, at least in part. Whenever her voice sounded from far off, the dog would go to the open window to help her find her way. For only that horrible howling, puncturing the night like an arrow, could guide her; the farmer's own, human, voice was of no avail.

For a long time the farmer lived thus, enjoying the mild companionship of the dog by day and the beloved voice of his dead wife by night. But the dog was growing old. During their walks through the fields he noticed that she trudged ever more slowly, breathing with effort. Yet fiercely devoted, she strove to keep up with him, would not desert his path. One day the farmer sensed she was no longer behind him; he went back a short distance and found her collapsed on the ground. He carried her back to the house, settled her on a rug in front of the fire, and gave her water from his cupped hand till she closed her eyes and died. He buried her under a tree near the barn.

Now the farmer suffered an excruciating loneliness. In daylight he walked alone and in the dark he knew the agony of hearing his wife's voice calling out there, unable to find him without the howling to guide her. Many nights the voice called, raw with pleading, while the farmer shouted out the window to no avail. As the voice despaired and faded he would shut the window with bitter tears in his throat. The voice stopped seeking him. He pondered whether it was worse to have no gifts at all, or to have gifts given and so cruelly withdrawn.

Then one night as he lay sleepless, there came the awful voice of the dog, howling far across the fields. The farmer rushed to the window. The dog's voice came steadily closer, finding its way with ease. Although he could neither stroke her nor play with her, and although she kept silent once in the room, the farmer took comfort and rested more calmly, feeling her presence. He reflected, though, how strange it was to have as companion a voice that had best not make itself heard, for very ugliness.

On a moonlit night when the dog had come, the farmer was sitting at the window when he heard his wife's voice again, calling over the fields. He leaped to his feet and called back as loudly as he could. Suddenly from right beside him came the lacerating howl of the dog, slicing into the still night. He longed to hug her in gratitude, but there was nothing to the touch. Just as before, the dog's voice howled until the wife's voice found its way into the room. The farmer was trembling with emotion; he longed to embrace her, but again he had to content himself with what he was given.

His wife's voice was joyous too; but scarcely had she begun to speak of this recovery of each other than her voice was overpowered by the dog's insistent howl. Sternly, the farmer commanded the animal to be silent, but for the first time she refused to obey him. The wife's voice grew higher, urgent: she was calling for help. Her words became screams, then pure shrieks of sound swooping through the air; meanwhile the howling reached an unearthly pitch, filling up the room, exulting in its rough, wild fury kept at bay so long. The farmer veered about in a frenzy of helplessness, arms outstretched and flailing for something to touch. The wife's terrified shrieks got short and staccato, like the plucking of a taut string against the prolonged howls tearing into the dark. Madly, the farmer raced about, hands plunging and stabbing at the empty night. Till at last there was one drawn-out, descending note wailed in unison with the dog's rapid panting, and then both voices sank and subsided, and there was nothing.

When the townspeople came to investigate they found the farmer gone, the house abandoned. The bedroom was all in disorder, as if a rampaging wind had whipped things up and left them to fall where they might. From near the window, reported some, came now and then a hoarse, panting noise, like a beast out of breath.

I USED TO

LIVE HERE

ONCE

Jean Rhys

She was standing by the river looking at the stepping stones and remembering each one. There was the round unsteady stone, the pointed one, the flat one in the middle—the safe stone where you could stand and look round. The next wasn't so safe for when the river was full the water flowed over it and even when it showed dry it was slippery. But after that it was easy and soon she was standing on the other side.

The road was much wider than it used to be but the work had been done carelessly. The felled trees had not been cleared away and the bushes looked trampled. Yet it was the same road and she walked along feeling extraordinarily happy.

It was a fine day, a blue day. The only thing was that the sky had a glassy look that she didn't remember. That was the only word she could think of. Glassy. She turned the corner, saw that what had been the old pavé had been taken up, and there too the road was much wider, but it had the same unfinished look.

She came to the worn stone steps that led up to the house and her heart began to beat. The screw pine was gone, so was the mock summer house called the ajoupa, but the clove tree was still there and at the top of the steps the rough lawn stretched away, just as she remembered it. She stopped and looked towards the house that had been added to and painted white. It was strange to see a car standing in front of it.

There were two children under the big mango tree, a boy and a little girl, and she waved to them and called 'Hello' but they didn't answer her or turn their heads. Very fair children, as Europeans born in the West Indies so often are: as if the white blood is asserting itself against all odds.

The grass was yellow in the hot sunlight as she walked towards them. When she was quite close she called again, shyly: 'Hello.' Then, 'I used to live here once,' she said.

Still they didn't answer. When she said for the third time 'Hello' she was quite near them. Her arms went out instinctively with the longing to touch them.

It was the boy who turned. His grey eyes looked straight into hers. His expression didn't change. He said: 'Hasn't it gone cold all of a sudden. D'you notice? Let's go in.' 'Yes, let's,' said the girl.

Her arms fell to her sides as she watched them running across the grass to the house. That was the first time she knew.

THE

JOLLY

CORNER

Henry James

I

"Every one asks me what I 'think' of everything," said Spencer
Brydon; "and I make answer as I can—begging or dodging the
question, putting them off with any nonsense. It wouldn't
matter to any of them really," he went on, "for, even were it
possible to meet in that stand-and-deliver way so silly a demand on so big a subject, my 'thoughts' would still be almost
altogether about something that concerns only myself." He was
talking to Miss Staverton, with whom for a couple of months
now he had availed himself of every possible occasion to talk;
this disposition and this resource, this comfort and support, as
the situation in fact presented itself, having promptly enough
taken the first place in the considerable array of rather
unattenuated surprises attending his so strangely belated return to America. Everything was somehow a surprise; and that
might be natural when one had so long and so consistently
neglected everything, taken pains to give surprises so much
margin for play. He had given them more than thirty years—
thirty-three, to be exact; and they now seemed to him to have
organised their performance quite on the scale of that license.
He had been twenty-three on leaving New York—he was fifty-
six today: unless indeed he were to reckon as he had sometimes, since his repatriation, found himself feeling; in which
case he would have lived longer than is often allotted to man.
It would have taken a century, he repeatedly said to himself,

and said also to Alice Staverton, it would have taken a longer absence and a more averted mind than those even of which he had been guilty, to pile up the differences, the newnesses, the queernesses, above all the bignesses, for the better or the worse, that at present assaulted his vision wherever he looked.

The great fact all the while however had been the incalculability; since he *had* supposed himself, from decade to decade, to be allowing, and in the most liberal and intelligent manner, for brilliancy of change. He actually saw that he had allowed for nothing; he missed what he would have been sure of finding, he found what he would never have imagined. Proportions and values were upside-down; the ugly things he had expected; the ugly things of his far-away youth, when he had too promptly waked up to a sense of the ugly—these uncanny phenomena placed him rather, as it happened, under the charm; whereas the "swagger" things, the modern, the monstrous, the famous things, those he had more particularly, like thousands of ingenuous enquirers every year, come over to see, were exactly his sources of dismay. They were as so many set traps for displeasure, above all for reaction, of which his restless tread was constantly pressing the spring. It was interesting, doubtless, the whole show, but it would have been too disconcerting hadn't a certain finer truth saved the situation. He had distinctly not, in this steadier light, come over *all* for the monstrosities; he had come, not only in the last analysis but quite on the face of the act, under an impulse with which they had nothing to do. He had come—putting the thing pompously—to look at his "property," which he had thus for a third of a century not been within four thousand miles of; or, expressing it less sordidly, he had yielded to the humour of seeing again his house on the jolly corner, as he usually, and quite fondly, described it—the one in which he had first seen the light, in which various members of his family had lived and had died, in which the holidays of his overschooled boyhood had been passed and the few social flowers of his chilled adolescence gathered, and which, alienated then for so long a period, had, through the successive deaths of his two brothers and the termination of old arrangements, come wholly into his hands. He was the owner of another, not quite so "good"—the jolly corner having been, from far back, superlatively extended and consecrated; and the value of the pair represented his main capital, with an income consisting, in these later years, of their respective rents which (thanks precisely to their original excellent type) had never been depressingly low. He could live in "Europe," as he had been in the habit of living, on the product of these flourishing New York leases, and all the better since, that of the second structure, the mere number in its long row, having within a twelvemonth fallen in, renovation at a high advance had proved beautifully possible.

These were items of property indeed, but he had found himself since his arrival distinguishing more than ever between them. The house within the street, two bristling blocks westward, was already in course of reconstruction as a tall mass of flats; he had acceded, some time before, to overtures for this conversion—in which, now that it was going forward, it had been not the least of astonishments to find himself able, on the spot, and though without a previous ounce of such experience, to participate with a certain intelligence, almost with a certain authority. He had lived his life with his back so turned to such concerns and his face addressed to those of so different an order that he scarce knew what to make of this lively stir, in a compartment of his mind never yet penetrated, of a capacity for business and a sense for construction. These virtues, so common all round him now, had been dormant in his own organism—where it might be said of them perhaps that they had slept the sleep of the just. At present, in the splendid autumn weather—the autumn at least was a pure boon in the terrible place—he loafed about his "work" undeterred, secretly agitated; not in the least "minding" that the whole proposition, as they said, was vulgar and sordid, and ready to climb ladders, to walk the plank, to handle materials and look wise about them, to ask questions, in fine, and challenge explanations and really "go into" figures.

It amused, it verily quite charmed him; and, by the same stroke, it amused, and even more, Alice Staverton, though perhaps charming her perceptibly less. She wasn't however going to be better off for it, as *he* was—and so astonishingly much: nothing was now likely, he knew, even to make her better-off than she found herself, in the afternoon of life, as the delicately frugal possessor and tenant of the small house in Irving Place to which she had subtly managed to cling through her almost unbroken New York career. If he knew the way to it

now better than to any other address among the dreadful
multiplied numberings which seemed to him to reduce the
whole place to some vast ledger-page, overgrown, fantastic,
of ruled and criss-crossed lines and figures—if he had formed,
for his consolation, that habit, it was really not a little because
of the charm of his having encountered and recognised, in the
vast wilderness of the wholesale, breaking through the mere
gross generalisation of wealth and force and success, a small
still scene where items and shades, all delicate things, kept the
sharpness of the notes of a high voice perfectly trained, and
where economy hung about like the scent of a garden. His old
friend lived with one maid and herself dusted her relics and
trimmed her lamps and polished her silver; she stood off, in
the awful modern crush, when she could, but she sallied forth
and did battle when the challenge was really to "spirit," the
spirit she after all confessed to, proudly and a little shyly, as to
that of the better time, that of *their* common, their quite
far-away and antediluvian social period and order. She made
use of the street-cars when need be, the terrible things that
people scrambled for as the panic-stricken at sea scramble for
the boats; she affronted, inscrutably, under stress, all the public concussions and ordeals; and yet, with that slim mystifying
grace of her appearance, which defied you to say if she were a
fair young woman who looked older through trouble, or a fine
smooth older one who looked young through successful indifference; with her precious reference, above all, to memories
and histories into which he could enter, she was as exquisite
for him as some pale pressed flower (a rarity to begin with),
and, failing other sweetnesses, she was a sufficient reward of
his effort. They had communities of knowledge, "their" knowledge (this discriminating possessive was always on her lips) of
presences of the other age, presences all overlaid, in his case,
by the experience of a man and the freedom of a wanderer,
overlaid by pleasure, by infidelity, by passages of life that were
strange and dim to her, just by "Europe" in short, but still
unobscured, still exposed and cherished, under that pious visitation of the spirit from which she had never been diverted.

      She had come with him one day to see how his "apartment-
house" was rising; he had helped her over gaps and explained
to her plans, and while they were there had happened to have,
before her, a brief but lively discussion with the man in charge,

the representative of the building-firm that had undertaken his
work. He had found himself quite "standing-up" to this person-
age over a failure on the latter's part to observe some detail of
one of their noted conditions, and had so lucidly argued his
case that, besides ever so prettily flushing, at the time, for
sympathy in his triumph, she had afterwards said to him (though
to a slightly greater effect of irony) that he had clearly for too
many years neglected a real gift. If he had but stayed at home
he would have anticipated the inventor of the sky-scraper. If he
had but stayed at home he would have discovered his genius in
time really to start some new variety of awful architectural hare
and run it till it burrowed in a gold-mine. He was to remember
these words, while the weeks elapsed, for the small silver ring
they had sounded over the queerest and deepest of his own
lately most disguised and most muffled vibrations.

It had begun to be present to him after the first fortnight, it
had broken out with the oddest abruptness, this particular
wanton wonderment: it met him there—and this was the image
under which he himself judged the matter, or at least, not a
little, thrilled and flushed with it—very much as he might have
been met by some strange figure, some unexpected occupant,
at a turn of one of the dim passages of an empty house. The
quaint analogy quite hauntingly remained with him, when he
didn't indeed rather improve it by still intenser form: that of
his opening a door behind which he would have made sure of
finding nothing, a door into a room shuttered and void, and
yet so coming, with a great suppressed start, on some quite
erect confronting presence, sometimes planted in the middle of the place and facing him through the dusk. After that
visit to the house in construction he walked with his companion
to see the other and always so much the better one, which in
the eastward direction formed one of the corners, the "jolly"
one precisely, of the street now so generally dishonoured and
disfigured in its westward reaches, and of the comparatively
conservative Avenue. The Avenue still had pretensions, as
Miss Staverton said, to decency; the old people had mostly
gone, the old names were unknown, and here and there an old
association seemed to stray, all vaguely, like some very aged
person, out too late, whom you might meet and feel the
impulse to watch or follow, in kindness, for safe restoration to
shelter.

They went in together, our friends; he admitted himself with his key, as he kept no one there, he explained, preferring, for his reasons, to leave the place empty, under a simple arrangement with a good woman living in the neighbourhood and who came for a daily hour to open windows and dust and sweep. Spencer Brydon had his reasons and was growingly aware of them; they seemed to him better each time he was there, though he didn't name them all to his companion, any more than he told her as yet how often, how quite absurdly often, he himself came. He only let her see for the present, while they walked through the great blank rooms, that absolute vacancy reigned and that, from top to bottom, there was nothing but Mrs. Muldoon's broomstick, in a corner, to tempt the burglar. Mrs. Muldoon was then on the premises, and she loquaciously attended the visitors, preceding them from room to room and pushing back shutters and throwing up sashes—all to show them, as she remarked, how little there was to see. There was little indeed to see in the great gaunt shell where the main dispositions and the general apportionment of space, the style of an age of ampler allowances, had nevertheless for its master their honest pleading message, affecting him as some good old servant's, some lifelong retainer's appeal for a character, or even for a retiring-pension; yet it was also a remark of Mrs. Muldoon's that, glad as she was to oblige him by her noonday round, there was a request she greatly hoped he would never make of her. If he should wish her for any reason to come in after dark she would just tell him, if he "plased," that he must ask it of somebody else.

The fact that there was nothing to see didn't militate for the worthy woman against what one *might* see, and she put it frankly to Miss Staverton that no lady could be expected to like, could she? "scraping up to thim top storeys in the ayvil hours." The gas and electric light were off the house, and she fairly evoked a gruesome vision of her march through the great grey rooms—so many of them as there were too!—with her glimmering taper. Miss Staverton met her honest glare with a smile and the profession that she herself certainly would recoil from such an adventure. Spencer Brydon meanwhile held his peace—for the moment; the question of the "evil" hours in his old home had already become too grave for him. He had begun some time since to "crape," and he knew just why a packet of candles addressed to that pursuit had been stowed by his own hand, three weeks before, at the back of a drawer of the fine old sideboard that occupied, as a "fixture," the deep recess in the dining-room. Just now he laughed at his companions—quickly however changing the subject; for the reason that, in the first place, his laugh struck him even at that moment as starting the odd echo, the conscious human resonance (he scarce knew how to qualify it) that sounds made while he was there alone sent back to his ear or his fancy; and that, in the second, he imagined Alice Staverton for the instant on the point of asking him, with a divination, if he ever so prowled. There were divinations he was unprepared for, and he had at all events averted enquiry by the time Mrs. Muldoon had left them, passing on to other parts.

There was happily enough to say, on so consecrated a spot, that could be said freely and fairly; so that a whole train of declarations was precipitated by his friend's having herself broken out, after a yearning look round: "But I hope you don't mean they want you to pull *this* to pieces!" His answer came, promptly, with his re-awakened wrath: it was of course exactly what they wanted, and what they were "at" him for, daily, with the iteration of people who couldn't for their life understand a man's liability to decent feelings. He had found the place, just as it stood and beyond what he could express, an interest and a joy. There were values other than the beastly rent-values, and in short, in short—! But it was thus Miss Staverton took him up. "In short you're to make so good a thing of your sky-scraper that, living in luxury on *those* ill-gotten gains, you can afford for a while to be sentimental here!" Her smile had for him, with the words, the particular mild irony with which he found half her talk suffused; an irony without bitterness and that came, exactly, from her having so much imagination—not, like the cheap sarcasms with which one heard most people, about the world of "society," bid for the reputation of clever-ness, from nobody's really having any. It was agreeable to him at this very moment to be sure that when he had answered, after a brief demur, "Well yes: so, precisely, you may put it!" her imagination would still do him justice. He explained that even if never a dollar were to come to him from the other house he would nevertheless cherish this one; and he dwelt, further, while they lingered and wandered, on the fact of the stupefaction he was already exciting, the positive mystification he felt himself create.

He spoke of the value of all he read into it, into the mere sight of the walls, mere shapes of the rooms, mere sound of the floors, mere feel, in his hand, of the old silver-plated knobs of the several mahogany doors, which suggested the pressure of the palms of the dead; the seventy years of the past in fine that these things represented, the annals of nearly three generations, counting his grandfather's, the one that had ended there, and the impalpable ashes of his long-extinct youth, afloat in the very air like microscopic motes. She listened to everything; she was a woman who answered intimately but who utterly didn't chatter. She scattered abroad therefore no cloud of words; she could assent, she could agree, above all she could encourage, without doing that. Only at the last she went a little further than he had done himself. "And then how do you know? You may still, after all, want to live here." It rather indeed pulled him up, for it wasn't what he had been thinking, at least in her sense of the words. "You mean I may decide to stay on for the sake of it?"

"Well, *with* such a home—!" But, quite beautifully, she had too much tact to dot so monstrous an *i*, and it was precisely an illustration of the way she didn't rattle. How could any one—of any wit—insist on any one else's "wanting" to live in New York?

"Oh," he said, "I *might* have lived here (since I had my opportunity early in life); I might have put in here all these years. Then everything would have been different enough— and, I dare say, 'funny' enough. But that's another matter. And then the beauty of it—I mean of my perversity, of my refusal to agree to a 'deal'—is just in the total absence of a reason. Don't you see that if I had a reason about the matter at all it would *have* to be the other way, and would then be inevitably a reason of dollars? There are no reasons here *but* of dollars. Let us therefore have none whatever—not the ghost of one."

They were back in the hall then for departure, but from where they stood the vista was large, through an open door, into the great square main saloon, with its almost antique felicity of brave spaces between windows. Her eyes came back from that reach and met his own a moment. "Are you very sure the 'ghost' of one doesn't, much rather, serve—?"

He had a positive sense of turning pale. But it was as near as they were then to come. For he made answer, he believed, between a glare and a grin: "Oh ghosts—of course the place must swarm with them! I should be ashamed of it if it didn't. Poor Mrs. Muldoon's right, and it's why I haven't asked her to do more than look in."

Miss Staverton's gaze again lost itself, and things she didn't utter, it was clear, came and went in her mind. She might even for the minute, off there in the fine room, have imagined some element dimly gathering. Simplified like the death-mask of a handsome face, it perhaps produced for her just then an effect akin to the stir of an expression in the "set" commemorative plaster. Yet whatever her impression may have been she produced instead a vague platitude. "Well, if it were only furnished and lived in—!"

She appeared to imply that in case of its being still furnished he might have been a little less opposed to the idea of a return. But she passed straight into the vestibule, as if to leave her words behind her, and the next moment he had opened the house-door and was standing with her on the steps. He closed the door and, while he re-pocketed his key, looking up and down, they took in the comparatively harsh actuality of the Avenue, which reminded him of the assault of the outer light of the Desert on the traveller emerging from an Egyptian tomb. But he risked before they stepped into the street his gathered answer to her speech. "For me it *is* lived in. For me it *is* furnished." At which it was easy for her to sigh "Ah yes—!" all vaguely and discreetly; since his parents and his favourite sister, to say nothing of other kin, in numbers, had run their course and met their end there. That represented, within the walls, ineffaceable life.

It was a few days after this that, during an hour passed with her again, he had expressed his impatience of the too flattering curiosity—among the people he met—about his appreciation of New York. He had arrived at none at all that was socially producible, and as for that matter of his "thinking" (thinking the better or the worse of anything there) he was wholly taken up with one subject of thought. It was mere vain egoism, and it was moreover, if she liked, a morbid obsession. He found all things come back to the question of what he personally might have been, how he might have led his life and "turned out," if

he had not so, at the outset, given it up. And confessing for the
first time to the intensity within him of this absurd speculation—
which but proved also, no doubt, the habit of too selfishly
thinking—he affirmed the impotence there of any other source
of interest, any other native appeal. "What would it have made
of me, what would it have made of me? I keep for ever
wondering, all idiotically; as if I could possibly know! I see
what it has made of dozens of others, those I meet, and it
positively aches within me, to the point of exasperation, that it
would have made something of me as well. Only I can't make
out *what*, and the worry of it, the small rage of curiosity never
to be satisfied, brings back what I remember to have felt, once
or twice, after judging best, for reasons, to burn some important letter unopened. I've been sorry, I've hated it—I've never
known what was in the letter. You may of course say it's a
trifle—!"

"I don't say it's a trifle," Miss Staverton gravely interrupted.

She was seated by her fire, and before her, on his feet and
restless, he turned to and fro between this intensity of his idea
and a fitful and unseeing inspection, through his single eye-
glass, of the dear little old objects on her chimney-piece. Her
interruption made him for an instant look at her harder. "I
shouldn't care if you did!" he laughed, however; "and it's only a
figure, at any rate, for the way I now feel. *Not* to have followed
my perverse young course—and almost in the teeth of my father's curse, as I may say; not to have kept it up, so, 'over
there,' from that day to this, without a doubt or a pang; not,
above all, to have liked it, to have loved it, so much, loved it,
no doubt, with such an abysmal conceit of my own preference:
some variation from *that*, I say, must have produced some
different effect for my life and for my 'form.' I should have
stuck here—if it had been possible; and I was too young, at
twenty-three, to judge, *pour deux sous*, whether it *were* possible. If I had waited I might have seen it was, and then I might
have been, by staying here, something nearer to one of these
types who have been hammered so hard and made so keen by
their conditions. It isn't that I admire them so much—the
question of any charm in them, or of any charm, beyond that of
the rank money-passion, exerted by their conditions *for* them,
has nothing to do with the matter: it's only a question of what
fantastic, yet perfectly possible, development of my own nature

I mayn't have missed. It comes over me that I had then a strange *alter ego* deep down somewhere within me, as the full-blown flower is in the small tight bud, and that I just took the course, I just transferred him to the climate, that blighted him for once and for ever."

"And you wonder about the flower," Miss Staverton said. "So do I, if you want to know; and so I've been wondering these several weeks. I believe in the flower," she continued, "I felt it would have been quite splendid, quite huge and monstrous."

"Monstrous above all!" her visitor echoed; "and I imagine, by the same stroke, quite hideous and offensive."

"You don't believe that," she returned; "if you did you wouldn't wonder. You'd know, and that would be enough for you. What you feel—and what I feel *for* you—is that you'd have had power."

"You'd have liked me that way?" he asked.

She barely hung fire. "How should I not have liked you?"

"I see. You'd have liked me, have preferred me, a billionaire!"

"How should I not have liked you?" she simply again asked.

He stood before her still—her question kept him motionless. He took it in, so much there was of it; and indeed his not otherwise meeting it testified to that. "I know at least what I am," he simply went on; "the other side of the medal's clear enough. I've not been edifying—I believe I'm thought in a hundred quarters to have been barely decent. I've followed strange paths and worshipped strange gods; it must have come to you again and again—in fact you've admitted to me as much—that I was leading, at any time these thirty years, a selfish frivolous scandalous life. And you see what it has made of me."

She just waited, smiling at him. "You see what it has made of *me*."

"Oh you're a person whom nothing can have altered. You were born to be what you are, anywhere, anyway: you've the perfection nothing else could have blighted. And don't you see how, without my exile, I shouldn't have been waiting till now—?" But he pulled up for the strange pang.

"The great thing to see," she presently said, "seems to me to be that it has spoiled nothing. It hasn't spoiled your being here at last. It hasn't spoiled this. It hasn't spoiled your speaking—" She also however faltered.

He wondered at everything her controlled emotion might mean. "Do you believe then—too dreadfully!—that I *am* as good as I might ever have been?"

"Oh no! Far from it!" With which she got up from her chair and was nearer to him. "But I don't care," she smiled.

"You mean I'm good enough?"

She considered a little. "Will you believe it if I say so? I mean will you let that settle your question for you?" And then as if making out in his face that he drew back from this, that he had some idea which, however absurd, he couldn't yet bargain away: "Oh you don't care either—but very differently: you don't care for anything but yourself."

Spencer Brydon recognised it—it was in fact what he had absolutely professed. Yet he importantly qualified. "*He* isn't myself. He's the just so totally other person. But I do want to see him," he added. "And I can. And I shall."

Their eyes met for a minute while he guessed from something in hers that she divined his strange sense. But neither of them otherwise expressed it, and her apparent understanding, with no protesting shock, no easy derision, touched him more deeply than anything yet, constituting for his stifled perversity, on the spot, an element that was like breathable air. What she said however was unexpected. "Well, *I've* seen him."

"You—?"

"I've seen him in a dream."

"Oh a 'dream'—!" It let him down.

"But twice over," she continued, "I saw him as I see you now."

"You've dreamed the same dream—?"

"Twice over," she repeated. "The very same."

This did somehow a little speak to him, as it also gratified him. "You dream about me at that rate?"

"Ah about *him!*" she smiled.

His eyes again sounded her. "Then you know all about him." And as she said nothing more: "What's the wretch like?"

She hesitated, and it was as if he were pressing her so hard that, resisting for reasons of her own, she had to turn away. "I'll tell you some other time!"

II

It was after this that there was most of a virtue for him, most of a cultivated charm, most of a preposterous secret thrill, in the particular form of surrender to his obsession and of address to what he more and more believed to be his privilege. It was what in these weeks he was living for—since he really felt life to begin but after Mrs. Muldoon had retired from the scene and, visiting the ample house from attic to cellar, making sure he was alone, he knew himself in safe possession and, as he tacitly expressed it, let himself go. He sometimes came twice in the twenty-four hours; the moments he liked best were those of gathering dusk, of the short autumn twilight; this was the time of which, again and again, he found himself hoping most. Then he could, as seemed to him, most intimately wander and wait, linger and listen, feel his fine attention, never in his life before so fine, on the pulse of the great vague place: he preferred the lampless hour and only wished he might have prolonged each day the deep crepuscular spell. Later—rarely much before midnight, but then for a considerable vigil—he watched with his glimmering light; moving slowly, holding it high, playing it far, rejoicing above all, as much as he might, in open vistas, reaches of communication between rooms and by passages; the long straight chance or show, as he would have called it, for the revelation he pretended to invite. It was a practice he found he could perfectly "work" without exciting remark; no one was in the least the wiser for it; even Alice Staverton, who was moreover a well of discretion, didn't quite fully imagine.

He let himself in and let himself out with the assurance of calm proprietorship; and accident so far favoured him that, if a fat Avenue "officer" had happened on occasion to see him entering at eleven-thirty, he had never yet, to the best of his belief, been noticed as emerging at two. He walked there on the crisp November nights, arrived regularly at the evening's end; it was as easy to do this after dining out as to take his way to a club or to his hotel. When he left his club, if he hadn't been dining out, it was ostensibly to go to his hotel; and when he left his hotel, if he had spent a part of the evening there, it was ostensibly to go to his club. Everything was easy in fine; everything conspired and promoted; there was truly even in

the strain of his experience something that glossed over, something that salved and simplified, all the rest of consciousness.
He circulated, talked, renewed, loosely and pleasantly, old
relations—met indeed, so far as he could, new expectations
and seemed to make out on the whole that in spite of the
career, of such different contacts, which he had spoken of to Miss
Staverton as ministering so little, for those who might have
watched it, to edification, he was positively rather liked than
not. He was a dim secondary social success—and all with
people who had truly not an idea of him. It was all mere
surface sound, this murmur of their welcome, this popping of
their corks—just as his gestures of response were the extravagant shadows, emphatic in proportion as they meant little, of
some game of *ombres chinoises*. He projected himself all day,
in thought, straight over the bristling line of hard unconscious
heads and into the other, the real, the waiting life; the life that,
as soon as he had heard behind him the click of his great
house-door, began for him, on the jolly corner, as beguilingly
as the slow opening bars of some rich music follows the tap of
the conductor's wand.

He always caught the first effect of the steel point of his stick
on the old marble of the hall pavement, large black-and-white
squares that he remembered as the admiration of his childhood
and that had then made in him, as he now saw, for the growth
of an early conception of style. This effect was the dim rever-
berating tinkle as of some far-off bell hung who should say
where?—in the depths of the house, of the past, of that mystical other world that might have flourished for him had he not,
for weal or woe, abandoned it. On this impression he did ever
the same thing; he put his stick noiselessly away in a corner—
feeling the place once more in the likeness of some great glass
bowl, all precious concave crystal, set delicately humming by
the play of a moist finger round its edge. The concave crystal
held, as it were, this mystical other world, and the indescriba-
bly fine murmur of its rim was the sigh there, the scarce
audible pathetic wail to his strained ear, of all the old baffled
forsworn possibilities. What he did therefore by this appeal of
his hushed presence was to wake them into such measure of
ghostly life as they might still enjoy. They were shy, all but
unappeasably shy, but they weren't really sinister; at least they
weren't as he had hitherto felt them—before they had taken

the Form he so yearned to make them take, the Form he at
moments saw himself in the light of fairly hunting on tiptoe,
the points of his evening-shoes, from room to room and from
storey to storey.

That was the essence of his vision—which was all rank folly,
if one would, while he was out of the house and otherwise
occupied, but which took on the vast verisimilitude as soon as
he was placed and posted. He knew what he meant and what
he wanted; it was as clear as the figure on a cheque presented
in demand for cash. His *alter ego* "walked"—that was the note
of his image of him, while his image of his motive for his own
odd pastime was the desire to waylay him and meet him. He
roamed, slowly, warily, but all restlessly, he himself did—Mrs.
Muldoon had been right, absolutely, with her figure of their
"craping"; and the presence he watched for would roam restlessly too. But it would be as cautious and as shifty; the
conviction of its probable, in fact its already quite sensible,
quite audible evasion of pursuit grew for him from night to
night, laying on him finally a rigour to which nothing in his life
had been comparable. It had been the theory of many
superficially-judging persons, he knew, that he was wasting
that life in a surrender to sensations, but he had tasted of no
pleasure so fine as his actual tension, had been introduced to
no sport that demanded at once the patience and the nerve of
this stalking of a creature more subtle, yet at bay perhaps more
formidable, than any beast of the forest. The terms, the com-
parisons, the very practices of the chase positively came again
into play; there were even moments when passages of his
occasional experience as a sportsman, stirred memories, from
his younger time, of moor and mountain and desert, revived
for him—and to the increase of his keenness—by the tremendous force of analogy. He found himself at moments—once he
had placed his single light on some mantel-shelf or in some
recess—stepping back into shelter or shade, effacing himself
behind a door or in an embrasure, as he had sought of old the
vantage of rock and tree; he found himself holding his breath
and living in the joy of the instant, the supreme suspense
created by big game alone.

He wasn't afraid (though putting himself the question as he
believed gentlemen on Bengal tiger-shoots or in close quarters
with the great bear of the Rockies had been known to confess

to having put it); and this indeed—since here at least he might
be frank!—because of the impression, so intimate and so strange,
that he himself produced as yet a dread, produced certainly a
strain, beyond the liveliest he was likely to feel. They fell for
him into categories, they fairly became familiar, the signs, for
his own perception, of the alarm his presence and his vigilance
created; though leaving him always to remark, portentously, on
his probably having formed a relation, his probably enjoying a
consciousness, unique in the experience of man. People enough,
first and last, had been in terror of apparitions, but who had
ever before so turned the tables and become himself, in the
apparitional world, an incalculable terror? He might have found
this sublime had he quite dared to think of it; but he didn't too
much insist, truly, on that side of his privilege. With habit and
repetition he gained to an extraordinary degree the power to
penetrate the dusk of distances and the darkness of corners, to
resolve back into their innocence the treacheries of uncertain
light, the evil-looking forms taken in the gloom by mere shadows, by accidents of the air, by shifting effects of perspective;
putting down his dim luminary he could still wander on without it, pass into other rooms and, only knowing it was there
behind him in case of need, see his way about, visually project
for his purpose a comparative clearness. It made him feel, this
acquired faculty, like some monstrous stealthy cat; he wondered if he would have glared at these moments with large
shining yellow eyes, and what it mightn't verily be, for the
poor hard-pressed *alter ego*, to be confronted with such a type.

He liked however the open shutters; he opened everywhere
those Mrs. Muldoon had closed, closing them as carefully
afterwards, so that she shouldn't notice: he liked—oh, this he
did like, and above all in the upper rooms!—the sense of the
hard silver of the autumn stars through the window-panes, and
scarcely less the flare of the street-lamps below, the white
electric lustre which it would have taken curtains to keep out.
This was human actual social; this was of the world he had lived
in, and he was more at his ease certainly for the countenance,
coldly general and impersonal, that all the while and in spite of
his detachment it seemed to give him. He had support of
course mostly in the rooms at the wide front and the prolonged
side; it failed him considerably in the central shades and the
parts at the back. But if he sometimes, on his rounds, was glad

of his optical reach, so none the less often the rear of the house affected him as the very jungle of his prey. The place was there more subdivided; a large "extension" in particular, where small rooms for servants had been multiplied, abounded in nooks and corners, in closets and passages, in the ramifications especially of an ample back staircase over which he leaned many a time, to look far down—not deterred from his gravity even while aware that he might, for a spectator, have figured some solemn simpleton playing at hide-and-seek. Outside in fact he might himself make that ironic *rapprochement;* but within the walls, and in spite of the clear windows, his consistency was proof against the cynical light of New York.

It had belonged to that idea of the exasperated consciousness of his victim to become a real test for him; since he had quite put it to himself from the first that, oh distinctly! he could "cultivate" his whole perception. He had felt it as above all open to cultivation—which indeed was but another name for his manner of spending his time. He was bringing it on, bringing it to perfection, by practice; in consequence of which it had grown so fine that he was now aware of impressions, attestations of his general postulate, that couldn't have broken upon him at once. This was the case more specifically with a phenomenon at last quite frequent for him in the upper rooms, the recognition—absolutely unmistakable, and by a turn dating from a particular hour, his resumption of his campaign after a diplomatic drop, a calculated absence of three nights—of his being definitely followed, tracked at a distance carefully taken and to the express end that he should the less confidently, less arrogantly, appear to himself merely to pursue. It worried, it finally quite broke him up, for it proved, of all the conceivable impressions, the one least suited to his book. He was kept in sight while remaining himself—as regards the essence of his position—sightless, and his only recourse then was in abrupt turns, rapid recoveries of ground. He wheeled about, retracing his steps, as if he might so catch in his face at least the stirred air of some other quick revolution. It was indeed true that his fully dislocalised thought of these manœuvres recalled to him Pantaloon, at the Christmas farce, buffeted and tricked from behind by ubiquitous Harlequin; but it left intact the influence of the conditions themselves each time he was reexposed to them, so that in fact this association, had he suffered it to

become constant, would on a certain side have but ministered
to his intenser gravity. He had made, as I have said, to create
on the premises the baseless sense of a reprieve, his three
absences; and the result of the third was to confirm the after-
effect of the second.

On his return, that night—the night succeeding his last
intermission—he stood in the hall and looked up the staircase
with a certainty more intimate than any he had yet known.
"He's *there*, at the top, and waiting—not, as in general, falling
back for disappearance. He's holding his ground, and it's the
first time—which is a proof, isn't it? that something has happened for him." So Brydon argued with his hand on the banister and his foot on the lowest stair; in which position he felt as
never before the air chilled by his logic. He himself turned
cold in it, for he seemed of a sudden to know what now was
involved. "Harder pressed?—yes, he takes it in, with its thus
making clear to him that I've come, as they say, 'to stay.' He
finally doesn't like and can't bear it, in the sense, I mean, that
his wrath, his menaced interest, now balances with his dread.
I've hunted him till he has 'turned': that, up there, is what has
happened—he's the fanged or the antlered animal brought at
last to bay." There came to him, as I say—but determined by
an influence beyond my notation!—the acuteness of this certainty; under which however the next moment he had broken
into a sweat that he would as little have consented to attribute
to fear as he would have dared immediately to act upon it for
enterprise. It marked none the less a prodigious thrill, a thrill
that represented sudden dismay, no doubt, but also represented, and with the self-same throb, the strangest, the most
joyous, possibly the next minute almost the proudest, duplica-
tion of consciousness.

"He has been dodging, retreating, hiding, but now, worked
up to anger, he'll fight!"—this intense impression made a single mouthful, as it were, of terror and applause. But what was
wonderous was that the applause, for the felt fact, was so
eager, since, if it was his other self he was running to earth,
this ineffable identity was thus in the last resort not unworthy
of him. It bristled there—somewhere near at hand, however
unseen still—as the hunted thing, even as the trodden worm of
the adage *must* at last bristle; and Brydon at this instant tasted
probably of a sensation more complex than had ever before

found itself consistent with sanity. It was as if it would have shamed him that a character so associated with his own should triumphantly succeed in just skulking, should to the end not risk the open, so that the drop of this danger was, on the spot, a great lift of the whole situation. Yet with another rare shift of the same subtlety he was already trying to measure by how much more he himself might now be in peril of fear; so rejoicing that he could, in another form, actively inspire that fear, and simultaneously quaking for the form in which he might passively know it.

The apprehension of knowing it must after a little have grown in him, and the strangest moment of his adventure perhaps, the most memorable or really most interesting, afterwards, of his crisis, was the lapse of certain instants of concentrated conscious *combat,* the sense of a need to hold on to something, even after the manner of a man slipping and slipping on some awful incline; the vivid impulse, above all, to move, to act, to charge, somehow and upon something—to show himself, in a word, that he wasn't afraid. The state of "holding-on" was thus the state to which he was momentarily reduced; if there had been anything, in the great vacancy, to seize, he would presently have been aware of having clutched it as he might under a shock at home have clutched the nearest chair-back. He had been surprised at any rate—of this he *was* aware—into something unprecedented since his original appropriation of the place; he had closed his eyes, held them tight, for a long minute, as with that instinct of dismay and that terror of vision. When he opened them the room, the other contiguous rooms, extraordinarily, seemed lighter—so light, almost, that at first he took the change for day. He stood firm, however that might be, just where he had paused; his resistance had helped him—it was as if there were something he had tided over. He knew after a little what this was—it had been in the imminent danger of flight. He had stiffened his will against going; without this he would have made for the stairs, and it seemed to him that, still with his eyes closed, he would have descended them, would have known how, straight and swiftly, to the bottom.

Well, as he had held out, here he was—still at the top, among the more intricate upper rooms and with the gauntlet of the others, of all the rest of the house, still to run when it should be his time to go. He would go at his time—only at his time: didn't he go every night very much at the same hour? He took out his watch—there was light for that: it was scarcely a quarter past one, and he had never withdrawn so soon. He reached his lodgings for the most part at two—with his walk of a quarter of an hour. He would wait for the last quarter—he wouldn't stir till then; and he kept his watch there with his eyes on it, reflecting while he held it that this deliberate wait, a wait with an effort, which he recognised, would serve perfectly for the attestation he desired to make. It would prove his courage— unless indeed the latter might most be proved by his budging at last from his place. What he mainly felt now was that, since he hadn't originally scuttled, he had his dignities—which had never in his life seemed so many—all to preserve and to carry aloft. This was before him in truth as a physical image, an image almost worthy of an age of greater romance. That remark indeed glimmered for him only to glow the next instant with a finer light; since what age of romance, after all, could have matched either the state of his mind or, "objectively," as they said, the wonder of his situation? The only difference would have been that, brandishing his dignities over his head as in a parchment scroll, he might then—that is in the heroic time— have proceeded downstairs with a drawn sword in his other grasp.

At present, really, the light he had set down on the mantel of the next room would have to figure his sword; which utensil, in the course of a minute, he had taken the requisite number of steps to possess himself of. The door between the rooms was open, and from the second another door opened to a third. These rooms, as he remembered, gave all three upon a common corridor as well, but there was a fourth, beyond them, without issue save through the preceding. To have moved, to have heard his step again, was appreciably a help; though even in recognising this he lingered once more a little by the chimney-piece on which his light had rested. When he next moved, just hesitating where to turn, he found himself considering a circumstance that, after his first and comparatively vague apprehension of it, produced in him the start that often attends some pang of recollection, the violent shock of having ceased happily to forget. He had come into sight of the door in which the brief chain of communication ended and which he now surveyed

from the nearer threshold, the one not directly facing it. Placed
at some distance to the left of this point, it would have admitted him to the last room of the four, the room without other
approach or egress, had it not, to his intimate conviction, been
closed *since* his former visitation, the matter probably of a
quarter of an hour before. He stared with all his eyes at the
wonder of the fact, arrested again where he stood and again
holding his breath while he sounded its sense. Surely it had
been *subsequently* closed—that is it had been on his previous
passage indubitably open!

He took it full in the face that something had happened
between—that he couldn't not have noticed before (by which
he meant on his original tour of all the rooms that evening) that
such a barrier had exceptionally presented itself. He had indeed since that moment undergone an agitation so extraordinary that it might have muddled for him any earlier view; and
he tried to convince himself that he might perhaps then have
gone into the room and, inadvertently, automatically, on coming out, have drawn the door after him. The difficulty was that
this exactly was what he never did; it was against his whole
policy, as he might have said, the essence of which was to keep
vistas clear. He had them from the first, as he was well aware,
quite on the brain: the strange apparition, at the far end of one
of them, of his baffled "prey" (which had become by so sharp
an irony so little the term now to apply!) was the form of
success his imagination had most cherished, projecting into it
always a refinement of beauty. He had known fifty times the
start of perception that had afterwards dropped; had fifty times
gasped to himself "There!" under some fond brief hallucina-
tion. The house, as the case stood, admirably lent itself; he
might wonder at the taste, the native architecture of the particular time, which could rejoice so in the multiplication of doors—
the opposite extreme to the modern, the actual almost complete
proscription of them; but it had fairly contributed to provoke
this obsession of the presence encountered telescopically, as he
might say, focussed and studied in diminishing perspective and
as by a rest for the elbow.

It was with these considerations that his present attention
was charged—they perfectly availed to make what he saw
portentous. He *couldn't*, by any lapse, have blocked that
aperture; and if he hadn't, if it was unthinkable, why what else

was clear but that there had been another agent? Another
agent?—he had been catching, as he felt, a moment back, the
very breath of him; but when had he been so close as in this
simple, this logical, this completely personal act? It was so
logical, that is, that one might have *taken* it for personal; yet
for what did Brydon take it, he asked himself, while, softly
panting, he felt his eyes almost leave their sockets. Ah this
time at last they *were*, the two, the opposed projections of him,
in presence; and this time, as much as one would, the question
of danger loomed. With it rose, as not before, the question of
courage—for what he knew the blank face of the door to say to
him was "Show us how much you have!" It stared, it glared
back at him with that challenge; it put to him the two alternatives: should he just push it open or not? Oh to have this
consciousness was to *think*—and to think, Brydon knew, as he
stood there, was, with the lapsing moments, not to have acted!
Not to have acted—that was the misery and the pang—was
even still not to act; was in fact *all* to feel the thing in another,
in a new and terrible way. How long did he pause and how
long did he debate? There was presently nothing to measure it;
for his vibration had already changed—as just by the effect of
its intensity. Shut up there, at bay, defiant, and with the
prodigy of the thing palpably proveably *done*, thus giving notice like some stark signboard—under that accession of accent
the situation itself had turned; and Brydon at last remarkably
made up his mind on what it had turned to.

It had turned altogether to a different admonition; to a
supreme hint, for him, of the value of Discretion! This slowly
dawned, no doubt—for it could take its time; so perfectly, on
his threshold, had he been stayed, so little as yet had he either
advanced or retreated. It was the strangest of all things that
now when, by his taking ten steps and applying his hand to a
latch, or even his shoulder and his knee, if necessary, to a
panel, all the hunger of his prime need might have been met,
his high curiosity crowned, his unrest assuaged—it was amazing, but it was also exquisite and rare, that insistence should
have, at a touch, quite dropped from him. Discretion—he
jumped at that; and yet not, verily, at such a pitch, because it
saved his nerves or his skin, but because, much more valuably,
it saved the situation. When I say he "jumped" at it I feel the
consonance of this term with the fact that—at the end indeed of

I know not how long—he did move again, he crossed straight to the door. He wouldn't touch it—it seemed now that he might *if* he would: he would only just wait there a little, to show, to prove, that he wouldn't. He had thus another station, close to the thin partition by which revelation was denied him; but with his eyes bent and his hands held off in a mere intensity of stillness. He listened as if there had been something to hear, but this attitude, while it lasted, was his own communication. "If you won't then—good: I spare you and I give up. You affect me as by the appeal positively for pity: you convince me that for reasons rigid and sublime—what do I know?—we both of us should have suffered. I respect them then, and, though moved and privileged as, I believe, it has never been given to man, I retire, I renounce—never, on my honour, to try again. So rest for ever—and let *me!*"

That, for Brydon was the deep sense of this last demonstration—solemn, measured, directed, as he felt it to be. He brought it to a close, he turned away; and now verily he knew how deeply he had been stirred. He retraced his steps, taking up his candle, burnt, he observed, well-nigh to the socket, and marking again, lighten it as he would, the distinctness of his footfall; after which, in a moment, he knew himself at the other side of the house. He did here what he had not yet done at these hours—he opened half a casement, one of those in the front, and let in the air of the night; a thing he would have taken at any time previous for a sharp rupture of his spell. His spell was broken now, and it didn't matter—broken by his concession and his surrender, which made it idle henceforth that he should ever come back. The empty street—its other life so marked even by the great lamplit vacancy—was within call, within touch; he stayed there as to be in it again, high above it though he was still perched; he watched as for some comforting common fact, some vulgar human note, the passage of a scavenger or a thief, some night-bird however base. He would have blessed that sign of life; he would have welcomed positively the slow approach of his friend the policeman, whom he had hitherto only sought to avoid, and was not sure that if the patrol had come into sight he mightn't have felt the impulse to get into relation with it, to hail it, on some pretext, from his fourth floor.

The pretext that wouldn't have been too silly or too compromising, the explanation that would have saved his dignity and kept his name, in such a case, out of the papers, was not definite to him: he was so occupied with the thought of recording his Discretion—as an effect of the vow he had just uttered to his intimate adversary—that the importance of this loomed large and something had overtaken all ironically his sense of proportion. If there had been a ladder applied to the front of the house, even one of the vertiginous perpendiculars employed by painters and roofers and sometimes left standing overnight, he would have managed somehow, astride of the window-sill, to compass by outstretched leg and arm that mode of descent. If there had been some such uncanny thing as he had found in his room at hotels, a workable fire-escape in the form of notched cable or a canvas shoot, he would have availed himself of it as a proof—well, of his present delicacy. He nursed that sentiment, as the question stood, a little in vain, and even—at the end of he scarce knew, once more, how long—found it, as by the action on his mind of the failure of response of the outer world, sinking back to vague anguish. It seemed to him he had waited an age for some stir of the great grim hush; the life of the town was itself under a spell—so unnaturally, up and down the whole prospect of known and rather ugly objects, the blankness and the silence lasted. Had they ever, he asked himself, the hard-faced houses, which had begun to look livid in the dim dawn, had they ever spoken so little to any need of his spirit? Great builded voids, great crowded stillnesses put on, often, in the heart of cities, for the small hours, a sort of sinister mask, and it was of this large collective negation that Brydon presently became conscious— all the more that the break of day was, almost incredibly, now at hand, proving to him what a night he had made of it.

He looked again at his watch, saw what had become of his time-values (he had taken hours for minutes—not, as in other tense situations, minutes for hours) and the strange air of the streets was but the weak, the sullen flush of a dawn in which everything was still locked up. His choked appeal from his own open window had been the sole note of life, and he could but break off at last as for a worse despair. Yet while so deeply demoralised he was capable again of an impulse denoting—at least by his present measure—extraordinary resolution; of retracing his steps to the spot where he had turned cold with the extinction of his last pulse of doubt as to there being in the place another presence than his own. This required an effort strong enough to sicken him; but he had his reason, which overmastered for the moment everything else. There was the whole of the rest of the house to traverse, and how should he screw himself to that if the door he had seen closed were at present open? He could hold to the idea that the closing had practically been for him an act of mercy, a chance offered him to descend, depart, get off the ground and never again profane it. This conception held together, it worked; but what it meant for him depended now clearly on the amount of forbearance his recent action, or rather his recent inaction, had engendered. The image of the "presence," whatever it was, waiting there for him to go—this image had not yet been so concrete for his nerves as when he stopped short of the point at which certainty would have come to him. For, with all his resolution, or more exactly with all his dread, he did stop short—he hung back from really seeing. The risk was too great and his fear too definite: it took at this moment an awful specific form.

He knew—yes, as he had never known anything—that, *should* he see the door open, it would all too abjectly be the end of him. It would mean that the agent of his shame—for his shame was the deep abjection—was once more at large and in general possession; and what glared him thus in the face was the act that this would determine for him. It would send him straight about to the window he had left open, and by that window, be long ladder and dangling rope as absent as they would, he saw himself uncontrollably insanely fatally take his way to the street. The hideous chance of this he at least could avert; but he could only avert it by recoiling in time from assurance. He had the whole house to deal with, this fact was still there; only he now knew that uncertainty alone could start him. He stole back from where he had checked himself—merely to do so was suddenly like safety—and, making blindly for the greater staircase, left gaping rooms and sounding passages behind. Here was the top of the stairs, with a fine large dim descent and three spacious landings to mark off. His instinct was all for mildness, but his feet were harsh on the floors, and, strangely, when he had in a couple of minutes become aware of this, it counted somehow for help. He couldn't have spoken, the tone of his voice would have scared him, and the common conceit or

resource of "whistling in the dark" (whether literally or figura-
tively) have appeared basely vulgar; yet he liked none the less
to hear himself go, and when he had reached his first landing—
taking it all with no rush, but quite steadily—that stage of
success drew from him a gasp of relief.

The house, withal, seemed immense, the scale of space again
inordinate; the open rooms, to no one of which his eyes de-
flected, gloomed in their shuttered state like mouths of caverns; only the high skylight that formed the crown of the deep
well created for him a medium in which he could advance, but
which might have been, for queerness of colour, some watery
under-world. He tried to think of something noble, as that his
property was really grand, a splendid possession; but this no-
bleness took the form too of the clear delight with which he
was finally to sacrifice it. They might come in now, the build-
ers, the destroyers—they might come as soon as they would.
At the end of two flights he had dropped to another zone, and
from the middle of the third, with only one more left, he
recognised the influence of the lower windows, of half-drawn
blinds, of the occasional gleam of street-lamps, of the glazed
spaces of the vestibule. This was the bottom of the sea, which
showed an illumination of its own and which he even saw
paved—when at a given moment he drew up to sink a long
look over the banisters—with the marble squares of his childhood. By that time indubitably he felt, as he might have said in
a commoner cause, better; it had allowed him to stop and draw
breath, and the ease increased with the sight of the old black-
and-white slabs. But what he most felt was that now surely,
with the element of impunity pulling him as by hard firm
hands, the case was settled for what he might have seen above
had he dared that last look. The closed door, blessedly remote
now, was still closed—and he had only in short to reach that of
the house.

He came down further, he crossed the passage forming the
access to the last flight; and if here again he stopped an instant
it was almost for the sharpness of the thrill of assured escape. It
made him shut his eyes—which opened again to the straight
slope of the remainder of the stairs. Here was impunity still,
but impunity almost excessive; inasmuch as the side-lights and
the high fan-tracery of the entrance were glimmering straight
into the hall; an appearance produced, he the next instant saw,

by the fact that the vestibule gaped wide, that the hinged halves of the inner door had been thrown far back. Out of that again the *question* sprang at him, making his eyes, as he felt, half-start from his head, as they had done, at the top of the house, before the sign of the other door. If he had left that one open, hadn't he left this one closed, and wasn't he now in *most* immediate presence of some inconceivable occult activity? It was as sharp, the question, as a knife in his side, but the answer hung fire still and seemed to lose itself in the vague darkness to which the thin admitted dawn, glimmering archwise over the whole outer door, made a semicircular margin, a cold silvery nimbus that seemed to play a little as he looked—to shift and expand and contract.

It was as if there had been something within it, protected by indistinctness and corresponding in extent with the opaque surface behind, the painted panels of the last barrier to his escape, of which the key was in his pocket. The indistinctness mocked him even while he stared, affected him as somehow shrouding or challenging certitude, so that after faltering an instant on his step he let himself go with the sense that here *was* at last something to meet, to touch, to take, to know— something all unnatural and dreadful, but to advance upon which was the condition for him either of liberation or of supreme defeat. The penumbra, dense and dark, was the virtual screen of a figure which stood in it as still as some image erect in a niche or as some black-vizored sentinel guarding a treasure. Brydon was to know afterwards, was to recall and make out, the particular thing he had believed during the rest of his descent. He saw, in its great grey glimmering margin, the central vagueness diminish, and he felt it to be taking the very form toward which, for so many days, the passion of his curiosity had yearned. It gloomed, it loomed, it was something, it was somebody, the prodigy of a personal presence.

Rigid and conscious, spectral yet human, a man of his own substance and stature waited there to measure himself with his power to dismay. This only could it be—this only till he recognised, with his advance, that what made the face dim was the pair of raised hands that covered it and in which, so far from being offered in defiance, it was buried as for dark deprecation. So Brydon, before him, took him in; with every fact of him now, in the higher light, hard and acute—his planted stillness, his vivid truth, his grizzled bent head and white masking hands, his queer actuality of evening-dress, of dangling double eye-glass, of gleaming silk lappet and white linen, of pearl button and gold watch-guard and polished shoe. No portrait by a great modern master could have presented him with more intensity, thrust him out of his frame with more art, as if there had been "treatment," of the consummate sort, in his every shade and salience. The revulsion, for our friend, had become, before he knew it, immense—this drop, in the act of apprehension, to the sense of his adversary's inscrutable manœuvre. That meaning at least, while he gaped, it offered him; for he could but gape at his other self in this other anguish, gape as a proof that *he*, standing there for the achieved, the enjoyed, the triumphant life, couldn't be faced in his triumph. Wasn't the proof in the splendid covering hands, strong and completely spread?—so spread and so intentional that, in spite of a special verity that surpassed every other, the fact that one of these hands had lost two fingers, which were reduced to stumps, as if accidentally shot away, the face was effectually guarded and saved.

"Saved," though, *would* it be?—Brydon breathed his wonder till the very impunity of his attitude and the very insistence of his eyes produced, as he felt, a sudden stir which showed the next instant as a deeper portent, which the head raised itself, the betrayal of a braver purpose. The hands, as he looked, began to move, to open; then, as if deciding in a flash, dropped from the face and left it uncovered and presented. Horror, with the sight, had leaped into Brydon's throat, gasping there in a sound he couldn't utter; for the bared identity was too hideous as *his,* and his glare was the passion of his protest. The face, *that* face, Spencer Brydon's?—he searched it still, but looking away from it in dismay and denial, falling straight from his height of sublimity. It was unknown, inconceivable, awful, disconnected from any possibility—! He had been "sold," he inwardly moaned, stalking such game as this: the presence before him was a presence, the horror within him a horror, but the waste of his nights had been only grotesque and the success of his adventure an irony. Such an identity fitted his at *no* point, made its alternative monstrous. A thousand times yes, as it came upon him nearer now—the face was the face of a stranger. It came upon him nearer now, quite as one of those expanding fantastic images projected by the magic lantern of childhood; for the stranger, whoever he might be, odious, blatant, vulgar, had advanced as for aggression, and he knew himself give ground. Then harder pressed still, sick with the force of his shock, and falling back as under the hot breath and the roused passion of a life larger than his own, a rage of personality before which his own collapsed, he felt the whole vision turn to darkness and his very feet give way. His head went round; he was going; he had gone.

III

What had next brought him back, clearly—though after how long?—was Mrs. Muldoon's voice, coming to him from quite near, from so near that he seemed presently to see her as kneeling on the ground before him while he lay looking up at her; himself not wholly on the ground, but half-raised and upheld—conscious, yes, of tenderness of support and, more particularly, of a head pillowed in extraordinary softness and faintly refreshing fragrance. He considered, he wondered, his wit but half at his service; then another face intervened, bending more directly over him, and he finally knew that Alice Staverton had made her lap an ample and perfect cushion to him, and that she had to this end seated herself on the lowest degree of the staircase, the rest of his long person remaining stretched on his old black-and-white slabs. They were cold, these marble squares of his youth; but *he* somehow was not, in this rich return of consciousness—the most wonderful hour, little by little, that he had ever known, leaving him, as it did, so gratefully, so abysmally passive, and yet as with a treasure of intelligence waiting all round him for quiet appropriation; dissolved, he might call it, in the air of the place and producing the golden glow of a late autumn afternoon. He had come back, yes—come back from further away than any man but himself had ever travelled; but it was strange how with this sense what he had come back *to* seemed really the great thing, and as if his prodigious journey had been all for the sake of it. Slowly but surely his consciousness grew, his vision of his state thus completing itself: he had been miraculously *carried* back—lifted and carefully borne as from where he had been picked up, the uttermost end of an interminable grey passage. Even with this he was suffered to rest, and what had now brought him to knowledge was the break in the long mild motion.

It had brought him to knowledge, to knowledge—yes, this was the beauty of his state; which came to resemble more and more that of a man who has gone to sleep on some news of a great inheritance, and then, after dreaming it away, after profaning it with matters strange to it, has waked up again to serenity of certitude and has only to lie and watch it grow. This was the drift of his patience—that he had only to let it shine on him. He must moreover, with intermissions, still have been lifted and borne; since why and how else should he have known himself, later on, with the afternoon glow intenser, no longer at the foot of his stairs—situated as these now seemed at that dark other end of his tunnel—but on a deep window-bench of his high saloon, over which had been spread, couch-fashion, a mantle of soft stuff lined with grey fur that was familiar to his eyes and that one of his hands kept fondly feeling as for its pledge of truth. Mrs. Muldoon's face had gone, but the other, the second he had recognised, hung over him in a way that showed how he was still propped and pillowed. He took it all in, and the more he took it the more it seemed to suffice: he was as much at peace as if he had had food and drink. It was the two women who had found him, on Mrs. Muldoon's having plied, at her usual hour, her latch-key—and on her having above all arrived while Miss Staverton still lingered near the house. She had been turning away, all anxiety, from worrying the vain bell-handle—her calculation having been of the hour of the good woman's visit; but the latter, blessedly, had come up while she was still there, and they had entered together. He had then lain, beyond the vestibule, very much as he was lying now—quite, that is, as he appeared to have fallen, but all so wondrously without bruise or gash; only in a depth of stupor. What he most took in, however, at present, with the steadier clearance, was that Alice Staverton had for a long unspeakable moment not doubted he was dead.

"It must have been that I *was*." He made it out as she held him. "Yes—I can only have died. You brought me literally to life. Only," he wondered, his eyes rising to her, "only, in the name of all the benedictions, how?"

It took her but an instant to bend her face and kiss him, and something in the manner of it, and in the way her hands clasped and locked his head while he felt the cool charity and virtue of her lips, something in all this beatitude somehow answered everything. "And now I keep you," she said.

"Oh keep me, keep me!" he pleaded while her face still hung over him: in response to which it dropped again and stayed close, clingingly close. It was the seal of their situation—of which he tasted the impress for a long blissful moment in silence. But he came back. "Yet how did you know—?"

"I was uneasy. You were to have come, you remember—and you had sent no word."

"Yes, I remember—I was to have gone to you at one today." It caught on to their "old" life and relation—which were so near and so far. "I was still out there in my strange darkness—where was it, what was it? I must have stayed there so long." He could but wonder at the depth and the duration of his swoon.

"Since last night?" she asked with a shade of fear for her possible indiscretion.

"Since this morning—it must have been: the cold dim dawn of today. Where have I been," he vaguely wailed, "where have I been?" He felt her hold him close, and it was as if this helped him now to make in all security his mild moan. "What a long dark day!"

All in her tenderness she had waited a moment. "In the cold dim dawn?" she quavered.

But he had already gone on piecing together the parts of the whole prodigy. "As I didn't turn up you came straight—?"

She barely cast about. "I went first to your hotel—where they told me of your absence. You had dined out last evening and hadn't been back since. But they appeared to know you had been at your club."

"So you had the idea of *this*—?"

"Of what?" she asked in a moment.

"Well—of what has happened."

"I believed at least you'd have been here. I've known, all along," she said, "that you've been coming."

" 'Known' it—?"

"Well, I've believed it. I said nothing to you after that talk we had a month ago—but I felt sure. I knew you *would*," she declared.

"That I'd persist, you mean?"

"That you'd see him."

"Ah but I didn't!" cried Brydon with his long wail. "There's somebody—an awful beast; whom I brought, too horribly, to bay. But it's not me."

At this she bent over him again, and her eyes were in his eyes. "No—it's not you." And it was as if, while her face hovered, he might have made out in it, hadn't it been so near, some particular meaning blurred by a smile. "No, thank heaven," she repeated—"it's not you! Of course it wasn't to have been."

"Ah but it *was*," he gently insisted. And he stared before him now as he had been staring for so many weeks. "I was to have known myself."

"You couldn't!" she returned consolingly. And then reverting, and as if to account further for what she had herself done, "But it wasn't only *that*, that you hadn't been at home," she went on. "I waited till the hour at which we had found Mrs. Muldoon that day of my going with you; and she arrived, as I've told you, while, failing to bring any one to the door, I lingered in my despair on the steps. After a little, if she hadn't come, by such a mercy, I should have found means to hunt her up. But it wasn't," said Alice Staverton, as if once more with her fine intention—"it wasn't only that."

His eyes, as he lay, turned back to her. "What more then?"

She met it, the wonder she had stirred. "In the cold dim dawn, you say? Well, in the cold dim dawn of this morning I too saw you."

"Saw *me*—?"

"Saw *him*," said Alice Staverton. "It must have been at the same moment."

He lay an instant taking it in—as if he wished to be quite reasonable. "At the same moment?"

"Yes—in my dream again, the same one I've named to you. He came back to me. Then I knew it for a sign. He had come to you."

At this Brydon raised himself; he had to see her better. She helped him when she understood his movement, and he sat up, steadying himself beside her there on the window-bench and with his right hand grasping her left. "*He* didn't come to me."

"You came to yourself," she beautifully smiled.

"Ah I've come to myself now—thanks to you, dearest. But

this brute, with his awful face—this brute's a black stranger. He's none of *me*, even as I *might* have been," Brydon sturdily declared.

But she kept the clearness that was like the breath of infallibility. "Isn't the whole point that you'd have been different?"

He almost scowled for it. "As different as *that*—?"

Her look again was more beautiful to him than the things of this world. "Haven't you exactly wanted to know *how* different? So this morning," she said, "you appeared to me."

"Like *him?*"

"A black stranger!"

"Then how did you know it was I?"

"Because, as I told you weeks ago, my mind, my imagination, had worked so over what you might, what you mightn't have been—to show you, you see, how I've thought of you. In the midst of that you came to me—that my wonder might be answered. So I knew," she went on; "and believed that, since the question held you too so fast, as you told me that day, you too would see for yourself. And when this morning I again saw I knew it would be because you had—and also then, from the first moment, because you somehow wanted me. *He* seemed to tell me of that. So why," she strangely smiled, "shouldn't I like him?"

It brought Spencer Brydon to his feet. "You 'like' that horror—?"

"I *could* have liked him. And to me," she said, "he was no horror. I had accepted him."

" 'Accepted'—?" Brydon oddly sounded.

"Before, for the interest of his difference—yes. And as *I* didn't disown him, as *I* knew him—which you at last, confronted with him in his difference, so cruelly didn't, my dear— well, he must have been, you see, less dreadful to me. And it may have pleased him that I pitied him."

She was beside him on her feet, but still holding his hand— still with her arm supporting him. But though it all brought for him thus a dim light, "You 'pitied' him?" he grudgingly, resentfully asked.

"He has been unhappy; he has been ravaged," she said.

"And haven't I been unhappy? Am not I—you've only to look at me!—ravaged?"

"Ah I don't say I like him *better*," she granted after a thought.

"But he's grim, he's worn—and things have happened to him. He doesn't make shift, for sight, with your charming monocle."

"No"—it struck Brydon: "I couldn't have sported mine 'downtown.' They'd have guyed me there."

"His great convex pince-nez—I saw it, I recognised the kind—is for his poor ruined sight. And his poor right hand—!"

"Ah!" Brydon winced—whether for his proved identity or for his lost fingers. Then, "He has a million a year," he lucidly added. "But he hasn't you."

"And he isn't—no, he isn't—*you!*" she murmured as he drew her to his breast.

FIRST

DARK

Elizabeth Spencer

When Tom Beavers started coming back to Richton, Mississippi, on weekends, after the war was over, everybody in town
was surprised and pleased. They had never noticed him much
before he paid them this compliment; now they could not say
enough nice things. There was not much left in Richton for him
to call family—just his aunt who had raised him, Miss Rita
Beavers, old as God, ugly as sin, deaf as a post. So he must be
fond of the town, they reasoned; certainly it was a pretty old
place. Far too many young men had left it and never come
back at all.

He would drive in every Friday night from Jackson, where
he worked. All weekend, his Ford, dusty of flank, like a hard-
ridden horse, would sit parked down the hill near Miss Rita's
old wire front gate, which sagged from the top hinge and had
worn a span in the ground. On Saturday morning, he would
head for the drugstore, then the post office; then he would be
observed walking here and there around the streets under the
shade trees. It was as though he were looking for something.

He wore steel taps on his heels, and in the still the click of
them on the sidewalks would sound across the big front lawns
and all the way up to the porches of the houses, where two
ladies might be sitting behind a row of ferns. They would
identify him to one another, murmuring in their fine little
voices, and say it was just too bad there was nothing here for
young people. It was just a shame they didn't have one or two

181

more old houses, here, for a Pilgrimage—look how Natchez had waked up.

One Saturday morning in early October, Tom Beavers sat at the counter in the drugstore and reminded Totsie Poteet, the drugstore clerk, of a ghost story. Did he remember the strange old man who used to appear to people who were coming into Richton along the Jackson road at twilight—what they called "first dark"?

"Sure I remember," said Totsie. "Old Cud'n Jimmy Wiltshire used to tell us about him every time we went 'possum hunting. I could see him plain as I can see you, the way he used to tell it. Tall, with a top hat on, yeah, and waiting in the weeds alongside the road ditch, so'n you couldn't tell if he wasn't taller than any mortal man could be, because you couldn't tell if he was standing down in the ditch or not. It would look like he just grew up out of the weeds. Then he'd signal to you."

"Them that stopped never saw anybody," said Tom Beavers, stirring his coffee. "There were lots of folks besides Mr. Jimmy that saw him."

"There was, let me see . . ." Totsie enumerated others— some men, some women, some known to drink, others who never touched a drop. There was no way to explain it. "There was that story the road gang told. Do you remember, or were you off at school? It was while they were straightening the road out to the highway—taking the curves out and building a new bridge. Anyway, they said that one night at quitting time, along in the winter and just about dark, this old guy signaled to some of 'em. They said they went over and he asked them to move a bulldozer they had left across the road, because he had a wagon back behind on a little dirt road, with a sick nigger girl in it. Had to get to the doctor and this was the only way. They claimed they knew didn't nobody live back there on that little old road, but niggers can come from anywhere. So they moved the bulldozer and cleared back a whole lot of other stuff, and waited and waited. Not only didn't no wagon ever come, but the man that had stopped them, he was gone, too. They was right shook up over it. You never heard that one?"

"No, I never did." Tom Beavers said this with his eyes looking up over his coffee cup, as though he sat behind a hand of cards. His lashes and brows were heavier than was ordinary, and worked as a veil might, to keep you away from knowing exactly what he was thinking.

"They said he was tall and had a hat on." The screen door flapped to announce a customer, but Totsie kept on talking. "But whether he was a white man or a real light-colored nigger they couldn't say. Some said one and some said another. I figured they'd been pulling on the jug a little earlier than usual. You know why? I never heard of *our* ghost *saying* nothing. Did you, Tom?"

He moved away on the last words, the way a clerk will, talking back over his shoulder and ahead of him to his new customer at the same time, as though he had two voices and two heads. "And what'll it be today, Miss Frances?"

The young woman standing at the counter had a prescription already out of her bag. She stood with it poised between her fingers, but her attention was drawn toward Tom Beavers, his coffee cup, and the conversation she had interrupted. She was a girl whom no ordinary description would fit. One would have to know first of all who she was: Frances Harvey. After that, it was all right for her to be a little odd-looking, with her reddish hair that curled back from her brow, her light eyes, and her high, pale temples. This is not the material for being pretty, but in Frances Harvey it was what could sometimes be beauty. Her family home was laden with history that nobody but the Harveys could remember. It would have been on a Pilgrimage if Richton had had one. Frances still lived in it, looking after an invalid mother.

"What were you-all talking about?" she wanted to know.

"About that ghost they used to tell about," said Totsie, holding out his hand for the prescription. "The one people used to see just outside of town, on the Jackson road."

"But why?" she demanded. "Why were you talking about him?"

"Tom, here—" the clerk began, but Tom Beavers interrupted him.

"I was asking because I was curious," he said. He had been studying her from the corner of his eye. Her face was beginning to show the wear of her mother's long illness, but that couldn't be called change. Changing was something she didn't seem to have done, her own style being the only one natural to her.

"I was asking," he went on, "because I saw him." He turned away from her somewhat too direct gaze and said to Totsie

Poteet, whose mouth had fallen open, "It was where the new road runs close to the old road, and as far as I could tell he was right on the part of the old road where people always used to see him."

"But when?" Francis Harvey demanded.

"Last night," he told her. "Just around first dark. Driving home."

A wealth of quick feeling came up in her face. "So did I! Driving home from Jackson! I saw him, too!"

For some people, a liking for the same phonograph record or for Mayan archaeology is enough of an excuse to get together. Possibly, seeing the same ghost was no more than that. Anyway, a week later, on Saturday at first dark, Frances Harvey and Tom Beavers were sitting together in a car parked just off the highway, near the spot where they agreed the ghost had appeared. The season was that long, peculiar one between summer and fall, and there were so many crickets and tree frogs going full tilt in their periphery that their voices could hardly be distinguished from the background noises, though they both would have heard a single footfall in the grass. An edge of autumn was in the air at night, and Frances had put on a tweed jacket at the last minute, so the smell of moth balls was in the car, brisk and most unghostlike.

But Tom Beavers was not going to forget the value of the ghost, whether it put in an appearance or not. His questions led Frances into reminiscence.

"No, I never saw him before the other night," she admitted. "The Negroes used to talk in the kitchen, and Regina and I—you know my sister Regina—would sit there listening, scared to go and scared to stay. Then finally going to bed upstairs was no relief, either, because sometimes Aunt Henrietta was visiting us, and *she'd* seen it. Or if she wasn't visiting us, the front room next to us, where she stayed, would be empty, which was worse. There was no way to lock ourselves in, and besides, what was there to lock out? We'd lie all night like two sticks in bed, and shiver. Papa finally had to take a hand. He called us in and sat us down and said that the whole thing was easy to explain—it was all automobiles. What their headlights did with the dust and shadows out on the Jackson road. 'Oh, but Sammie and Jerry!' we said, with great big eyes, sitting side by side on the sofa, with our tennis shoes flat on the floor."

"Who were Sammie and Jerry?" asked Tom Beavers.

"Sammie was our cook. Jerry was her son, or husband, or something. Anyway, they certainly didn't have cars. Papa called them in. They were standing side by side by the bookcase, and Regina and I were on the sofa—four pairs of big eyes, and Papa pointing his finger. Papa said, 'Now, you made up these stories about ghosts, didn't you?' 'Yes, sir,' said Sammie. 'We made them up.' 'Yes, sir,' said Jerry. 'We sho did.' 'Well, then, you can just stop it,' Papa said. 'See how peaked these children look?' Sammie and Jerry were terribly polite to us for a week, and we got in the car and rode up and down the Jackson road at first dark to see if the headlights really did it. But we never saw anything. We didn't tell Papa, but headlights had nothing whatever to do with it."

"You had your own *car* then?" He couldn't believe it.

"Oh no!" She was emphatic. "We were too young for that. Too young to drive, really, but we did anyway."

She leaned over to let him give her cigarette a light, and saw his hand tremble. Was he afraid of the ghost or of her? She would have to stay away from talking family.

Frances remembered Tommy Beavers from her childhood—a small boy going home from school down a muddy side road alone, walking right down the middle of the road. His old aunt's house was at the bottom of a hill. It was damp there, and the yard was always muddy, with big fat chicken tracks all over it, like Egyptian writing. How did Frances know? She could not remember going there, ever. Miss Rita Beavers was said to order cold ham, mustard, bread, and condensed milk from the grocery store. "I doubt if that child ever has anything hot," Frances's mother had said once. He was always neatly dressed in the same knee pants, high socks, and checked shirt, and sat several rows ahead of Frances in study hall, right in the middle of his seat. He was three grades behind her; in those days, that much younger seemed very young indeed. What had happened to his parents? There was some story, but it was not terribly interesting, and, his people being of no importance, she had forgotten.

"I think it's past time for our ghost," she said. "He's never out so late at night."

"He gets hungry, like me," said Tom Beavers. "Are you hungry, Frances?"

They agreed on a highway restaurant where an orchestra played on weekends. Everyone went there now.

From the moment they drew up on the graveled entrance, cheerful lights and a blare of music chased the spooks from their heads. Tom Beavers ordered well and danced well, as it turned out. Wasn't there something she had heard about his being "smart"? By "smart," Southerners mean intellectual, and they say it in an almost condescending way, smart being what you are when you can't be anything else, but it is better, at least, than being nothing. Frances Harvey had been away enough not to look at things from a completely Southern point of view, and she was encouraged to discover that she and Tom had other things in common besides a ghost, though all stemming, perhaps, from the imagination it took to see one.

They agreed about books and favorite movies and longing to see more plays. She sighed that life in Richton was so confining, but he assured her that Jackson could be just as bad; *it* was getting to be like any Middle Western city, he said, while Richton at least had a sense of the past. This was the main reason, he went on, gaining confidence in the jumble of commonplace noises—dishes, music, and a couple of drinkers chattering behind them—that he had started coming back to Richton so often. He wanted to keep a connection with the past. He lived in a modern apartment, worked in a soundproof office—he could be in any city. But Richton was where he had been born and raised, and nothing could be more old-fashioned. Too many people seemed to have their lives cut in two. He was earnest in desiring that this should not happen to him.

"You'd better be careful," Frances said lightly. Her mood did not incline her to profound conversation. "There's more than one ghost in Richton. You may turn into one yourself, like the rest of us."

"It's the last thing I'd think of you," he was quick to assure her.

Had Tommy Beavers really said such a thing, in such a natural, charming way? Was Frances Harvey really so pleased? Not only was she pleased but, feeling warmly alive amid the music and small lights, she agreed with him. She could not have agreed with him more.

"I hear that Thomas Beavers has gotten to be a very attractive man," Frances Harvey's mother said unexpectedly one afternoon.

Frances had been reading aloud—Jane Austen this time. Theirs was one house where the leather-bound sets were actually read. In Jane Austen, men and women seesawed back and forth for two or three hundred pages until they struck a point of balance; then they got married. She had just put aside the book, at the end of a chapter, and risen to lower the shade against the slant of afternoon sun. "Or so Cud'n Jennie and Mrs. Giles Antley and Miss Fannie Stapleton have been coming and telling you," she said.

"People talk, of course, but the consensus is favorable," Mrs. Harvey said. "Wonders never cease; his mother ran away with a brush salesman. But nobody can make out what he's up to, coming back to Richton."

"Does he have to be 'up to' anything?" Frances asked.

"Men are always up to something," said the old lady at once. She added, more slowly, "In Thomas's case, maybe it isn't anything it oughtn't to be. They say he reads a lot. He may just have taken up with some sort of idea."

Frances stole a long glance at her mother's face on the pillow. Age and illness had reduced the image of Mrs. Harvey to a kind of caricature, centered on a mouth that Frances could not help comparing to that of a fish. There was a tension around its rim, as though it were outlined in bone, and the underlip even stuck out a little. The mouth ate, it took medicine, it asked for things, it gasped when breath was short, it commented. But when it commented, it ceased to be just a mouth and became part of Mrs. Harvey, that witty tyrant with the infallible memory for the right detail, who was at her terrible best about men.

"And what could he be thinking of?" she was wont to inquire when some man had acted foolishly. No one could ever defend accurately the man in question, and the only conclusion was Mrs. Harvey's; namely, that he wasn't thinking, if, indeed, he could. Although she had never been a belle, never a flirt, her popularity with men was always formidable. She would be observed talking marathons with one in a corner, and could you ever be sure, when they both burst into laughter, that they had not just exchanged the most shocking stories? "Of course, he—" she would begin later, back with the family, and the masculinity that had just been encouraged to strut and preen a little was quickly shown up as idiotic. Perhaps Mrs. Harvey

hoped by this method to train her daughters away from a lot of
sentimental nonsense that was their birthright as pretty Southern girls in a house with a lawn that moonlight fell on and that
was often lit also by Japanese lanterns hung for parties. "Oh,
he's not like that, Mama!" the little girls would cry. They were
already alert for heroes who would ride up and cart them off.
"Well, then, you watch," she would say. Sure enough, if you
watched, she would be right.

Mrs. Harvey's younger daughter, Regina, was a credit to her
mother's long campaign; she married well. The old lady, however, never tired of pointing out behind her son-in-law's back
that his fondness for money was ill-concealed, that he had the
longest feet she'd ever seen, and that he sometimes made
grammatical errors.

Her elder daughter, Frances, on a trip to Europe, fell in
love, alas! The gentleman was of French extraction but Swiss
citizenship, and Frances did not marry him, because he was
already married—that much filtered back to Richton. In response to a cable, she had returned home one hot July in time
to witness her father's wasted face and last weeks of life. That
same September, the war began. When peace came, Richton
wanted to know if Frances Harvey would go back to Europe.
Certain subtly complicated European matters, little understood in Richton, seemed to be obstructing Romance; one of
them was probably named Money. Meanwhile, Frances's mother
took to bed, in what was generally known to be her last illness.

So no one crossed the ocean, but eventually Tom Beavers
came up to Mrs. Harvey's room one afternoon, to tea.

Though almost all her other faculties were seriously im-
paired, in ear and tongue Mrs. Harvey was as sound as a young
beagle, and she could still weave a more interesting conversation than most people who go about every day and look at the
world. She was of the old school of Southern lady talkers; she
vexed you with no ideas, she tried to protect you from even a
moment of silence. In the old days, when a bright company
filled the downstairs rooms, she could keep the ball rolling
amongst a crowd. Everyone—all the men especially—got their
word in, but the flow of things came back to her. If one of
those twenty-minutes-to-or-after silences fell—and even with
her they did occur—people would turn and look at her daughter Frances. "And what do you think?" some kind-eyed gentle-

man would ask. Frances did not credit that she had the sort of face people would turn to, and so did not know how to take advantage of it. What did she think? Well, to answer that honestly took a moment of reflection—a fatal moment, it always turned out. Her mother would be up instructing the maid, offering someone an ashtray or another goody, or remarking outright, "Frances is so timid. She never says a word."

Tom Beavers stayed not only past teatime that day but for a drink as well. Mrs. Harvey was induced to take a glass of sherry, and now her bed became her enormous throne. Her keenest suffering as an invalid was occasioned by the absence of men. "What is a house without a man in it?" she would often cry. From her eagerness to be charming to Frances's guest that afternoon, it seemed that she would have married Tom Beavers herself if he had asked her. The amber liquid set in her small four-sided glass glowed like a jewel, and her diamond flashed; she had put on her best ring for the company. What a pity no longer to show her ankle, that delicious bone, so remarkably slender for so ample a frame.

Since the time had flown so, they all agreed enthusiastically that Tom should wait downstairs while Frances got ready to go out to dinner with him. He was hardly past the stair landing before the old lady was seized by such a fit of coughing that she could hardly speak. "It's been—it's been too much—too *much* for me!" she gasped out.

But after Frances had found the proper sedative for her, she was calmed, and insisted on having her say.

"Thomas Beavers has a good job with an insurance company in Jackson," she informed her daughter, as though Frances were incapable of finding out anything for herself. "He makes a good appearance. He is the kind of man"—she paused—"who would value a wife of good family." She stopped, panting for breath. It was this complimenting a man behind his back that was too much for her—as much out of character, and hence as much of a strain, as if she had got out of bed and tried to tap-dance.

"Heavens, Mama," Frances said, and almost giggled.

At this, the old lady, thinking the girl had made light of her suitor, half screamed at her, "Don't be so critical, Frances! You can't be so critical of men!" and fell into an even more terrible spasm of coughing. Frances had to lift her from the pillow and hold her straight until the fit passed and her breath returned. Then Mrs. Harvey's old, dry, crooked, ineradicably feminine hand was laid on her daughter's arm, and when she spoke again she shook the arm to emphasize her words.

"When your father knew he didn't have long to live," she whispered, "we discussed whether to send for you or not. You know you were his favorite, Frances. 'Suppose our girl is happy over there,' he said. 'I wouldn't want to bring her back on my account.' I said you had to have the right to choose whether to come back or not. You'd never forgive us, I said, if you didn't have the right to choose."

Frances could visualize this very conversation taking place between her parents; she could see them, decorous and serious, talking over the fact of his approaching death as though it were a piece of property for agreeable disposition in the family. She could never remember him without thinking, with a smile, how he used to come home on Sunday from church (he being the only one of them who went) and how, immediately after hanging his hat and cane in the hall, he would say, "Let all things proceed in orderly progression to their final confusion. How long before dinner?" No, she had had to come home. Some humor had always existed between them—her father and her—and humor, of all things, cannot be betrayed.

"I meant to go back," said Frances now. "But there was the war. At first I kept waiting for it to be over. I still wake up at night sometimes thinking, I wonder how much longer before the war will be over. And then—" She stopped short. For the fact was that her lover had been married to somebody else, and her mother was the very person capable of pointing that out to her. Even in the old lady's present silence she heard the unspoken thought, and got up nervously from the bed, loosing herself from the hand on her arm, smoothing her reddish hair where it was inclined to straggle. "And then he wrote me that he had gone back to his wife. Her family and his had always been close, and the war brought them back together. This was in Switzerland—naturally, he couldn't stay on in Paris during the war. There were the children, too—all of them were Catholic. Oh, I do understand how it happened."

Mrs. Harvey turned her head impatiently on the pillow. She dabbed at her moist upper lip with a crumpled linen handkerchief; her diamond flashed once in motion. "War, religion, wife, children—yes. But men do what they want to."

Could anyone make Frances as angry as her mother could? "Believe what you like then! You always know so much better than I do. *You* would have managed things somehow. Oh, you would have had your way!"

"Frances," said Mrs. Harvey, "I'm an old woman." The hand holding the handkerchief fell wearily, and her eyelids dropped shut. "If you should want to marry Thomas Beavers and bring him here, I will accept it. There will be no distinctions. Next, I suppose, we will be having his old deaf aunt for tea. I hope she has a hearing aid. I haven't got the strength to holler at her."

"I don't think any of these plans are necessary, Mama."

The eyelids slowly lifted. "None?"

"None."

Mrs. Harvey's breathing was as audible as a voice. She spoke, at last, without scorn, honestly. "I cannot bear the thought of leaving you alone. You, nor the house, nor your place in it—alone. I foresaw Tom Beavers here! What has he got that's better than you and this place? I knew he would come!"

Terrible as her mother's meanness was, it was not half so terrible as her love. Answering nothing, explaining nothing, Frances stood without giving in. She trembled, and tears ran down her cheeks. The two women looked at each other helplessly across the darkening room.

In the car, later that night, Tom Beavers asked, "Is your mother trying to get rid of me?" They had passed an unsatisfactory evening, and he was not going away without knowing why.

"No, it's just the other way around," said Frances, in her candid way. "She wants you so much she'd like to eat you up. She wants you in the house. Couldn't you tell?"

"She once chased me out of the yard," he recalled.

"Not really!"

They turned into Harvey Street (that was actually the name of it), and when he had drawn the car up before the dark front steps, he related the incident. He told her that Mrs. Harvey had been standing just there in the yard, talking to some visitor who was leaving by inches, the way ladies used to—ten minutes' more talk for every forward step. He, a boy not more than

nine, had been crossing a corner of the lawn where a faint path
had already been worn; he had had nothing to do with wearing
the path and had taken it quite innocently and openly. "You,
boy!" Mrs. Harvey's fan was an enormous painted thing. She
had furled it with a clack so loud he could still hear it. "You
don't cut through my yard again! Now, you stop where you are
and you go all the way back and around by the walk, and don't
you ever do that again." He went back and all the way around.
She was fanning comfortably as he passed. "Old Miss Rita
Beavers' nephew," he heard her say, and though he did not
speak of it now to Frances, Mrs. Harvey's rich tone had been
as stuffed with wickedness as a fruitcake with goodies. In it you
could have found so many things: that, of course, he didn't
know any better, that he was poor, that she knew his first name
but would not deign to mention it, that she meant him to
understand all this and more. Her fan was probably still somewhere in the house, he reflected. If he ever opened the wrong
door, it might fall from above and brain him. It seemed impossible that nowadays he could even have the chance to open the
wrong door in the Harvey house. With its graceful rooms and
big lawn, its camellias and magnolia trees, the house had been
one of the enchanted castles of his childhood, and Frances and
Regina Harvey had been two princesses running about the
lawn one Saturday morning drying their hair with big white
towels and not noticing when he passed.

There was a strong wind that evening. On the way home,
Frances and Tom had noticed how the night was streaming,
but whether with mist or dust or the smoke from some far-off
fire in the dry winter woods they could not tell. As they stood
on the sidewalk, the clouds raced over them, and moonlight
now and again came through. A limb rubbed against a high
cornice. Inside the screened area of the porch, the swing
jangled in its iron chains. Frances's coat blew about her, and
her hair blew. She felt herself to be no different from anything
there that the wind was blowing on, her happiness of no
relevance in the dark torrent of nature.

"I can't leave her, Tom. But I can't ask you to live with her,
either. Of all the horrible ideas! She'd make demands, take all
my time, laugh at you behind your back—she has to run
everything. You'd hate me in a week."

He did not try to pretty up the picture, because he had a

feeling that it was all too accurate. Now, obviously, was the time she should go on to say there was no good his waiting around through the years for her. But hearts are not noted for practicality, and Frances stood with her hair blowing, her hands stuck in her coat pockets, and did not go on to say anything. Tom pulled her close to him—in, as it were, out of the wind.

"I'll be coming by next weekend, just like I've been doing. And the next one, too," he said. "We'll just leave it that way, if it's O.K. with you."

"Oh yes, it is, Tom!" Never so satisfied to be weak, she kissed him and ran inside.

He stood watching on the walk until her light flashed on. Well, he had got what he was looking for; a connection with the past, he had said. It was right upstairs, a splendid old mass of dictatorial female flesh, thinking about him. Well, they could go on, he and Frances, sitting on either side of the sickbed, drinking tea and sipping sherry with streaks of gray broadening on their brows, while the familiar seasons came and went. So he thought. Like Frances, he believed that the old lady had a stranglehold on life.

Suddenly, in March, Mrs. Harvey died.

A heavy spring funeral, with lots of roses and other scented flowers in the house, is the worst kind of all. There is something so recklessly fecund about a south Mississippi spring that death becomes just another word in the dictionary, along with swarms of others, and even so pure and white a thing as a gardenia has too heavy a scent and may suggest decay. Mrs. Harvey, amid such odors, sank to rest with a determined pomp, surrounded by admiring eyes.

While Tom Beavers did not "sit with the family" at this time, he was often observed with the Harveys, and there was whispered speculation among those who were at the church and the cemetery that the Harvey house might soon come into new hands, "after a decent interval." No one would undertake to judge for a Harvey how long an interval was decent.

Frances suffered from insomnia in the weeks that followed, and at night she wandered about the spring-swollen air of the old house, smelling now spring and now death. "Let all things proceed in orderly progression to their final confusion." She

had always thought that the final confusion referred to death,
but now she began to think that it could happen any time; that
final confusion, having found the door ajar, could come into a
house and show no inclination to leave. The worrisome thing,
the thing it all came back to, was her mother's clothes. They
were numerous, expensive, and famous, and Mrs. Harvey had
never discarded any of them. If you opened a closet door,
hatboxes as big as crates towered above your head. The shiny
black trim of a great shawl stuck out of a wardrobe door just
below the lock. Beneath the lid of a cedar chest, the bright
eyes of a tippet were ready to twinkle at you. And the jewels!
Frances's sister had restrained her from burying them all on
their mother, and had even gone off with a wad of them
tangled up like fishing tackle in an envelope, on the ground of
promises made now and again in the course of the years.

("Regina," said Frances, "what else were you two talking
about besides jewelry?" "I don't remember," said Regina, getting mad.

"Frances makes me so mad," said Regina to her husband as
they were driving home. "I guess I can love Mama and jewelry, too. Mama certainly loved *us* and jewelry, too.")

One afternoon, Frances went out to the cemetery to take
two wreaths sent by somebody who had "just heard." She
drove out along the winding cemetery road, stopping the car a
good distance before she reached the gate, in order to walk
through the woods. The dogwood was beautiful that year. She
saw a field where a house used to stand but had burned down;
its cedar trees remained, and two bushes of bridal wreath
marked where the front gate had swung. She stopped to admire the clusters of white bloom massing up through the
young, feathery leaf and stronger now than the leaf itself. In
the woods, the redbud was a smoke along shadowy ridges, and
the dogwood drifted in layers, like snow suspended to give you
all the time you needed to wonder at it. But why, she wondered, do they call it bridal *wreath?* It's not a wreath but a
little bouquet. Wreaths are for funerals, anyway. As if to prove
it, she looked down at the two she held, one in each hand. She
walked on, and such complete desolation came over her that it
was more of a wonder than anything in the woods—more,
even, than death.

As she returned to the car from the two parallel graves, she met a thin, elderly, very light-skinned Negro man in the road. He inquired if she would mind moving her car so that he could pass. He said that there was a sick colored girl in his wagon, whom he was driving in to the doctor. He pointed out politely that she had left her car right in the middle of the road. "Oh, I'm terribly sorry," said Frances, and hurried off toward the car.

That night, reading late in bed, she thought, I could have given her a ride into town. No wonder they talk about us up North. A mile into town in a wagon! She might have been having a baby. She became conscience-stricken about it—foolishly so, she realized, but if you start worrying about something in a house like the one Frances Harvey lived in, in the dead of night, alone, you will go on worrying about it until dawn. She was out of sleeping pills.

She remembered having bought a fresh box of sedatives for her mother the day before she died. She got up and went into her mother's closed room, where the bed had been dismantled for airing, its wooden parts propped along the walls. On the closet shelf she found the shoe box into which she had packed away the familiar articles of the bedside table. Inside she found the small enameled-cardboard box, with the date and prescription inked on the cover of Totsie Poteet's somewhat prissy handwriting, but the box was empty. She was surprised, for she realized that her mother could have used only one or two of the pills. Frances was so determined to get some sleep that she searched the entire little store of things in the shoe box quite heartlessly, but there were no pills. She returned to her room and tried to read, but could not, and so smoked instead and stared out at the dawn-blackened sky. The house sighed. She could not take her mind off the Negro girl. If she died . . . When it was light, she dressed and got into the car.

In town, the postman was unlocking the post office to sort the early mail. "I declare," he said to the rural mail carrier who arrived a few minutes later, "Miss Frances Harvey is driving herself crazy. Going back out yonder to the cemetery, and it not seven o'clock in the morning."

"Aw," said the rural deliveryman skeptically, looking at the empty road.

"That's right. I was here and seen her. You wait there, you'll see her come back. She'll drive herself nuts. Them old maids like that, left in them old houses—crazy and sweet, or crazy and mean, or just plain crazy. They just ain't locked up like them that's down in the asylum. That's the only difference."

"Miss Frances Harvey ain't no more than thirty-two, -three years old."

"Then she's just got more time to get crazier in. You'll see."

That day was Friday, and Tom Beavers, back from Jackson, came up Frances Harvey's sidewalk, as usual, at exactly a quarter past seven in the evening. Frances was not "going out" yet, and Regina had telephoned her long distance to say that "in all probability" she should not be receiving gentlemen "in." "What would Mama say?" Regina asked. Frances said she didn't know, which was not true, and went right on cooking dinners for Tom every weekend.

In the dining room that night, she sat across one corner of the long table from Tom. The useless length of polished cherry stretched away from them into the shadows as sadly as a road. Her plate pushed back, her chin resting on one palm, Frances stirred her coffee and said, "I don't know what on earth to do with all of Mama's clothes. I can't give them away, I can't sell them, I can't burn them, and the attic is full already. What can I do?"

"You look better tonight," said Tom.

"I slept," said Frances. "I slept and slept. From early this morning until just 'while ago. I never slept so well."

Then she told him about the Negro near the cemetery the previous afternoon, and how she had driven back out there as soon as dawn came, and found him again. He had been walking across the open field near the remains of the house that had burned down. There was no path to him from her, and she had hurried across ground uneven from old plowing and covered with the kind of small, tender grass it takes a very skillful mule to crop. "Wait!" she had cried. "Please wait!" The Negro had stopped and waited for her to reach him. "Your daughter?" she asked, out of breath.

"Daughter?" he repeated.

"The colored girl that was in the wagon yesterday. She was sick, you said, so I wondered. I could have taken her to town in the car, but I just didn't think. I wanted to know, how is she? Is she very sick?"

He had removed his old felt nigger hat as she approached him. "She a whole lot better, Miss Frances. She going to be all right now." Then he smiled at her. He did not say thank you, or anything more. Frances turned and walked back to the road and the car. And exactly as though the recovery of the Negro girl in the wagon had been her own recovery, she felt the return of a quiet breath and a steady pulse, and sensed the blessed stirring of a morning breeze. Up in her room, she had barely time to draw an old quilt over her before she fell asleep.

"When I woke, I knew about Mama," she said now to Tom. By the deepened intensity of her voice and eyes, it was plain that this was the important part. "It isn't right to say I *knew*," she went on, "because I had known all the time—ever since last night. I just realized it, that's all. I realized she had killed herself. It had to be that."

He listened soberly through the story about the box of sedatives. "But why?" he asked her. "It maybe looks that way, but what would be her reason for doing it?"

"Well, you see—" Frances said, and stopped.

Tom Beavers talked quietly on. "She didn't suffer. With what she had, she could have lived five, ten, who knows how many years. She was well cared for. Not hard up, I wouldn't say. Why?"

The pressure of his questioning could be insistent, and her trust in him, even if he was nobody but old Miss Rita Beavers' nephew, was well-nigh complete. "Because of you and me," she said, finally. "I'm certain of it, Tom. She didn't want to stand in our way. She never knew how to express love, you see." Frances controlled herself with an effort.

He did not reply, but sat industriously balancing a match folder on the tines of an unused serving fork. Anyone who had passed a lonely childhood in the company of an old deaf aunt is not inclined to doubt things hastily, and Tom Beavers would not have said he disbelieved anything Frances had told him. In fact, it seemed only too real to him. Almost before his eyes, that imperial, practical old hand went fumbling for the pills in the dark. But there had been much more to it than just love, he reflected. Bitterness, too, and pride, and control. And humor, perhaps, and the memory of a frightened little boy chased out of the yard by a twitch of her fan. Being invited to tea was one thing; suicide was quite another. Times had certainly changed, he thought.

But, of course, he could not say that he believed it, either. There was only Frances to go by. The match folder came to balance and rested on the tines. He glanced up at her, and a chill walked up his spine, for she was too serene. Cheek on palm, a lock of reddish hair fallen forward, she was staring at nothing with the absorbed silence of a child, or of a sweet, silver-haired old lady engaged in memory. Soon he might find that more and more of her was vanishing beneath this placid surface.

He himself did not know what he had seen that Friday evening so many months ago—what the figure had been that stood forward from the roadside at the tilt of the curve and urgently waved an arm to him. By the time he had braked and backed, the man had disappeared. Maybe it had been somebody drunk (for Richton had plenty of those to offer), walking it off in the cool of the woods at first dark. No such doubts had occurred to Frances. And what if he told her now the story Totsie had related of the road gang and the sick Negro girl in the wagon? Another labyrinth would open before her; she would never get out.

In Richton, the door to the past was always wide open, and what came in through it and went out of it had made people "different." But it scarcely ever happens, even in Richton, that one is able to see the precise moment when fact becomes faith, when life turns into legend, and people start to bend their finest loyalties to make themselves bemused custodians of the grave. Tom Beavers saw that moment now, in the profile of this dreaming girl, and he knew there was no time to lose.

He dropped the match folder into his coat pocket. "I think we should be leaving, Frances."

"Oh well, I don't know about going yet," she said. "People criticize you so. Regina even had the nerve to telephone. Word had got all the way to her that you came here to have supper with me and we were alone in the house. When I tell the maid I want biscuits made up for two people, she looks like 'What would yo' mama say?'"

"I mean," he said, "I think it's time we left for good."

"And never came back?" It was exactly like Frances to balk at going to a movie but seriously consider an elopement.

"Well, never is a long time. I like to see about Aunt Rita every once in a great while. She can't remember from one time to the next whether it's two days or two years since I last came."

She glanced about the walls and at the furniture, the pictures, and the silver. "But I thought you would want to live here, Tom. It never occurred to me. I know it never occurred to Mama . . . This house . . . It can't be just left."

"It's a fine old house," he agreed. "But what would you do with all your mother's clothes?"

Her freckled hand remained beside the porcelain cup for what seemed a long time. He waited and made no move toward her; he felt her uncertainty keenly, but he believed that some people should not be startled out of a spell.

"It's just as you said," he went on, finally. "You can't give them away, you can't sell them, you can't burn them, and you can't put them in the attic, because the attic is full already. So what are you going to do?"

Between them, the single candle flame achieved a silent altitude. Then, politely, as on any other night, though shaking back her hair in a decided way, she said, "Just let me get my coat, Tom."

She locked the door when they left, and put the key under the mat—a last obsequy to the house. Their hearts were bounding ahead faster than they could walk down the sidewalk or drive off in the car, and, mindful, perhaps, of what happened to people who did, they did not look back.

Had they done so, they would have seen that the Harvey house was more beautiful than ever. All unconscious of its rejection by so mere a person as Tom Beavers, it seemed, instead, to have got rid of what did not suit it, to be free, at last, to enter with abandon the land of mourning and shadows and memory.

MISSING

PERSON

Peter Taylor

*Virgil Minor, a novelist, has come home to St. Louis to deliver
a public lecture. Flo Abbot, his old sweetheart, is now a widow
and the mother of three children. Ginny, the baby sitter, is
fifteen. Flo's three children are Janey, Joey, and Gibby, aged
eleven, eight, and five, respectively.*

*Ginny is alone in the wide, sumptuous sitting room. She is
slumped on the couch, center, her eyes fixed on the television
screen, right and toward the front. The television volume is
high. Male and female voices are heard thereon, though not so
distinctly as to make the lines understandable. Ginny's school
books and papers are scattered on the coffee table. There is
also an empty soft drink bottle and a liberal sprinkling of
potato chips. As the television voices are lowered and softened
with unmistakable tenderness, Ginny stretches forward toward
the screen. Suddenly she hears the sound of voices in the hall
behind her, left and rear. She springs up, cuts off the television set, shoves the soft drink bottle under the couch, pushes
the last potato chips into her mouth. She is sitting on the
couch, bent over her books as V and Flo enter from left, rear.
They are dressed in formal evening clothes.*

V

What a strange evening it was for me, seeing all those old
friends again! Flo, my dear—

200

FLO

(moving center)

Why, Ginny, you're alone. I thought I heard someone here with you—or the television.

GINNY

(shrugging)

No, Mrs. Abbot, I've been slaving over this homework.

V

Flo, my dearest Flo, how really bewildering this has all been for me.

FLO

(She is looking earnestly, questioningly, at GINNY, but smiles as she speaks to V.)

V, I am not your "dearest Flo," and you will give Ginny here the wrong idea . . . *(to GINNY)* This is Mr. Virgil Minor, Ginny. Mr. Minor and I are old friends. He and I have known each other since we were no older than you are. He's visiting back here from New York, and seeing so many old friends has left him feeling sentimental toward all of us.

V

(frowning)

Not precisely sentimental, Flo. It's just—

FLO

(to GINNY)

How are the children? Did they go to bed all right?

GINNY

Oh, I know who Virgil Minor is.

FLO

(examining pad on telephone table)

Any telephone calls?

GINNY

I saw his picture in this afternoon's paper. He was here to give a lecture over at the University. Everybody in St. Louis knows

about you, Mr. Minor. One of your books is on our English
reading list. Some of the teachers think you're "too mature" for
us to read, but I think young people ought to read contempo-
rary books, don't you? I haven't read the one of yours in our
library yet, but I'm certainly going to now that we've met. It
will make it so interesting, knowing the author.

V

I'm glad something will make it interesting. Tonight it doesn't
seem very real to me that I am the author of those books.
There have been moments all day when I felt I had never left
here. And one can't help wondering—

FLO
(interrupting)

Now let's see, how much do I owe you, Ginny? It's nearly
midnight. That makes it about five dollars.

GINNY *has gathered her books and papers and now begins getting into her coat.*

V

How this room takes me back . . . Miss Abbot lived in this
house when she was growing up, Ginny. We had splendid
times here.

GINNY
(accepting money)

It was nice meeting you, Mr. Minor. I'll tell my English
teacher.

V

Yes, but don't tell the teachers who think I'm too mature.

FLO

Can you let yourself out, Ginny? The lights are all on. *(to* V)
Ginny lives next door. She's John and Patty Moore's child. You
may remember John.

V

Let's see. John Moore?

GINNY
(*shrugging*)
He's just a St. Louis businessman. Why should Virgil Minor remember *him?*

FLO
(*laughing*)
What's wrong with being a St. Louis businessman, Ginny? Don't forget my husband was a businessman, too.

GINNY
I mean—like—well, you know—compared to a real author. Good night. (*Exit*)

FLO
I'm just going to have a look-in at the children.

V
How old are they, Flo?

FLO
Five, eight, and eleven. There they are. (*pointing to photographs on table, lingering over them*) They hardly need a sitter any more. Jane there is eleven. It's just—somehow—in this big old house . . . I won't be a minute. (*Exit*)

V
(*wandering about the room, looking at the pictures on the tables and walls*)
A widow with half-grown children. (*glancing out window*) And right here on Lindell Boulevard. It's unbelievable. And yet it seems inevitable, somehow, for Flo. A beautiful widow with three children, and in the old house looking out over Forest Park. (*He turns back into the room, walks about, then suddenly sits down in a comfortable chair and puts his feet up.*) Well here I am! I can almost imagine— (*suddenly rising from the chair, laughing sadly*) Oh, but not quite. Not quite. (*He walks about again, picks up framed photographs from a table.*) Ah, I didn't quite expect this! (*eyeing it critically*) Yours truly at nineteen.

FLO

How embarrassing! Had I known you were going to give me a
lift home tonight I would have put that away. But it's excus-
able, I think. One has a right to display pictures of one's
friends when they become famous.

V

Then you've just begun to display this again . . . in recent
years?

FLO

Only since your pictures have begun appearing everywhere.
It's fun to remind people that I knew you once . . . *(mixing
drink)* Is it bourbon for you, still?

V

No, Scotch.

FLO

Ah, you've switched.

V
(still looking at photograph)

It's the same old frame I gave it to you in. A period piece now,
but in excellent condition. Am I right to imagine it lying
somewhere in a drawer for a number of years?

FLO

You are.

V

And only brought out again after . . . your husband's death.

He glances up at the portrait of FLO's *husband, which
hangs above the mantel.* FLO *interrupts her drink mixing
and comes over to him.*

FLO

For a man who is generally indirect, you can, on occasion, ask
very direct questions.

V

There are things one has to know in order to understand *other* things.

FLO

What other things?

V

The other side of the coin.

FLO

Don't speak to me in riddles, V. I'm just the dumb girl who didn't want to leave home. You have to be ever so direct with her.

V

Quit posturing, Flo. You don't deceive me. I feel we really have taken up just where we left off. And I *will* be direct. You are extremely attractive to me. *(He comes to chair and throws himself into it again.)* Bring my slippers . . . Light my pipe . . . I can see how you have redecorated and made everything your own here. And yet it's the same, too. It's so elegant, so attractive, so comfortable, so reassuring.

FLO

You need reassuring, V?

V

Continually. *(rising)* The picture is irresistible—that is, the whole scene: We come home to a baby sitter—a neighbor girl—waiting to welcome us. The three kids are sound asleep. Our nightcaps are all but ready for us over there on the neat little bar arrangement.

FLO

You're making love to me, V. Or to my life. *(laughs)* The answer is: Yes, I do love you still. *(She gives him a slight peck on the cheek.)* I loved you through all the years. But the fact remains, you could never see living the kind of cozy, bourgeois life I wanted to live here in St. Louis, and I could never live the life you yearned for and have found—there up East . . . in Europe, in the great world.

V

It's not so simple as that.

FLO
Yes, it's so simple as that. *(smiling fondly, putting her hand on his)* And that, my dear friend, is why I could not let you address me as "your dear Flo" in the presence of little Ginny Moore just now. St. Louis is still St. Louis. Ginny didn't know that it was quite by chance that you brought me home in your taxi. Ginny didn't know that we would be calling another taxi for you in half an hour or so. I only trust *(suddenly laughing)* that since Ginny lives next door, somebody over there will hear your taxi when it comes for you.

V
But, Flo, it wasn't "quite by chance" that I brought you home in my taxi. I had been scheming all day to make this opportunity for us to be together and talk—without other people.

FLO *turns rather abruptly and walks back toward the cabinet where she was mixing drinks earlier. She pauses close to the television set and runs her hand along its top. She hesitates, and then speaks.*

FLO
The TV is still warm. That's the sort of petty and ignoble observation my life leads me to make. The baby sitter was not telling the truth, and so I must wonder if she is generally reliable. She is not forbidden to watch TV while sitting for me, and so why should she try to deceive me . . . See what a bore my life is—for someone like you, that is.

V
(following her across the room, going ahead of her and mixing the drinks)
On the contrary, I find it a fascinating question. Maybe Ginny's not allowed to watch television at home on school nights. And so she automatically switched it off at the approach of adults. Or maybe she simply wanted you to think her mind was on higher things. Most of us do that.

FLO

That sounds very sensible. You might be good with young people— or permissive, at least. You were good with little children even when you were a boy—or sometimes you were. Do you have any children, V?

V

Me? Oh, no!

FLO

Are you married . . . now?

V

No, not now.

FLO

You're between marriages?

V

Maybe so. I don't think of it that way . . . Look here, Flo, would we really be criticized here in St. Louis for my simply bringing you home this way at midnight and having a drink with you?

FLO

That would depend upon whether you were married or were between marriages.

V

You . . . they . . . are very legalistic about it, aren't they?

FLO

I am—usually. I would never have invited any other man inside for a drink at this hour—or any hour—without knowing for sure he was unattached.

V

But you don't care how many times he has been attached—or may yet be attached?

FLO

In your case I don't . . . V, I never thought you should leave St. Louis. I never thought you really *needed* to. I remember another side to you that would have been content here the way the rest of us are.

V

Yes, I can almost remember him.

FLO

Him?

V

Yes, him. That side of me. Yes, yes. I would like to remember him better than I do. I would like to see how he has turned out.

FLO

Oh, I'm serious, V. I'm not playing a game with you. You *could* come back here even yet, couldn't you? This is where your roots are. This is where the good old family business is. You still own your interest in that, I imagine. In fact, I know you do. I have bought shares in it myself since I have been a widow and manager of my own affairs. There is a place for you in that office, and there is a side of you—

V

True. All you say is true. There *was* another side to me once. When we are young we all have more sides than one. When we are young we have lots of possibilities. Lots of potentiality. It seems almost impossible that those other aspects of one's self besides the one you finally concentrate upon, don't go on developing somewhere. I've kept thinking all day today about that other side of me you refer to. Was he around somewhere? Would I see him? Ever since I stepped off the plane I've found myself watching for him.

FLO

Some man like the man you might have become?

V

It's not quite so vague as that. Or not quite so specific. I have the feeling he is here in town, the very one. If I could just see him.

FLO *laughs*

V

I know it's silly. But I've had the feeling I might come on him at every turn, in every group I've joined. But he's missing. He doesn't seem to be here. That's part of what's made it such a bewildering day—such a sad day. It's as though someone got left out of the gatherings. Everyone else is there, all the old faces, but *he*—*his* face is missing. If I could meet him face to face—that missing other side of me—then he and I might become friends again. *Anything* might be possible.

FLO

Yes, I should think so. If that happened, *anything* might be possible.

A child's cry from above.

FLO

That's one of the children.

She puts down her drink and crosses the room toward the doorway to the hall. He begins to follow her.

V

Shall I come?

FLO

No, no. Someone's fallen out of bed or something. (*She lingers in the doorway.*)

V

Fallen out of bed? At their ages?

FLO
(*smiling at him*)
You've forgotten how long children go on being children. Especially children without a father—especially the boys. (*Exit.*)

V crosses the room and takes up his own photograph again. Presently he hears a noise—a sudden, brief banging. He looks up and glances in the direction of the doorway.

V
(raising his voice)

Flo?

He puts down the photograph and drink and crosses to doorway.

V
(calling)

Flo?

FLO
(from a distance, upstairs)

Yes, I'm coming.

He returns to pick up his drink. He stands with his head cocked to one side, listening for a repetition of the noise. FLO enters.

FLO

What is it? What's happening?

V

Nothing, I think. But what happened up there? What was it?

FLO

Oh, it was nothing at all. Gibby cried out in his sleep, I think. He has a tendency to do that. He's my youngest.

V

But there *was* a noise just now. While you were with them.

FLO

I didn't hear it. It must have been outside. I think there's some wind. Now, where *were* we? And where is my drink? We aren't making much headway with those drinks.

V

Are you suggesting that I drink up? And be on my way?

FLO

On the contrary. Come and sit down. I think we should make it an all-night session. Do you think it's true that men make mistakes in what they do with their lives but that it's never too late to correct their mistakes? That's only a rhetorical question. *I* think it's so. And I propose to you that you come back home and discover another life for yourself.

V

That sounds like a *real* proposal.

FLO

It's a proposal with conditions. You would have to reassess the decision you made fifteen years ago.

V

(He rises and walks about.)

I suspect you have sensed it—just since I got here, or maybe guessed it earlier from a greater distance, that this is a time in my life when reassessment may be in order. The complications of the kind of life I've lived up till now—a series of marriages and/or love affairs—well, they are not as easily dealt with by a man approaching forty as by a younger man. In the years when you are first doing your important work, it seems that you couldn't be doing it without the stimulation of those love affairs. But later you begin to doubt whether or not it is so. You know, I wrote the first chapter of my first book on the broad arm of a certain chair at my father's house, just two blocks away from here. I developed an awful superstition about that chair and had to sit there every morning in just that position in order to finish the book. Later on, I even tried to persuade Father to let me take the chair away with me. When I explained to him why, he looked at me as though I were crazy—and refused. But that's how it is. When our work goes well, when we're inspired, we get the notion that our surroundings and the other

conditions of our life have something to do with it. But that's
not so. I know a writer who is tone deaf and who therefore
maintains that to write good prose one *must* be tone deaf. And
a painter who is a homosexual and who is convinced that one
must be queer in order to paint. But there comes a time when
your pattern of work is clearly what counts and you know that
what you need from life is not stimulation but rather the
tranquillity and the quiet satisfaction of life that will allow you
to work.

FLO

No, V, I don't quite like the sound of that. If it's *my* proposal
you think of accepting, you must not think of life here as a kind
of retirement for you. You must think of it as an alternative to
the choice you made fifteen years ago. You must see perhaps that
you made a mistake and that there is a possible life here for you.

V

Believe me, Flo, I see the good life here clearly enough. But
first I want to see *me* in it, I want to see if my other side which
would have stayed here and would have become me—would
also have done my work. One glimpse of him would be enough
to let me know. This afternoon I took two hours off. Supposedly for napping in my hotel room. Instead, I visited alone the
old haunts of my rebellious adolescence, of my early young
manhood. Ah, how they have cleaned up the old waterfront!
And Olive Street! And, yes, I went through Gaslight Square
and laughed aloud at its phoniness. But I kept searching, half
expecting him around every corner I turned. And then suddenly it came to me *where* I would find him, if *any*where.

A silence.

FLO

And he isn't here?

Again there is a child's cry, more shrill this time.

FLO

That's not usual for one of my children. You must excuse me
again, V.

(She runs from the room. V stands in the doorway and listens. There is the sound of a rainstorm, with wind. He goes to a window and looks out. FLO's voice is heard.)

FLO

V? Are you down there?

He hurries to the doorway.

V

Yes, I'm here. Shall I come up?

FLO

No, I thought I heard the front door close. I was afraid you might have left.

V

I haven't thought of going. And you were right, my dear. There *is* a storm, with wind.

FLO

I'll be right down.

V returns to the center of the room. The lights flicker. They go out altogether for a moment. When they come on, FLO's eleven-year-old daughter JANIE stands in the doorway.

V

Hello there. Who are you?

JANIE

I'm Janie. I'm on the way to the kitchen to fetch a spoon for Mother. You're Mr. Minor, aren't you?

V

Yes, I am. Come in and see me, Janie. It's nice to meet you. How pretty you are. I like a girl who has long hair. You're very pretty.

JANIE

I'm too fat to be really pretty. But I've just given my hair a hundred strokes.

V

That's a lot of strokes. What does a girl like you think about when she's stroking her hair, Janie?

JANIE

I think about the future. I want to be a ballerina. Sometimes I stand on my toes while I'm stroking my hair.

V

Ah, a ballerina!

JANIE

I suppose that sounds trite to you.

V

Not at all. It sounds wonderful. It must have been your dancing I heard upstairs just now.

JANIE

No, not tonight. I only stroked my hair tonight. I woke up and couldn't go back to sleep, and so I stroked my hair sitting up in bed.

V

Well, what's going on upstairs?

JANIE

Oh, Mother thinks Gibby is sick. He's my younger brother, the youngest. He's only five and a big baby. He's had two nightmares in the past ten minutes or so. He's the scary type and wakes everybody else up when he's scared. He thought he saw somebody out in the hall just now when Mother was taking him to the bathroom. You weren't standing at the foot of the stairs, were you?

V

No, I wasn't.

JANIE

I didn't think you were. There was nobody there. Besides being scary, Gibby tends to tell stories. Mother says it's just a stage he's going through, but I doubt it.

The lights go off again and when they come on, JANIE is gone. FLO's voice is heard.

FLO
(from upstairs)

Janie! When are you coming with that spoon?

V
(moving to doorway)

I'm afraid I detained her, Flo. How charming she is. *(lights flicker)*

FLO

You mightn't think so if you were waiting for her to bring you a teaspoon at midnight. But I'll be down in just a minute, V, if you can wait.

V

Ah, I can wait.

He turns back into the room and walks about with a light step, his arms folded. He stops and takes up the children's photographs, one by one, and looks at each approvingly. Then he goes and with a certain abandon throws himself into the same chair as before. He sits with his eyes closed. Suddenly FLO and the two little boys appear in the doorway. She holds the five-year-old, his face hidden on her shoulder.

FLO

Why, V, you've gone to sleep.

V
(opening his eyes)

No, but I think I'm dreaming. What a lovely picture. I dare not move for fear the vision will vanish.

FLO

We've come looking for Janie. She's so absent-minded you can't send her on the simplest errand.

V
(rising and coming toward her)
So this is Gibby and—

FLO

And Joey.

GIBBY *slowly lifts his head and steals a glance at* V. *He utters a prolonged whisper, points a finger at* V *and speaks aloud.*

GIBBY

That's him. The one in the hall. *(He hides his face again.)*

FLO

Were you in the hall?

V

No . . . Well, maybe I was. Who knows. Let me hold Gibby. He's a very big boy for you to be carrying about.

JOEY

He's a big baby.

V

Let me shake your hand, Joey. It's good to see you.

(As they shake hands, GIBBY *steals another glance, then looks openly at* V *and puts out his arms.)*

GIBBY

No, it *wasn't* you. It was a *great* big man.

JOEY
(as V *takes* GIBBY*)*
He's such a scary cat.

V

That's all right, (*moving to chair, where he sits down with* GIBBY *on his lap. He is followed by* JOEY.) I was scared when I was little, too.

JOEY

I don't believe you were. You're just saying that.

V

No, really I was. Weren't you, when you were little?

JOEY

Well, maybe I was. I guess probably I was. You live in New York, don't you?

V

I do.

JOEY

Do you like Kennedy or Newark or LaGuardia best?

V

I think I like Newark. Which do you like?

JOEY

I haven't been to any of them. But I know the names of all the airports in all the big places in the United States.

V

Let's test him, Gibby.

GIBBY

All right.

V

What shall we ask him first? (*GIBBY whispers in his ear.*) Good. How about Chicago, Joey?

JOEY

Oh, that's too easy. Gibby knows I know that. It's O'Hare.

V

Well, how about Washington?

JOEY

That's easy, too. National and Dulles.

FLO

Stop while you're winning, Joey. Run to the kitchen and see
what's keeping Janie.

  Exit JOEY, *running.*

V

And now for this fellow. Say, Gibby, have you ever been
hypnotized?

GIBBY

No. Can you hypnotize people?

V

Watch. *(extends his arm, holds palm toward the two of them,
crooks fingers and sets fingers in motion)* You're feeling very
sleepy. *(closes his own eyes and pretends to nod)* I put myself
to sleep by mistake. (GIBBY *bursts into giggles.)*

GIBBY

He was only pretending, wasn't he, Mother?

V

Well, then, let's try something else. Can you pat the top of
your head and rub your own stomach at the same time? (GIBBY
attempts it.) No, you're patting both . . . No, you're rubbing
both. *(They both laugh.* FLO *looks on.)*

  Enter JOEY, *running.*

JOEY

Here's the spoon. What's Gibby doing?

V

Magic. Magic. He's performing magic.

FLO

That's enough from all of you. Come on, boys. But where's Janie?

JOEY

She's in the kitchen, having a bowl of corn flakes.

FLO

Oh! Just what a fat girl needs!

JOEY

And you should see the sugar piled on it!

V
(watching from chair)

Good night, boys.

GIBBY and JOEY

Good night, good night. *(They throw their arms about his neck and kiss him.)*

Exit FLO *and the boys.* V *sits watching the doorway. Presently* JANIE *reappears there.*

V

Ah, another vision! *(He rises and goes to her.)*

JANIE

Good night, Mr. Minor.

V

You're a very charming little girl, Janie. May I kiss you good night? *(He bends and kisses her on the forehead.)*

JANIE

Come to see us again.

V

Thank you, Janie. Thank you.

As JANIE *turns back into the hall,* V *watches her. He watches as she ascends the stair. The lights flicker periodically. He throws her a kiss, upward to the top of the stairs, and he whispers:* "Good night." *He turns back into the room. The lights go off for a moment. When they flash on again he is standing face to face with a man of his own height and coloring, though somewhat heavier and wearing a double-breasted business suit.*

V

Well, I'll be damned!! And who are you? You can't be— *(gesturing toward portrait of* FLO's *late husband, above the mantel)* No. For a moment I thought you were a ghost.

MP

Don't you recognize me?

V

Oh, God! Oh, yes! *(taking several steps backward)* So here you are, after all. So you've come to the party.

MP

You can dispense with the levity.

V

Yes, I might say *you* have put on some weight.

MP

You artists and writers are all alike. You've got to be so god-damned clever under all circumstances.

V

Well, seeing you is sufficiently sobering.

MP

Cut it out, will you? Do you think it's any pleasure to me to see you? I could have predicted just how you'd look nowadays. But what business have you got being *here?*

V
(still backing away)
Anyhow, it's of great interest to me to see you.

MP

Then, why do you keep backing off?

V

I want to get you in perspective. I want to see you in this room.

MP

Oh, I'm forgetting myself. May I fix you a drink? (*taking up glass*)

V

No, thanks. I have one over there . . . You make yourself very much at home, don't you?

MP

What do you mean? I *am* at home. Flo and I came directly here from our honeymoon. We've never lived anywhere else. She *had* to live in this house. I was man enough to give in to her.

V

You and Flo?

MP

Yes, *me* and Flo. Look here, I thought you understood. I thought you wanted to see me. That's what I've been hearing from you all day. It hasn't been easy for me to arrange matters, either. And we haven't got all night, you know.

V
(*taking up his drink*)
Oh, I *did* want to see you . . . What's it like? That's what I want to know.

MP

What's it like? Or what am *I* like?

V

What would *I* be like here?

MP
(laughing)

You couldn't be here. That's the whole point, isn't it? But I'm
not going to answer your twenty questions. You're forgetting:
You didn't want speculations. You wanted to *see* me here. That
was all. So you see me. And now tell me: Was it worth
upsetting the weather and the whole family for it? *(He drinks.)*

V

I don't know what to say. I think I envy you your having what
you have. But I don't think I envy you your being you.

MP

I can return the compliment.

V

No offense, then?

MP

No offense. But as for your envying my having what I have. I'm
glad you got a load of it tonight.

V

What do you mean?

MP

Those children! Wonderful children, of course, but my God,
they can take it out of you if you're around very much. And
can't you see how they're taking it out of her? And this house!
Oh, Christ-a-mighty! Well, she wanted to stay in this house
and bring up the children the way we were brought up. It's
cost me something—even me. *(laughing)* I've had to do things
you couldn't have brought yourself to do.

V
(setting down his glass)

It's been worth it, though?

MP

Worth it? It's cost about fifty thousand dollars a year. What's
worth that? Anything? There have been private schools, the

Country Club, the Racquet Club. Not to mention a summer place in Michigan, a winter house in Florida, and trips abroad. Then think what's ahead: a debut for the girl, Yale for all the boys. It costs a man something, I tell you.

V

That's not what I mean by "worth it." Don't you know what I mean?

MP

How should I know what a fellow like you means? Why come bothering me about the worth of all this? You've had every-thing else, haven't you?

MP *lifts his glass and drinks. As he throws back his head, there is a blackout. When the lights come up again, V is standing where* MP *stood. He is in the same position* MP *was in when the lights went out, holding the glass to his mouth. He puts the glass down slowly on the bar. He goes and picks up the other glass from the table and sets it on the bar also.* FLO *stands in the doorway, watching him.*

FLO

I'm glad you had another drink. (*She comes forward and takes up her own drink.*)

V

I'm way ahead.

FLO

I've never seen the children so upset—or, rather, so excited. I'm sorry I let them spoil this meeting for us.

V

It's time to run along, I suppose . . . Yes, it's very late.

FLO

I called a taxi for you before I came down.

V

How did you happen to do that?

FLO

A look on your face I saw before I went up with the boys—just a shadow of doubt, perhaps.

V

So little and so slight . . . and yet it was enough?

FLO

Enough to make me call a taxi, yes.

V

Well. Well, it was thoughtful of you.

FLO

You sound so— Please don't feel any bitterness—or pity—toward me. You must try to understand.

V

No, it is you who will have to try to understand. Because finally, my dear, I've seen him.

A silence.

FLO

I was afraid you would.

V

Even before we came here tonight you were afraid I would?

FLO

He's always here, I suppose.

V

And has always been here?

FLO

Yes. If only you had been here to give him life.

V

You loathe him?

FLO

No, *that's* what *you* must try to understand. I love him still.

V

But not me.

She turns away and puts her hands to her face.

FLO

I wanted *him.*

Though her back is turned to him, he stands looking at her. There is the sound of the taxi's horn outside.

V

It's terrible . . . the narrowness.

She drops her hands and turns back to him.

FLO
(wounded)

Mine?

V

No. Nor mine. Ours . . . ours.

He takes up his coat and goes out quickly. FLO drops down on a straight chair, puts her head in the crook of her arm on the chair back, and weeps.

THE BELL

IN

THE FOG

Gertrude Atherton

I

The great author had realized one of the dreams of his ambitious youth, the possession of an ancestral hall in England. It was not so much the good American's reverence for ancestors that inspired the longing to consort with the ghosts of an ancient line, as artistic appreciation of the mellowness, the dignity, the aristocratic aloofness of walls that have sheltered, and furniture that has embraced, generations and generations of the dead. To mere wealth, only his astute and incomparably modern brain yielded respect; his ego raised its goose-flesh at the sight of rooms furnished with a single check, conciliatory as the taste might be. The dumping of the old interiors of Europe into the glistening shells of the United States not only roused him almost to passionate protest, but offended his patriotism—which he classified among his unworked ideals. The average American was not an artist, therefore he had no excuse for even the affectation of cosmopolitanism. Heaven knew he was national enough in everything else, from his accent to his lack of repose; let his surroundings be in keeping.

Orth had left the United States soon after his first successes, and, his art being too great to be confounded with locality, he had long since ceased to be spoken of as an American author. All civilized Europe furnished stages for his puppets, and, if never picturesque nor impassioned, his originality was as overwhelming as his style. His subtleties might not always be

226

understood—indeed, as a rule, they were not—but the musical mystery of his language and the penetrating charm of his lofty and cultivated mind induced raptures in the initiated, forever denied to those who failed to appreciate him.

His following was not a large one, but it was very distinguished. The aristocracies of the earth gave to it; and not to understand and admire Ralph Orth was deliberately to relegate one's self to the ranks. But the elect are few, and they frequently subscribe to the circulating libraries; on the Continent, they buy the Tauchnitz edition; and had not Mr. Orth inherited a sufficiency of ancestral dollars to enable him to keep rooms in Jermyn Street, and the wardrobe of an Englishman of leisure, he might have been forced to consider the tastes of the middle-class at a desk in Hampstead. But, as it mercifully was, the fashionable and exclusive sets of London knew and sought him. He was too wary to become a fad, and too sophisticated to grate or bore; consquently, his popularity continued evenly from year to year, and long since he had come to be regarded as one of them. He was not keenly addicted to sport, but he could handle a gun, and all men respected his dignity and breeding. They cared less for his books than women did, perhaps because patience is not a characteristic of their sex. I am alluding, however, in the instance, to men-of-the-world. A group of young literary men—and one or two women—put him on a pedestal and kissed the earth before it. Naturally, they imitated him, and as this flattered him, and he had a kindly heart deep among the cere-cloths of his formalities, he sooner or later wrote "appreciations" of them all, which nobody living could understand, but which owing to the subtitle and signature answered every purpose.

With all this, however, he was not utterly content. From the 12th of August until late in the winter—when he did not go to Homburg and the Riviera—he visited the best houses in England, slept in state chambers, and meditated in historic parks; but the country was his one passion, and he longed for his own acres.

He was turning fifty when his great-aunt died and made him her heir: "as a poor reward for his immortal services to literature," read the will of this phenomenally appreciative relative. The estate was a large one. There was a rush for his books; new editions were announced. He smiled with cynicism, not unmixed with sadness; but he was very grateful for the money, and as soon as his fastidious taste would permit he bought him a country-seat.

The place gratified all his ideals and dreams—for he had romanced about his sometime English possession as he had never dreamed of women. It had once been the property of the Church, and the ruin of cloister and chapel above the ancient wood was sharp against the low pale sky. Even the house itself was Tudor, but wealth from generation to generation had kept it in repair; and the lawns were as velvety, the hedges as rigid, the trees as aged as any in his own works. It was not a castle nor a great property, but it was quite perfect; and for a long while he felt like a bridegroom on a succession of honeymoons. He often laid his hand against the rough ivied walls in a lingering caress.

After a time, he returned the hospitalities of his friends, and his invitations, given with the exclusiveness of his great distinction, were never refused. Americans visiting England eagerly sought for letters to him; and if they were sometimes benumbed by that cold and formal presence, and awed by the silences of Chillingsworth—the few who entered there—they thrilled in anticipation of verbal triumphs, and forthwith bought an entire set of his books. It was characteristic that they dared not ask him for his autograph.

Although women invariably described him as "brilliant," a few men affirmed that he was gentle and lovable, and any one of them was well content to spend weeks at Chillingsworth with no other companion. But, on the whole, he was rather a lonely man.

It occurred to him how lonely he was one gay June morning when the sunlight was streaming through his narrow windows, illuminating tapestries and armor, the family portraits of the young profligate from whom he had made this splendid purchase, dusting its gold on the black wood of wainscot and floor. He was in the gallery at the moment, studying one of his two favorite portraits, a gallant little lad in the green costume of Robin Hood. The boy's expression was imperious and radiant, and he had that perfect beauty which in any disposition appealed so powerfully to the author. But as Orth stared to-day at the brilliant youth, of whose life he knew nothing, he suddenly became aware of a human stirring at the foundations of his aesthetic pleasure.

"I wish he were alive and here," he thought, with a sigh. "What a jolly little companion he would be! And this fine old mansion would make a far more complementary setting for him than for me."

He turned away abruptly, only to find himself face to face with the portrait of a little girl who was quite unlike the boy, yet so perfect in her own way, and so unmistakably painted by the same hand, that he had long since concluded they had been brother and sister. She was angelically fair, and, young as she was—she could not have been more than six years old—her dark-blue eyes had a beauty of mind which must have been remarkable twenty years later. Her pouting mouth was like a little scarlet serpent, her skin almost transparent, her pale hair fell waving—not curled with the orthodoxy of childhood—about her tender bare shoulders. She wore a long white frock, and clasped tightly against her breast a doll far more gorgeously arrayed than herself. Behind her were the ruins and the woods of Chillingsworth.

Orth had studied this portrait many times, for the sake of an art which he understood almost as well as his own; but to-day he saw only the lovely child. He forgot even the boy in the intensity of this new and personal absorption.

"Did she live to grow up, I wonder?" he thought. "She should have made a remarkable, even a famous woman, with those eyes and that brow, but—could the spirit within that ethereal frame stand the enlightenments of maturity? Would not that mind—purged, perhaps, in a long probation from the dross of other existences—flee in disgust from the common-place problems of a woman's life? Such perfect beings should die while they are still perfect. Still, it is possible that this little girl, whoever she was, was idealized by the artist, who painted into her his own dream of exquisite childhood."

Again he turned away impatiently. "I believe I am rather fond of children," he admitted. "I catch myself watching them on the street when they are pretty enough. Well, who does not like them?" he added, with some defiance.

He went back to his work; he was chiselling a story which was to be the foremost excuse of a magazine as yet unborn. At the end of half an hour he threw down his wondrous instru-

ment—which looked not unlike an ordinary pen—and making
no attempt to disobey the desire that possessed him, went back
to the gallery. The dark splendid boy, the angelic little girl were
all he saw—even of the several children in that roll call of the
past—and they seemed to look straight down his eyes into
depths where the fragmentary ghosts of unrecorded ancestors
gave faint musical response.

"The dead's kindly recognition of the dead," he thought.
"But I wish these children were alive."

For a week he haunted the gallery, and the children haunted
him. Then he became impatient and angry. "I am mooning like
barren woman," he exclaimed. "I must take the briefest way of
getting those youngsters off my mind.

With the help of his secretary, he ransacked the library, and
finally brought to light the gallery catalogue which had been
named in the inventory. He discovered that his children were
the Viscount Tancred and the Lady Blanche Mortlake, son and
daughter of the second Earl of Teignmouth. Little wiser than
before, he sat down at once and wrote to the present earl,
asking for some account of the lives of the children. He awaited
the answer with more restlessness than he usually permitted
himself, and took long walks, ostentatiously avoiding the gallery.

"I believe those youngsters have obsessed me," he thought,
more than once. "They certainly are beautiful enough, and the
last time I looked at them in that waning light they were fairly
alive. Would that they were, and scampering about this park."

Lord Teignmouth, who was intensely grateful to him, answered promptly.

"I am afraid," he wrote, "that I don't know much about my
ancestors—those who didn't do something or other; but I have
a vague remembrance of having been told by an aunt of mine,
who lives on the family traditions—she isn't married—that the
little chap was drowned in the river, and that the little girl died
too—I mean when she *was* a little girl—wasted away, or
something—I'm such a beastly idiot about expressing myself,
that I wouldn't dare to write to you at all if you weren't really
great. That is actually all I can tell you, and I am afraid the
painter was their only biographer."

The author was gratified that the girl had died young, but
grieved for the boy. Although he had avoided the gallery of
late, his practised imagination had evoked from the throngs of

history the high-handed and brilliant, surely adventurous career of the third Earl of Teignmouth. He had pondered upon
the deep delights of directing such a mind and character, and
had caught himself envying the dust that was older still. When
he read of the lad's early death, in spite of his regret that such
promise should have come to naught, he admitted to a secret
thrill of satisfaction that the boy had so soon ceased to belong
to any one. Then he smiled with both sadness and humor.

"What an old fool I am!" he admitted. "I believe I not only
wish those children were alive, but that they were my own."

The frank admission proved fatal. He made straight for the
gallery. The boy, after the interval of separation, seemed more
spiritedly alive than ever, the little girl to suggest, with her
faint appealing smile, that she would like to be taken up and
cuddled. "I must try another way," he thought, desperately,
after that long communion. "I must write them out of me."

He went back to the library and locked up the *tour de force*
which had ceased to command his classic faculty. At once, he
began to write the story of the brief lives of the children, much
to the amazement of that faculty, which was little accustomed
to the simplicities. Nevertheless, before he had written three
chapters, he knew that he was at work upon a masterpiece—
and more: he was experiencing a pleasure so keen that once
and again his hand trembled, and he saw the page through a
mist. Although his characters had always been objective to
himself and his more patient readers, none knew better than
he—a man of no delusions—that they were so remote and
exclusive as barely to escape being mere mentalities; they were
never the pulsing living creations of the more full-blooded
genius. But he had been content to have it so. His creations
might find and leave him cold, but he had known his highest
satisfaction in chiselling the statuettes, extracting subtle and
elevating harmonies, while combining words as no man of his
tongue had combined them before.

But the children were not statuettes. He had loved and
brooded over them long ere he had thought to tuck them into
his pen, and on its first stroke they danced out alive. The old
mansion echoed with their laughter, with their delightful and
original pranks. Mr. Orth knew nothing of children, therefore all the pranks he invented were as original as his faculty.
The little girl clung to his hand or knee as they both followed

the adventurous course of their common idol, the boy. When
Orth realized how alive they were, he opened each room of his
home to them in turn, that evermore he might have sacred
and poignant memories with all parts of the stately mansion
where he must dwell alone to the end. He selected their
bedrooms, and hovered over them—not through infantile dis-
orders, which were beyond even his imagination,—but through
those painful intervals incident upon the enterprising spirit of
the boy and the devoted obedience of the girl to fraternal
command. He ignored the second Lord Teignmouth; he was
himself their father, and he admired himself extravagantly for
the first time; art had chastened him long since. Oddly
enough, the children had no mother, not even the memory of
one.

He wrote the book more slowly than was his wont, and spent
delightful hours pondering upon the chapter of the morrow.
He looked forward to the conclusion with a sort of terror, and
made up his mind that when the inevitable last word was
written he should start at once for Homburg. Incalculable
times a day he went to the gallery, for he no longer had any
desire to write the children out of his mind, and his eyes
hungered for them. They were his now. It was with an effort
that he sometimes humorously reminded himself that another
man had fathered them, and that their little skeletons were
under the choir of the chapel. Not even for peace of mind
would he have descended into the vaults of the lords of
Chillingsworth and looked upon the marble effigies of his children. Nevertheless, when in a superhumorous mood, he dwelt
upon his high satisfaction in having been enabled by his great-
aunt to purchase all that was left of them.

For two months he lived in his fool's paradise, and then he
knew that the book must end. He nerved himself to nurse the
little girl through her wasting illness, and when he clasped her
hands, his own shook, his knees trembled. Desolation settled
upon the house, and he wished he had left one corner of it to
which he could retreat unhaunted by the child's presence. He
took long tramps, avoiding the river with a sensation next to
panic. It was two days before he got back to his table, and then
he had made up his mind to let the boy live. To kill him off, too,
was more than his augmented stock of human nature could
endure. After all, the lad's death had been purely accidental,

wanton. It was just that he should live—with one of the author's inimitable suggestions of future greatness; but, at the end, the parting was almost as bitter as the other. Orth knew then how men feel when their sons go forth to encounter the world and ask no more of the old companionship.

The author's boxes were packed. He sent the manuscript to his publisher an hour after it was finished—he could not have given it a final reading to have saved it from failure—directed his secretary to examine the proof under a microscope, and left the next morning for Homburg. There, in inmost circles, he forgot his children. He visited in several of the great houses of the Continent until November; then returned to London to find his book the literary topic of the day. His secretary handed him the reviews; and for once in a way he read the finalities of the nameless. He found himself hailed as a genius, and compared in astonished phrases to the prodigiously clever talent which the world for twenty years had isolated under the name of Ralph Orth. This pleased him, for every writer is human enough to wish to be hailed as a genius, and immediately. Many are, and many wait; it depends upon the fashion of the moment, and the needs and bias of those who write of writers. Orth had waited twenty years; but his past was bedecked with the headstones of geniuses long since forgotten. He was gratified to come thus publicly into his estate, but soon reminded himself that all the adulation of which a belated world was capable could not give him one thrill of the pleasure which the companionship of that book had given him, while creating. It was the keenest pleasure in his memory, and when a man is fifty and has written many books, that is saying a great deal.

He allowed what society was in town to lavish honors upon him for something over a month, then cancelled all his engagements and went to Chillingsworth.

His estate was in Hertfordshire, that county of gentle hills and tangled lanes, of ancient oaks and wide wild heaths, of historic houses, and dark woods, and green fields innumerable—a Wordsworthian shire, steeped in the deepest peace of England. As Orth drove towards his own gates he had the typical English sunset to gaze upon, a red streak with a church spire against it. His woods were silent. In the fields, the cows stood as if conscious of their part. The ivy on his old gray towers had been young with his children.

He spent a haunted night, but the next day stranger happenings began.

II

He rose early, and went for one of his long walks. England seems to cry out to be walked upon, and Orth, like others of the transplanted, experienced to the full the country's gift of foot-restlessness and mental calm. Calm flees, however, when the ego is rampant, and to-day, as upon others too recent. Orth's soul was as restless as his feet. He had walked for two hours when he entered the wood of his neighbor's estate, a domain seldom honored by him, as it, too, had been bought by an American—a flighty hunting widow, who displeased the fastidious taste of the author. He heard the children's voices, and turned with the quick prompting of retreat.

As he did so, he came face to face, on the narrow path, with a little girl. For the moment he was possessed by the most hideous sensation which can visit a man's being—abject terror. He believed that body and soul were disintegrating. The child before him was his child, the original of a portrait in which the artist, dead two centuries ago, had missed exact fidelity, after all. The difference, even his rolling vision took note, lay in the warm pure living whiteness and the deeper spiritual suggestion of the child in his path. Fortunately for his self-respect, the surrender lasted but a moment. The little girl spoke.

"You look real sick," she said. "Shall I lead you home?"

The voice was soft and sweet, but the intonation, the vernacular, were American, and not of the highest class. The shock was, if possible, more agonizing than the other, but this time Orth rose to the occasion.

"Who are you?" he demanded, with asperity. "What is your name? Where do you live?"

The child smiled, an angelic smile, although she was evidently amused. "I never had so many questions asked me all at once," she said. "But I don't mind, and I'm glad you're not sick. I'm Mrs. Jennie Root's little girl—my father's dead. My name is Blanche—you *are* sick! No?—and I live in Rome, New York State. We've come over here to visit pa's relations."

Orth took the child's hand in his. It was very warm and soft.

"Take me to your mother," he said firmly; "now, at once.

You can return and play afterwards. And as I wouldn't have you disappointed for the world, I'll send to town to-day for a beautiful doll."

The little girl, whose face had fallen, flashed her delight, but walked with great dignity beside him. He groaned in his depths as he saw they were pointing for the widow's house, but made up his mind that he would know the history of the child and of all her ancestors, if he had to sit down at table with his obnoxious neighbor. To his surprise, however, the child did not lead him into the park, but towards one of the old stone houses of the tenantry.

"Pa's great-great-great-grandfather lived there," she remarked, with all the American's pride of ancestry. Orth did not smile, however. Only the warm clasp of the hand in his, the soft thrilling voice of his still mysterious companion, prevented him from feeling as if moving through the mazes of one of his own famous ghost stories.

The child ushered him into the dining-room, where an old man was seated at the table reading his Bible. The room was at least eight hundred years old. The ceiling was supported by the trunk of a tree, black, and probably petrified. The windows had still their diamond panes, separated, no doubt, by the original lead. Beyond was a large kitchen in which were several women. The old man, who looked patriarchal enough to have laid the foundations of his dwelling, glanced up and regarded his visitor without hospitality. His expression softened as his eyes moved to the child.

"Who 'ave ye brought?" he asked. He removed his spectacles. "Ah!" He rose, and offered the author a chair. At the same moment, the women entered the room.

"Of course you've fallen in love with Blanche, sir," said one of them. "Everybody does."

"Yes, that is it. Quite so." Confusion still prevailing among his faculties, he clung to the naked truth. "This little girl has interested and startled me because she bears a precise resemblance to one of the portraits in Chillingsworth—painted about two hundred years ago. Such extraordinary likenesses do not occur without reason, as a rule, and, as I admired my portrait so deeply that I have written a story about it, you will not think it unnatural if I am more than curious to discover the reason for this resemblance. The little girl tells me that her ancestors lived in this very house, and as my little girl lived next door, so to speak, there undoubtedly is a natural reason for the resemblance."

His host closed the Bible, put his spectacles in his pocket, and hobbled out of the house.

"He'll never talk of family secrets," said an elderly woman, who introduced herself as the old man's daughter, and had placed bread and milk before the guest. "There are secrets in every family, and we have ours, but he'll never tell those old tales. All I can tell you is that an ancestor of little Blanche went to wreck and ruin because of some fine lady's doings, and killed himself. The story is that his boys turned out bad. One of them saw his crime, and never got over the shock; he was foolish like, after. The mother was a poor scared sort of creature, and hadn't much influence over the other boy. There seemed to be blight on all the man's descendants, until one of them went to America. Since then, they haven't prospered, exactly, but they've done better, and they don't drink so heavy."

"They haven't done so well," remarked a worn patient-looking woman. Orth typed her as belonging to the small middle-class of an interior town of the eastern United States.

"You are not the child's mother?"

"Yes, sir. Everybody is surprised; you needn't apologize. She doesn't look like any of us, although her brothers and sisters are good enough for anybody to be proud of. But we all think she strayed in by mistake, for she looks like any lady's child, and, of course, we're only middle-class."

Orth gasped. It was the first time he had ever heard a native American use the term middle-class with a personal application. For the moment, he forgot the child. His analytical mind raked in the new specimen. He questioned, and learned that the woman's husband had kept a hat store in Rome, New York; that her boys were clerks, her girls in stores, or type-writing. They kept her and little Blanche—who had come after her other children were well grown—in comfort; and they were all very happy together. The boys broke out, occasionally; but, on the whole, were the best in the world, and her girls were worthy of far better than they had. All were robust, except Blanche. "She coming so late, when I was no longer young, makes her delicate," she remarked, with a slight blush, the signal of her chaste Americanism; "but I guess she'll get along all right. She couldn't have better care if she was a queen's child."

Orth, who had gratefully consumed the bread and milk, rose. "Is that really all you can tell me?" he asked.

"That's all," replied the daughter of the house. "And you couldn't pry open father's mouth."

Orth shook hands cordially with all of them, for he could be charming when he chose. He offered to escort the little girl back to her playmates in the woods, and she took prompt possession of his hand. As he was leaving, he turned suddenly to Mrs. Root. "Why did you call her Blanche?" he asked.

"She was so white and dainty, she just looked it."

Orth took the next train for London, and from Lord Teignmouth obtained the address of the aunt who lived on the family traditions, and a cordial note of introduction to her. He then spent an hour anticipating, in a toy shop, the whims and pleasures of a child—an incident of paternity which his book-children had not inspired. He bought the finest doll, piano, French dishes, cooking apparatus, and playhouse in the shop, and signed a check for thirty pounds with a sensation of positive rapture. Then he took the train for Lancashire, where the Lady Mildred Mortlake lived in another ancestral home.

Possibly there are few imaginative writers who have not a leaning, secret or avowed, to the occult. The creative gift is in very close relationship with the Great Force behind the universe; for aught we know, may be an atom thereof. It is not strange, therefore, that the lesser and closer of the unseen forces should send their vibrations to it occasionally; or, at all events, that the imagination should incline its ear to the most mysterious and picturesque of all beliefs. Orth frankly dallied with the old dogma. He formulated no personal faith of any sort, but his creative faculty, that ego within an ego, had made more than one excursion into the invisible and brought back literary treasure.

The Lady Mildred received with sweetness and warmth the generous contributor to the family sieve, and listened with fluttering interest to all he had not told the world—she had read the book—and to the strange, Americanized sequel.

"I am all at sea," concluded Orth. "What had my little girl to do with the tragedy? What relation was she to the lady who drove the young man to destruction—?"

"The closest," interrupted Lady Mildred. "She was herself!"

Orth stared at her. Again he had a confused sense of disintegration. Lady Mildred, gratified by the success of her bolt, proceeded less dramatically:

"Wally was up here just after I read your book, and I discovered he had given you the wrong history of the picture. Not that he knew it. It is a story we have left untold as often as possible, and I tell it to you only because you would probably become a monomaniac if I didn't. Blanche Mortlake—that Blanche—there had been several of her name, but there has not been one since—did not die in childhood, but lived to be twenty-four. She was an angelic child, but little angels sometimes grow up into very naughty girls. I believe she was delicate as a child, which probably gave her that spiritual look. Perhaps she was spoiled and flattered, until her poor little soul was stifled, which is likely. At all events, she was the coquette of her day—she seemed to care for nothing but breaking hearts; and she did not stop when she married, either. She hated her husband, and became reckless. She had no children. So far, the tale is not an uncommon one; but the worst, and what makes the ugliest stain in our annals, is to come.

"She was alone one summer at Chillingsworth—where she had taken temporary refuge from her husband—and she amused herself—some say, fell in love—with a young man of the yeomanry, a tenant of the next estate. His name was Root. He, so it comes down to us, was a magnificent specimen of his kind, and in those days the yeomanry gave us our great soldiers. His beauty of face was quite as remarkable as his physique; he led all the rural youth in sport, and was a bit above his class in every way. He had a wife in no way remarkable, and two little boys, but was always more with his friends than his family. Where he and Blanche Mortlake met I don't know—in the woods, probably, although it has been said that he had the run of the house. But, at all events, he was wild about her, and she pretended to be about him. Perhaps she was, for women have stooped before and since. Some women can be stormed by a fine man in any circumstances; but, although I am a woman of the world, and not easy to shock, there are some things I tolerate so hardly that it is all I can do to bring myself to believe in them; and stooping is one. Well, they were the scandal of the county for months, and then, either because she had tired of her new toy, or his grammar grated after the first glamour, or because she feared her husband, who was returning from the Continent, she broke off with him and returned to town. He followed her, and forced his way into her house. It is said she melted, but made him swear never to attempt to see her again. He returned to his home, and killed himself. A few months later she took her own life. That is all I know."

"It is quite enough for me," said Orth.

The next night, as his train travelled over the great waste of Lancashire, a thousand chimneys were spouting forth columns of fire. Where the sky was not red it was black. The place looked like hell. Another time Orth's imagination would have gathered immediate inspiration from this wildest region of England. The fair and peaceful counties of the south had nothing to compare in infernal grandeur with these acres of flaming columns. The chimneys were invisible in the lower darkness of the night; the fires might have leaped straight from the angry caldron of the earth.

But Orth was in a subjective world, searching for all he had ever heard of occultism. He recalled that the sinful dead are doomed, according to this belief, to linger for vast reaches of time in that borderland which is close to earth, eventually sent back to work out their final salvation; that they work it out among the descendants of the people they have wronged; that suicide is held by the devotees of occultism to be a cardinal sin, abhorred and execrated.

Authors are far closer to the truths enfolded in mystery than ordinary people, because of that very audacity of imagination which irritates their plodding critics. As only those who dare to make mistakes succeed greatly, only those who shake free the wings of the imagination brush, once in a way, the secrets of the great pale world. If such writers go wrong, it is not for the mere brains to tell them so.

Upon Orth's return to Chillingsworth, he called at once upon the child, and found her happy among his gifts. She put her arms about his neck, and covered his serene unlined face with soft kisses. This completed the conquest. Orth from that moment adored her as a child, irrespective of the psychological problem.

Gradually he managed to monopolize her. From long walks it was but a step to take her home for luncheon. The hours of her visits lengthened. He had a room fitted up as a nursery and filled with the wonders of toyland. He took her to London to see the pantomimes; two days before Christmas, to buy presents for her relatives; and together they strung them upon the most wonderful Christmas-tree that the old hall of Chillingsworth had ever embraced. She had a donkey-cart, and a trained nurse, disguised as a maid, to wait upon her. Before a month had passed she was living in state at Chillingsworth and paying daily visits to her mother. Mrs. Root was deeply flattered, and apparently well content. Orth told her plainly that he should make the child independent, and educate her, meanwhile. Mrs. Root intended to spend six months in England, and Orth was in no hurry to alarm her by broaching his ultimate design.

He reformed Blanche's accent and vocabulary, and read to her out of books which would have addled the brains of most little maids of six; but she seemed to enjoy them, although she seldom made a comment. He was always ready to play games with her, but she was a gentle little thing, and moreover, tired easily. She preferred to sit in the depths of a big chair, toasting her bare toes at the log-fire in the hall, while her friend read or talked to her. Although she was thoughtful, and when left to herself, given to dreaming, his patient observation could detect nothing uncanny about her. Moreover, she had a quick sense of humor, she was easily amused, and could laugh as merrily as any child in the world. He was resigning all hope of further development on the shadowy side when one day he took her to the picture-gallery.

It was the first warm day of summer. The gallery was not heated, and he had not dared to take his frail visitor into its chilly spaces during the winter and spring. Although he had wished to see the effect of the picture on the child, he had shrunk from the bare possibility of the very developments the mental part of him craved; the other was warmed and satisfied for the first time, and held itself aloof from disturbance. But one day the sun streamed through the old windows, and, obeying a sudden impulse, he led Blanche to the gallery.

It was some time before he approached the child of his earlier love. Again he hesitated. He pointed out many other fine pictures, and Blanche smiled appreciatively at his remarks, that were wise in criticism and interesting in matter. He never knew just how much she understood, but the very fact that there were depths in the child beyond his probing riveted his chains.

Suddenly he wheeled about and waved his hand to her prototype. "What do you think of that?" he asked. "You remember, I told you of the likeness the day I met you."

She looked indifferently at the picture, but he noticed that her color changed oddly; its pure white tone gave place to an equally delicate gray.

"I have seen it before," she said. "I came in here one day to look at it. And I have been quite often since. You never forbade me," she added, looking at him appealingly, but dropping her eyes quickly. "And I like the little girl—and the boy—very much."

"Do you? Why?"

"I don't know"—a formula in which she had taken refuge before. Still her candid eyes were lowered; but she was quite calm. Orth, instead of questioning, merely fixed his eyes upon her, and waited. In a moment she stirred uneasily, but she did not laugh nervously, as another child would have done. He had never seen her self-possession ruffled, and he had begun to doubt he ever should. She was full of human warmth and affection. She seemed made for love, and every creature who came within her ken adored her, from the author himself down to the litter of puppies presented to her by the stable-boy a few weeks since; but her serenity would hardly be enhanced by death.

She raised her eyes finally, but not to his. She looked at the portrait.

"Did you know that there was another picture behind?" she asked.

"No," replied Orth, turning cold. "How did you know it?"

"One day I touched a spring in the frame, and this picture came forward. Shall I show you?"

"Yes!" And crossing curiosity and the involuntary shrinking from impending phenomena was a sensation of aesthetic disgust that *he* should be treated to a secret spring.

The little girl touched hers, and that other Blanche sprang aside so quickly that she might have been impelled by a sharp blow from behind. Orth narrowed his eyes and stared at what she revealed. He felt that his own Blanche was watching him, and set his features, although his breath was short.

There was the Lady Blanche Mortlake in the splendor of her young womanhood, beyond a doubt. Gone were all traces of her spiritual childhood, except, perhaps, in the shadows of the mouth; but more than fulfilled were the promises of her mind. Assuredly, the woman had been as brilliant and gifted as she had been restless and passionate. She wore her very pearls with arrogance, her very hands were tense with eager life, her whole being breathed mutiny.

Orth turned abruptly to Blanche, who had transferred her attention to the picture.

"What a tragedy is there!" he exclaimed, with a fierce attempt at lightness. "Think of a woman having all that pent up within her two centuries ago! And at the mercy of a stupid family, no doubt, and a still stupider husband. No wonder— To-day, a woman like that might not be a model for all the virtues, but she certainly would use her gifts and become famous, the while living her life too fully to have any place in it for yeomen and such, or even for the trivial business of breaking hearts." He put his finger under Blanche's chin, and raised her face, but he could not compel her gaze. "You are the exact image of that little girl," he said, "except that you are even purer and finer. She had no chance, none whatever. You live in the woman's age. Your opportunities will be infinite. I shall see to it that they are. What you wish to be you shall be. There will be no pent-up energies here to burst out into disaster for yourself and others. You shall be trained to self-control—that is, if you ever develop self-will, dear child—every faculty shall be educated, every school of life you desire knowledge through shall be open to you. You shall become that finest flower of civilization, a woman who knows how to use her independence."

She raised her eyes slowly, and gave him a look which stirred the roots of sensation—a long look of unspeakable melancholy. Her chest rose once; then she set her lips tightly, and dropped her eyes.

"What do you mean?" he cried, roughly, for his soul was chattering. "Is—it—do you—?" He dared not go too far, and concluded lamely, "You mean you fear that your mother will not give you to me when she goes—you have divined that I wish to adopt you? Answer me, will you?"

But she only lowered her head and turned away, and he, fearing to frighten or repel her, apologized for his abruptness, restored the outer picture to its place, and led her from the gallery.

He sent her at once to the nursery, and when she came down to luncheon and took her place at his right hand, she was as natural and childlike as ever. For some days he restrained his curiosity, but one evening, as they were sitting before the fire in the hall listening to the storm, and just after he had told her the story of the erl-king, he took her on his knee and asked her gently if she would not tell him what had been in her thoughts when he had drawn her brilliant future. Again her face turned gray, and she dropped her eyes.

"I cannot," she said. "I—perhaps—I don't know."

"Was it what I suggested?"

She shook her head, then looked at him with a shrinking appeal which forced him to drop the subject.

He went the next day alone to the gallery, and looked long at the portrait of the woman. She stirred no response in him. Nor could he feel that the woman of Blanche's future would stir the man in him. The paternal was all he had to give, but that was hers forever.

He went out into the park and found Blanche digging in her garden, very dirty and absorbed. The next afternoon, however, entering the hall noiselessly, he saw her sitting in her big chair, gazing out into nothing visible, her whole face settled in melancholy. He asked her if she were ill, and she recalled herself at once, but confessed to feeling tired. Soon after this he noticed that she lingered longer in the comfortable depths of her chair, and seldom went out, except with himself. She insisted that she was quite well, but after he had surprised her again looking as sad as if she had renounced every joy of childhood, he summoned from London a doctor renowned for his success with children.

The scientist questioned and examined her. When she had left the room he shrugged his shoulders.

"She might have been born with ten years of life in her, or she might grow up into a buxom woman," he said. "I confess I cannot tell. She appears to be sound enough, but I have no X-rays in my eyes, and for all I know she may be on the verge of decay. She certainly has the look of those who die young. I have never seen so spiritual a child. But I can put my finger on nothing. Keep her out-of-doors, don't give her sweets, and don't let her catch anything if you can help it."

Orth and the child spent the long warm days of summer under the trees of the park, or driving in the quiet lanes. Guests were unbidden, and his pen was idle. All that was human in him had gone out to Blanche. He loved her, and she was a perpetual delight to him. The rest of the world received the large measure of his indifference. There was no further change in her, and apprehension slept and let him sleep. He had persuaded Mrs. Root to remain in England for a year. He sent her theater tickets every week, and placed a horse and phaeton at her disposal. She was enjoying herself and seeing less and less of Blanche. He took the child to Bournemouth for a fortnight, and again to Scotland, both of which outings bene-fited as much as they pleased her. She had begun to tyrannize over him amiably, and she carried herself quite royally. But she was always sweet and truthful, and these qualities, com-bined with that something in the depths of her mind which defied his explorations, held him captive. She was devoted to him, and cared for no other companion, although she was demonstrative to her mother when they met.

It was in the tenth month of this idyl of the lonely man and the lonely child that Mrs. Root flurriedly entered the library of Chillingsworth, where Orth happened to be alone.

"Oh, sir," she exclaimed, "I must go home. My daughter Grace writes me—she should have done it before—that the boys are not behaving as well as they should—she didn't tell me, as I was having such a good time she just hated to worry me—Heaven knows I've had enough worry—but now I must go—I just couldn't stay—boys are an awful responsibility—girls ain't a circumstance to them, although mine are a handful sometimes."

Orth had written about too many women to interrupt the flow. He let her talk until she paused to recuperate her forces. Then he said quietly:

"I am sorry this has come so suddenly, for it forces me to broach a subject at once which I would rather have postponed until the idea had taken possession of you by degrees—"

"I know what it is you want to say, sir," she broke in, "and I've reproached myself that I haven't warned you before, but I didn't like to be the one to speak first. You want Blanche—of course, I couldn't help seeing that; but I can't let her go, sir, indeed, I can't."

"Yes," he said, firmly, "I want to adopt Blanche, and I hardly think you can refuse, for you must know how greatly it will be to her advantage. She is a wonderful child; you have never been blind to that; she should have every opportunity, not only of money, but of association. If I adopt her legally, I shall, of course, make her my heir, and—there is no reason why she should not grow up as great a lady as any in England."

The poor woman turned white, and burst into tears. "I've sat up nights and nights, struggling," she said, when she could speak. "That, and missing her. I couldn't stand in her light, and I let her stay. I know I oughtn't to, now—I mean, stand in her light—but, sir, she is dearer than all the others put together."

"Then live here in England—at least, for some years longer. I will gladly relieve your children of your support, and you can see Blanche as often as you choose."

"I can't do that, sir. After all, she is only one, and there are six others. I can't desert them. They all need me, if only to keep them together—three girls unmarried and out in the world, and three boys just a little inclined to be wild. There is another point, sir—I don't exactly know how to say it."

"Well?" asked Orth, kindly. This American woman thought him the ideal gentleman, although the mistress of the estate on which she visited called him a boor and a snob.

"It is—well—you must know—you can imagine—that her brothers and sisters just worship Blanche. They save their dimes to buy her everything she wants—or used to want. Heaven knows what will satisfy her now, although I can't see that she's one bit spoiled. But she's just like a religion to them; they're not much on church. I'll tell you, sir, what I couldn't say to any one else, not even to these relations who've been so kind to me—but there's wildness, just a streak, in all my children, and I believe, I know, it's Blanche that keeps them straight. My girls get bitter, sometimes; work all the week and little fun, not caring for common men and no chance to marry gentlemen; and sometimes they break out and talk dreadful; then, when they're over it, they say they'll live for Blanche— they've said it over and over, and they mean it. Every sacrifice they've made for her—and they've made many—has done them good. It isn't that Blanche ever says a word of the preachy sort, or has anything of the Sunday-school child about her, or even tries to smooth them down when they're excited. It's just herself. The only thing she ever does is sometimes to draw herself up and look scornful, and that nearly kills them. Little as she is, they're crazy about having her respect. I've grown superstitious about her. Until she came I used to get frightened, terribly, sometimes, and I believe she came for that. So—you see! I know Blanche is too fine for us and ought to have the best; but, then, they are to be considered, too. They have their rights, and they've got much more good than bad in them. I don't know! I don't know! It's kept me awake many nights."

Orth rose abruptly. "Perhaps you will take some further time to think it over," he said. "You can stay a few weeks longer—the matter cannot be so pressing as that."

The woman rose. "I've thought this," she said; "let Blanche decide. I believe she knows more than any of us. I believe that whichever way she decided would be right. I won't say anything to her, so you won't think I'm working on her feelings; and I can trust you. But she'll know."

"Why do you think that?" asked Orth, sharply. "There is nothing uncanny about the child. She is not yet seven years old. Why should you place such a responsibility upon her?"

"Do you think she's like other children?"

"I know nothing of other children."

"I do, sir. I've raised six. And I've seen hundreds of others. I never was one to be a fool about my own, but Blanche isn't like any other child living—I'm certain of it."

"What *do* you think?"

And the woman answered, according to her lights: "I think she's an angel, and came to us because we needed her."

"And I think she is Blanche Mortlake working out the last of her salvation," thought the author; but he made no reply, and was alone in a moment.

It was several days before he spoke to Blanche, and then, one morning, when she was sitting on her mat on the lawn with the light full upon her, he told her abruptly that her mother must return home.

To his surprise, but utterable delight, she burst into tears and flung herself into his arms.

"You need not leave me," he said, when he could find his

own voice. "You can stay here always and be my little girl. It all rests with you."

"I can't stay," she sobbed. "I can't!"

"And that is what made you so sad once or twice?" he asked, with a double eagerness.

She made no reply.

"Oh!" he said, passionately, "give me your confidence, Blanche. You are the only breathing thing that I love."

"If I could I would," she said. "But I don't know—not quite."

"How much do you know?"

But she sobbed again and would not answer. He dared not risk too much. After all, the physical barrier between the past and the present was very young.

"Well, well, then, we will talk about the other matter. I will not pretend to disguise the fact that your mother is distressed at the idea of parting from you, and thinks it would be as sad for your brothers and sisters, whom she says you influence for their good. Do you think that you do?"

"Yes."

"How do you know this?"

"Do you know why you know everything?"

"No, my dear, and I have great respect for your instincts. But your sisters and brothers are now old enough to take care of themselves. They must be of poor stuff if they cannot live properly without the aid of a child. Moreover, they will be marrying soon. That will also mean that your mother will have many little grandchildren to console her for your loss. I will be the one bereft, if you leave me. I am the only one who really needs you. I don't say I will go to the bad, as you may have very foolishly persuaded yourself your family will do without you, but I trust to your instincts to make you realize how unhappy, how inconsolable I shall be. I shall be the loneliest man on earth!"

She rubbed her face deeper into his flannels, and tightened her embrace. "Can't you come, too?" she asked.

"No; you must live with me wholly or not at all. Your people are not my people, their ways are not my ways. We should not get along. And if you lived with me over there you might as well stay here, for your influence over them would be quite as removed. Moreover, if they are of the right stuff, the memory of you will be quite as potent for good as your actual presence."

"Not unless I died."

Again something within him trembled. "Do you believe you are going to die young?" he blurted out.

But she would not answer.

He entered the nursery abruptly the next day and found her packing her dolls. When she saw him, she sat down and began to weep hopelessly. He knew then that his fate was sealed. And when, a year later, he received her last little scrawl, he was almost glad that she went when she did.

THE

WEDDING CAKE

COUPLE

Howard Lewis Russell

George Dapper first noticed them on the first of July. He remembered the date so well because it was so damnably hot—ninety-seven degrees, ninety percent humidity and no trace of a breeze. George, a man never comfortable even under optimum conditions, was rolling with sweat only seconds after stepping from the cool glass obelisk that employed him. He yanked loose his tie and peeled his coat off. The street was a river of black gum. Greasy fumes of carbon monoxide swayed through the air like the wavy waters of a desert mirage, caressing the city with deceptive refreshment.

Pulling out a handkerchief, George patted his face, wondering whether it wouldn't be such a bad idea to take a cab the seven blocks to Penn Station. Of course it would mean spending perhaps two dollars—possibly even three with a tip—provided he could find a cab in the first place, which wasn't likely. On the other hand, the words "heart attack" lurked ominously in the back of his mind. Already George was older than his father had been when he'd had his first (a spectre that only loomed more ghoulishly all the time). Then again, waiting for a cab might mean missing his train, which George's wife wouldn't be too happy about, not that she'd care if he dropped dead in the street. For her, though, good ammunition was where one found it.

It was while George was leaning against a blue postal box, weighing this dilemma, that he saw them.

They were a couple—beautiful, happy, seemingly exempt

249

from the unmerciful heat and obliviously content, as though
they were the world's nucleus and all else was but protoplasm.
They could have been any age, arbitrate of youth, looking to
have just stepped out of a fashion magazine. The woman was
slim and sleek and the very epitome of vogue—a sculpted face,
airbrushed complexion, and long geometrical blonde hair that
bounced as though electrically operated. The man was just as
beautiful, just as stylized—chiseled bones, symmetrical features and teasing clothes, suggestive of a pranksterish nature.

They held hands loosely at George's street corner, waiting
for the walk signal—she laughing, he smiling, and neither one
noticing George at their left staring enviously. "How can they
not sweat?" he thought, looking around at the rest of the
panting crowd, just to confirm that he wasn't alone in his
perspiration. He inched a little closer to the couple, praying
the light wouldn't change.

Their nails were perfectly manicured, like glimmering talons, and attached to perfect fingers that tapered gracefully
from their streamlined bodies. And of course, unlike George,
they had no wrinkles on their faces, nor did their abdomens sag
around the middle. "How old are they?" he wondered. Closer
scrutiny revealed no trace of stubble on the man's face. It was
as unmarred as a baby's. And the woman's skin was so faultless
it didn't even look real, resembling instead some sort of man-
made synthetic, smooth and flawless. In fact, they had no lines
in their skin at all, not as far as George could detect. Not even
in the joints of their fingers or the insides of their wrists, or the
backs of their elbows. None! They reminded George of the
plastic figurines that adorn the tops of wedding cakes. He
wondered if perfection recognized itself as such and, if so, was
it simply taken for granted? Or was it thanked on one's knees
every day?

He had the sudden urge to grab the woman, just to touch
her, to see what she felt like, to actually *feel*, if only once in his
life, real, God-given impeccancy. "Do it," he thought. "Just do
it. You can always say excuse me, I'm sorry . . . hurry!"

But the light changed, and the wedding cake couple glided
obliviously across the street where they disappeared into the
masses, never having even noticed the overweight, middle-
aged figure who had so completely, for however briefly, adored
them.

*   *   *

By supper time, George had completely forgotten about the couple. As usual, his day had been too boring for him to want to remember any of it, and any deviation from the theme, no matter how interesting, was always irretrievably buried by day's end under a mountain of frustrations; i.e., heat that wilted his energy, cabs that didn't stop, trains that left him behind. His griping wife usually added a few extra boulders, as did his obesity and his age.

Although only forty-four, George Dapper was the type of individual who began to depreciate once out of the womb. Childhood had been a series of bizarre accidents, unusual illnesses and too many cookies. Puberty had been no better— scarring pimples, a receding hairline, expandable waistlines and uncontrollable body sounds. By the time George was exiting his teens, he'd become the class scapegoat and school laughing-stock. Naturally, he had to develop an armor, and being George, he chose urban society's most contemptible type of armor—a bland, meek, blend-in-with-the-walls personality, equipped with anemic skin, flaccid eyes, and a high twittering voice.

So it was little wonder that George told no one, when by coincidence (or so he first thought) he happened to see the wedding cake couple again the next day, a Saturday . . . then again the next, and the next after that. People might laugh and accuse him of having an over-stressed imagination, and laugh-ter meant ridicule, and ridicule meant that George wasn't as good as everybody else. Thus he kept quiet about it, not even telling his wife (a woman renown for her stupefying lack of curiosity anyhow).

That Saturday, the second day George saw them, he'd awak-ened with a minimal amount of aches and cracking joints and decided to join a health spa. It was something he'd been planning to do for years, although really he had no conception of what was actually expected of one at such a place, but he was in a healthful mood. Lithuania, his stringy, stingy excuse for a wife, snarled at him over her morning vodka as he left. "Don't show up any of the regulars, Georgie."

George said nothing in return. Their marriage had, years before, disintegrated into the stuff of farce. Now it was a union held together through sheer inertia, one promulgated by the comfort of mutual lethargy—they had just never bothered to get a divorce.

George closed the front door a little too loudly and found that his car had a flat. Rather than change it himself, which would only give Lithuania fuel in which to gloat—if not over his mechanical incompetence, then at least over the further proof of his ongoing lucklessness—he drove to a service station about a half mile away.

As it was being repaired and he was leaning against a gas pump cursing the heat, he saw the couple come out of an ice cream parlor across the intersection. They were both dressed in flowing white and holding pink ice cream cones. The woman wore clear sandals and had a big floppy hat the size of a manhole cover fluttering on her head. The man wore strange green metal bracelets about his ankles that clattered when he walked. They were laughing as they billowed through the traffic. Neither one seemed too interested in the ice cream which, despite the heat, defiantly refused to melt onto their manicured hands, spurring George to wonder just how long that ice cream would stay frozen if it were his.

Suddenly, he sucked in his breath, jumping away from the gas pump as though someone had thrown a cigarette at his feet—they were coming across the street toward him. His throat tightened. Effervescently they drifted, their loose white garments flapping like angel wings in a breeze George couldn't detect. But just as they got to the curb on his side, they turned away, and George Dapper breathed a sigh of great relief. As they floated out of sight, he wondered why he was glad they hadn't seen him. He also observed that they never once touched their ice cream against their lips, which still refused to melt.

"Okay, that'll be twelve bucks mister . . . hey buddy!"

"What? Oh yes."

George forgot to join a health spa that day.

The next time he saw them, the following day, George and Lithuania had gone to the Metropolitan Museum. Lithuania hated art, but at least the museum offered her an excellent chance to deface the masterpieces. While no one was looking, she would scrape her fingernails across an oil or dabble a little nail polish on a bust. But she was always quick about it, making sure that roving cameras and roving eyes were looking elsewhere. It was an uncompromising sensation.

George noticed nothing in the room of Egyptian artifacts as Lithuania, quicker than a striking cobra, slashed Nefertiti's turban with her favorite shade, Cherries in the Snow. George was too dumbfounded by the sight of the beautiful couple. They slid, like statues on castors, across the parquet floor and vanished into a room of Greek vases. "Come on," snorted Lithuania triumphantly, "I'm ready to get out of here."

"But, but we can't leave yet," stammered George, taking Lithuania by the hand. "What about the Greek vases?" He began leading her through the crowd, straining to get a better look at the couple.

Lithuania jerked her arm away, glancing furtively over one shoulder at a uniformed guard slouched in a chair. "Vases! We've got vases at home if it's dishes you want, and there are plenty that need washing, too. Now hurry up! This old junk makes me nervous."

Following her out, George thought what a strange coincidence it was that he should see the wedding cake couple three days in a row, and they'd yet to see him! It was so exhilarating somehow, almost like he was a spy.

The exhilaration, however, was to be short lived. As George saw them again the next day on his lunch hour. And again the next. He began to wonder if, in fact, their roles weren't reversed, and it was *he* who was being spied upon. But why? It simply made no sense. He wasn't an important person—a prince or dignitary, or world peace keeper. And he didn't play around on his wife (although God knew he had every reason), and he certainly wasn't involved in any underworld crimes or espionage or otherwise shady subterfuges. He was just plain old George Dapper—an accountant for a book binding company who went to bed at ten o'clock every night, never touched liquor, and gave blood once every two months. So why would anyone want to spy on him? "It has to be only a bizarre coincidence," he thought. "They've never even seen me."

But then a terrible revelation crossed his mind. *Maybe they want you to think that, George. Maybe you've just never seen them see you.*

"No," he assured himself, "it's only a coincidence. I'm positive."

Nonetheless, George didn't sleep well that night at all. Lithuania, on the other hand, after having spent a leisurely day at the Museum of Natural History, slept like a fossil.

The crepe myrtles on George's tiny lawn were in full bloom, announcing that summer had reached its zenith, and would henceforth slide downward until it dropped into a wash of cool gold sometime in early October. George Dapper, too, was on the downhill slide. He'd begun to lose weight, which certainly he needed to do, but the circumstances surrounding the loss only made him appear pasty and haggard. There was a pinched look about him, an appearance only punctuated by eyes that had begun to involuntarily twitch and dart from left to right, as if constantly on the lookout for something and fearful he might find it. In fact, this was his fear exactly. For over a month and a half now, not a day had passed that George did not, at some point in any given twenty-four hours, see the wedding cake couple. Furthermore, they *never* saw him!

After the first week or so, George had meant to walk over and say something to them. He didn't know what, for he was an abysmal conversationalist when it came to introductions, but it seemed that whenever he got up his courage, an obstacle would mysteriously drop into his path—a crowd of people would appear from nowhere, a bus would block his view, an old acquaintance not seen in years would run into him. Once, when he was particularly close to them, a child even grabbed hold of his leg and asked where its mother was. It was as though they were untouchable somehow, creating their own diversions to keep him at bay.

Slowly, George found himself living for that moment in the day when he would see them. No longer was it a question of if, only a question of when. Sometimes he saw them in the early morning, just walking and laughing, rain or not, never with an umbrella and dry of course. Sometimes he would see them during his lunch hour, feeding morsels to the pigeons or splashing their hands at the edge of a fountain—apparently they didn't work. And sometimes he wouldn't see them until after dark, leaving a boutique or chic specialty shop (always empty handed). But invariably he saw them once a day. Never twice, only once. And until he saw them he was a nervous wreck, continually worrying over where and when it would happen.

But afterwards he was okay. He could concentrate and breathe easily . . . that is, until the next day.

It was around Labor Day that George finally got a golden opportunity to speak to them. He had lost twenty-three pounds. His jaws sagged and his eyes were more flaccid than ever, giving him the appearance of a creature that was more amphibian than mammal. He was in Macy's on his lunch hour, hunting a birthday present for Lithuania—of all things, she'd asked for a complete line of Revlon nail polishes. "And I *mean* every last one of them, too. I don't care if it comes in two hundred different shades!" George had found most of them, but some of the oranges were kind of rare, which presented a problem. Either he'd have to search every store in Manhattan until he found them, which might take days, or else he'd have to take the risk that Lithuania wouldn't notice—a *very* big risk. So it was while he was wandering aimlessly about Macy's Cellar, agonizing over this, that George's twitching head caught sight of the pair descending the escalator. They floated down much as the Gods would from Mount Olympus, with satisfied smirks on their faces, as though they had just stuffed themselves on ambrosia and were now ready to wreak havoc upon the mortals.

George began to shake as if an earthquake had entered his body. This time, the woman was wearing a paper jumpsuit the color of aluminum. One earring hung from her left ear the size of a Christmas ornament, in which swam a goldfish in green water. The man had on painter's overalls, wrinkle free, and meticulously splotched like a Jackson Pollock with brilliant enamel in shades of autumn. He clutched a black rabbit.

Go over to them, George. Demand to know why they're following you.

"But are they?"

They have to be.

"Then why are they so open about it? Why every single day?"

They're trying to drive you insane, George. And they'll succeed if you let them. Don't! Be strong for once in your life.

George turned white as he watched them stroll into Kitchenwares about twenty yards away.

Do it!

"I will. I will go speak to them. I will." And regally, head held high, he began marching toward the copper kettles and wooden spoons. At fifteen yards he could see that the woman was wearing purple lipstick. At ten yards he could make out that the man's necklace was made of coral. At five yards, the sprinkler system sprang to life and havoc ensued. Housewives screamed. Security scrambled. Cashiers sighed with disgust. The woman laughed, the man smiled, they gazed into each other's eyes and then vanished into the confusion. George stood dripping and soggy by the steamers like a squished frog, his eyes as wide as woks.

By Halloween, George was in need of a vacation in the most desperate way. In fact, his boss insisted, even going so far as to buy the airline tickets. George, once a short rotund man, had, in only four months, dropped from two hundred twelve pounds down to one hundred thirty-five. Still short, he was anything but rotund—a stuttering, emaciated jellyfish who jumped anytime someone entered a room or said hello. Yes, he would accept his boss' gracious gesture. He'd go abroad, too, and he *would not* follow an itinerary. "Let's just see if they can find me there!"

"We're going to Europe," he stammered to Lithuania one night as she sat glued to the soaps, her fingers soaking in a bowl of syrupy pink liquid that rested in her lap. "We'll be gone for a month. Mr. Himmler even gave me the plane tickets. Wasn't that nice?"

"I won't go," said Lithuania simply, not taking her eyes off the screen. She retracted a thumb from the liquid, examined it quickly, then submerged it again. "I hate traveling."

"But, dear, I need a vacation."

Lithuania made no comment. Even she had noticed George didn't appear to be in the best of health lately—not that he ever had, at least as long as she'd known him—but now he looked almost green. Nonetheless, she refused. Weakness was something she just could not tolerate, weak men especially. How she had ever ended up marrying such a pillar of sawdust, she couldn't imagine.

"I simply will not be subjected to unhygienic foreigners," she said. "Especially ones who can't even speak English!"

George began grasping at straws. "But . . . but think how

lovely it will be this time of year. Think how you'll broaden your education."

Lithuania took a quick peek at her other thumb. Satisfied, she pulled both hands out of the goop and let them drip over the bowl a few seconds. "People who drive on the wrong side of the road can't teach me anything. I'm smart enough as it is." She wiped her hands on a towel. "Exceedingly smart," she added.

"But, dear," George whined, looking confused and defeated. He sank into an easy chair, all the air leaving his lungs in a slow deflated sigh. "How can you not want to see the Eiffel Tower, the Elgin Marbles, the David, or the Louvre?"

"The Louvre!"

Suddenly, Lithuania was extremely interested.

George settled luxuriously into his hotel room overlooking the Seine, after a harrowing flight. He had seen them at Kennedy. They were standing at a large window near one of the TWA passenger gates as George's plane waited in line for takeoff. He saw them from his seat (thank God they weren't on the plane) just standing with cocktails in their hands. George stared at them a full ten minutes, but never once did they take a sip.

"What are you looking at?" hissed Lithuania. "There's nothing out there to see. We haven't even taken off yet. Now tell one of these waitresses you'd like a vodka!"

But now he was in Paris, thousands of miles from the wedding cake couple, and he just dared them to find where he was. George chuckled delightedly, then ordered a very caloric breakfast from room service. "Safe at last."

Paris was so lovely in the fall. Translucent leaves in malleable hues of red and gold flitted elusively about the cobbled streets, where vendors sold flowers out of season. It was George's first day in the City of Lights, and he wanted to bury his face in the ordered bouquets of papery blossoms. He even bought a cluster of lavender phlox for Lithuania, who was visiting the Louvre for the third time that day. Maybe the dead bloom of their marriage still had not dropped its last petal after all. He had never before realized she was so interested in art.

Something was wrong, however. A queasy sense of *déjà vu* enveloped George as he turned to pay the burly woman behind the flower cart. The flesh on his back began to crawl and goose pimples washed down his legs . . . they were behind him. "No," he thought. "No, it can't be." He put up a pretense of calmness as he counted out his francs to the woman, yet it didn't help matters that she kept looking over his shoulder as he pressed the coins into her hand.

Finally he couldn't stand it anymore, and whipped about just in time to see the backs of a man and woman casually disappear into the Metro. He didn't see their faces, but the woman had a geometrical hairstyle, and the man wore strange green metal bracelets around his ankles that clattered when he walked.

The remainder of George's recuperative European holiday was spent in desperate flight between world capitals. He and Lithuania left Paris that afternoon and flew immediately to Rome. George sat dazed and catatonic the entire flight, pallid as talcum. Lithuania went wild at the Forum. She used up three bottles of Cherries in the Snow, and a half bottle of her less favorite but just as purposeful, Cranberry Ice. Her ecstasy upon seeing the Colliseum nearly caused her to swoon. It *did* cause George to swoon, but not until he saw a beautiful couple of flawless skin cuddling beneath the Arch of Constantine.

The next day, at Grand Place in Brussels, while taking a photograph of the glowering Lithuania, George dropped his camera into a puddle and ruined a whole roll of film. This, just after a familiar couple happened to wander in front of the frame. Lithuania was livid over George's clumsiness.

The day after that, in Dublin, George developed a delirious case of hiccups after spotting a beautiful bunch of green balloons ascend above the rooftops and melt into the clouds. The source of this abandoned aeronautics was none other than a man and woman in matching plastic moo-moos of an emerald shade, on whose shoulders perched a pair of scarlet macaws.

But it wasn't until George was in London, a day later, at the British Museum to be exact, that he slid limp, rambling, and exhausted to the floor. Stomachal screws twisted and wrenched his defenseless butterflies until they howled in agony. The final turn occurred when George was standing near the Rosetta Stone. Lithuania was "viewing" the Marbles at the time. She had even bought two extra bottles of polish for the event, but just as she whipped out her brush, she heard the screams.

George Dapper was none too sympathetically escorted to the door. Lithuania followed, a river of obscenities flowing from her mouth.

"I . . . couldn't . . . help it," he stuttered. "I saw . . . some people. They made me . . . nervous."

"So what's new!" Lithuania barked. "Popcorn at the movies makes you nervous! Violence in the springtime makes you nervous! And now, ordinary people off the streets make you nervous! Does anything *not* make you nervous, George?" She next dropped her two bottles of polish back into her purse, which up until then, she'd been rolling angrily between her palms. Stalking off ahead of George, she shouted back, "Just take me home!"

"Y . . . yes, dear."

As Thanksgiving came and went, so did the last vestiges of George's health. He had lost fifteen more pounds during his European nightmare, and another ten since then. Where before the trip he could have passed for being merely undernourished, he now had the look of a scarecrow on stilts. His skin was the odd color and texture of moldy burlap, and it hung from his wooden bones in just about the same folds. His thinning hair, now oily and uneven, swirled wildly about his head, as though crows were in the process of constructing a nest in it. His eyes actually bulged from their sockets, and he found he had trouble even standing up for more than a few moments at a time.

He quit his job, to the outcries of Lithuania, who was seeming less and less like a human being every day, and more and more like some sort of snarling, clawing animal. She seemed to George strangely uncurious and uncaring of his decline in health. "Has she not even noticed?" he wondered.

Maybe she has noticed, George. Maybe she's glad. Ever think of that?

"No," he thought, "even Lithuania has a heart."

Well, why has she never seen the wedding cake couple? Answer me that. Not once in Europe did she notice them. Not once . . . or did she?

George trusted no one anymore. Yet he simply could not let a couple of laughing mannequins destroy his life.

Come on, George. They haven't done a thing to you.

"But they're everywhere I go."

So are lots of other people, too.

"The same ones? Every day?"

It's only a coincidence. Nothing more.

"For five months? Every single day! A coincidence? I can't take it anymore I'm telling you. And I'm not going out of this house again. They wouldn't dare come up to the door, would they? No. No, that would mean they'd have to speak to me, and they don't want that . . . I'm not going to look out the windows either. If I do, even for a second, I know they'll be there. Oh, maybe not right there, staring at me, but they'll happen to be driving down the street at just that moment, or walking, or riding bicycles. I don't know how they'd know precisely when I'd look out the window, but they would. You can bet on that. And oh, how they'd love to see the expression on my face, pretending all along they don't see me at all, and laughing. God, how they'd laugh. But I'll show them. Yes sir, I will. I'll lock myself up in this house, and I won't move!"

Which is exactly what George did. He sat down in his favorite armchair, unmoving, holding a butcher's knife, staring at the walls. Hours ticked by and, of course, nothing happened. Eventually, daylight faded into a purplish dusk. Still nothing. Occasionally, Lithuania would shamble in and out of the room, snorting, then shamble back into the catacombs whence she came. At least she never mentioned the butcher's knife, so maybe he didn't look as ridiculous as he felt after all. The night dragged slowly on. His anxiety began to grow.

"If I can make it to midnight," he thought. "If I can just make it to midnight, maybe the spell or curse, or whatever it is, will be broken."

Two more hours passed. Nothing.

An hour later, Lithuania shambled in again and asked if the Lincoln Memorial planned on going to bed that evening. No response. She gave him a malevolent shrug, sucking in her cheeks while she arched her eyebrows, then left. By 11:45, George was sweating uncontrollably.

"They're out there, just outside the door, listening. I know they are. They're laughing at me, too. They're peeping under the door and laughing at me. They think I'm just *so* funny."

Don't let them get to you, George. Just fifteen more minutes. That's all. Fifteen more minutes and the curse will be broken.

But at 11:55, with only five minutes to go, George suddenly heard a noise outside the door. The wind? A bird? He was certain he heard something. It wasn't just his imagination.

The clatter of green metal bracelets?

George vaulted from his chair, tortured rage searing through his eyes. He flung open the door and poised his knife high above his head . . . nothing. Just a starry sky and a chilly November breeze. He galloped into the street, holding his knife in front of him with both hands, turning round and round in slow circles. "I know you're here!" he shouted. "Show your faces . . . I'll kill you both!"

"George Dapper!" shrieked Lithuania, running out from the house as though it were in flames. "Have you gone psychotic?" A wake of stray hair rollers and bobby pins trailed her into the street. "Get back inside before the neighbors see you. And give me that damned knife before you kill yourself!" She snatched the saber from his hands and stalked quickly back into the house, lest any passers-by should see her associating with the insane.

George, bewildered and simpering, stumbled back up the lawn wringing his hands. As he got to the door, a pair of light beams brushed across the side of the house. George turned his head just in time to see a flash of headlights hang a corner about a block away. To the untrained eye, at such a distance with such little light, they would have been nothing more than a pair of silhouettes sitting in the front seat. They could have been anybody . . . anybody.

But George Dapper knew better, and his screams lasted a full hour.

Christmas crept to George's house like two pairs of icy eyes, always seeing but never seen. They were everywhere by now, George was sure of it. They were even in his house. Oh, he never actually *saw* them in there—they usually saved that for his unwary moments during the day—but he heard them at night, creeping and slithering about like beautiful but dangerous toys.

Sounds once airily attributed to the settling foundation or the wind whistling, or windows rattling, now took on hideous sources. The foundation wasn't settling at all. It was the beautiful man digging holes around the edge of the house. And what

George thought was only the wind, was really the hissing from the adders he had planted in the holes. And the windows didn't rattle either. They never had. It was the beautiful woman. She was clawing at the windows with her manicured talons, waiting. She was waiting to catch George off guard, and then she would dive through the glass and rip him to shreds!

George celebrated New Year's Eve by stuffing Lithuania's empty vodka bottles down any holes he could find in the lawn. The nasty adders weren't going to hiss at him anymore. Let the monsters starve to death! Every now and then, George would raise his bony head into the air and twist it quickly around, searching for the familiar faces which most certainly were watching him. "Take that you slimy eels," he'd say, jabbing another bottle down an abandoned chipmunk's tunnel. "What time will it be today my pretty friends? Lunch time perhaps? Or will I have to wait until dinner. Or even later? We'll see," he'd chortle. "We shall see."

As it happened, it was later, much later. Almost midnight. George felt surprisingly calm that evening, despite the fact that he hadn't seen his friends all day. At ten o'clock, clutching a bottle of champagne, he gently pulled the drapes and closed the door to his bedroom. (Lithuania had, years before, insisted on her own "boudoir.") Then, serenely pulling the covers over him, he switched on the television with his toe. "Maybe, just maybe, and if I don't think about them, I can make it tonight." He popped the cork and poured himself a bracer for the new year.

That's right, George, slow and easy.

At eleven the reruns began to come on, and George felt himself drifting into sleep. His tired lids slowly descended as Lucy and Ricky played coy around the pool of their Hollywood hotel. The Mertzes weren't around. Gradually, the shapes around the pool began to blur into one solid, fuzzy mass. George was just pulling the sheets around his shoulders to flip onto his stomach, when suddenly, his eyes bulged open in terror.

"Not on television!" he screamed. "No, no it can't be!"

But there they were, caught by the camera for one fleeting second as extras lounging around the pool . . . and they weren't one day younger.

George sprung from his bed, his face pasty and veined.

Garbled, choking sounds came out of gasping lungs. Lithuania sauntered into his room blowing her nails dry.

"Hallucinations again, Georgie?"

It was bitterly cold the day George was buried. The ground was so frozen, it had taken three men the better part of a morning to dig the grave. Icy clouds of breath hovered around the few family members and former co-workers who'd bothered to come. The minister's teeth chattered as he delivered the eulogy, his hands as white as vanilla ice cream. Everyone wished for the service to end as quickly as possible, and their cars waited idling.

As the casket floated soundlessly into its hole, Lithuania, careful of her nails, obligatorily picked up a small lump of dirt and, like it was acid in her hands, quickly threw it at the lid. Then stepping back, she smeared a handkerchief across her palms and paused her weeping long enough to scowl at a laughing couple walking opposite a wrought iron fence at the cemetery's edge. They held hands, kicking merrily at the snow on the sidewalk, apparently oblivious to the funeral. "What a breach of taste," she thought disgustedly, wiping a tear from her cheek. She shot them a disapproving stare, hoping to catch their attention. But they didn't notice her. They merely laughed.

"Probably newlyweds," she shrugged, and thought no more about them . . . until the next day.

THE

DAEMON

LOVER

Shirley Jackson

She had not slept well; from one-thirty, when Jamie left and she went lingeringly to bed, until seven, when she at last allowed herself to get up and make coffee, she had slept fitfully, stirring awake to open her eyes and look into the half-darkness, remembering over and over, slipping again into a feverish dream. She spent almost an hour over her coffee—they were to have a real breakfast on the way—and then, unless she wanted to dress early, had nothing to do. She washed her coffee cup and made the bed, looking carefully over the clothes she planned to wear, worried unnecessarily, at the window, over whether it would be a fine day. She sat down to read, thought that she might write a letter to her sister instead, and began, in her finest handwriting, "Dearest Anne, by the time you get this I will be married. Doesn't it sound funny? I can hardly believe it myself, but when I tell you how it happened, you'll see it's even stranger than that. . . ."

Sitting, pen in hand, she hesitated over what to say next, read the lines already written, and tore up the letter. She went to the window and saw that it was undeniably a fine day. It occurred to her that perhaps she ought not to wear the blue silk dress; it was too plain, almost severe, and she wanted to be soft, feminine. Anxiously she pulled through the dresses in the closet, and hesitated over a print she had worn the summer before; it was too young for her, and it had a ruffled neck, and it was very early in the year for a print dress, but still. . . .

She hung the two dresses side by side on the outside of the

closet door and opened the glass doors carefully closed upon the small closet that was her kitchenette. She turned on the burner under the coffeepot, and went to the window; it was sunny. When the coffeepot began to crackle she came back and poured herself coffee, into a clean cup. I'll have a headache if I don't get some solid food soon, she thought, all this coffee, smoking too much, no real breakfast. A headache on her wedding day; she went and got the tin box of aspirin from the bathroom closet and slipped it into her blue pocketbook. She'd have to change to a brown pocketbook if she wore the print dress, and the only brown pocketbook she had was shabby. Helplessly, she stood looking from the blue pocketbook to the print dress, and then put the pocketbook down and went and got her cofee and sat down near the window, drinking her coffee, and looking carefully around the one-room apartment. They planned to come back here tonight and everything must be correct. With sudden horror she realized that she had forgotten to put clean sheets on the bed; the laundry was freshly back and she took clean sheets and pillow cases from the top shelf of the closet and stripped the bed, working quickly to avoid thinking consciously of why she was changing the sheets. The bed was a studio bed, with a cover to make it look like a couch, and when it was finished no one would have known she had just put clean sheets on it. She took the old sheets and pillow cases into the bathroom and stuffed them down into the hamper, and put the bathroom towels in the hamper too, and clean towels on the bathroom racks. Her coffee was cold when she came back to it, but she drank it anyway.

When she looked at the clock, finally, and saw that it was after nine, she began at last to hurry. She took a bath, and used one of the clean towels, which she put into the hamper and replaced with a clean one. She dressed carefully, all her underwear fresh and most of it new; she put everything she had worn the day before, including her nightgown, into the hamper. When she was ready for her dress, she hesitated before the closet door. The blue dress was certainly decent, and clean, and fairly becoming, but she had worn it several times with Jamie, and there was nothing about it which made it special for a wedding day. The print dress was overly pretty, and new to Jamie, and yet wearing such a print this early in the year was certainly rushing the season. Finally she thought, This is my wedding day, I can dress as I please, and she took the print dress down from the hanger. When she slipped it on over her head it felt fresh and light, but when she looked at herself in the mirror she remembered that the ruffles around the neck did not show her throat to any great advantage, and the wide swinging skirt looked irresistibly made for a girl, for someone who would run freely, dance, swing it with her hips when she walked. Looking at herself in the mirror she thought with revulsion, It's as though I was trying to make myself look prettier than I am, just for him; he'll think I want to look younger because he's marrying me; and she tore the print dress off so quickly that a seam under the arm ripped. In the old blue dress she felt comfortable and familiar, but unexciting. It isn't what you're wearing that matters, she told herself firmly, and turned in dismay to the closet to see if there might be anything else. There was nothing even remotely suitable for her marrying Jamie, and for a minute she thought of going out quickly to some little shop nearby, to get a dress. Then she saw that it was close on ten, and she had no time for more than her hair and her make-up. Her hair was easy, pulled back into a knot at the nape of her neck, but her make-up was another delicate balance between looking as well as possible, and deceiving as little. She could not try to disguise the sallowness of her skin, or the lines around her eyes, today, when it might look as though she were only doing it for her wedding, and yet she could not bear the thought of Jamie's bringing to marriage anyone who looked haggard and lined. You're thirty-four years old after *all*, she told herself cruelly in the bathroom mirror. Thirty, it said on the license.

It was two minutes after ten; she was not satisfied with her clothes, her face, her apartment. She heated the coffee again and sat down in the chair by the window. Can't do anything more now, she thought, no sense trying to improve anything the last minute.

Reconciled, settled, she tried to think of Jamie and could not see his face clearly, or hear his voice. It's always that way with someone you love, she thought, and let her mind slip past today and tomorrow, into the farther future, when Jamie was established with his writing and she had given up her job, the golden house-in-the-country future they had been preparing for the last week. "I used to be a wonderful cook," she had promised Jamie, "with a little time and practice I could remember how to make angel-food cake. And fried chicken," she said, knowing how the words would stay in Jamie's mind, half-tenderly. "And Hollandaise sauce."

Ten-thirty. She stood up and went purposefully to the phone. She dialed, and waited, and the girl's metallic voice said, ". . . the time will be exactly ten-twenty-nine." Half-consciously she set her clock back a minute; she was remembering her own voice saying last night, in the doorway: "Ten o'clock then. I'll be ready. Is it really *true?*"

And Jamie laughing down the hallway.

By eleven o'clock she had sewed up the ripped seam in the print dress and put her sewing-box away carefully in the closet. With the print dress on, she was sitting by the window, drinking another cup of coffee. I could have taken more time over my dressing after all, she thought; but by now it was so late he might come any minute, and she did not dare try to repair anything without starting all over. There was nothing to eat in the apartment except the food she had carefully stocked up for their life beginning together: the unopened package of bacon, the dozen eggs in their box, the unopened bread and the unopened butter; they were for breakfast tomorrow. She thought of running downstairs to the drugstore for something to eat, leaving a note on the door. Then she decided to wait a little longer.

By eleven-thirty she was so dizzy and weak that she had to go downstairs. If Jamie had had a phone she would have called him then. Instead, she opened her desk and wrote a note: "Jamie, have gone downstairs to the drugstore. Back in five minutes." Her pen leaked onto her fingers and she went into the bathroom and washed, using a clean towel which she replaced. She tacked the note on the door, surveyed the apartment once more to make sure that everything was perfect, and closed the door without locking it, in case he should come.

In the drugstore she found that there was nothing she wanted to eat except more coffee, and she left it half-finished because she suddenly realized that Jamie was probably upstairs waiting and impatient, anxious to get started.

But upstairs everything was prepared and quiet, as she had left it, her note unread on the door, the air in the apartment a little stale from too many cigarettes. She opened the window and sat down next to it until she realized that she had been asleep and it was twenty minutes to one.

Now, suddenly, she was frightened. Waking without preparation into the room of waiting and readiness, everything clean and untouched since ten o'clock, she was frightened, and felt an urgent need to hurry. She got up from the chair and almost ran across the room to the bathroom, dashed cold water on her face, and used a clean towel; this time she put the towel carelessly back on the rack without changing it; time enough for that later. Hatless, still in the print dress with a coat thrown on over it, the wrong blue pocketbook with the aspirin inside in her hand, she locked the apartment door behind her, no note this time, and ran down the stairs. She caught a taxi on the corner and gave the driver Jamie's address.

It was no distance at all; she could have walked it if she had not been so weak, but in the taxi she suddenly realized how imprudent it would be to drive brazenly up to Jamie's door, demanding him. She asked the driver, therefore, to let her off at a corner near Jamie's address and, after paying him, waited till he drove away before she started to walk down the block. She had never been here before; the building was pleasant and old, and Jamie's name was not on any of the mailboxes in the vestibule, nor on the doorbells. She checked the address; it was right, and finally she rang the bell marked "Superintendent." After a minute or two the door buzzer rang and she opened the door and went into the dark hall where she hesitated until a door at the end opened and someone said, "Yes?"

She knew at the same moment that she had no idea what to ask, so she moved forward toward the figure waiting against the light of the open doorway. When she was very near, the figure said, "Yes?" again and she saw that it was a man in his shirtsleeves, unable to see her any more clearly than she could see him.

With sudden courage she said, "I'm trying to get in touch with someone who lives in this building and I can't find the name outside."

"What's the name you wanted?" the man asked, and she realized she would have to answer.

"James Harris," she said. "Harris."

The man was silent for a minute and then he said, "Harris."

He turned around to the room inside the lighted doorway and said, "Margie, come here a minute."

"What now?" a voice said from inside, and after a wait long enough for someone to get out of a comfortable chair a woman joined him in the doorway, regarding the dark hall. "Lady here," the man said. "Lady looking for a guy name of Harris, lives here. Anyone in the building?"

"No," the woman said. Her voice sounded amused. "No men named Harris here."

"Sorry," the man said. He started to close the door. "You got the wrong house, lady," he said, and added in a lower voice, "or the wrong guy," and he and the woman laughed.

When the door was almost shut and she was alone in the dark hall she said to the thin lighted crack still showing, "But he *does* live here; I know it."

"Look," the woman said, opening the door again a little, "it happens all the time."

"Please don't make any mistake," she said, and her voice was very dignified, with thirty-four years of accumulated pride. "I'm afraid you don't understand."

"What did he look like?" the woman said wearily, the door still only part open.

"He's rather tall, and fair. He wears a blue suit very often. He's a writer."

"No," the woman said, and then, "Could he have lived on the third floor?"

"I'm not sure."

"There was a fellow," the woman said reflectively. "He wore a blue suit a lot, lived on the third floor for a while. The Roysters lent him their apartment while they were visiting her folks upstate."

"That might be it; I thought, though. . . ."

"This one wore a blue suit mostly, but I don't know how tall he was," the woman said. "He stayed there about a month."

"A month ago is when—"

"You ask the Roysters," the woman said. "They come back this morning. Apartment 3B."

The door closed, definitely. The hall was very dark and the stairs looked darker.

On the second floor there was a little light from a skylight far above. The apartment doors lined up, four on the floor, uncommunicative and silent. There was a bottle of milk outside 2C.

On the third floor, she waited for a minute. There was the sound of music beyond the door of 3B, and she could hear voices. Finally she knocked, and knocked again. The door was opened and the music swept out at her, an early afternoon symphony broadcast. "How do you do," she said politely to this woman in the doorway. "Mrs. Royster?"

"That's right." The woman was wearing a housecoat and last night's make-up.

"I wonder if I might talk to you for a minute?"

"Sure," Mrs. Royster said, not moving.

"About Mr. Harris."

"*What* Mr. Harris?" Mrs. Royster said flatly.

"Mr. James Harris. The gentleman who borrowed your apartment."

"O Lord," Mrs. Royster said. She seemed to open her eyes for the first time. "What'd he do?"

"Nothing. I'm just trying to get in touch with him."

"O Lord," Mrs. Royster said again. Then she opened the door wider and said, "Come in," and then, "Ralph!"

Inside, the apartment was still full of music, and there were suitcases half unpacked on the couch, on the chairs, on the floor. A table in the corner was spread with the remains of a meal, and the young man sitting there, for a minute resembling Jamie, got up and came across the room.

"What about it?" he said.

"Mr. Royster," she said. It was difficult to talk against the music. "The superintendent downstairs told me that this was where Mr. James Harris has been living."

"Sure," he said. "If that was his name."

"I thought you lent him the apartment," she said, surprised.

"*I* don't know anything about him," Mr. Royster said. "He's one of Dottie's friends."

"Not *my* friends," Mrs. Royster said. "No friend of mine." She had gone over to the table and was spreading peanut butter on a piece of bread. She took a bite and said thickly, waving the bread and peanut butter at her husband, "Not *my* friend."

"You picked him up at one of those damn meetings," Mr. Royster said. He shoved a suitcase off the chair next to the radio and sat down, picking up a magazine from the floor next to him. "I never said more'n ten words to him."

"You said it was okay to lend him the place," Mrs. Royster said before she took another bite. "You never said a word against him, after *all.*"

"*I* don't say anything about *your* friends," Mr. Royster said.

"If he'd of been a friend of mine you would have said *plenty*, believe me," Mrs. Royster said darkly. She took another bite and said, "Believe me, he would have said *plenty.*"

"That's all I want to hear," Mr. Royster said, over the top of the magazine. "No more, now."

"You see." Mrs. Royster pointed the bread and peanut butter at her husband. "That's the way it is, day and night."

There was silence except for the music bellowing out of the radio next to Mr. Royster, and then she said, in a voice she hardly trusted to be heard over the radio noise, "Has he gone, then?"

"Who?" Mrs. Royster demanded, looking up from the peanut butter jar.

"Mr. James Harris."

"Him? He must've left this morning, before we got back. No sign of him anywhere."

"Gone?"

"Everything was fine, though, perfectly fine. I told you," she said to Mr. Royster, "I told you he'd take care of everything fine. I can always tell."

"You were lucky," Mr. Royster said.

"Not a thing out of place," Mrs. Royster said. She waved her bread and peanut butter inclusively. "Everything just the way we left it," she said.

"Do you know where he is now?"

"Not the slightest idea," Mrs. Royster said cheerfully. "But, like I said, he left everything fine. Why?" she asked suddenly. "You looking for *him?*"

"It's very important."

"I'm sorry he's not here," Mrs. Royster said. She stepped forward politely when she saw her visitor turn toward the door.

"Maybe the super saw him," Mr. Royster said into the magazine.

When the door was closed behind her the hall was dark again, but the sound of the radio was deadened. She was halfway down the first flight of stairs when the door was opened and Mrs. Royster shouted down the stairwell, "If I see him I'll tell him you were looking for him."

What can I do? she thought, out on the street again. It was impossible to go home, not with Jamie somewhere between here and there. She stood on the sidewalk so long that a woman, leaning out of a window across the way, turned and called to someone inside to come see. Finally, on an impulse, she went into the small delicatessen next door to the apartment house, on the side that led to her own apartment. There was a small man reading a newspaper, leaning against the counter; when she came in he looked up and came down inside the counter to meet her.

Over the glass case of cold meats and cheese she said, timidly, "I'm trying to get in touch with a man who lived in the apartment house next door, and I just wondered if you know him."

"Whyn't you ask the people there?" the man said, his eyes narrow, inspecting her.

It's because I'm not buying anything, she thought, and she said, "I'm sorry. I asked them, but they don't know anything about him. They think he left this morning."

"I don't know what you want *me* to do," he said, moving a little back toward his newspaper. "I'm not here to keep track of guys going in and out next door."

She said quickly, "I thought you might have noticed, that's all. He would have been coming past here, a little before ten o'clock. He was rather tall, and he usually wore a blue suit."

"Now how many men in blue suits go past here every day, lady?" the man demanded. "You think I got nothing to do but—"

"I'm sorry," she said. She heard him say, "For God's sake," as she went out the door.

As she walked toward the corner, she thought, he must have come this way, it's the way he'd go to get to my house, it's the only way for him to walk. She tried to think of Jamie: where would he have crossed the street? What sort of person was he actually—would he cross in front of his own apartment house, at random in the middle of the block, at the corner?

On the corner was a newsstand; they might have seen him there. She hurried on and waited while a man bought a paper and a woman asked directions. When the newsstand man looked at her she said, "Can you possibly tell me if a rather tall young man in a blue suit went past here this morning around ten o'clock?" When the man only looked at her, his eyes wide and his mouth a little open, she thought, he thinks it's a joke, or a trick, and she said urgently, "It's very important, please believe me. I'm not teasing you."

"*Look*, lady," the man began, and she said eagerly, "He's a writer. He might have bought magazines here."

"What you want him for?" the man asked. He looked at her, smiling, and she realized that there was another man waiting in back of her and the newsdealer's smile included him. "Never mind," she said, but the newsdealer said, "Listen, maybe he did come by here." His smile was knowing and his eyes shifted over her shoulder to the man in back of her. She was suddenly horribly aware of her over-young print dress, and pulled her coat around her quickly. The newsdealer said, with vast thoughtfulness, "Now I don't know for sure, mind you, but there might have been someone like your gentleman friend coming by this morning."

"About ten?"

"About ten," the newsdealer agreed. "Tall fellow, blue suit. I wouldn't be at all surprised."

"Which way did he go?" she said eagerly. "Uptown?"

"Uptown," the newsdealer said, nodding. "He went uptown. That's just exactly it. What can I do for you, sir?"

She stepped back, holding her coat around her. The man who had been standing behind her looked at her over his shoulder and then he and the newsdealer looked at one another. She wondered for a minute whether or not to tip the newsdealer but when both men began to laugh she moved hurriedly on across the street.

Uptown, she thought, that's right, and she started up the avenue, thinking: He wouldn't have to cross the avenue, just go up six blocks and turn down my street, so long as he started uptown. About a block farther on she passed a florist's shop; there was a wedding display in the window and she thought, This is my wedding day after all, he might have gotten flowers to bring me, and she went inside. The florist came out of the back of the shop, smiling and sleek, and she said, before he could speak, so that he wouldn't have a chance to think she was buying anything: "It's *terribly* important that I get in touch with a gentleman who may have stopped in here to buy flowers this morning. *Terribly* important."

She stopped for breath, and the florist said, "Yes, what sort of flowers were they?"

"I don't know," she said, surprised. "He never—" She stopped and said, "He was a rather tall young man, in a blue suit. It was about ten o'clock."

"I see," the florist said. "Well, *really*, I'm afraid . . ."

"But it's *so* important," she said. "He may have been in a hurry," she added helpfully.

"Well," the florist said. He smiled genially, showing all his small teeth. "For a *lady*," he said. He went to a stand and opened a large book. "Where were they to be sent?" he asked.

"Why," she said, "I don't think he'd have sent them. You see, he was coming—that is, he'd *bring* them."

"Madam," the florist said; he was offended. His smile became deprecatory, and he went on, "Really, you must realize that unless I have *something* to go on. . . ."

"*Please* try to remember," she begged. "He was tall, and had a blue suit, and it was about ten this morning."

The florist closed his eyes, one finger to his mouth, and thought deeply. Then he shook his head. "I simply *can't*," he said.

"Thank you," she said despondently, and started for the door, when the florist said, in a shrill, excited voice, "Wait! Wait just a moment, madam." She turned and the florist, thinking again, said finally, "Chrysanthemums?" He looked at her inquiringly.

"Oh, *no*," she said; her voice shook a little and she waited for a minute before she went on. "Not for an occasion like this, I'm sure."

The florist tightened his lips and looked away coldly. "Well, of *course* I don't know the *occasion*," he said, "but I'm almost certain that the gentleman you were inquiring for came in this morning and purchased chrysanthemums. No delivery."

"You're *sure*?" she asked.

"Positive," the florist said emphatically. "That was absolutely the man." He smiled brilliantly, and she smiled back and said, "Well, thank you very much."

He escorted her to the door. "Nice corsage?" he said, as they went through the shop. "Red roses? Gardenias?"

"It was very kind of you to help me," she said at the door.

"Ladies always look their best in flowers," he said, bending his head toward her. "Orchids, perhaps?"

"No, thank you," she said, and he said, "I hope you find your young man," and gave it a nasty sound.

Going on up the street she thought, Everyone thinks it's so *funny*: and she pulled her coat tighter around her, so that only the ruffle around the bottom of the print dress was showing.

There was a policeman on the corner, and she thought, Why don't I go to the police—you go to the police for a missing person. And then thought, What a fool I'd look like. She had a quick picture of herself standing in a police station, saying, "Yes, we were going to be married today, but he didn't come," and the policemen, three or four of them standing around listening, looking at her, at the print dress, at her too-bright make-up, smiling at one another. She couldn't tell them any more than that, could not say, "Yes, it looks silly, doesn't it, me all dressed up and trying to find the young man who promised to marry me, but what about all of it you don't know? I have more than this, more than you can see: talent, perhaps, and humor of a sort, and I'm a lady and I have pride and affection and delicacy and a certain clear view of life that might make a man satisfied and productive and happy; there's more than you think when you look at me."

The police were obviously impossible, leaving out Jamie and what he might think when he heard she'd set the police after him. "No, no," she said aloud, hurrying her steps, and someone passing stopped and looked after her.

On the coming corner—she was three blocks from her own street—was a shoeshine stand, an old man sitting almost asleep in one of the chairs. She stopped in front of him and waited, and after a minute he opened his eyes and smiled at her.

"Look," she said, the words coming before she thought of them, "I'm sorry to bother you, but I'm looking for a young man who came up this way about ten this morning, did you see him?" And she began her description, "Tall, blue suit, carrying a bunch of flowers?"

The old man began to nod before she was finished. "I saw him," he said. "Friend of yours?"

"Yes," she said, and smiled back involuntarily.

The old man blinked his eyes and said, "I remember I thought, You're going to see your girl, young fellow. They all go to see their girls," he said, and shook his head tolerantly.

"Which way did he go? Straight on up the avenue?"

"That's right," the old man said. "Got a shine, had his flowers, all dressed up, in an awful hurry. You got a girl, I thought."

"Thank you," she said, fumbling in her pocket for her loose change.

"She sure must of been glad to see him, the way he looked," the old man said.

"Thank you," she said again, and brought her hand empty from her pocket.

For the first time she was really sure he would be waiting for her, and she hurried up the three blocks, the skirt of the print dress swinging under her coat, and turned into her own block. From the corner she could not see her own windows, could not see Jamie looking out, waiting for her, and going down the block she was almost running to get to him. Her key trembled in her fingers at the downstairs door, and as she glanced into the drugstore she thought of her panic, drinking coffee there this morning, and almost laughed. At her own door she could wait no longer, but began to say, "Jamie, I'm here, I was so worried," even before the door was open.

Her own apartment was waiting for her, silent, barren, afternoon shadows lengthening from the window. For a minute she saw only the empty coffee cup, thought, He has been here waiting, before she recognized it as her own, left from the morning. She looked all over the room, into the closet, into the bathroom.

"I never saw him," the clerk in the drugstore said. "I know because I would of noticed the flowers. No one like that's been in."

The old man at the shoeshine stand woke up again to see her standing in front of him. "Hello again," he said, and smiled.

"Are you *sure?*" she demanded. "Did he go on up the avenue?"

"I watched him," the old man said, dignified against her tone. "I thought, There's a young man's got a girl, and I watched him right into the house."

"What house?" she said remotely.

"Right there," the old man said. He leaned forward to point. "The next block. With his flowers and his shine and going to see his girl. Right into her house."

"Which one?" she said.

"About the middle of the block," the old man said. He looked at her with suspicion, and said, "What you trying to do, anyway?"

She almost ran, without stopping to say "Thank you." Up on the next block she walked quickly, searching the houses from the outside to see if Jamie looked from a window, listening to hear his laughter somewhere inside.

A woman was sitting in front of one of the houses, pushing a baby carriage monotonously back and forth the length of her arm. The baby inside slept, moving back and forth.

The question was fluent, by now. "I'm sorry, but did you see a young man go into one of these houses about ten this morning? He was tall, wearing a blue suit, carrying a bunch of flowers."

A boy about twelve stopped to listen, turning intently from one to the other, occasionally glancing at the baby.

"Listen," the woman said tiredly, "the kid has his bath at ten. Would I see strange men walking around? I ask you."

"Big bunch of flowers?" the boy asked, pulling at her coat. "Big bunch of flowers? I seen him, missus."

She looked down and the boy grinned insolently at her. "Which house did he go in?" she asked wearily.

"You gonna divorce him?" the boy asked insistently.

"That's not nice to ask the lady," the woman rocking the carriage said.

"Listen," the boy said, "I seen him. He went in there." He pointed to the house next door. "I followed him," the boy said. "He give me a quarter." The boy dropped his voice to a growl, and said, " 'This is a big day for me, kid,' he says. Give me a quarter."

She gave him a dollar bill. "Where?" she said.

"Top floor," the boy said. "I followed him till he give me the quarter. Way to the top." He backed up the sidewalk, out of reach, with the dollar bill. "You gonna divorce him?" he asked again.

"Was he carrying flowers?"

"Yeah," the boy said. He began to screech. "You gonna divorce him, missus? You got something on him?" He went careening down the street, howling, "She's got something on the poor guy," and the woman rocking the baby laughed.

The street door of the apartment house was unlocked; there were no bells in the outer vestibule, and no lists of names. The stairs were narrow and dirty; there were two doors on the top floor. The front one was the right one; there was a crumpled florist's paper on the floor outside the door, and a knotted paper ribbon, like a clue, like the final clue in the paper-chase.

She knocked, and thought she heard voices inside, and she thought, suddenly, with terror, What shall I say if Jamie is there, if he comes to the door? The voices seemed suddenly still. She knocked again and there was silence, except for something that might have been laughter far away. He could have seen me from the window, she thought, it's the front apartment and that little boy made a dreadful noise. She waited, and knocked again, but there was silence.

Finally she went to the other door on the floor, and knocked. The door swung open beneath her hand and she saw the empty attic room, bare lath on the walls, floorboards unpainted. She stepped just inside, looking around; the room was filled with bags of plaster, piles of old newspapers, a broken trunk. There was a noise which she suddenly realized was a rat, and then she saw it, sitting very close to her, near the wall, its evil face alert, bright eyes watching her. She stumbled in her haste to be out with the door closed, and the skirt of the print dress caught and tore.

She knew there was someone inside the other apartment, because she was sure she could hear low voices and sometimes laughter. She came back many times, every day for the first week. She came on her way to work, in the mornings; in the evenings, on her way to dinner alone, but no matter how often or how firmly she knocked, no one ever came to the door.

A

HAUNTED

HOUSE

Virginia Woolf

Whatever hour you woke there was a door shutting. From room to room they went, hand in hand, lifting here, opening there, making sure—a ghostly couple.

"Here we left it," she said. And he added, "Oh, but here too!" "It's upstairs," she murmured. "And in the garden," he whispered. "Quietly," they said, "or we shall wake them."

But it wasn't that you woke us. Oh, no. "They're looking for it; they're drawing the curtain," one might say, and so read on a page or two. "Now they've found it," one would be certain, stopping the pencil on the margin. And then, tired of reading, one might rise and see for oneself, the house all empty, the doors standing open, only the wood pigeons bubbling with content and the hum of the threshing machine sounding from the farm. "What did I come in here for? What did I want to find?" My hands were empty. "Perhaps it's upstairs then?" The apples were in the loft. And so down again, the garden still as ever, only the book had slipped into the grass.

But they had found it in the drawing-room. Not that one could ever see them. The window panes reflected apples, reflected roses; all the leaves were green in the glass. If they moved in the drawing-room, the apple only turned its yellow side. Yet, the moment after, if the door was opened, spread about the floor, hung upon the walls, pendant from the ceiling— what? My hands were empty. The shadow of a thrush crossed the carpet; from the deepest wells of silence the wood pigeon drew its bubble of sound. "Safe, safe, safe," the pulse of the

house beat softly. "The treasure buried; the room . . ." the
pulse stopped short. Oh, was that the buried treasure?

A moment later the light had faded. Out in the garden then?
But the trees spun darkness for a wandering beam of sun. So
fine, so rare, coolly sunk beneath the surface the beam I sought
always burnt behind the glass. Death was the glass; death was
between us; coming to the woman first, hundreds of years ago,
leaving the house, sealing all the windows; the rooms were
darkened. He left it, left her, went North, went East, saw the
stars turned in the Southern sky; sought the house, found it
dropped beneath the Downs. "Safe, safe, safe," the pulse of
the house beat gladly. "The Treasure yours."

The wind roars up the avenue. Trees stoop and bend this
way and that. Moonbeams splash and spill wildly in the rain.
But the beam of the lamp falls straight from the window. The
candle burns stiff and still. Wandering through the house,
opening the windows, whispering not to wake us, the ghostly
couple seek their joy.

"Here we slept," she says. And he adds, "Kisses without
number." "Waking in the morning—" "Silver between the
trees—" "Upstairs—" "In the garden—" "When summer came—"
"In winter snowtime—" The doors go shutting far in the distance, gently knocking like the pulse of a heart.

Nearer they come; cease at the doorway. The wind falls, the
rain slides silver down the glass. Our eyes darken; we hear no
steps beside us; we see no lady spread her ghostly cloak. His
hands shield the lantern. "Look," he breathes. "Sound asleep.
Love upon their lips."

Stooping, holding their silver lamp above us, long they look
and deeply. Long they pause. The wind drives straightly; the
flame stoops slightly. Wild beams of moonlight cross both
floor and wall, and, meeting, stain the faces bent; the faces
pondering; the faces that search the sleepers and seek their
hidden joy.

"Safe, safe, safe," the heart of the house beats proudly.
"Long years—" he sighs. "Again you found me." "Here," she
murmurs, "sleeping; in the garden reading; laughing, rolling
apples in the loft. Here we left our treasure—" Stooping, their
light lifts the lids upon my eyes. "Safe! safe! safe!" the pulse of
the house beats wildly. Waking, I cry "Oh, is this *your* buried
treasure? The light in the heart."

UP

NORTH

Mavis Gallant

When they woke up in the train, their bed was black with soot
and there was soot in his Mum's blondie hair. They were miles
north of Montreal, which had, already, sunk beneath his remembrance. "D'you know what I sor in the night?" said Dennis. He had to keep his back turned while she dressed. They
were both in the same berth, to save money. He was small,
and didn't take up much room, but when he woke up in that
sooty autumn dawn, he found he was squashed flat against the
side of the train. His Mum was afraid of falling out and into the
aisle; they had a lower berth, but she didn't trust the strength
of the curtain. Now she was dressing, and sobbing; really
sobbing. For this was worse than anything she had ever been
through, she told him. She had been right through the worst of
the air raids, yet this was the worst, this waking in the cold,
this dark, dirty dawn, everything dirty she touched, her
clothes—oh, her clothes!—and now having to dress as she lay
flat on her back. She daren't sit up. She might knock her
head.

"You know what I sor?" said the child patiently. "Well, the
train must of stopped, see, and some little men with bundles
on their backs got on. Other men was holding lanterns. They
were all little. They were all talking French."

"Shut up," said Mum. "Do you hear me?"

"Sor them," said the boy.

"You and your bloody elves."

"They was people."

281

"Little men with bundles," said Mum, trying to dress again. "You start your fairy tales with your Dad and I don't know what *he'll* give you."

It was this mythical, towering, half-remembered figure they were now travelling to join up north.

Roy McLaughlin, travelling on the same train, saw the pair, presently, out of his small red-lidded eyes. Den and his Mum were dressed and as clean as they could make themselves, and sitting at the end of the car. McLaughlin was the last person to get up, and he climbed down from his solitary green-curtained cubicle conspicuous and alone. He had to pad the length of the car in a trench coat and city shoes—he had never owned slippers, bathrobe, or pajamas—past the passengers, who were drawn with fatigue, pale under the lights. They were men, mostly; some soldiers. The Second World War had been finished, in Europe, a year and five months. It was a dirty, rickety train going up to Abitibi. McLaughlin was returning to a construction camp after three weeks in Montreal. He saw the girl, riding with her back to the engine, doing her nails, and his faculties absently registered "Limey bride" as he went by. The kid, looking out the window, turned and stared. McLaughlin thought "Pest," but only because children and other men's wives made him nervous and sour when they were brought around camp on a job.

After McLaughlin had dressed and had swallowed a drink in the washroom—for he was sick and trembling after his holiday— he came and sat down opposite the blond girl. He did not bother to explain that he had to sit somewhere while his berth was being dismantled. His arms were covered with coarse red hair; he had rolled up the sleeves of his khaki shirt. He spread his pale, heavy hands on his knees. The child stood between them, fingertips on the sooty window sill, looking out at the breaking day. Once, the train stopped for a long time; the engine was being changed, McLaughlin said. They had been rolling north but were now turning west. At six o'clock, in about an hour, Dennis and his mother would have to get down, and onto another train, and go north once more. Dennis could not see any station where they were now. There was a swamp with bristling black rushes, red as ink. It was the autumn sunrise; cold, red. It was so strange to him, so singular, that he could not have said an hour later which feature of the scene was in the foreground or to the left or right. Two women wearing army battle jackets over their dresses, with their hair piled up in front, like his mother's, called and giggled to someone they had put on the train. They were fat and dark—grinny. His mother looked at them with detestation, recognizing what they were; for she hated whores. She had always acted on the desire of the moment, without thought of gain, and she had taken the consequences (Dennis) without complaint. Dennis saw that she was hating the women, and so he looked elsewhere. On a wooden fence sat four or five men in open shirts and patched trousers. They had dull, dark hair, and let their mouths sag as though they were too tired or too sleepy to keep them closed. Something about them was displeasing to the child, and he thought that this was an ugly place with ugly people. It was also a dirty place; every time Dennis put his hands on the window sill they came off black.

"Come down any time to see a train go by," said McLaughlin, meaning those men. "Get up in the *night* to see a train."

The train moved. It was still dark enough outside for Dennis to see his face in the window and for the light from the windows to fall in pale squares on the upturned vanishing faces and on the little trees. Dennis heard his mother's new friend say, "Well, there's different possibilities." They passed into an unchanging landscape of swamp and bracken and stunted trees. Then the lights inside the train were put out and he saw that the sky was blue and bright. His mother and McLaughlin, seen in the window, had been remote and bodiless; through their transparent profiles he had seen the yellowed trees going by. Now he could not see their faces at all.

"He's been back in Canada since the end of the war. He was wounded. Den hardly knows him," he heard his mother say. "I couldn't come. I had to wait my turn. We were over a thousand war brides on that ship. He was with Aluminium when he first came back." She pronounced the five vowels in the word.

"You'll be all right there," said McLaughlin. "It's a big place. Schools. All company."

"Pardon me?"

"I mean it all belongs to Aluminum. Only if that's where you're going you happen to be on the wrong train."

"He isn't there now. He hates towns. He seems to move about a great deal. He drives a bulldozer, you see."

"Owns it?" said McLaughlin.

"Why, I shouldn't *think* so. Drives for another man, I think he said."

The boy's father fell into the vast pool of casual labor, drifters; there was a social hierarchy in the north, just as in Heaven. McLaughlin was an engineer. He took another look at the boy: black hair, blue eyes. The hair was coarse, straight, rather dull; Indian hair. The mother was a blonde; touched up a bit, but still blond.

"What name?" said McLaughlin on the upward note of someone who has asked the same question twice.

"Cameron. Donald Cameron."

That meant nothing, still; McLaughlin had worked in a place on James Bay where the Indians were named MacDonald and Ogilvie and had an unconquered genetic strain of blue eyes.

"D'you know about any ghosts?" said the boy, turning to McLaughlin. McLaughlin's eyes were paler than his own, which were a deep slate blue, like the eyes of a newly born child. McLaughlin saw the way he held his footing on the rocking train, putting out a few fingers to the window sill only for the form of the thing. He looked all at once ridiculous and dishonored in his cheap English clothes—the little jacket, the Tweedledum cap on his head. He outdistanced his clothes; he was better than they were. But he was rushing on this train into an existence where his clothes would be too good for him.

"D'you know about any ghosts?" said the boy again.

"Oh, sure," said McLaughlin, and shivered, for he still felt sick, even though he was sharing a bottle with the Limey bride. He said, "Indians see them," which was as close as he could come to being crafty. But there was no reaction out of the mother; she was not English for nothing.

"You seen any?"

"*I'm* not an Indian," McLaughlin started to say; instead he said, "Well, yes. I saw the ghost, or something like the ghost, of a dog I had."

They looked at each other, and the boy's mother said, "Stop that, you two. Stop that this minute."

"I'll tell you a strange thing about Dennis," said his mother. "It's this. There's times he gives me the creeps."

Dennis was lying on the seat beside her with his head on her lap.

She said, "If I don't like it I can clear out. I was a waitress. There's always work."

"Or find another man," McLaughlin said. "Only it won't be me, girlie. I'll be far away."

"Den says that when the train stopped he saw a lot of elves," she said, complaining.

"Not elves—men," said Dennis. "Some of them had mattresses rolled up on their backs. They were little and bent over. They were talking French. They were going up north."

McLaughlin coughed and said, "He means settlers. They were sent up on this same train during the depression. But that's nine, ten years ago. It was supposed to clear the unemployed out of the towns, get them off relief. But there wasn't anything up here then. The winters were terrible. A lot of them died."

"He couldn't know that," said Mum edgily. "For that matter, how can he tell what is French? He's never heard any."

"No, he couldn't know. It was around ten years ago, when times were bad."

"Are they good now?"

"Jeez, after a *war?*" He shoved his hand in the pocket of his shirt, where he kept a roll, and he let her see the edge of it.

She made no comment, but put her hand on Den's head and said to him, "You didn't see anyone. Now shut up."

"Sor 'em," the boy said in a voice as low as he could descend without falling into a whisper.

"You'll see what your Dad'll give you when you tell lies." But she was halfhearted about the threat and did not quite believe in it. She had been attracted to the scenery, whose persistent sameness she could no longer ignore. "It's not proper country," she said. "It's bare."

"Not enough for me," said McLaughlin. "Too many people. I keep on moving north."

"I want to see some Indians," said Dennis, sitting up.

"There aren't any," his mother said. "Only in films."

"I don't like Canada." He held her arm. "Let's go home now."

"It's the train whistle. It's so sad. It gets him down."

The train slowed, jerked, flung them against each other, and came to a stop. It was quite day now; their faces were plain and clear, as if drawn without shading on white paper. McLaughlin

felt responsible for them, even compassionate; the change in
him made the boy afraid.

"We're getting down, Den," said his Mum, with great, wide
eyes. "We take another train. See? It'll be grand. Do you hear
what Mum's telling you?"

He was determined not to leave the train, and clung to the
window sill, which was too smooth and narrow to provide a
grip; McLaughlin had no difficulty getting him away. "I'll give
you a present," he said hurriedly. But he slapped all his
pockets and found nothing to give. He did not think of the
money, and his watch had been stolen in Montreal. The woman
and the boy struggled out with their baggage, and McLaughlin,
who had descended first so as to help them down, reached up
and swung the boy in his arms.

"The Indians!" the boy cried, clinging to the train, to air; to
anything. His face was momentarily muffled by McLaughlin's
shirt. His cap fell to the ground. He screamed, "Where's
Mum? I never saw *anything!*"

"You saw Indians," said McLaughlin. "On the rail fence, at
that long stop. Look, don't worry your mother. Don't keep
telling her what you haven't seen. You'll be seeing plenty of
everything now."

THE MYSTERIES

OF THE

JOY RIO

Tennessee Williams

Perhaps because he was a watch repairman, Mr. Gonzales had grown to be rather indifferent to time. A single watch or clock can be a powerful influence on a man, but when a man lives among as many watches and clocks as crowded the tiny, dim shop of Mr. Gonzales, some lagging behind, some skipping ahead, but all ticking monotonously on in their witless fashion, the multitude of them may be likely to deprive them of importance, as a gem loses its value when there are too many just like it which are too easily or cheaply obtainable. At any rate, Mr. Gonzales kept very irregular hours, if he could be said to keep any hours at all, and if he had not been where he was for such a long time, his trade would have suffered badly. But Mr. Gonzales had occupied his tiny shop for more than twenty years, since he had come to the city as a boy of nineteen to work as an apprentice to the original owner of the shop, a very strange and fat man of German descent named Kroger, Emiel Kroger, who had now been dead a long time. Emiel Kroger, being a romantically practical Teuton, had taken time, the commodity he worked with, with intense seriousness. In practically all his behavior he had imitated a perfectly adjusted fat silver watch. Mr. Gonzales, who was then young enough to be known as Pablo, had been his only sustained flirtation with the confusing, quicksilver world that exists outside of regularities. He had met Pablo during a watchmakers' convention in Dallas, Texas, where Pablo, who had illegally come into the country from Mexico a few days before, was drifting hungrily about the

287

streets, and at that time Mr. Gonzales, Pablo, had not grown
plump but had a lustrous dark grace which had completely
bewitched Mr. Kroger. For as I have noted already, Mr.
Kroger was a fat and strange man, subject to the kind of
bewitchment that the graceful young Pablo could cast. The
spell was so strong that it interrupted the fleeting and furtive
practices of a lifetime in Mr. Kroger and induced him to take
the boy home with him, to his shop-residence, where Pablo,
now grown to the mature and fleshy proportions of Mr. Gonzales, had lived ever since, for three years before the death of his
protector and for more than seventeen years after that, as the
inheritor of shop-residence, clocks, watches, and everything
else that Mr. Kroger had owned except a few pieces of dining-
room silver which Emiel Kroger had left as a token bequest to
a married sister in Toledo.

Some of these facts are of dubious pertinence to the little
history which is to be unfolded. The important one is the fact
that Mr. Gonzales had managed to drift enviably apart from the
regularities that rule most other lives. Some days he would not
open his shop at all and some days he would open it only for an
hour or two in the morning, or in the late evening when other
shops had closed, and in spite of these caprices he managed to
continue to get along fairly well, due to the excellence of his
work, when he did it, the fact that he was so well established in
his own quiet way, the advantage of his location in a neighborhood where nearly everybody had an old alarm-clock which
had to be kept in condition to order their lives (this community being one inhabited mostly by people with small-paying
jobs), but it was also due in measurable part to the fact that the
thrifty Mr. Kroger, when he finally succumbed to a chronic
disease of the bowels, had left a tidy sum in government
bonds, and this capital, bringing in about a hundred and seventy dollars a month, would have kept Mr. Gonzales going
along in a commonplace but comfortable fashion even if he had
declined to do anything whatsoever. It was a pity that the late,
or rather long-ago, Mr. Kroger, had not understood what a
fundamentally peaceable sort of young man he had taken under
his wing. Too bad he couldn't have guessed how perfectly
everything suited Pablo Gonzales. But youth does not betray
its true nature as palpably as the later years do, and Mr.
Kroger had taken the animated allure of his young protégé, the

flickering lights in his eyes and his quick, nervous movements, his very grace and slimness, as meaning something difficult to keep hold of. And as the old gentleman declined in health, as he did quite steadily during the three years that Pablo lived with him, he was never certain that the incalculably precious bird flown into his nest was not one of sudden passage but rather the kind that prefers to keep a faithful commitment to a single place, the nest-building kind, and not only that, but the very-rare-indeed-kind that gives love back as generously as he takes it. The long-ago Mr. Kroger had paid little attention to his illness, even when it entered the stage of acute pain, so intense was his absorption in what he thought was the tricky business of holding Pablo close to him. If only he had known that for all this time after his decease the boy would still be in the watchshop, how it might have relieved him! But on the other hand, maybe this anxiety, mixed as it was with so much tenderness and sad delight, was actually a blessing, standing as it did between the dying old man and a concern with death.

Pablo had never flown. But the sweet bird of youth had flown from Pablo Gonzales, leaving him rather sad, with a soft yellow face that was just as round as the moon. Clocks and watches he fixed with marvelous delicacy and precision, but he paid no attention to them; he had grown as obliviously accustomed to their many small noises as someone grows to the sound of waves who has always lived by the sea. Although he wasn't aware of it, it was actually light by which he told time, and always in the afternoons when the light had begun to fail (through the narrow window and narrower, dusty skylight at the back of the shop), Mr. Gonzales automatically rose from his stooped position over littered table and gooseneck lamp, took off his close-seeing glasses with magnifying lenses, and took to the street. He did not go far and he always went in the same direction, across town toward the river where there was an old opera house, now converted into a third-rate cinema, which specialized in the showing of cowboy pictures and other films of the sort that have a special appeal to children and male adolescents. The name of this moviehouse was the Joy Rio, a name peculiar enough but nowhere nearly so peculiar as the place itself.

The old opera house was a miniature of all the great opera houses of the old world, which is to say its interior was faded gilt and incredibly old and abused red damask which extended upwards through at least three tiers and possibly five. The upper stairs, that is, the stairs beyond the first gallery, were roped off and unlighted and the top of the theater was so peculiarly dusky, even with the silver screen flickering far below it, that Mr. Gonzales, used as he was to close work, could not have made it out from below. Once he had been there when the lights came on in the Joy Rio, but the coming on of the lights had so enormously confused and embarrassed him, that looking up was the last thing in the world he felt like doing. He had buried his nose in the collar of his coat and had scuttled out as quickly as a cockroach makes for the nearest shadow when a kitchen light comes on.

I have already suggested that there was something a bit special and obscure about Mr. Gonzales' habitual attendance at the Joy Rio, and that was my intention. For Mr. Gonzales had inherited more than the material possessions of his dead benefactor: he had also come into custody of his old protector's fleeting and furtive practices in dark places, the practices which Emiel Kroger had given up only when Pablo had come into his fading existence. The old man had left Mr. Gonzales the full gift of his shame, and now Mr. Gonzales did the sad, lonely things that Mr. Kroger had done for such a long time before his one lasting love came to him. Mr. Kroger had even practiced those things in the same place in which they were practiced now by Mr. Gonzales, in the many mysterious recesses of the Joy Rio, and Mr. Gonzales knew about this. He knew about it because Mr. Kroger had told him. Emiel Kroger had confessed his whole life and soul to Pablo Gonzales. It was his theory, the theory of most immoralists, that the soul becomes intolerably burdened with lies that have to be told to the world in order to be permitted to live in the world, and that unless this burden is relieved by entire honesty with *some one* person, who is trusted and adored, the soul will finally collapse beneath its weight of falsity. Much of the final months of the life of Emiel Kroger, increasingly dimmed by morphia, were devoted to these whispered confessions to his adored apprentice, and it was as if he had breathed the guilty soul of his past into the ears and brain and blood of the youth who listened, and not long after the death of Mr. Kroger, Pablo, who had stayed slim until then, had begun to accumulate fat. He never became anywhere nearly so gross as Emiel Kroger had been, but his delicate frame disappeared sadly from view among the irrelevant curves of a sallow plumpness. One by one the perfections which he had owned were folded away as Pablo put on fat as a widow puts on black garments. For a year beauty lingered about him, ghostly, continually fading, and then it went out altogether, and at twenty-five he was already the nondescriptly plump and moonfaced little man that he now was at forty, and if in his waking hours somebody to whom he would have to give a true answer had enquired of him, Pablo Gonzales, how much do you think about the dead Mr. Kroger, he probably would have shrugged and said, *Not much now. It's such a long time ago*. But if the question were asked him while he slept, the guileless heart of the sleeper would have responded, *Always, always!*

II

Now across the great marble stairs, that rose above the first gallery of the Joy Rio to the uncertain number of galleries above it, there had been fastened a greasy and rotting length of old velvet rope at the center of which was hung a sign that said to *Keep Out*. But that rope had not always been there. It had been there about twenty years, but the late Mr. Kroger had known the Joy Rio in the days before the flight of stairs was roped off. In those days the mysterious upper galleries of the Joy Rio had been a sort of fiddler's green where practically every device and fashion of carnality had run riot in a gloom so thick that a chance partner could only be discovered by touch. There were not rows of benches (as there were now on the orchestra level and the one gallery still kept in use), but strings of tiny boxes, extending in semicircles from one side of the great proscenium to the other. In some of these boxes broken-legged chairs might be found lying on their sides and shreds of old hangings still clung to the sliding brass loops at the entrances. According to Emiel Kroger, who is our only authority on these mysteries which share his remoteness in time, one lived up there, in the upper reaches of the Joy Rio, an almost sightless existence where the other senses, the senses of smell and touch and hearing, had to develop a preternatural keenness in order to spare one from making awkward mistakes,

such as taking hold of the knee of a boy when it was a girl's
knee one looked for, and where sometimes little scenes of
panic occurred when a mistake of gender or of compatibility
had been carried to a point where radical correction was called
for. There had been many fights, there had even been rape and
murder in those ancient boxes, till finally the obscure management of the Joy Rio had been compelled by the pressure of
notoriety to shut down that part of the immense old building
which had offered its principal enticement, and the Joy Rio,
which had flourished until then, had then gone into sharp
decline. It had been closed down and then reopened and
closed down and reopened again. For several years it had
opened and shut like a nervous lady's fan. Those were the
years in which Mr. Kroger was dying. After his death the fitful
era subsided, and now for about ten years the Joy Rio had been
continually active as a third-rate cinema, closed only for one
week during a threatened epidemic of poliomyelitis some years
past and once for a few days when a small fire had damaged the
projection booth. But nothing happened there now of a nature
to provoke a disturbance. There were no complaints to the
management or the police, and the dark glory of the upper
galleries was a legend in such memories as that of the late
Emiel Kroger and the present Pablo Gonzales, and one by one,
of course, those memories died out and the legend died out
with them. Places like the Joy Rio and the legends about them
make one more than usually aware of the short bloom and the
long fading out of things. The angel of such a place is a fat
silver angel of sixty-three years in a shiny dark-blue alpaca
jacket, with short, fat fingers that leave á damp mark where
they touch, that sweat and tremble as they caress between
whispers, an angel of such a kind as would be kicked out of
heaven and laughed out of hell and admitted to earth only by a
grace of its habitual slyness, its gift for making itself a counter-
feit being, and the connivance of those that a quarter tip and an
old yellow smile can corrupt.

But the reformation of the Joy Rio was somewhat less than
absolute. It had reformed only to the point of ostensible virtue,
and in the back rows of the first gallery at certain hours in the
afternoon and very late at night were things going on of the
sort Mr. Gonzales sometimes looked for. At those hours the
Joy Rio contained few patrons, and since the seats in the

orchestra were in far better condition, those who had come to sit comfortably watching the picture would naturally remain downstairs; the few that elected to sit in the nearly deserted rows of the first gallery did so either because smoking was permitted in that section—or *because* . . .

There was a danger, of course, there always is a danger with places and things like that, but Mr. Gonzales was a tentative person not given to leaping before he looked. If a patron had entered the first gallery only in order to smoke, you could usually count on his occupying a seat along the aisle. If the patron had bothered to edge his way toward the center of a row of seats irregular as the jawbone of poor Yorick, one could assume as infallibly as one can assume anything in a universe where chance is the one invariable, that he had chosen his seat with something more than a cigarette in mind. Mr. Gonzales did not take many chances. This was a respect in which he paid due homage to the wise old spirit of the late Emiel Kroger, that romantically practical Teuton who used to murmur to Pablo, between sleeping and waking, a sort of incantation that went like this: Sometimes you will find it and other times you won't find it and the times you don't find it are the times when you have got to be careful. Those are the times you have got to remember that other times you *will* find it, not *this* time but the *next* time, or the time *after* that, and then you've got to be able to go home without it, yes, those times are the times when you have got to be able to go home without it, go home *alone* without it . . .

Pablo didn't know, then, that he would ever have need of this practical wisdom that his benefactor had drawn from his almost lifelong pursuit of a pleasure which was almost as unreal and basically unsatisfactory as an embrace in a dream. Pablo didn't know then that he would inherit so much from the old man who took care of him, and at that time, when Emiel Kroger, in the dimness of morphia and weakness following hemorrhage, had poured into the delicate ear of his apprentice, drop by slow, liquid drop, this distillation of all he had learned in the years before he found Pablo, the boy had felt for this whisper the same horror and pity that he felt for the mortal disease in the flesh of his benefactor, and only gradually, in the long years since the man and his whisper had ceased, had the singsong rigmarole begun to have sense for him, a practical

wisdom that such a man as Pablo had turned into, a man such
as Mr. Gonzales, could live by safely and quietly and still find
pleasure . . .

III

Mr. Gonzales was careful, and for careful people life has a
tendency to take on the character of an almost arid plain with
only here and there, at wide intervals, the solitary palm tree
and its shadow and the spring alongside it. Mr. Kroger's life
had been much the same until he had come across Pablo at the
watchmakers' convention in Dallas. But so far in Mr. Gonzales'
life there had been no Pablo. In his life there had been only
Mr. Kroger and the sort of things that Mr. Kroger had looked
for and sometimes found but most times continued patiently to
look for in the great expanse of arid country which his lifetime
had been before the discovery of Pablo. And since it is not my
intention to spin this story out any longer than its content
seems to call for, I am not going to attempt to sustain your
interest in it with a description of the few palm trees on the
uneventful desert through which the successor to Emiel Kroger wandered after the death of the man who had been his life.
But I am going to remove you rather precipitately to a summer
afternoon which we will call *Now* when Mr. Gonzales learned
that he was dying, and not only dying but dying of the same
trouble that had put the period under the question mark of
Emiel Kroger. The scene, if I can call it that, takes place in a
doctor's office. After some hedging on the part of the doctor,
the word malignant is uttered. The hand is placed on the
shoulder, almost contemptuously comforting, and Mr. Gonzales is assured that surgery is unnecessary because the condition
is not susceptible to any help but that of drugs to relax the
afflicted organs. And after that the scene is abruptly blacked
out . . .

Now it is a year later. Mr. Gonzales has recovered more or
less from the shocking information that he received from his
doctor. He has been repairing watches and clocks almost as
well as ever, and there has been remarkably little alteration in
his way of life. Only a little more frequently is the shop closed.
It is apparent, now, that the disease from which he suffers does
not intend to destroy him any more suddenly than it destroyed

the man before him. It grows slowly, the growth, and in fact it has recently shown signs of what is called a remission. There is no pain, hardly any and hardly ever. The most palpable symptom is loss of appetite and, as a result of that, after all this time, the graceful approximation of Pablo's delicate structure has come back out of the irrelevant contours which had engulfed it after the long-ago death of Emiel Kroger. The mirrors are not very good in the dim little residence-shop, where he lives in his long wait for death, and when he looks in them, Mr. Gonzales sees the boy that was loved by the man whom he loved. It is almost Pablo. Pablo has almost returned from Mr. Gonzales.

And then one afternoon . . .

IV

The new usher at the Joy Rio was a boy of seventeen and the little Jewish manager had told him that he must pay particular attention to the roped-off staircase to see to it that nobody slipped upstairs to the forbidden region of the upper galleries, but this boy was in love with a girl named Gladys who came to the Joy Rio every afternoon, now that school was let out for the summer, and loitered around the entrance where George, the usher, was stationed. She wore a thin, almost transparent, white blouse with nothing much underneath it. Her skirt was usually of sheer silken material that followed her heart-shaped loins as raptly as George's hand followed them when he embraced her in the dark ladies' room on the balcony level of the Joy Rio. Sensual delirium possessed him those afternoons when Gladys loitered near him. But the recently changed management of the Joy Rio was not a strict one, and in the summer vigilance was more than commonly relaxed. George stayed near the downstairs entrance, twitching restively in his tight, faded uniform till Gladys drifted in from the afternoon streets on a slow tide of lilac perfume. She would seem not to see him as she sauntered up the aisle he indicated with his flashlight and took a seat in the back of the orchestra section where he could find her easily when the "coast was clear," or if he kept her waiting too long and she was more than usually bored with the film, she would stroll back out to the lobby and inquire in her childish drawl, Where is the ladies' room, please? Some-

times he would curse her fiercely under his breath because she
hadn't waited. But he would have to direct her to the staircase,
and she would go up there and wait for him, and the knowledge that she was up there waiting would finally overpower his
prudence to the point where he would even abandon his station if the little manager, Mr. Katz, had his office door wide
open. The ladies' room was otherwise not in use. Its light-
switch was broken, or if it was repaired, the bulbs would be
mysteriously missing. When ladies other than Gladys enquired
about it, George would say gruffly, The ladies' room's out of
order. It made an almost perfect retreat for the young lovers.
The door left ajar gave warning of footsteps on the grand
marble staircase in time for George to come out with his hands
in his pockets before whoever was coming could catch him at
it. But these interruptions would sometimes infuriate him,
especially when a patron would insist on borrowing his flashlight to use the cabinet in the room where Gladys waited with
her crumpled silk skirt gathered high about her flanks (leaning
against the invisible dried-up washbasin) which were the blazing black heart of the insatiably concave summer.

In the old days Mr. Gonzales used to go to the Joy Rio in the
late afternoons but since his illness he had been going earlier
because the days tired him earlier, especially the steaming
days of August which were now in progress. Mr. Gonzales
knew about George and Gladys; he made it his business, of
course, to know everything there was to know about the Joy
Rio, which was his earthly heaven, and, of course, George also
knew about Mr. Gonzales; he knew why Mr. Gonzales gave
him a fifty cent tip every time he enquired his way to the men's
room upstairs, each time as if he had never gone upstairs
before. Sometimes George muttered something under his breath,
but the tributes collected from patrons like Mr. Gonzales had
so far ensured his complicity in their venal practices. But then
one day in August, on one of the very hottest and blindingly
bright afternoons, George was so absorbed in the delights of
Gladys that Mr. Gonzales had arrived at the top of the stairs to
the balcony before George heard his footsteps. Then he heard
them and he clamped a sweating palm over the mouth of
Gladys which was full of stammerings of his name and the
name of God. He waited, but Mr. Gonzales also waited. Mr.
Gonzales was actually waiting at the top of the stairs to recover

his breath from the climb, but George, who could see him, now, through the door kept slightly ajar, suspected that he was waiting to catch him coming out of his secret place. A fury burst in the boy. He thrust Gladys violently back against the washbasin and charged out of the room without even bothering to button his fly. He rushed up to the slight figure waiting near the stairs and began to shout a dreadful word at Mr. Gonzales, the word "morphodite." His voice was shrill as a jungle bird's, shouting this word "morphodite." Mr. Gonzales kept backing away from him, with the lightness and grace of his youth, he kept stepping backwards from the livid face and threatening fists of the usher, all the time murmuring, No, no, no, no, no. The youth stood between him and the stairs below so it was toward the upper staircase that Mr. Gonzales took flight. All at once, as quickly and lightly as ever Pablo had moved, he darted under the length of velvet rope with the sign "Keep Out." George's pursuit was interrupted by the manager of the theater, who seized his arm so fiercely that the shoulder-seam of the uniform burst apart. This started another disturbance under the cover of which Mr. Gonzales fled farther and farther up the forbidden staircase into regions of deepening shadow. There were several points at which he might safely have stopped but his flight had now gathered an irresistible momentum and his legs moved like pistons bearing him up and up, and then—

At the very top of the staircase he was intercepted. He half turned back when he saw the dim figure waiting above, he almost turned and scrambled back down the grand marble staircase, when the name of his youth was called to him in a tone so commanding that he stopped and waited without daring to look up again.

Pablo, said Mr. Kroger, come on up here, Pablo.

Mr. Gonzales obeyed, but now the false power that his terror had given him was drained out of his body and he climbed with effort. At the top of the stairs where Emiel Kroger waited, he would have sunk exhausted to his knees if the old man hadn't sustained him with a firm hand at his elbow.

Mr. Kroger said, This way, Pablo. He led him into the Stygian blackness of one of the little boxes in the once-golden horseshoe of the topmost tier. Now sit down, he commanded.

Pablo was too breathless to say anything except, Yes, and
Mr. Kroger leaned over him and unbuttoned his collar for him,
unfastened the clasp of his belt, all the while murmuring,
There now, there now, Pablo.

The panic disappeared under those soothing old fingers and
the breathing slowed down and stopped hurting the chest as if
a fox was caught in it, and then at last Mr. Kroger began to
lecture the boy as he used to, Pablo, he murmured, don't ever
be so afraid of being lonely that you forget to be careful. Don't
forget that you will find it sometimes but other times you won't
be lucky, and those are the times when you have got to be
patient, since patience is what you must have when you don't
have luck.

The lecture continued softly, reassuringly familiar and repet-
itive as the tick of a bedroom clock in his ear, and if his ancient
protector and instructor, Emiel Kroger, had not kept all the
while soothing him with the moist, hot touch of his tremulous
fingers, the gradual, the very gradual dimming out of things,
his fading out of existence, would have terrified Pablo. But the
ancient voice and fingers, as if they had never left him, kept on
unbuttoning, touching, soothing, repeating the ancient lesson,
saying it over and over like a penitent counting prayer beads.
Sometimes you will have it and sometimes you won't have it, so
don't be anxious about it. You must always be able to go home
alone without it. Those are the times when you have got to
remember that other times you will have it and it doesn't matter
if sometimes you don't have it and have to go home without it,
go home alone without it, go home alone without it. The gentle
advice went on, and as it went on, Mr. Gonzales drifted away
from everything but the wise old voice in his ear, even at last
from that, but not till he was entirely comforted by it.

GHOST

AND FLESH,

WATER AND DIRT

William Goyen

Was somebody here while ago acallin for you. . . .

O don't say that, don't tell me who . . . was he fair and had a wrinkle in his chin? I wonder was he the one . . . describe me his look, whether the eyes were pale light-colored and swimmin and wild and shifty; did he bend a little at the shoulders was his face agrievin what did he say where did he go, whichaway, hush don't tell me; wish I could keep him but I cain't, so go, go (but come back).

Cause you know honey there's a time to go round and tell and there's a time to set still (and let a ghost grieve ya); so listen to me while I tell, cause I'm in my time a tellin and you better run fast if you don wanna hear what I tell, cause I'm goin ta tell . . .

Dreamt last night again I saw pore Raymon Emmons, all last night seen im plain as day. There uz tears in iz glassy eyes and iz face uz all meltin away. O I was broken of my sleep and of my night disturbed, for I dreamt of pore Raymon Emmons live as ever.

He came on the sleepin porch where I was sleepin (and he's there to stay) ridin a purple horse (like King was), and then he got off and tied im to the bedstead and come and stood over me and commenced iz talkin. All night long he uz talkin and talkin, his speech (whatever he uz sayin) uz like steam streamin outa the mouth of a kettle, streamin and streamin and streamin. At first I said in my dream, 'Will you do me the favor of tellin

299

me just who in the world you can be, will you please show the
kindness to tell me who you can be, breakin my sleep and
disturbin my rest?' 'I'm Raymon Emmons,' the steamin voice
said, 'and I'm here to stay; putt out my things that you've putt
away, putt out my oatmeal bowl and putt hot oatmeal in it, get
out my rubberboots when it rains, iron my clothes and fix my
supper . . . I never died and I'm here to stay.'

*(Oh go way ole ghost of Raymon Emmons, whisperin in my
ear on the pilla at night; go way ole ghost and lemme be! Quit
standin over me like that, all night standin there sayin somethin
to me . . . behave ghost of Raymon Emmons, behave yoself and
lemme be! Lemme get out and go round, lemme put on those
big ole rubberboots and go clompin. . . .)*

Now you shoulda known that Raymon Emmons. *There* was
somebody, I'm tellin you. Oh he uz a bright thang, quick 'n
fair, tall, about six feet, real lean and a devlish face full of
snappin eyes, he had eyes all over his face, didn't miss a thang,
that man, saw everthang; and a clean brow. He was a rayroad
man, worked for the Guff Coast Lines all iz life, our house
always smelt like a train.

When I first knew of him he was livin at the Boardinhouse
acrost from the depot (oh that uz years and years ago), and I uz
in town and wearin my first pumps when he stopped me on the
corner and ast me to do him the favor of tellin him the size a
my foot. I was not afraid atall to look at him and say the size a
my foot uz my own affair and would he show the kindness to
not be so fresh. But when he said I only want to know because
there's somebody livin up in New Waverley about your size
and age and I want to send a birthday present of some houseshoes
to, I said that's different; and we went into Richardson's store,
to the back where the shoes were, and tried on shoes till he
found the kind and size to fit me and this person in New
Waverley. I didn't tell im that the pumps I'uz wearin were
Sistah's and not my size (when I got home and Mama said
why'd it take you so long? I said it uz because I had to walk so
slow in Sistah's pumps).

Next time I saw him in town (and I made it a point to look
for him, was why I come to town), I went up to him and said
do you want to measure my foot again Raymon Emmons, ha!
And he said any day in the week I'd measure that pretty foot;
and we went into Richardson's and he bought *me* a pair of

white summer pumps with a pink tie (and I gave Sistah's pumps back to her). Miz Richardson said my lands Margy you buyin lotsa shoes lately, are you goin to take a trip (O I took a trip, and one I come back from, too).

We had other meetins and was plainly in love; and when we married, runnin off to Groveton to do it, everbody in town said things about the marriage because he uz thirty and I uz seventeen.

We moved to this house owned by the Picketts, with a good big clothesyard and a swing on the porch, and I made it real nice for me and Raymon Emmons, made curtains with fringe, putt jardinears on the front bannisters and painted the fern buckets. We furnished those unfurnished rooms with our brand new lives, and started goin along.

Between those years and this one I'm tellin about them in, there seems a space as wide and vacant and silent as the Neches River, with my life *then* standin on one bank and my life *now* standin on the other, lookin acrost at each other like two different people wonderin who the other can really be.

How did Raymon Emmons die? Walked right through a winda and tore hisself all to smithereens. Walked right through a second-story winda at the depot and fell broken on the tracks—nothin much left a Raymon Emmons after he walked through that winda—broken his crown, hon, broken his crown. But he lingered for three days in Victry Hospital and then passed, sayin just before he passed away, turnin towards me, 'I hope you're satisfied. . . .'

Why did he die? From grievin over his daughter and mine, Chitta was her name, that fell off a horse they uz both ridin on the Emmonses' farm. Horse's name was King and we had im shot.

Buried im next to Chitta's grave with iz insurance, two funerals in as many weeks, then set aroun blue in our house, cryin all day and cryin half the night, sleep all broken and disturbed of my rest, thinkin oh if he'd come knockin at that door right now I'd let him in, oh I'd let Raymon Emmons in! After he died, I set aroun sayin who's gonna meet all the hours in a day with me, whatever is in each one—*all those hours*—who's gonna be with me in the mornin, in the ashy afternoons

that we always have here, in the nights of lightnin who's goan
be lyin there, seen in the flashes and makin me feel as safe as if
he uz a lightnin rod (and honey he *wuz*); who's gonna be like a
light turned on in a dark room when I go in, who's gonna be at
the door when I open it, who's goin to be there when I wake
up or when I go to sleep, who's goin to call my name? I cain't
stand a life of just me and our furniture in a room, who's gonna
be with me? Honey it's true that you never miss water till the
well runs dry, tiz truly true.

Went to talk to the preacher, but he uz no earthly help,
regalin me with iz pretty talk, he's got a tongue that will trill
out a story pretty as a bird on a bobwire fence—but meanin
what?—sayin 'the wicked walk on every hand when the vilest
men are exalted'—now what uz that mean?—; went to set and
talk with Fursta Evans in her Millinary Shop (who's had her
share of tumult in her sad life, but never shows it) but she uz
no good, sayin 'Girl pick up the pieces and go on . . . here try
on this real cute hat' (that woman had nothin but hats on her
mind—even though she taught me *my* life, grant cha *that*—for
brains she's got hats). Went to the graves on Sundays carryin
potplants and cryin over the mounds, one long wide one and
one little un—how sad are the little graves a childrun, childrun
ought not to have to die it's not right to bring death to childrun,
they're just little toys grownups play with or neglect (thas how
some of em die, too, honey, but won't say no more bout that);
but all childrun go to Heaven so guess it's best—the grasshoppers flyin all round me (they say graveyard grasshoppers spit
tobacco juice and if it gets in your eye it'll putt your eye out)
and an armadilla diggin in the crepemyrtle bushes—sayin 'dirt
lay light on Raymon Emmons and iz child,' and thinkin 'all my
life is dirt I've got a family of dirt.' And then I come back to set
and scratch aroun like an armadilla myself in these rooms,
alone; but honey that uz no good either.

And then one day, I guess it uz a year after my family died,
there uz a knock on my door and it uz Fursta Evans knockin
when I opened it to see. And she said 'honey, now listen I've
come to visit with you and to try to tell you somethin: why are
you so glued to Raymon Emmonses memry when you never
cared a hoot bout him while he was on earth, you despised all
the Emmonses, said they was just trash, wouldn't go to the
farm on Christmas or Thanksgivin, wouldn't set next to em in

church, broke pore Raymon Emmons's heart because you'd never let Chitta stay with her grandparents and when you finely did the Lord purnished you for bein so hateful by takin Chitta. Then you blamed it on Raymon Emmons, hounded im night and day, said he killed Chitta, drove him stark ravin mad. While Raymon Emmons was live you'd never even give him the time a day, wouldn't lift a hand for him, you never would cross the street for him, to you he uz just a dog in the yard, and you know it, and now that he's dead you grieve yo life away and suddenly fall in love with im.' Oh she tole me good and proper—said, 'you never loved him till you lost im, till it uz too late, said now set up and listen to me and get some brains in yo head, chile.' Said, 'cause listen honey, I've had four husbands in my time, two of em died and two of em quit me, but each one of em I thought was goin to be the *only* one, and I took each one for that, then let him go when he uz gone, kept goin round, kept ready, we got to honey, left the gate wide open for anybody to come through, friend or stranger, ran with the hare and hunted with the hound, honey we got to *greet* life not grieve life,' is what she said.

'Well,' I said, 'I guess that's the way life is, you don't know what you have till you don't have it any longer, till you've lost it, till it's too late.'

'Anyway,' Fursta said, 'little cattle little care—you're beginnin again now, fresh and empty handed, it's later and it's shorter, yo life, but go on from *here* not *there*,' she said. 'You've had one kind of a life, had a husband, putt him in iz grave (now leave im there!), had a child and putt her away, too; start over, hon, the world don't know it, the world's fresh as ever— it's a new day, putt some powder on yo face and start goin roun. Get you a job, and try that; or take you a trip. . . .'

'But I got to stay in this house,' I said. 'Feel like I cain't budge. Raymon Emmons is here, live as ever, and I cain't get away from him. He keeps me fastened to this house.'

'Oh poot,' Fursta said, lightin a cigarette. 'Honey, you're losin ya mine. Now listen here, put on those big ole rubberboots and go clompin, go steppin high and wide—cause listen here, if ya don't they'll have ya up in the Asylum at Rusk sure's as shootin, specially if you go on talkin about this ghost of Raymon Emmons the way you do.'

'But if I started goin roun, what would people say?'

'You can tell em it's none of their beeswax. Cause listen honey, the years uv passed and are passin and you in ever one of em, passin too, and not gettin any younger—yo hair's gettin bunchy and the lines clawed roun yo mouth and eyes by the glassy claws of cryin sharp tears. We got to paint ourselves up and go on, young *outside*, anyway—cause listen honey the sun comes up and the sun crosses over and *goes down*—and while the sun's up we got to get on that fence and crow. Cause night muss fall—and then thas all. Come on, les go roun; have us a Sataday night weddin ever Sataday night; forget this ole patched-faced ghost I hear you talkin about. . . .'

'In this town?' I said. 'I hate this ole town, always rain fallin—'cept this ain't rain it's rainin, Fursta, it's rainin mildew. . . .'

'O deliver me!' Fursta shouted out, and putt out her cigarette, 'you won't do. Are you afraid you'll *melt?*'

'I wish I'd melt—and run down the drains. Wish I uz rain, fallin on the dirt of certain graves I know and seepin down into the dirt, could lie in the dirt with Raymon Emmons on one side and Chitta on the other. Wish I uz dirt. . . .'

'I wish you are just crazy,' Fursta said. 'Come on, you're gonna take a trip. You're gonna get on a train and take a nonstop trip and get off at the end a the line and start all over again new as a New Year's Baby, baby. I'm gonna see to that.'

'Not on no train, all the king's men couldn't get me to ride a train again, no siree. . . .'

'Oh no train my foot,' said Fursta.

'But what'll I use for money please tell me,' I said.

'With Raymon Emmons's insurance of course—it didn't take all of it to bury him, I know. Put some acreage tween you and yo past life, and maybe some new friends and scenery too, and pull down the shade on all the water that's gone under the bridge; and come back here a new woman. Then if ya want tew you can come into my millinary shop with me.'

'Oh,' I said, 'is the world still there? Since Raymon Emmons walked through that winda seems the whole world's gone, the whole world went out through that winda when he walked through it.'

Closed the house, sayin 'goodbye ghost of Raymon Emmons,' bought my ticket at the depot, deafenin my ears to the sound of the tickin telegraph machine, got on a train and headed west to California. Day and night the trainwheels on the traintracks said *Raymon Emmons Raymon Emmons Raymon Emmons*, and I looked through the winda at dirt and desert, miles and miles of dirt, thinkin I wish I uz dirt I wish I uz dirt. O I uz vile with grief.

In California the sun was out, wide, and everbody and everthing lighted up; and oh honey the world *was* still there. I decided to stay awhile. I started my new life with Raymon Emmons's insurance money. It uz in San Diego, by the ocean and with mountains of dirt standin gold in the blue waters. A war had come. I was alone for awhile, but not for long. Got me a job in an airplane factory, met a lotta girls, met a lotta men. I worked in fusilodges.

There uz this Nick Natowski, a brown clean Pollock from Chicago, real wile, real Satanish. What kind of a life did he start me into? I don't know how it started, but it did, and in a flash we uz everwhere together, dancin and swimmin and *everthing*. He uz in the war and in the U.S. Navy, but we didn't think of the war or of water. I just liked him tight as a glove in iz uniform, I just liked him laughin, honey, I just liked him *ever* way he was, and that uz all I knew. And then one night he said, 'Margy I'm goin to tell you somethin, goin on a boat, be gone a long long time, goin in a week.' Oh I cried and had a nervous fit and said, 'Why do you have to go when there's these thousands of others all aroun San Diego that could go?' and he said, 'We're goin away to Coronada for that week, you and me, and what happens there will be enough to keep and save for the whole time we're apart.' We went, honey, Nick and me, to Coronada, I mean we really *went*. Lived like a king and queen—where uz my life behind me that I thought of onct and a while like a story somebody was whisperin to me?—laughed and loved and I cried; and after that week at Coronada, Nick left for sea on his boat, to the war, sayin I want you to know baby I'm leavin you my allotment.

I was blue, so blue, all over again, but this time it uz diffrent someway, guess cause I uz blue for somethin live this time and not dead under dirt, I don't know; anyway I kept goin roun, kept my job in fusilodges and kept goin roun. There was this friend of Nick Natowski's called George, and we went together some. 'But why doesn't Nick Natowski write me,

George?' I said. 'Because he cain't yet,' George said, 'but just wait and he'll write.' I kept waitin but no letter ever came, and the reason he didn't write when he could of, finely, was because his boat was sunk and Nick Natowski in it.

Oh what have I ever done in this world, I said, to send my soul to torment? Lost one to dirt and one to water, makes my life a life of mud, why was I ever put to such a test as this O Lord, I said. I'm goin back home to where I started, gonna get on that train and backtrack to where I started from, want to look at dirt awhile, can't stand to look at water. I rode the train back. Somethin drew me back like I'd been pastured on a rope in California.

Come back to this house, opened it up and aired it all out, and when I got back you know who was there in that house? That ole faithful ghost of Raymon Emmons. He'd been there, waitin, while I went aroun, in my goin round time, and was there to have me back. While I uz gone he'd covered everythin in our house with the breath a ghosts, fine ghost dust over the tables and chairs and a curtain of ghost lace over my bed on the sleepinporch.

Took me this job in Richardson's Shoe Shop (this town's big now and got money in it, the war 'n oil made it rich, ud never know it was the same if you hadn't known it before; and Fursta Evans married to a rich widower), set there fittin shoes on measured feet all day—it all started in a shoestore measurin feet and it ended that way—can you feature that? Went home at night to my you-know-what.

Comes ridin onto the sleepinporch ever night regular as clockwork, ties iz horse to the bedstead and I say hello Raymon Emmons and we start our conversation. Don't ask me what he says or what I say, but ever night is a night full of talkin, and it lasts the whole night through. Oh onct in a while I get real blue and want to hide away and just set with Raymon Emmons in my house, cain't budge, don't see daylight nor dark, putt away my wearin clothes, couldn't walk outa that door if my life depended on it. But I set real still and let it all be, claimed by that ghost until he unclaims me—and then I get up and go roun, free, and that's why I'm here, settin with you here in the Pass Time Club, drinkin this beer and tellin you all I've told.

*   *   *

Honey, why am I tellin all this? Oh all our lives! So many things to tell. And I keep em to myself a long long time, tight as a drum, won't open my mouth, just set in my blue house with that ole ghost agrievin me, until there comes a time of tellin, a time to tell, a time to putt on those big ole rubberboots.

Now I believe in *tellin*, while we're live and goin roun; when the tellin time comes I say spew it out, we just got to tell things, things in our lives, things that've happened, things we've fancied and things we dream about or are haunted by. Cause you know honey the time to shut you mouth and set moultin and mildewed in yo room, grieved by a ghost and fastened to a chair, comes back roun again, don't worry honey, it comes roun again. There's a time ta tell and a time ta set still ta let a ghost grieve ya. So listen to me while I tell, cause I'm in my time atellin, and you better run fast if you don wanna hear what I tell, cause I'm goin ta tell. . . .

The world is changed, let's drink ower beer and have us a time, tell and tell and tell, let's get that hot bird in a cole bottle tonight. Cause next time you think you'll see me and hear me tell, you won't: I'll be flat where I cain't budge again, like I wuz all that year, settin and hidin way . . . until the time comes round again when I can say oh go way ole ghost of Raymon Emmons, go way ole ghost and lemme be!

Cause I've learned this and I'm gonna tell ya: there's a time for live things and a time for dead, for ghosts and for flesh 'n bones: all life is just a sharin of ghosts and flesh. Us humans are part ghost and part flesh—part fire and part ash—but I think maybe the ghost part is the longest lastin, the fire blazes but the ashes last forever. I had fire in California (and water putt it out) and ash in Texis (and it went to dirt); but I say now, while I'm tellin you, there's a world both places, a world where there's ghosts and a world where there's flesh, and I believe the real right way is to take our worlds, of ghosts or of flesh, take each one as they come and take what comes in em: take a ghost and grieve with im, settin still; and take the flesh 'n bones and go roun; and even run out to meet what worlds come in to our lives, strangers (like you), and ghosts (like Raymon Emmons) and lovers (like Nick Natowski) . . . and be what each world wants us to be.

And I think that ghosts, if you set still with em long enough, can give you over to flesh 'n bones; and that flesh 'n bones, if you go roun when it's time, can send you back to a faithful ghost. One provides the other.

Saw pore Raymon Emmons all last night, all last night seen im plain as day.

THE

CELESTIAL

OMNIBUS

E. M. Forster

The boy who resided at Agathox Lodge, 28, Buckingham Park Road, Surbiton, had often been puzzled by the old sign-post that stood almost opposite. He asked his mother about it, and she replied that it was a joke, and not a very nice one, which had been made many years back by some naughty young men, and that the police ought to remove it. For there were two strange things about this sign-post: firstly, it pointed up a blank alley, and, secondly, it had painted on it, in faded characters, the words, "To Heaven."

"What kind of young men were they?" he asked.

"I think your father told me that one of them wrote verses, and was expelled from the University and came to grief in other ways. Still, it was a long time ago. You must ask your father about it. He will say the same as I do, that it was put up as a joke."

"So it doesn't mean anything at all?"

She sent him up-stairs to put on his best things, for the Bonses were coming to tea, and he was to hand the cake-stand.

It struck him, as he wrenched on his tightening trousers, that he might do worse than ask Mr. Bons about the sign-post. His father, though very kind, always laughed at him—shrieked with laughter whenever he or any other child asked a question or spoke. But Mr. Bons was serious as well as kind. He had a beautiful house and lent one books, he was a churchwarden, and a candidate for the County Council; he had donated to the Free Library enormously, he presided over the Literary Society, and had Members of Parliament to stop with him—in short, he was probably the wisest person alive.

Yet even Mr. Bons could only say that the signpost was a joke— the joke of a person named Shelley.

"Of course!" cried the mother; "I told you so, dear. That was the name."

"Had you never heard of Shelley?" asked Mr. Bons.

"No," said the boy, and hung his head.

"But is there no Shelley in the house?"

"Why, yes!" exclaimed the lady, in much agitation. "Dear Mr. Bons, we aren't such Philistines as that. Two at the least. One a wedding present, and the other, smaller print, in one of the spare rooms."

"I believe we have seven Shelleys," said Mr. Bons, with a slow smile. Then he brushed the cake crumbs off his stomach, and, together with his daughter, rose to go.

The boy, obeying a wink from his mother, saw them all the way to the garden gate, and when they had gone he did not at once return to the house, but gazed for a little up and down Buckingham Park Road.

His parents lived at the right end of it. After No. 39 the quality of the houses dropped very suddenly, and 64 had not even a separate servants' entrance. But at the present moment the whole road looked rather pretty, for the sun had just set in splendour, and the inequalities of rent were drowned in a saffron afterglow. Small birds twittered, and the breadwinners' train shrieked musically down through the cutting—that wonderful cutting which has drawn to itself the whole beauty out of Surbiton, and clad itself, like any Alpine valley, with the glory of the fir and the silver birch and the primrose. It was this cutting that had first stirred desires within the boy—desires for something just a little different, he knew not what, desires that would return whenever things were sunlit, as they were this evening, running up and down inside him, up and down, up and down, till he would feel quite unusual all over, and as likely as not would want to cry. This evening he was even sillier, for he slipped across the road towards the sign-post and began to run up the blank alley.

The alley runs between high walls—the walls of the gardens of "Ivanhoe" and "Belle Vista" respectively. It smells a little all the way, and is scarcely twenty yards long, including the turn at the end. So not unnaturally the boy soon came to a stand-still. "I'd like to kick that Shelley," he exclaimed, and glanced idly at a piece of paper which was pasted on the wall. Rather an odd piece of paper, and he read it carefully before he turned back. This is what he read:

S. AND C. R. C. C.

Alteration in Service.

Owing to lack of patronage the Company are regretfully com-pelled to suspend the hourly service, and to retain only the

Sunrise and Sunset Omnibuses,

which will run as usual. It is to be hoped that the public will patronize an arrangement which is intended for their conve-nience. As an extra inducement, the Company will, for the first time, now issue

Return Tickets(available one day only), which may be ob-tained of the driver. Passengers are again reminded that no tickets are issued at the other end, and that no complaints in this connection will receive consideration from the Company. Nor will the Company be responsible for any negligence or stupidity on the part of Passengers, nor for Hailstorms, Light-ning, Loss of Tickets nor for any Act of God.

For the Direction.

Now he had never seen this notice before, nor could he imagine where the omnibus went to. S. of course was for Surbiton, and R.C.C. meant Road Car Company. But what was the meaning of the other C.? Coombe and Malden, perhaps, or possibly "City." Yet it could not hope to compete with the South-Western. The whole thing, the boy reflected, was run on hopelessly unbusiness-like lines. Why no tickets from the other end? And what an hour to start! Then he realized that unless the notice was a hoax, an omnibus must have been starting just as he was wishing the Bonses goodbye. He peered at the ground through the gathering dusk, and there he saw what might or might not be the marks of wheels. Yet nothing had come out of the alley. And he had never seen an omnibus

at any time in the Buckingham Park Road. No: it must be a
hoax, like the sign-posts, like the fairy tales, like the dreams
upon which he would wake suddenly in the night. And with a
sigh he stepped from the alley—right into the arms of his
father.

Oh, how his father laughed! "Poor, poor Popsey!" he cried.
"Diddums! Diddums! Diddums think he'd walky-palky up to
Evvink!" And his mother, also convulsed with laughter, ap-
peared on the steps of Agathox Lodge. "Don't, Bob!" she gasped.
"Don't be so naughty! Oh, you'll kill me! Oh, leave the boy
alone!"

But all the evening the joke was kept up. The father im-
plored to be taken too. Was it a very tiring walk? Need one
wipe one's shoes on the door-mat? And the boy went to bed
feeling faint and sore, and thankful for only one thing—that he
had not said a word about the omnibus. It was a hoax, yet
through his dreams it grew more and more real, and the streets
of Surbiton, through which he saw it driving, seemed instead
to become hoaxes and shadows. And very early in the morning
he woke with a cry, for he had had a glimpse of its destination.

He struck a match, and its light fell not only on his watch but
also on his calendar, so that he knew it to be half-an-hour to
sunrise. It was pitch dark, for the fog had come down from
London in the night, and all Surbiton was wrapped in its
embraces. Yet he sprang out and dressed himself, for he was
determined to settle once for all which was real: the omnibus
or the streets. "I shall be a fool one way or the other," he
thought, "until I know." Soon he was shivering in the road
under the gas lamp that guarded the entrance to the alley.

To enter the alley itself required some courage. Not only was
it horribly dark, but he now realized that it was an impossible
terminus for an omnibus. If it had not been for a policeman,
whom he heard approaching through the fog, he would never
have made the attempt. The next moment he had made the
attempt and failed. Nothing. Nothing but a blank alley and a
very silly boy gaping at its dirty floor. It *was* a hoax. "I'll tell
papa and mamma," he decided. "I deserve it. I deserve that
they should know. I am too silly to be alive." And he went
back to the gate of Agathox Lodge.

There he remembered that his watch was fast. The sun was
not risen; it would not rise for two minutes. "Give the bus

every chance," he thought cynically, and returned into the alley.

But the omnibus was there.

II

It had two horses, whose sides were still smoking from their journey, and its two great lamps shone through the fog against the alley's walls, changing their cobwebs and moss into tissues of fairyland. The driver was huddled up in a cape. He faced the blank wall, and how he had managed to drive in so neatly and so silently was one of the many things that the boy never discovered. Nor could he imagine how ever he would drive out.

"Please," his voice quavered through the foul brown air, "please, is that an omnibus?"

"Omnibus est," said the driver, without turning round. There was a moment's silence. The policeman passed, coughing, by the entrance of the alley. The boy crouched in the shadow, for he did not want to be found out. He was pretty sure, too, that it was a Pirate; nothing else, he reasoned, would go from such odd places and at such odd hours.

"About when do you start?" He tried to sound nonchalant.

"At sunrise."

"How far do you go?"

"The whole way."

"And can I have a return ticket which will bring me all the way back?"

"You can."

"Do you know, I half think I'll come." The driver made no answer. The sun must have risen, for he unhitched the brake. And scarcely had the boy jumped in before the omnibus was off.

How? Did it turn? There was no room. Did it go forward? There was a blank wall. Yet it was moving—moving at a stately pace through the fog, which had turned from brown to yellow. The thought of warm bed and warmer breakfast made the boy feel faint. He wished he had not come. His parents would not have approved. He would have gone back to them if the weather had not made it impossible. The solitude was terrible; he was the only passenger. And the omnibus, though well-built, was cold and somewhat musty. He drew his coat round him, and in so doing chanced to feel his pocket. It was empty. He had forgotten his purse.

"Stop!" he shouted. "Stop!" And then, being of a polite disposition, he glanced up at the painted notice-board so that he might call the driver by name. "Mr. Browne! stop; O, do please stop!"

Mr. Browne did not stop, but he opened a little window and looked in at the boy. His face was a surprise, so kind it was and modest.

"Mr. Browne, I've left my purse behind. I've not got a penny. I can't pay for the ticket. Will you take my watch, please? I am in the most awful hole."

"Tickets on this line," said the driver, "whether single or return, can be purchased by coinage from no terrene mint. And a chronometer, though it had solaced the vigils of Charlemagne, or measured the slumbers of Laura, can acquire by no mutation the double-cake that charms the fangless Cerberus of Heaven!" So saying, he handed in the necessary ticket, and, while the boy said "Thank you," continued: "Titular pretensions, I know it well, are vanity. Yet they merit no censure when uttered on a laughing lip, and in an homonymous world are in some sort useful, since they do serve to distinguish one Jack from his fellow. Remember me, therefore, as Sir Thomas Browne."

"Are you a Sir? Oh, sorry!" He had heard of these gentlemen drivers. "It *is* good of you about the ticket. But if you go on at this rate, however does your bus pay?"

"It does not pay. It was not intended to pay. Many are the faults of my equipage; it is compounded too curiously of foreign woods; its cushions tickle erudition rather than promote repose; and my horses are nourished not on the evergreen pastures of the moment, but on the dried bents and clovers of Latinity. But that it pays!—that error at all events was never intended and never attained."

"Sorry again," said the boy rather hopelessly. Sir Thomas looked sad, fearing that, even for a moment, he had been the cause of sadness. He invited the boy to come up and sit beside him on the box, and together they journeyed on through the fog, which was now changing from yellow to white. There were no houses by the road; so it must be either Putney Heath or Wimbledon Common.

"Have you been a driver always?"

"I was a physician once."

"But why did you stop? Weren't you good?"

"As a healer of bodies I had scant success, and several score of my patients preceded me. But as a healer of the spirit I have succeeded beyond my hopes and my deserts. For though my draughts were not better nor subtler than those of other men, yet, by reason of the cunning goblets wherein I offered them, the queasy soul was oft times tempted to sip and be refreshed."

"The queasy soul," he murmured; "if the sun sets with trees in front of it, and you suddenly come strange all over, is that a queasy soul?"

"Have you felt that?"

"Why yes."

After a pause he told the boy a little, a very little, about the journey's end. But they did not chatter much, for the boy, when he liked a person, would as soon sit silent in his company as speak, and this, he discovered, was also the mind of Sir Thomas Browne and of many others with whom he was to be acquainted. He heard, however, about the young man Shelley, who was now quite a famous person, with a carriage of his own, and about some of the other drivers who are in the service of the Company. Meanwhile the light grew stronger, though the fog did not disperse. It was now more like mist than fog, and at times would travel quickly across them, as if it was part of a cloud. They had been ascending, too, in a most puzzling way; for over two hours the horses had been pulling against the collar, and even if it were Richmond Hill they ought to have been at the top long ago. Perhaps it was Epsom, or even the North Downs; yet the air seemed keener than that which blows on either. And as to the name of their destination, Sir Thomas Browne was silent.

Crash!

"Thunder, by Jove!" said the boy, "and not so far off either. Listen to the echoes! It's more like mountains."

He thought, not very vividly, of his father and mother. He saw them sitting down to sausages and listening to the storm. He saw his own empty place. Then there would be questions, alarms, theories, jokes, consolations. They would expect him back at lunch. To lunch he would not come, nor to tea, but he would be in for dinner, and so his day's truancy would be over. If he had had his purse he would have bought them presents— not that he should have known what to get them.

Crash!

The peal and the lightning came together. The cloud quivered as if it were alive, and torn streamers of mist rushed past. "Are you afraid?" asked Sir Thomas Browne.

"What is there to be afraid of? Is it much farther?"

The horses of the omnibus stopped just as a ball of fire burst up and exploded with a ringing noise that was deafening but clear, like the noise of a blacksmith's forge. All the cloud was shattered.

"Oh, listen, Sir Thomas Browne! No, I mean look; we shall get a view at last. No, I mean listen; that sounds like a rainbow!"

The noise had died into the faintest murmur, beneath which another murmur grew, spreading stealthily, steadily, in a curve that widened but did not vary. And in widening curves a rainbow was spreading from the horses' feet into the dissolving mists.

"But how beautiful! What colours! Where will it stop? It is more like the rainbows you can tread on. More like dreams."

The colour and the sound grew together. The rainbow spanned an enormous gulf. Clouds rushed under it and were pierced by it, and still it grew, reaching forward, conquering the darkness, until it touched something that seemed more solid than a cloud.

The boy stood up. "What is that out there?" he called. "What does it rest on, out at that other end?"

In the morning sunshine a precipice shone forth beyond the gulf. A precipice—or was it a castle? The horses moved. They set their feet upon the rainbow.

"Oh, look!" the boy shouted. "Oh, listen! Those caves—or are they gateways? Oh, look between those cliffs at those ledges. I see people! I see trees!"

"Look also below," whispered Sir Thomas. "Neglect not the diviner Acheron."

The boy looked below, past the flames of the rainbow that licked against their wheels. The gulf also had cleared, and in its depths there flowed an everlasting river. One sunbeam entered and struck a green pool, and as they passed over he saw three maidens rise to the surface of the pool, singing, and playing with something that glistened like a ring.

"You down in the water——" he called.

They answered, "You up on the bridge——" There was a burst of music. "You up on the bridge, good luck to you. Truth in the depth, truth on the height."

"You down in the water, what are you doing?"

Sir Thomas Browne replied: "They sport in the mancipiary possession of their gold"; and the omnibus arrived.

III

The boy was in disgrace. He sat locked up in the nursery of Agathox Lodge, learning poetry for a punishment. His father had said, "My boy! I can pardon anything but untruthfulness," and had caned him, saying at each stroke. "There is *no* omnibus, *no* driver, *no* bridge, *no* mountain; you are a *truant*, a *gutter snipe*, a *liar*." His father could be very stern at times. His mother had begged him to say he was sorry. But he could not say that. It was the greatest day of his life, in spite of the caning and the poetry at the end of it.

He had returned punctually at sunset—driven not by Sir Thomas Browne, but by a maiden lady who was full of quiet fun. They had talked of omnibuses and also of barouche landaus. How far away her gentle voice seemed now! Yet it was scarcely three hours since he had left her up the alley.

His mother called through the door. "Dear, you are to come down and to bring your poetry with you."

He came down, and found that Mr. Bons was in the smoking-room with his father. It had been a dinner party.

"Here is the great traveller!" said his father grimly. "Here is the young gentleman who drives in an omnibus over rainbows, while young ladies sing to him." Pleased with his wit, he laughed.

"After all," said Mr. Bons, smiling, "there is something a little like it in Wagner. It is odd how, in quite illiterate minds, you will find glimmers of Artistic Truth. The case interests me. Let me plead for the culprit. We have all romanced in our time, haven't we?"

"Hear how kind Mr. Bons is," said his mother, while his father said, "Very well. Let him say his Poem, and that will do.

He is going away to my sister on Tuesday, and *she* will cure him of this alley-slopering." (Laughter.) "Say your Poem."

The boy began. " 'Standing aloof in giant ignorance.' "

His father laughed again—roared. "One for you, my son! 'Standing aloof in giant ignorance!' I never knew these poets talked sense. Just describes you. Here, Bons, you go in for poetry. Put him through it, will you, while I fetch up the whisky?"

"Yes, give me the Keats," said Mr. Bons. "Let him say his Keats to me."

So for a few moments the wise man and the ignorant boy were left alone in the smoking-room.

" 'Standing aloof in giant ignorance, of thee I dream and of the Cyclades, as one who sits ashore and longs perchance to visit——' "

"Quite right. To visit what?"

" 'To visit dolphin coral in deep seas,' " said the boy, and burst into tears.

"Come, come! why do you cry?"

"Because—because all these words that only rhymed before, now that I've come back they're me."

Mr. Bons laid the Keats down. The case was more interesting than he had expected. "*You?*" he exclaimed. "This sonnet, *you?*"

"Yes—and look further on: 'Aye, on the shores of darkness there is light, and precipices show untrodden green.' It *is* so, sir. All these things are true."

"I never doubted it," said Mr. Bons, with closed eyes.

"You—then you believe me? You believe in the omnibus and the driver and the storm and that return ticket I got for nothing and——"

"Tut, tut! No more of your yarns, my boy. I meant that I never doubted the essential truth of Poetry. Some day, when you have read more, you will understand what I mean."

"But, Mr. Bons, it *is* so. There *is* light upon the shores of darkness. I have seen it coming. Light and a wind."

"Nonsense," said Mr. Bons.

"If I had stopped! They tempted me. They told me to give up my ticket—for you cannot come back if you lose your ticket. They called from the river for it, and indeed I was tempted, for I have never been so happy as among those precipices. But I thought of my mother and father, and that I must fetch them. Yet they will not come, though the road starts opposite our house. It has all happened as the people up there warned me, and Mr. Bons has disbelieved me like every one else. I have been caned. I shall never see that mountain again."

"What's that about me?" said Mr. Bons, sitting up in his chair very suddenly.

"I told them about you, and how clever you were, and how many books you had, and they said, 'Mr. Bons will certainly disbelieve you.'"

"Stuff and nonsense, my young friend. You grow impertinent. I—well—I will settle the matter. Not a word to your father. I will cure you. To-morrow evening I will myself call here to take you for a walk, and at sunset we will go up this alley opposite and hunt for your omnibus, you silly little boy."

His face grew serious, for the boy was not disconcerted, but leapt about the room singing, "Joy! joy! I told them you would believe me. We will drive together over the rainbow. I told them that you would come." After all, could there be anything in the story? Wagner? Keats? Shelley? Sir Thomas Browne? Certainly the case was interesting.

And on the morrow evening, though it was pouring with rain, Mr. Bons did not omit to call at Agathox Lodge.

The boy was ready, bubbling with excitement, and skipping about in a way that rather vexed the President of the Literary Society. They took a turn down Buckingham Park Road, and then—having seen that no one was watching them—slipped up the alley. Naturally enough (for the sun was setting) they ran straight against the omnibus.

"Good heavens!" exclaimed Mr. Bons. "Good gracious heavens!"

It was not the omnibus in which the boy had driven first, nor yet that in which he had returned. There were three horses— black, gray, and white, the gray being the finest. The driver, who turned round at the mention of goodness and of heaven, was a sallow man with terrifying jaws and sunken eyes. Mr. Bons, on seeing him, gave a cry as if of recognition, and began to tremble violently.

The boy jumped in.

"Is it possible?" cried Mr. Bons. "Is the impossible possible?"

"Sir; come in, sir. It is such a fine omnibus. Oh, here is his name—Dan some one."

Mr. Bons sprang in too. A blast of wind immediately slammed the omnibus door, and the shock jerked down all the omnibus blinds, which were very weak on their springs.

"Dan . . . Show me. Good gracious heavens! we're moving."

"Hooray!" said the boy.

Mr. Bons became flustered. He had not intended to be kidnapped. He could not find the door-handle, nor push up the blinds. The omnibus was quite dark, and by the time he had struck a match, night had come on outside also. They were moving rapidly.

"A strange, a memorable adventure," he said, surveying the interior of the omnibus, which was large, roomy, and constructed with extreme regularity, every part exactly answering to every other part. Over the door (the handle of which was outside) was written. "Lasciate ogni baldanza voi che entrate"—at least, that was what was written, but Mr. Bons said that it was Lashy arty something, and that baldanza was a mistake for speranza. His voice sounded as if he was in church. Meanwhile, the boy called to the cadaverous driver for two return tickets. They were handed in without a word. Mr. Bons covered his face with his hands and again trembled. "Do you know who that is!" he whispered, when the little window had shut upon them. "It is the impossible."

"Well, I don't like him as much as Sir Thomas Browne, though I shouldn't be surprised if he had even more in him."

"More in him?" He stamped irritably. "By accident you have made the greatest discovery of the century, and all you can say is that there is more in this man. Do you remember those vellum books in my library, stamped with red lilies? This—sit still, I bring you stupendous news!—*this is the man who wrote them.*"

The boy sat quite still. "I wonder if we shall see Mrs. Gamp?" he asked, after a civil pause.

"Mrs.——?"

"Mrs. Gamp and Mrs. Harris, I like Mrs. Harris. I came upon them quite suddenly. Mrs. Gamp's bandboxes have moved over the rainbow so badly. All the bottoms have fallen out, and two of the pippins off her bedstead tumbled into the stream."

"Out there sits the man who wrote my vellum books!" thundered Mr. Bons, "and you talk to me of Dickens and of Mrs. Gamp?"

"I know Mrs. Gamp so well," he apologized. "I could not help being glad to see her. I recognized her voice. She was telling Mrs. Harris about Mrs. Prig."

"Did you spend the whole day in her elevating company?"

"Oh, no. I raced. I met a man who took me out beyond to a race-course. You run, and there are dolphins out at sea."

"Indeed. Do you remember the man's name?"

"Achilles. No; he was later. Tom Jones."

Mr. Bons sighed heavily. "Well, my lad, you have made a miserable mess of it. Think of a cultured person with your opportunities! A cultured person would have known all these characters and known what to have said to each. He would not have wasted his time with a Mrs. Gamp or a Tom Jones. The creations of Homer, of Shakespeare, and of Him who drives us now, would alone have contented him. He would not have raced. He would have asked intelligent questions."

"But, Mr. Bons," said the boy humbly, "you will be a cultured person. I told them so."

"True, true, and I beg you not to disgrace me when we arrive. No gossiping. No running. Keep close to my side, and never speak to these Immortals unless they speak to you. Yes, and give me the return tickets. You will be losing them."

The boy surrendered the tickets, but felt a little sore. After all, he had found the way to this place. It was hard first to be disbelieved and then to be lectured. Meanwhile, the rain had stopped, and moonlight crept into the omnibus through the cracks in the blinds.

"But how is there to be a rainbow?" cried the boy.

"You distract me," snapped Mr. Bons. "I wish to meditate on beauty. I wish to goodness I was with a reverent and sympathetic person."

The lad bit his lip. He made a hundred good resolutions. He would imitate Mr. Bons all the visit. He would not laugh, or run, or sing, or do any of the vulgar things that must have disgusted his new friends last time. He would be very careful to pronounce their names properly, and to remember who knew whom. Achilles did not know Tom Jones—at least, so Mr. Bons said. The Duchess of Malfi was older than Mrs. Gamp—at least, so Mr. Bons said. He would be self-conscious, reticent, and prim. He would never say he liked any one. Yet, when the blind flew up at a chance touch of his head, all these good resolutions went to the winds, for the omnibus had reached the summit of a moonlit hill, and there was the chasm, and there, across it, stood the old precipices, dreaming, with their feet in the everlasting river. He exclaimed, "The mountain! Listen to the new tune in the water! Look at the camp fires in the ravines," and Mr. Bons, after a hasty glance, retorted, "Water? Camp fires? Ridiculous rubbish. Hold your tongue. There is nothing at all."

Yet, under his eyes, a rainbow formed, compounded not of sunlight and storm, but of moonlight and the spray of the river. The three horses put their feet upon it. He thought it the finest rainbow he had seen, but did not dare to say so, since Mr. Bons said that nothing was there. He leant out—the window had opened—and sang the tune that rose from the sleeping waters.

"The prelude to Rhinegold?" said Mr. Bons suddenly. "Who taught you these *leit motifs?*" He, too, looked out of the window. Then he behaved very oddly. He gave a choking cry, and fell back on to the omnibus floor. He writhed and kicked. His face was green.

"Does the bridge make you dizzy?" the boy asked.

"Dizzy!" gasped Mr. Bons. "I want to go back. Tell the driver."

But the driver shook his head.

"We are nearly there," said the boy. "They are asleep. Shall I call? They will be so pleased to see you, for I have prepared them."

Mr. Bons moaned. They moved over the lunar rainbow, which ever and ever broke away behind their wheels. How still the night was! Who would be sentry at the Gate?

"I am coming," he shouted, again forgetting the hundred resolutions. "I am returning—I, the boy."

"The boy is returning," cried a voice to other voices, who repeated, "The boy is returning."

"I am bringing Mr. Bons with me."

Silence.

"I should have said Mr. Bons is bringing me with him."

Profound silence.

"Who stands sentry?"

"Achilles."

And on the rocky causeway, close to the springing of the

rainbow bridge, he saw a young man who carried a wonderful shield.

"Mr. Bons, it is Achilles, armed."

"I want to go back," said Mr. Bons.

The last fragment of the rainbow melted, the wheels sang upon the living rock, the door of the omnibus burst open. Out leapt the boy—he could not resist—and sprang to meet the warrior, who, stooping suddenly, caught him on his shield.

"Achilles!" he cried, "let me get down, for I am ignorant and vulgar, and I must wait for that Mr. Bons of whom I told you yesterday."

But Achilles raised him aloft. He crouched on the wonderful shield, on heroes and burning cities, on vineyards graven in gold, on every dear passion, every joy, on the entire image of the Mountain that he had discovered, encircled, like it, with an everlasting stream. "No, no," he protested. "I am not worthy. It is Mr. Bons who must be up here."

But Mr. Bons was whimpering, and Achilles trumpeted and cried, "Stand upright upon my shield!"

"Sir, I did not mean to stand! something made me stand. Sir, why do you delay? Here is only the great Achilles, whom you knew."

Mr. Bons screamed, "I see no one. I see nothing. I want to go back." Then he cried to the driver, "Save me! Let me stop in your chariot. I have honoured you. I have quoted you. I have bound you in vellum. Take me back to my world."

The driver replied, "I am the means and not the end. I am the food and not the life. Stand by yourself, as that boy has stood. I cannot save you. For poetry is a spirit; and they that would worship it must worship in spirit and in truth."

Mr. Bons—he could not resist—crawled out of the beautiful omnibus. His face appeared, gaping horribly. His hands followed, one gripping the step, the other beating the air. Now his shoulders emerged, his chest, his stomach. With a shriek of "I see London," he fell—fell against the hard, moonlit rock, fell into it as if it were water, fell through it, vanished, and was seen by the boy no more.

"Where have you fallen to, Mr. Bons? Here is a procession arriving to honour you with music and torches. Here come the men and women whose names you know. The mountain is awake, the river is awake, over the race-course the sea is awaking those dolphins, and it is all for you. They want you——"

There was the touch of fresh leaves on his forehead. Some one had crowned him.

ΤΕΛΟΣ

From the *Kingston Gazette, Surbiton Times,*
and *Raynes Park Observer.*

The body of Mr. Septimus Bons has been found in a shockingly mutilated condition in the vicinity of the Bermondsey gas-works. The deceased's pockets contained a sovereign-purse, a silver cigar-case, a bijou pronouncing dictionary, and a couple of omnibus tickets. The unfortunate gentleman had apparently been hurled from a considerable height. Foul play is suspected, and a thorough investigation is pending by the authorities.

AFTERWARD

Edith Wharton

"Oh, there *is* one, of course, but you'll never know it."

The assertion, laughingly flung out six months earlier in a bright June garden, came back to Mary Boyne with a new perception of its significance as she stood, in the December dusk, waiting for the lamps to be brought into the library.

The words had been spoken by their friend Alida Stair, as they sat at tea on her lawn at Pangbourne, in reference to the very house of which the library in question was the central, the pivotal "feature." Mary Boyne and her husband, in quest of a country place in one of the southern or southwestern counties, had, on their arrival in England, carried their problem straight to Alida Stair, who had successfully solved it in her own case; but it was not until they had rejected, almost capriciously, several practical and judicious suggestions that she threw out: "Well, there's Lyng, in Dorsetshire. It belongs to Hugo's cousins, and you can get it for a song."

The reason she gave for its being obtainable on these terms—its remoteness from a station, its lack of electric light, hot water pipes, and other vulgar necessities—were exactly those pleading in its favor with two romantic Americans perversely in search of the economic drawbacks which were associated, in their tradition, with unusual architectural felicities.

"I should never believe I was living in an old house unless I was thoroughly uncomfortable," Ned Boyne, the more extravagant of the two, had jocosely insisted; "the least hint of convenience would make me think it had been bought out of an exhibition, with the pieces numbered, and set up again." And they had proceeded to enumerate, with humorous precision, their various doubts and demands, refusing to believe that the house their cousin recommended was *really* Tudor till they learned it had no heating system, or that the village church was literally in the grounds, till she assured them of the deplorable uncertainty of the water supply.

"It's too uncomfortable to be true!" Edward Boyne had continued to exult as the avowal of each disadvantage was successively wrung from her; but he had cut short his rhapsody to ask, with a relapse to distrust: "And the ghost? You've been concealing from us the fact that there is no ghost!"

Mary, at the moment, had laughed with him, yet almost with her laugh, being possessed of several sets of independent perceptions, had been struck by a note of flatness in Alida's answering hilarity.

"Oh, Dorsetshire's full of ghosts, you know."

"Yes, yes; but that won't do. I don't want to have to drive ten miles to see somebody else's ghost. I want one of my own on the premises. *Is* there a ghost at Lyng?"

His rejoinder had made Alida laugh again, and it was then that she had flung back tantalizingly: "Oh, there *is* one, of course, but you'll never know it."

"Never know it?" Boyne pulled her up. "But what in the world constitutes a ghost except the fact of its being known for one?"

"I can't say. But that's the story."

"That there's a ghost, but that nobody knows it's a ghost?"

"Well—not till afterward, at any rate."

"Till afterward?"

"Not till long long afterward."

"But if it's once been identified as an unearthly visitant, why hasn't it *signalement* been handed down in the family? How has it managed to preserve its incognito?"

Alida could only shake her head. "Don't ask me. But it has."

"And then suddenly"—Mary spoke up as if from cavernous depths of divination—"suddenly, long afterward, one says to one's self '*That was it?*' "

She was startled at the sepulchral sound with which her question fell on the banter of the other two, and she saw the shadow of the same surprise flit across Alida's pupils. "I suppose so. One just has to wait."

"Oh, hang waiting!" Ned broke in. "Life's too short for a ghost who can only be enjoyed in retrospect. Can't we do better than that, Mary?"

But it turned out that in the event they were not destined to, for within three months of their conversation with Mrs. Stair they were settled at Lyng, and the life they had yearned for, to the point of planning it in advance in all its daily details, had actually begun for them.

It was to sit, in the thick December dusk, by just such a widehooded fireplace, under just such black oak rafters, with the sense that beyond the mullioned panes the downs were darkened to a deeper solitude; it was for the ultimate indulgence of such sensations that Mary Boyne, abruptly exiled from New York by her husband's business, had endured for nearly fourteen years the soul-deadening ugliness of a Middle Western town, and that Boyne had ground on doggedly at his engineering till, with a suddenness that still made her blink, the prodigious windfall of the Blue Star Mine had put them at a stroke in possession of life and the leisure to taste it. They had never for a moment meant their new state to be one of idleness; but they meant to give themselves only to harmonious activities. She had her vision of painting and gardening (against a background of grey walls), he dreamed of the production of his long-planned book on the "Economic Basis of Culture"; and with such absorbing work ahead no existence could be too sequestered: they could not get far enough from the world, or plunge deep enough into the past.

Dorsetshire had attracted them from the first by an air of remoteness out of all proportion to its geographical position. But to the Boynes it was one of the ever-recurring wonders of the whole incredibly compressed island—a nest of counties, as they put it—that for the production of its effects so little of a given quality went so far: that so few miles made a distance, and so short a distance a difference.

"It's that," Ned had once enthusiastically explained, "that gives such depth to their effects, such relief to their contrasts. They've been able to lay the butter so thick on every delicious mouthful."

The butter had certainly been laid on thick at Lyng: the old

house hidden under a shoulder of the downs had almost all the
finer marks of commerce with a protracted past. The mere fact
that it was neither large nor exceptional made it, to the Boynes,
abound the more completely in its special charm—the charm of
having been for centuries a deep dim reservoir of life. The life
had probably not been of the most vivid order: for long peri-
ods, no doubt, it had fallen as noiselessly into the past as the
quiet drizzle of autumn fell, hour after hour, into the fish pond
between the yews; but these backwaters of existence sometimes breed, in their sluggish depths, strange acuities of emotion, and Mary Boyne had felt from the first mysterious stir of
intenser memories.

The feeling had never been stronger than on this particular
afternoon when, waiting in the library for the lamps to come,
she rose from her seat and stood among the shadows of the
hearth. Her husband had gone off, after luncheon, for one of
his long tramps on the downs. She had noticed of late that he
preferred to go alone; and, in the tried security of their personal relations, had been driven to conclude that his book was
bothering him, and that he needed the afternoons to turn over
in solitude the problems left from the morning's work. Certainly the book was not going as smoothly as she had thought it
would, and there were lines of perplexity between his eyes
such as had never been there in his engineering days. He had
often, then, looked fagged to the verge of illness, but the
native demon of worry had never branded his brow. Yet the
few pages he had so far read to her—the introduction, and a
summary of the opening chapter—showed a firm hold on his
subject, and an increasing confidence in his powers.

The fact threw her into deeper perplexity, since, now that he
had done with business and its disturbing contingencies, the
one other possible source of anxiety was eliminated. Unless it
were his health, then? But physically he had gained since they
had come to Dorsetshire, grown robuster, ruddier, and fresher
eyed. It was only within the last week that she had felt in him
the undefinable change which made her restless in his absence,
and as tongue-tied in his presence as though it were *she* who
had a secret to keep from him!

The thought that there *was* a secret somewhere between
them struck her with a sudden rap of wonder, and she looked
about her down the long room.

"Can it be the house?" she mused.

The room itself might have been full of secrets. They seemed to be piling themselves up, as evening fell, like the layers and layers of velvet shadow dropping from the low ceiling, the rows of books, the smoke-blurred sculpture of the hearth.

"Why, of course—the house is haunted!" she reflected.

The ghost—Alida's imperceptible ghost—after figuring largely in the banter of their first month or two at Lyng, had been gradually left aside as too ineffectual for imaginative use. Mary had, indeed, as became the tenant of a haunted house, made the customary inquiries among her rural neighbors, but, beyond a vague "They do say so, Ma'am," the villagers had nothing to impart. The elusive specter had apparently never had sufficient identity for a legend to crystallize about it, and after a time the Boynes had set the matter down to their profit-and-loss account, agreeing that Lyng was one of the few houses good enough in itself to dispense with supernatural enhancements.

"And I suppose, poor ineffectual demon, that's why it beats its beautiful wings in vain in the void," Mary had laughingly concluded.

"Or, rather," Ned answered in the same strain, "why, amid so much that's ghostly, it can never affirm its separate existence as *the* ghost." And thereupon their invisible housemate had finally dropped out of their references, which were numerous enough to make them soon unaware of the loss.

Now, as she stood on the hearth, the subject of their earlier curiosity revived in her with a new sense of its meaning—a sense gradually acquired through daily contact with the scene of the lurking mystery. It was the house itself, of course, that possessed the ghost-seeing faculty, that communed visually but secretly with its own past; if one could only get into close enough communion with the house, one might surprise its secret, and acquire the ghost sight on one's own account. Perhaps, in his long hours in this very room, where she never trespassed till the afternoon, her husband *had* acquired it already, and was silently carrying about the weight of whatever it had revealed to him. Mary was too well versed in the code of the spectral world not to know that one could not talk about the ghosts one saw: to do so was almost as great a breach of taste as to name a lady in a club. But this explanation did not really satisfy her. "What, after all, except for the fun of the shudder," she reflected, "would he really care for any of their old ghosts?" And thence she was thrown back once more on the fundamental dilemma: the fact that one's greater or less susceptibility to spectral influences had no particular bearing on the case, since, when one *did* see a ghost at Lyng, one did not know it.

"Not till long afterward," Alida Stair had said. Well, supposing Ned *had* seen one when they first came, and had known only within the last week what had happened to him? More and more under the spell of the hour, she threw back her thoughts to the early days of their tenancy, but at first only to recall a lively confusion of unpacking, settling, arranging of books, and calling to each other from remote corners of the house as, treasure after treasure, it revealed itself to them. It was in this particular connection that she presently recalled a certain soft afternoon of the previous October, when, passing from the first rapturous flurry of exploration to a detailed inspection of the old house, she had pressed (like a novel heroine) a panel that opened on a flight of corkscrew stairs leading to a flat ledge of the roof—the roof which, from below, seemed to slope away on all sides too abruptly for any but practiced feet to scale.

The view from this hidden coign was enchanting, and she had flown down to snatch Ned from his papers and give him the freedom of her discovery. She remembered still how, standing at her side, he had passed his arm about her while their gaze flew to the long tossed horizon line of the downs, and then dropped contentedly back to trace the arabesque of yew hedges about the fish pond, and the shadow of the cedar on the lawn.

"And now the other way," he had said, turning her about within his arm; and closely pressed to him, she had absorbed, like some long satisfying draught, the picture of the grey-walled court, the squat lions on the gates, and the lime avenue reaching up to the highroad under the downs.

It was just then, while they gazed and held each other, that she had felt his arm relax, and heard a sharp "Hullo!" that made her turn to glance at him.

Distinctly, yes, she now recalled that she had seen, as she glanced, a shadow of anxiety, of perplexity, rather, fall across his face; and, following his eyes, had beheld the figure of a

man—a man in loose greyish clothes, as it appeared to her—
who was sauntering down the lime avenue to the court with
the doubtful gait of a stranger who seeks his way. Her shortsighted eyes had given her but a blurred impression of slight-
ness and greyishness, with something foreign, or at least unlocal,
in the cut of the figure or its dress; but her husband had
apparently seen more—seen enough to make him push past
her with a hasty "Wait!" and dash down the stairs without
pausing to give her a hand.

A slight tendency to dizziness obliged her, after a provisional
clutch at the chimney against which they had been leaning, to
follow him first more cautiously; and when she had reached the
landing she paused again, for a less definite reason, leaning
over the banister to strain her eyes through the silence of the
brown sun-flecked depths. She lingered there till, somewhere
in those depths, she heard the closing of a door; then, mechan-
ically impelled, she went down the shallow flights of steps till
she reached the lower hall.

The front door stood open on the sunlight of the court, and
hall and court were empty. The library door was open, too, and
after listening in vain for any sound of voices within, she
crossed the threshold, and found her husband alone, vaguely
fingering the papers on his desk.

He looked up, as if surprised at her entrance, but the shadow
of anxiety had passed from his face, leaving it even, as she
fancied, a little brighter and clearer than usual.

"What was it? Who was it?" she asked.

"Who?" he repeated, with the surprise still all on his side.

"The man we saw coming toward the house."

He seemed to reflect. "The man? Why, I thought I saw
Peters; I dashed after him to say a word about the stable
drains, but he had disappeared before I could get down."

"Disappeared? But he seemed to be walking so slowly when
we saw him."

Boyne shrugged his shoulders. "So I thought; but he must
have got up steam in the interval. What do you say to our
trying a scramble up Meldon Steep before sunset?"

That was all. At the time the occurrence had been less than
nothing, had, indeed, been immediately obliterated by the magic
of their first vision from Meldon Steep, a height which they
had dreamed of climbing ever since they had first seen its bare

spine rising above the roof of Lyng. Doubtless it was the mere fact of the other incident's having occurred on the very day of their ascent to Meldon that had kept it stored away in the fold of memory from which it now emerged; for in itself it had no mark of the portentous. At the moment there could have been nothing more natural than that Ned should dash himself from the roof in the pursuit of dilatory tradesmen. It was the period when they were always on the watch for one or the other of the specialists employed about the place; always lying in wait for them, and rushing out at them with questions, reproaches, or reminders. And certainly in the distance the grey figure had looked like Peters.

Yet now, as she reviewed the scene, she felt her husband's explanation of it to have been invalidated by the look of anxiety on his face. Why had the familiar appearance of Peters made him anxious? Why, above all, if it was of such prime necessity to confer with him on the subject of the stable drains, had the failure to find him produced such a look of relief? Mary could not say that any one of these questions had occurred to her at the time, yet, from the promptness with which they now marshalled themselves at her summons, she had a sense that they must all along have been there, waiting their hour.

II

Weary with her thoughts, she moved to the window. The library was now quite dark, and she was surprised to see how much faint light the outer world still held.

As she peered out into it across the court, a figure shaped itself far down the perspective of bare limes: it looked a mere blot of deeper grey in the greyness, and for an instant, as it moved toward her, her heart thumped to the thought "It's the ghost!"

She had time, in that long instant, to feel suddenly that the man of whom, two months earlier, she had had a distant vision from the roof, was now, at his predestined hour, about to reveal himself as *not* having been Peters; and her spirit sank under the impending fear of the disclosure. But almost with the next tick of the clock the figure, gaining substance and character, showed itself even to her weak sight as her husband's; and she turned to meet him, as he entered, with the confession of her folly.

"It's really too absurd," she laughed out, "but I never *can* remember!"

"Remember what?" Boyne questioned as they drew together.

"That when one sees the Lyng ghost one never knows it."

Her hand was on his sleeve, and he kept it there, but with no response in his gesture or in the lines of his preoccupied face.

"Did you think you'd seen it?" he asked, after an appreciable interval.

"Why, I actually took *you* for it, my dear, in my mad determination to spot it!"

"Me—just now?" His arm dropped away, and he turned from her with a faint echo of her laugh. "Really, dearest, you'd better give it up, if that's the best you can do."

"Oh, yes, I give it up. Have *you?*" she asked, turning round on him abruptly.

The parlormaid had entered with letters and a lamp, and the light struck up into Boyne's face as he bent above the tray she presented.

"Have *you?*" Mary perversely insisted, when the servant had disappeared on her errand of illumination.

"Have I what?" he rejoined absently, the light bringing out the sharp stamp of worry between his brows as he turned over the letters.

"Given up trying to see the ghost." Her heart beat a little at the experiment she was making.

Her husband, laying his letters aside, moved away into the shadow of the hearth.

"I never tried," he said, tearing open the wrapper of a newspaper.

"Well, of course," Mary persisted, "the exasperating thing is that there's no use trying, since one can't be sure till so long afterward."

He was unfolding the paper as if he had hardly heard her; but after a pause, during which the sheets rustled spasmodically between his hands, he looked up to ask, "Have you any idea *how long?*"

Mary had sunk into a low chair beside the fireplace. From her seat she glanced over, startled, at her husband's profile, which was projected against the circle of lamplight.

"No; none. Have *you?*" she retorted, repeating her former phrase with an added stress of intention.

Boyne crumpled the paper into a bunch, and then, inconsequently, turned back with it toward the lamp.

"Lord, no! I only meant," he exclaimed, with a faint tinge of impatience, "is there any legend, any tradition, as to that?"

"Not that I know of," she answered; but the impulse to add "What makes you ask?" was checked by the reappearance of the parlormaid, with tea and a second lamp.

With the dispersal of shadows, and the repetition of the daily domestic office, Mary Boyne felt herself less oppressed by that sense of something mutely imminent which had darkened her afternoon. For a few moments she gave herself to the details of her task, and when she looked up from it she was struck to the point of bewilderment by the change in her husband's face. He had seated himself near the farther lamp, and was absorbed in the perusal of his letters; but was it something he had found in them, or merely the shifting of her own point of view, that had restored his features to their normal aspect? The longer she looked the more definitely the change affirmed itself. The lines of tension had vanished, and such traces of fatigue as lingered were of the kind easily attributable to steady mental effort. He glanced up, as if drawn by her gaze, and met her eyes with a smile.

"I'm dying for my tea, you know; and here's a letter for you," he said.

She took the letter he held out in exchange for the cup she proffered him, and, returning to her seat, broke the seal with the languid gesture of the reader whose interests are all enclosed in the circle of one cherished presence.

Her next conscious motion was that of starting to her feet, the letter falling to them as she rose, while she held out to her husband a newspaper clipping.

"Ned! What's this? What does it mean?"

He had risen at the same instant, almost as if hearing her cry before she uttered it; and for a perceptible space of time he and she studied each other, like adversaries watching for an advantage, across the space between her chair and his desk.

"What's what? You fairly made me jump!" Boyne said at length, moving toward her with a sudden half-exasperated laugh. The shadow of apprehension was on his face again, not

now a look of fixed foreboding, but a shifting vigilance of lips
and eyes that gave her the sense of his feeling himself invisibly
surrounded.

Her hand shook so that she could hardly give him the
clipping.

"This article—from the *Waukesha Sentinel*—that a man named
Elwell has brought suit against you—that there was something
wrong about the Blue Star Mine. I can't understand more than
half."

They continued to face each other as she spoke, and to her
astonishment she saw that her words had the almost immediate
effect of dissipating the strained watchfulness of his look.

"Oh, *that!*" He glanced down the printed slip, and then
folded it with the gesture of one who handles something harmless and familiar. "What's the matter with you this afternoon,
Mary? I thought you'd got bad news."

She stood before him with her undefinable terror subsiding
slowly under the reassurance of his tone.

"You knew about this, then—it's all right?"

"Certainly I knew about it; and it's all right."

"But what *is* it? I don't understand. What does this man
accuse you of?"

"Pretty nearly every crime in the calendar." Boyne had
tossed the clipping down, and thrown himself into an armchair
near the fire. "Do you want to hear the story? It's not particularly interesting—just a squabble over interests in the Blue
Star."

"But who is this Elwell? I don't know the name."

"Oh, he's a fellow I put into it—gave him a hand up. I told
you all about him at the time."

"I dare say. I must have forgotten." Vainly she strained back
among her memories. "But if you helped him, why does he
make this return?"

"Probably some shyster lawyer got hold of him and talked
him over. It's all rather technical and complicated. I thought
that kind of thing bored you."

His wife felt a sting of compunction. Theoretically, she dep-
recated the American wife's detachment from her husband's
professional interests, but in practice she had always found it
difficult to fix her attention on Boyne's report of the transac-
tions in which his varied interests involved him. Besides, she

had felt during their years of exile, that, in a community where
the amenities of living could be obtained only at the cost of
efforts as arduous as her husband's professional labor, such
brief leisure as he and she could command should be used as
an escape from immediate preoccupations, a flight to the life
they always dreamed of living. Once or twice, now that this
new life had actually drawn its magic circle about them, she
had asked herself if she had done right; but hitherto such
conjectures had been no more than the retrospective excursions of an active fancy. Now, for the first time, it startled her a
little to find how little she knew of the material foundation on
which her happiness was built.

She glanced at her husband, and was again reassured by the
composure of his face; yet she felt the need of more definite
grounds for her reassurance.

"But doesn't this suit worry you? Why have you never spoken to me about it?"

He answered both questions at once. "I didn't speak of it at
first because it *did* worry me—annoyed me, rather. But it's all
ancient history now. Your correspondent must have got hold of
a back number of the *Sentinel*."

She felt a quick thrill of relief. "You mean it's over? He's lost
his case?"

There was a just perceptible delay in Boyne's reply. "The
suit's been withdrawn—that's all."

But she persisted, as if to exonerate herself from the inward
charge of being too easily put off. "Withdrawn it because he
saw he had no chance?"

"Oh, he had no chance," Boyne answered.

She was still struggling with a dimly felt perplexity at the
back of her thoughts.

"How long ago was it withdrawn?"

He paused, as if with a slight return to his former uncertainty. "I've just had the news now; but I've been expecting
it."

"Just now—in one of your letters?"

"Yes; in one of my letters."

She made no answer, and was aware only, after a short
interval of waiting, that he had risen, and, strolling across the
room, had placed himself on the sofa at her side. She felt him,
as he did so, pass an arm about her, she felt his hand seek hers

and clasp it, and turning slowly, drawn by the warmth of his cheek, she met his smiling eyes.

"It's all right—it's all right?" she questioned, through the flood of her dissolving doubts; and "I give you my word it was never righter!" he laughed back at her, holding her close.

III

One of the strangest things she was afterward to recall out of all the next day's strangeness was the sudden and complete recovery of her sense of security.

It was in the air when she woke in her low-ceiled, dusky room; it went with her downstairs to the breakfast table, flashed out at her from the fire, and reduplicated itself from the flanks of the urn and the sturdy flutings of the Georgian teapot. It was as if in some roundabout way, all her diffused fears of the previous day, with their moment of sharp concentration about the newspaper article—as if this dim questioning of the future, and startled return upon the past, had between them liquidated the arrears of some haunting moral obligation. If she had indeed been careless of her husband's affairs, it was, her new state seemed to prove, because her faith in him instinctively justified such carelessness; and his right to her faith had now affirmed itself in the very face of menace and suspicion. She had never seen him more untroubled, more naturally and unconsciously himself, than after the cross-examination to which she had subjected him: it was almost as if he had been aware of her doubts, and had wanted the air cleared as much as she did.

It was as clear, thank heaven, as the bright outer light that surprised her almost with a touch of summer when she issued from the house for her daily round of the gardens. She had left Boyne at his desk, indulging herself, as she passed the library door, by a last peep at his quiet face, where he bent, pipe in mouth, about his papers; and now she had her own morning's task to perform. The task involved, on such charmed winter days, almost as much happy loitering about the different quarters of her domain as if spring were already at work there. There were such endless possibilities still before her, such opportunities to bring out the latent graces of the old place, without a single irreverent touch of alteration, that the winter was all too short to plan what spring and autumn executed.

And her recovered sense of safety gave, on this particular morning, a peculiar zest to her progress through the sweet still place. She went first to the kitchen garden, where the espaliered pear trees drew complicated patterns on the walls, and pigeons were fluttering and preening about the silvery-slated roof of their cot. There was something wrong about the piping of the hothouse, and she was expecting an authority from Dorchester, who was to drive out between trains and make a diagnosis of the boiler. But when she dipped into the damp heat of the greenhouses, among the spiced scents and waxy pinks and reds of old-fashioned exotics—even the flora of Lyng was in the note!—she learned that the great man had not arrived, and, the day being too rare to waste in an artificial atmosphere, she came out again and paced along the springy turf of the bowling green to the gardens behind the house. At their farther end rose a grass terrace, looking across the fish pond and yew hedges to the long house front with its twisted chimney stacks and blue roof angles all drenched in the pale gold moisture of the air.

Seen thus, across the level tracery of the gardens, it sent her, from open windows and hospitably smoking chimneys, the look of some warm human presence, of a mind slowly ripened on a sunny wall of experience. She had never before had such a sense of her intimacy with it, such a conviction that its secrets were all beneficent, kept, as they said to children, "for one's good," such a trust in its power to gather up her life and Ned's into the harmonious pattern of the long long story it sat there weaving in the sun.

She heard steps behind her, and turned, expecting to see the gardener accompanied by the engineer from Dorchester. But only one figure was in sight, that of a youngish slightly built man, who, for reasons she could not on the spot have given, did not remotely resemble her notion of an authority on hothouse boilers. The newcomer, on seeing her, lifted his hat, and paused with the air of a gentleman—perhaps a traveler—who wishes to make it known that his intrusion is involuntary. Lyng occasionally attracted the more cultivated traveler, and Mary half expected to see the stranger dissemble a camera, or justify his presence by producing it. But he made no gesture of any sort, and after a moment she asked, in a tone responding to the courteous hesitation of his attitude: "Is there anyone you wish to see?"

"I came to see Mr. Boyne," he answered. His intonation, rather than his accent, was faintly American, and Mary, at the note, looked at him more closely. The brim of his soft felt hat cast a shade on his face, which, thus obscured, wore to her shortsighted gaze a look of seriousness, as of a person arriving on business, and civilly but firmly aware of his rights.

Past experience had made her equally sensible to such claims; but she was jealous of her husband's morning hours, and doubtful of his having given anyone the right to intrude on them.

"Have you an appointment with my husband?" she asked.

The visitor hesitated, as if unprepared for the question.

"I think he expects me," he replied.

It was Mary's turn to hesitate. "You see this is his time for work: he never sees anyone in the morning."

He looked at her a moment without answering; then, as if accepting her decision, he began to move away. As he turned, Mary saw him pause and glance up at the peaceful house front. Something in his air suggested weariness and disappointment, the dejection of the traveler who has come from far off and whose hours are limited by the timetable. It occurred to her that if this were the case her refusal might have made his errand vain, and a sense of compunction caused her to hasten after him.

"May I ask if you have come a long way?"

He gave her the same grave look. "Yes—I have come a long way."

"Then, if you'll go to the house, no doubt my husband will see you now. You'll find him in the library."

She did not know why she had added the last phrase, except from a vague impulse to atone for her previous inhospitality. The visitor seemed about to express his thanks, but her attention was distracted by the approach of the gardener with a companion who bore all the marks of being the expert from Dorchester.

"This way," she said, waving the stranger to the house; and an instant later she had forgotten him in the absorption of her meeting with the boiler maker.

The encounter led to such far-reaching results that the engineer ended by finding it expedient to ignore his train, and

Mary was beguiled into spending the remainder of the morning
in absorbed confabulation among the flower pots. When the
colloquy ended, she was surprised to find that it was nearly
luncheon time, and she half expected, as she hurried back to
the house, to see her husband coming out to meet her. But she
found no one in the court but an undergardener raking the
gravel, and the hall, when she entered it, was so silent that she
guessed Boyne to be still at work.

Not wishing to disturb him, she turned into the drawing
room, and there, at her writing table, lost herself in renewed
calculations of the outlay to which the morning's conference
had pledged her. The fact that she could permit herself such
follies had not yet lost its novelty; and somehow, in contrast to
the vague fears of the previous days, it now seemed an element
of her recovered security, of the sense that, as Ned had said,
things in general had never been "righter."

She was still luxuriating in a lavish play of figures when the
parlormaid, from the threshold, roused her with an inquiry as
to the expediency of serving luncheon. It was one of their jokes
that Trimmle announced luncheon as if she were divulging a
state secret, and Mary, intent upon her papers, merely murmured an absent-minded assent.

She felt Trimmle wavering doubtfully on the threshold, as if
in rebuke of such unconsidered assent; then her retreating
steps sounded down the passage, and Mary, pushing away her
papers, crossed the hall and went to the library door. It was
still closed, and she wavered in her turn, disliking to disturb
her husband, yet anxious that he should not exceed his usual
measure of work. As she stood there, balancing her impulses,
Trimmle returned with the announcement of luncheon, and
Mary, thus impelled, opened the library door.

Boyne was not at his desk, and she peered about her, expecting to discover him before the bookshelves, somewhere
down the length of the room; but her call brought no response,
and gradually it became clear to her that he was not there.

She turned back to the parlormaid.

"Mr. Boyne must be upstairs. Please tell him that luncheon
is ready."

Trimmle appeared to hesitate between the obvious duty of
obedience and an equally obvious conviction of the foolishness
of the injunction laid on her. The struggle resulted in her

saying: "If you please, Madam, Mr. Boyne's not upstairs."

"Not in his room? Are you sure?"

"I'm sure, Madam."

Mary consulted the clock. "Where is he, then?"

"He's gone out," Trimmle announced, with the superior air of one who has respectfully waited for the question that a well-ordered mind would have put first.

Mary's conjecture had been right, then. Boyne must have gone to the gardens to meet her, and since she had missed him, it was clear that he had taken the shorter way by the south door, instead of going round to the court. She crossed the hall to the French window opening directly on the yew garden, but the parlormaid, after another moment of inner conflict, decided to bring out: "Please, Madam, Mr. Boyne didn't go that way."

Mary turned back. "Where *did* he go? And when?"

"He went out of the front door, up the drive, Madam." It was a matter of principle with Trimmle never to answer more than one question at a time.

"Up the drive? At this hour?" Mary went to the door herself, and glanced across the court through the tunnel of bare limes. But its perspective was as empty as when she had scanned it on entering.

"Did Mr. Boyne leave no message?"

Trimmle seemed to surrender herself to a last struggle with the forces of chaos.

"No, Madam. He just went out with the gentleman."

"The gentleman? What gentleman?" Mary wheeled about, as if to front this new factor.

"The gentleman who called, Madam," said Trimmle resignedly.

"When did a gentleman call? Do explain yourself, Trimmle!"

Only the fact that Mary was very hungry, and that she wanted to consult her husband about the greenhouses, would have caused her to lay so unusual an injunction on her attendant; and even now she was detached enough to note in Trimmle's eye the dawning defiance of the respectful subordinate who has been pressed too hard.

"I couldn't exactly say the hour, Madam, because I didn't let the gentleman in," she replied, with an air of discreetly ignoring the irregularity of her mistress's course.

"You didn't let him in?"

"No, Madam. When the bell rang I was dressing, and Agnes—"

"Go and ask Agnes, then," said Mary.

Trimmle still wore her look of patient magnanimity. "Agnes would not know, Madam, for she had unfortunately burnt her hand in trimming the wick of the new lamp from town" —Trimmle, as Mary was aware, had always been opposed to the new lamp—"and so Mrs. Dockett sent the kitchenmaid instead."

Mary looked again at the clock. "It's after two! Go and ask the kitchenmaid if Mr. Boyne left any word."

She went into luncheon without waiting, and Trimmle presently brought her there the kitchenmaid's statement that the gentleman had called about eleven o'clock, and that Mr. Boyne had gone out with him without leaving any message. The kitchenmaid did not even know the caller's name, for he had written it on a slip of paper, which he had folded and handed to her, with the injunction to deliver it at once to Mr. Boyne.

Mary finished her luncheon, still wondering, and when it was over, and Trimmle had brought the coffee to the drawing room, her wonder had deepened to a first faint tinge of disquietude. It was unlike Boyne to absent himself without explanation at so unwonted an hour, and the difficulty of identifying the visitor whose summons he had apparently obeyed made his disappearance the more unaccountable. Mary Boyne's experience as the wife of a busy engineer, subject to sudden calls and compelled to keep irregular hours, had trained her to the philosophic acceptance of surprises; but since Boyne's withdrawal from business he had adopted a Benedictine regularity of life. As if to make up for the dispersed and agitated years, with their "stand-up" lunches, and dinners rattled down to the joltings of the dining cars, he cultivated the last refinements of punctuality and monotony, discouraging his wife's fancy for the unexpected, and declaring that to a delicate taste there were infinite gradations of pleasure in the recurrences of habit.

Still, since no life can completely defend itself from the unforeseen, it was evident that all Boyne's precautions would sooner or later prove unavailable, and Mary concluded that he had cut short a tiresome visit by walking with his caller to the station, or at least accompanying him for part of the way.

This conclusion relieved her from further preoccupation, and she went out herself to take up her conference with the gardener. Thence she walked to the village post office, a mile or so away; and when she turned toward home the early twilight was setting in.

She had taken a footpath across the downs, and as Boyne, meanwhile, had probably returned from the station by the highroad, there was little likelihood of their meeting. She felt sure, however, of his having reached the house before her; so sure that, when she entered it herself, without even pausing to inquire of Trimmle, she made directly for the library. But the library was still empty, and with an unwonted exactness of visual memory she observed that the papers on her husband's desk lay precisely as they had lain when she had gone in to call him to luncheon.

Then of a sudden she was seized by a vague dread of the unknown. She had closed the door behind her on entering, and as she stood alone in the long silent room, her dread seemed to take shape and sound, to be there breathing and lurking among the shadows. Her shortsighted eyes strained through them, half-discerning an actual presence, something aloof, that watched and knew; and in the recoil from that intangible presence she threw herself on the bell rope and gave it a sharp pull.

The sharp summons brought Trimmle in precipitately with a lamp, and Mary breathed again at this sobering reappearance of the usual.

"You may bring tea if Mr. Boyne is in," she said, to justify her ring.

"Very well, Madam. But Mr. Boyne is not in," said Trimmle, putting down the lamp.

"Not in? You mean he's come back and gone out again?"

"No, Madam. He's never been back."

The dread stirred again, and Mary knew that now it had her fast.

"Not since he went out with—the gentleman?"

"Not since he went out with the gentleman."

"But who *was* the gentleman?" Mary insisted, with the shrill note of someone trying to be heard through a confusion of noises.

"That I couldn't say, Madam." Trimmle, standing there by the lamp, seemed suddenly to grow less round and rosy, as though eclipsed by the same creeping shade of apprehension.

"But the kitchenmaid knows—wasn't it the kitchenmaid who let him in?"

"She doesn't know either, Madam, for he wrote his name on a folded paper."

Mary, through her agitation, was aware that they were both designating the unknown visitor by a vague pronoun, instead of the conventional formula which, till then, had kept their allusions within the bounds of conformity. And at the same moment her mind caught at the suggestion of the folded paper.

"But he must have a name! Where's the paper?"

She moved to the desk, and began to turn over the documents that littered it. The first that caught her eye was an unfinished letter in her husband's hand, with his pen lying across it, as though dropped there at a sudden summons.

"My dear Parvis"—who was Parvis?—"I have just received your letter announcing Elwell's death, and while I suppose there is now no further risk of trouble, it might be safer—"

She tossed the sheet aside, and continued her search; but no folded paper was discoverable among the letters and pages of manuscript which had been swept together in a heap, as if by a hurried or a startled gesture.

"But the kitchenmaid *saw* him. Send her here," she commanded, wondering at her dullness in not thinking sooner of so simple a solution.

Trimmle vanished in a flash, as if thankful to be out of the room, and when she reappeared, conducting the agitated underling, Mary had regained her self-possession, and had her questions ready.

The gentleman was a stranger, yes—that she understood. But what had he said? And, above all, what had he looked like? The first question was easily enough answered, for the disconcerting reason that he had said so little—had merely asked for Mr. Boyne, and, scribbling something on a bit of paper, had requested that it should at once be carried in to him.

"Then you don't know what he wrote? You're not sure it *was* his name?"

The kitchenmaid was not sure, but supposed it was, since he had written it in answer to her inquiry as to whom she should announce.

"And when you carried the paper in to Mr. Boyne, what did he say?"

The kitchenmaid did not think that Mr. Boyne had said anything, but she could not be sure, for just as she had handed him the paper and he was opening it, she had become aware that the visitor had followed her into the library, and she had slipped out, leaving the two gentlemen together.

"But then, if you left them in the library, how do you know that they went out of the house?"

This question plunged the witness into a momentary inarticulateness, from which she was rescued by Trimmle, who, by means of ingenious circumlocutions, elicited the statement that before she could cross the hall to the back passage she had heard the two gentlemen behind her, and had seen them go out of the front door together.

"Then, if you saw the strange gentleman twice, you must be able to tell me what he looked like."

But with this final challenge to her powers of expression it became clear that the limit of the kitchenmaid's endurance had been reached. The obligation of going to the front door to "show in" a visitor was in itself so subversive of the fundamental order of things that it had thrown her faculties into hopeless disarray, and she could only stammer out, after various panting efforts: "His hat, mum, was different-like, as you might say—"

"Different? How different?" Mary flashed out, her own mind, in the same instant, leaping back to an image left on it that morning, and then lost under layers of subsequent impressions.

"His hat had a wide brim, you mean, and his face was pale—a youngish face?" Mary pressed her, with a white-lipped intensity of interrogation. But if the kitchenmaid found any adequate answer to this challenge, it was swept away for her listener down the rushing current of her own convictions. The stranger—the stranger in the garden! Why had Mary not thought of him before? She needed no one now to tell her that it was he who had called for her husband and gone away with him. But who was he, and why had Boyne obeyed him?

IV

It leaped out at her suddenly, like a grin out of the dark, that they had often called England so little—"such a confoundedly hard place to get lost in."

A confoundedly hard place to get lost in! That had been her

husband's phrase. And now, with the whole machinery of
official investigation sweeping its flashlights from shore to shore,
and across the dividing straits; now, with Boyne's name blazing
from the walls of every town and village, his portrait (how that
wrung her!) hawked up and down the country like the image of
a hunted criminal; now the little compact populous island, so
policed, surveyed, and administered, revealed itself as a
Sphinxlike guardian of abysmal mysteries, staring back into his
wife's anguished eyes as if with the wicked joy of knowing
something they would never know!

In the fortnight since Boyne's disappearance there had been
no word of him, no trace of his movements. Even the usual
misleading reports that raise expectancy in tortured bosoms
had been few and fleeting. No one but the kitchenmaid had
seen Boyne leave the house, and no one else had seen "the
gentleman" who accompanied him. All inquiries in the neighborhood failed to elicit the memory of a stranger's presence
that day in the neighborhood of Lyng. And no one had met
Edward Boyne, either alone or in company, in any of the
neighboring villages, or on the road across the downs, or at
either of the local railway stations. The sunny English noon
had swallowed him as completely as if he had gone out into
Cimmerian night.

Mary, while every official means of investigation was working at its highest pressure, had ransacked her husband's papers
for any trace of antecedent complications, of entanglements or
obligations unknown to her, that might throw a ray into the
darkness. But if any such had existed in the background of
Boyne's life, they had vanished like the slip of paper on which
the visitor had written his name. There remained no possible
thread of guidance except—if it were indeed an exception—the
letter which Boyne had apparently been in the act of writing
when he received his mysterious summons. That letter, read
and reread by his wife, and submitted by her to the police,
yielded little enough to feed conjecture.

"I have just heard of Elwell's death, and while I suppose
there is now no further risk of trouble, it might be safer—"
That was all. The "risk of trouble" was easily explained by the
newspaper clipping which had apprised Mary of the suit brought
against her husband by one of his associates in the Blue Star
enterprise. The only new information conveyed by the letter

was the fact of its showing Boyne, when he wrote it, to be still apprehensive of the results of the suit, though he had told his wife that it had been withdrawn, and though the letter itself proved that the plaintiff was dead. It took several days of cabling to fix the identity of the "Parvis" to whom the fragment was addressed, but even after these inquiries had shown him to be a Waukesha lawyer, no new facts concerning the Elwell suit were elicited. He appeared to have had no direct concern in it, but to have been conversant with the facts merely as an acquaintance, and possible intermediary; and he declared himself unable to guess with what object Boyne intended to seek his assistance.

This negative information, sole fruit of the first fortnight's search, was not increased by a jot during the slow weeks that followed. Mary knew that the investigations were still being carried on, but she had a vague sense of their gradually slackening, as the actual march of time seemed to slacken. It was as though the days, flying horror-struck from the shrouded image of the one inscrutable day, gained assurance as the distance lengthened, till at last they fell back into their normal gait. And so with the human imaginations at work on the dark event. No doubt it occupied them still, but week by week and hour by hour it grew less absorbing, took up less space, was slowly but inevitably crowded out of the foreground of consciousness by the new problems perpetually bubbling up from the cloudy caldron of human experience.

Even Mary Boyne's consciousness gradually felt the same lowering of velocity. It still swayed with the incessant oscillations of conjecture; but they were slower, more rhythmical in their beat. There were even moments of weariness when, like the victim of some poison which leaves the brain clear, but holds the body motionless, she saw herself domesticated with the Horror, accepting its perpetual presence as one of the fixed conditions of life.

These moments lengthened into hours and days, till she passed into a phase of stolid acquiescence. She watched the routine of daily life with the incurious eye of a savage on whom the meaningless processes of civilization make but the faintest impression. She had come to regard herself as part of the routine, a spoke of the wheel, revolving with its motion; she felt almost like the furniture of the room in which she sat, an

insensate object to be dusted and pushed about with the chairs
and tables. And this deepening apathy held her fast at Lyng,
in spite of the entreaties of friends and the usual medical
recommendation of "change." Her friends supposed that her
refusal to move was inspired by the belief that her husband
would one day return to the spot from which he had vanished,
and a beautiful legend grew up about this imaginary state of
waiting. But in reality she had no such belief: the depths of
anguish enclosing her were no longer lighted by flashes of
hope. She was sure that Boyne would never come back, that he
had gone out of her sight as completely as if Death itself had
waited that day on the threshold. She had even renounced,
one by one, the various theories as to his disappearance which
had been advanced by the press, the police, and her own
agonized imagination. In sheer lassitude her mind turned from
these alternatives of horror, and sank back into the blank fact
that he was gone.

No, she would never know what had become of him—no one
would ever know. But the house *knew*; the library in which she
spent her long lonely evenings knew. For it was here that the
last scene had been enacted, here that the stranger had come,
and spoken the word which had caused Boyne to rise and
follow him. The floor she trod had felt his tread; the books on
the shelves had seen his face; and there were moments when
the intense consciousness of the old dusky walls seemed about
to break out into some audible revelation of their secret. But
the revelation never came, and she knew it would never come.
Lyng was not one of the garrulous old houses that betray the
secrets entrusted to them. Its very legend proved that it had
always been the mute accomplice, the incorruptible custodian,
of the mysteries it had surprised. And Mary Boyne, sitting face
to face with its silence, felt the futility of seeking to break it by
any human means.

V

"I don't say it *wasn't* straight, and yet I don't say it *was*
straight. It was business."

Mary, at the words, lifted her head with a start, and looked
intently at the speaker.

When, half an hour before, a card with "Mr. Parvis" on it

had been brought up to her, she had been immediately aware that the name had been a part of her consciousness ever since she had read it at the head of Boyne's unfinished letter. In the library she had found awaiting her a small sallow man with a bald head and gold eyeglasses, and it sent a tremor through her to know that this was the person to whom her husband's last known thought had been directed.

Parvis, civilly, but without vain preamble—in the manner of a man who has his watch in his hand—had set forth the object of his visit. He had "run over" to England on business, and finding himself in the neighborhood of Dorchester, had not wished to leave it without paying his respects to Mrs. Boyne; and without asking her, if the occasion offered, what she meant to do about Bob Elwell's family.

The words touched the spring of some obscure dread in Mary's bosom. Did her visitor, after all, know what Boyne had meant by his unfinished phrase? She asked for an elucidation of his question, and noticed at once that he seemed surprised at her continued ignorance of the subject. Was it possible that she really knew as little as she said?

"I know nothing—you must tell me," she faltered out; and her visitor thereupon proceeded to unfold his story. It threw, even to her confused perceptions, and imperfectly initiated vision, a lurid glare on the whole hazy episode of the Blue Star Mine. Her husband had made his money in that brilliant speculation at the cost of "getting ahead" of someone less alert to seize the chance; and the victim of his ingenuity was young Robert Elwell, who had "put him on" to the Blue Star scheme.

Parvis, at Mary's first cry, had thrown her a sobering glance through his impartial glasses.

"Bob Elwell wasn't smart enough, that's all; if he had been, he might have turned round and served Boyne the same way. It's the kind of thing that happens every day in business. I guess it's what the scientists call the survival of the fittest—see?" said Mr. Parvis, evidently pleased with the aptness of his analogy.

Mary felt a physical shrinking from the next question she tried to frame: it was as though the words on her lips had a taste that nauseated her.

"But then—you accuse my husband of doing something dishonorable?"

Mr. Parvis surveyed the question dispassionately. "Oh, no, I don't. I don't even say it wasn't straight." He glanced up and down the long lines of books, as if one of them might have supplied him with the definition he sought. "I don't say it *wasn't* straight, and yet I don't say it *was* straight. It was business." After all, no definition in his category could be more comprehensive than that.

Mary sat staring at him with a look of terror. He seemed to her like the indifferent emissary of some evil power.

"But Mr. Elwell's lawyers apparently did not take your view, since I suppose the suit was withdrawn by their advice."

"Oh, yes; they knew he hadn't a leg to stand on, technically. It was when they advised him to withdraw the suit that he got desperate. You see, he'd borrowed most of the money he lost in the Blue Star, and he was up a tree. That's why he shot himself when they told him he had no show."

The horror was sweeping over Mary in great deafening waves.

"He shot himself? He killed himself because of *that?*"

"Well, he didn't kill himself, exactly. He dragged on two months before he died." Parvis emitted the statement as unemotionally as a gramophone grinding out its record.

"You mean that he tried to kill himself, and failed? And tried again?"

"Oh, he didn't have to *try* again," said Parvis grimly.

They sat opposite each other in silence, he swinging his eyeglasses thoughtfully about his finger, she, motionless, her arms stretched along her knees in an attitude of rigid tension.

"But if you knew all this," she began at length, hardly able to force her voice above a whisper, "how is it that when I wrote you at the time of my husband's disappearance you said you didn't understand his letter?"

Parvis received this without perceptible embarrassment: "Why, I didn't understand it—strictly speaking. And it wasn't the time to talk about it, if I had. The Elwell business was settled when the suit was withdrawn. Nothing I could have told you would have helped you to find your husband."

Mary continued to scrutinize him. "Then why are you telling me now?"

Still Parvis did not hesitate. "Well, to begin with, I supposed you knew more than you appear to—I mean about the circumstances of Elwell's death. And then people are talking of it now;

the whole matter's been raked up again. And I thought if you didn't know you ought to."

She remained silent, and he continued: "You see, it's only come out lately what a bad state Elwell's affairs were in. His wife's a proud woman, and she fought on as long as she could, going out to work, and taking sewing at home when she got too sick—something with the heart, I believe. But she had his mother to look after, and the children, and she broke down under it, and finally had to ask for help. That called attention to the case, and the papers took it up, and a subscription was started. Everybody out there liked Bob Elwell, and most of the prominent names in the place are down on the list, and people began to wonder why—"

Parvis broke off to fumble in an inner pocket. "Here," he continued, "here's an account of the whole thing from the *Sentinel*—a little sensational, of course. But I guess you'd better look it over."

He held out a newspaper to Mary, who unfolded it slowly, remembering, as she did so, the evening when, in that same room, the perusal of a clipping from the *Sentinel* had first shaken the depths of her security.

As she opened the paper, her eyes, shrinking from the glaring headlines, "Widow of Boyne's Victim Forced to Appeal for Aid," ran down the column of text to two portraits inserted in it. The first was her husband's, taken from a photograph made the year they had come to England. It was the picture of him that she liked best, the one that stood on the writing table upstairs in her bedroom. As the eyes in the photograph met hers, she felt it would be impossible to read what was said of him, and closed her lids with the sharpness of the pain.

"I thought if you felt disposed to put your name down—" she heard Parvis continue.

She opened her eyes with an effort, and they fell on the other portrait. It was that of a youngish man, slightly built, with features somewhat blurred by the shadow of a projecting hat brim. Where had she seen that outline before? She stared at it confusedly, her heart hammering in her ears. Then she gave a cry.

"This is the man—the man who came for my husband!"

She heard Parvis start to his feet, and was dimly aware that she had slipped backward into the corner of the sofa, and that he was bending above her in alarm. She straightened herself, and reached out for the paper, which she had dropped.

"It's the man! I should know him anywhere!" she persisted in a voice that sounded to her own ears like a scream.

Parvis's answer seemed to come to her from far off, down endless fog-muffled windings.

"Mrs. Boyne, you're not very well. Shall I call somebody? Shall I get a glass of water?"

"No, no, no!" She threw herself toward him, her hand frantically clutching the newspaper. "I tell you, it's the man! I *know* him! He spoke to me in the garden!"

Parvis took the journal from her, directing his glasses to the portrait. "It can't be, Mrs. Boyne. It's Robert Elwell."

"Robert Elwell?" Her white stare seemed to travel into space. "Then it was Robert Elwell who came for him."

"Came for Boyne? The day he went away from here?" Parvis's voice dropped as hers rose. He bent over, laying a fraternal hand on her, as if to coax her gently back into her seat. "Why, Elwell was dead! Don't you remember?"

Mary sat with her eyes fixed on the picture, unconscious of what he was saying.

"Don't you remember Boyne's unfinished letter to me—the one you found on his desk that day? It was written just after he'd heard of Elwell's death." She noticed an odd shake in Parvis's unemotional voice. "Surely you remember!" he urged her.

Yes, she remembered: that was the profoundest horror of it. Elwell had died the day before her husband's disappearance; and this was Elwell's portrait; and it was the portrait of the man who had spoken to her in the garden. She lifted her head and looked slowly about the library. The library could have borne witness that it was also the portrait of the man who had come in that day to call Boyne from his unfinished letter. Through the misty surgings of her brain she heard the faint boom of half-forgotten words—words spoken by Alida Stair on the lawn at Pangbourne before Boyne and his wife had ever seen the house at Lyng, or had imagined that they might one day live there.

"This was the man who spoke to me," she repeated.

She looked again at Parvis. He was trying to conceal his disturbance under what he probably imagined to be an expres-

sion of indulgent commiseration; but the edges of his lips were
blue. "He thinks me mad; but I'm not mad," she reflected; and
suddenly there flashed upon her a way of justifying her strange
affirmation.

She sat quiet, controlling the quiver of her lips, and waiting
till she could trust her voice; then she said, looking straight at
Parvis: "Will you answer me one question, please? When was
it that Robert Elwell tried to kill himself?"

"When—when?" Parvis stammered.

"Yes; the date. Please try to remember."

She saw that he was growing still more afraid of her. "I have
a reason," she insisted.

"Yes, yes. Only I can't remember. About two months before,
I should say."

"I want the date," she repeated.

Parvis picked up the newspaper. "We might see here," he
said, still humoring her. He ran his eyes down the page. "Here
it is. Last October—the—"

She caught the words from him. "The 20th, wasn't it?" With
a sharp look at her, he verified. "Yes, the 20th. Then you *did*
know?"

"I know now." Her gaze continued to travel past him. "Sunday, the 20th—that was the day he came first."

Parvis's voice was almost inaudible. "Came *here* first?"

"Yes."

"You saw him twice, then?"

"Yes, twice." She just breathed it at him. "He came first on
the 20th of October. I remember the date because it was the
day we went up Meldon Steep for the first time." She felt a
faint gasp of inward laughter at the thought that but for that
she might have forgotten.

Parvis continued to scrutinize her, as if trying to intercept
her gaze.

"We saw him from the roof," she went on. "He came down
the lime avenue toward the house. He was dressed just as he is
in that picture. My husband saw him first. He was frightened,
and ran down ahead of me; but there was no one there. He had
vanished."

"Elwell had vanished?" Parvis faltered.

"Yes." Their two whispers seemed to grope for each other.
"I couldn't think what had happened. I see now. He *tried* to

come then; but he wasn't dead enough—he couldn't reach us. He had to wait for two months to die; and then he came back again—and Ned went with him."

She nodded at Parvis with the look of triumph of a child who has worked out a difficult puzzle. But suddenly she lifted her hands with a desperate gesture, pressing them to her temples.

"Oh, my God! I sent him to Ned—I told him where to go! I sent him to this room!" she screamed.

She felt the walls of books rush toward her, like inward falling ruins; and she heard Parvis, a long way off, through the ruins, crying to her, and struggling to get at her. But she was numb to his touch, she did not know what he was saying. Through the tumult she heard but one clear note, the voice of Alida Stair, speaking on the lawn at Pangbourne.

"You won't know till afterward," it said. "You won't know till long, long afterward."

MIRIAM

Truman Capote

For several years, Mrs. H. T. Miller had lived alone in a pleasant apartment (two rooms with kitchenette) in a remodeled brownstone near the East River. She was a widow: Mr. H. T. Miller had left a reasonable amount of insurance. Her interests were narrow, she had no friends to speak of, and she rarely journeyed farther than the corner grocery. The other people in the house never seemed to notice her: her clothes were matter-of-fact, her hair iron-gray, clipped and casually waved; she did not use cosmetics, her features were plain and inconspicuous, and on her last birthday she was sixty-one. Her activities were seldom spontaneous: she kept the two rooms immaculate, smoked an occasional cigarette, prepared her own meals and tended a canary.

Then she met Miriam. It was snowing that night. Mrs. Miller had finished drying the supper dishes and was thumbing through an afternoon paper when she saw an advertisement of a picture playing at a neighborhood theater. The title sounded good, so she struggled into her beaver coat, laced her galoshes and left the apartment, leaving one light burning in the foyer: she found nothing more disturbing than a sensation of darkness.

The snow was fine, falling gently, not yet making an impression on the pavement. The wind from the river cut only at street crossings. Mrs. Miller hurried, her head bowed, oblivious as a mole burrowing a blind path. She stopped at a drugstore and bought a package of peppermints.

A long line stretched in front of the box office; she took her place at the end. There would be (a tired voice groaned) a short wait for all seats. Mrs. Miller rummaged in her leather handbag till she collected exactly the correct change for admission. The line seemed to be taking its own time and, looking around for some distraction, she suddenly became conscious of a little girl standing under the edge of the marquee.

Her hair was the longest and strangest Mrs. Miller had ever seen: absolutely silver-white, like an albino's. It flowed waist-length in smooth, loose lines. She was thin and fragilely constructed. There was a simple, special elegance in the way she stood with her thumbs in the pockets of a tailored plum-velvet coat.

Mrs. Miller felt oddly excited, and when the little girl glanced toward her, she smiled warmly. The little girl walked over and said, "Would you care to do me a favor?"

"I'd be glad to, if I can," said Mrs. Miller.

"Oh, it's quite easy. I merely want you to buy a ticket for me; they won't let me in otherwise. Here, I have the money." And gracefully she handed Mrs. Miller two dimes and a nickel.

They went into the theater together. An usherette directed them to a lounge; in twenty minutes the picture would be over.

"I feel just like a genuine criminal," said Mrs. Miller gaily, as she sat down. "I mean that sort of thing's against the law, isn't it? I do hope I haven't done the wrong thing. Your mother knows where you are, dear? I mean she does, doesn't she?"

The little girl said nothing. She unbuttoned her coat and folded it across her lap. Her dress underneath was prim and dark blue. A gold chain dangled about her neck, and her fingers, sensitive and musical-looking, toyed with it. Examining her more attentively, Mrs. Miller decided the truly distinctive feature was not her hair, but her eyes; they were hazel, steady, lacking any childlike quality whatsoever and, because of their size, seemed to consume her small face.

Mrs. Miller offered a peppermint. "What's your name, dear?"

"Miriam," she said, as though, in some curious way, it were information already familiar.

"Why, isn't that funny—my name's Miriam, too. And it's not a terribly common name either. Now, don't tell me your last name's Miller!"

"Just Miriam."

"But isn't that funny?"

"Moderately," said Miriam, and rolled the peppermint on her tongue.

Mrs. Miller flushed and shifted uncomfortably. "You have such a large vocabulary for such a little girl."

"Do I?"

"Well, yes," said Mrs. Miller, hastily changing the topic to: "Do you like the movies?"

"I really wouldn't know," said Miriam. "I've never been before."

Women began filling the lounge; the rumble of the newsreel bombs exploded in the distance. Mrs. Miller rose, tucking her purse under her arm. "I guess I'd better be running now if I want to get a seat," she said. "It was nice to have met you."

Miriam nodded ever so slightly.

It snowed all week. Wheels and footsteps moved soundlessly on the street, as if the business of living continued secretly behind a pale but impenetrable curtain. In the falling quiet there was no sky or earth, only snow lifting in the wind, frosting the window glass, chilling the rooms, deadening and hushing the city. At all hours it was necessary to keep a lamp lighted, and Mrs. Miller lost track of the days: Friday was no different from Saturday and on Sunday she went to the grocery: closed, of course.

That evening she scrambled eggs and fixed a bowl of tomato soup. Then, after putting on a flannel robe and cold-creaming her face, she propped herself up in bed with a hot-water bottle under her feet. She was reading the *Times* when the doorbell rang. At first she thought it must be a mistake and whoever it was would go away. But it rang and rang and settled to a persistent buzz. She looked at the clock: a little after eleven; it did not seem possible, she was always asleep by ten.

Climbing out of bed, she trotted barefoot across the living room. "I'm coming, please be patient." The latch was caught; she turned it this way and that way and the bell never paused an instant. "Stop it," she cried. The bolt gave way and she opened the door an inch. "What in heaven's name?"

"Hello," said Miriam.

"Oh . . . why, hello," said Mrs. Miller, stepping hesitantly into the hall. "You're that little girl."

"I thought you'd never answer, but I kept my finger on the button; I knew you were home. Aren't you glad to see me?"

Mrs. Miller did not know what to say. Miriam, she saw, wore the same plum-velvet coat and now she had also a beret to match; her white hair was braided in two shining plaits and looped at the ends with enormous white ribbons.

"Since I've waited so long, you could at least let me in," she said.

"It's awfully late. . . ."

Miriam regarded her blankly. "What difference does that make? Let me in. It's cold out here and I have on a silk dress." Then, with a gentle gesture, she urged Mrs. Miller aside and passed into the apartment.

She dropped her coat and beret on a chair. She was indeed wearing a silk dress. White silk. White silk in February. The skirt was beautifully pleated and the sleeves long; it made a faint rustle as she strolled about the room. "I like your place," she said. "I like the rug, blue's my favorite color." She touched a paper rose in a vase on the coffee table. "Imitation," she commented wanly. "How sad. Aren't imitations sad?" She seated herself on the sofa, daintily spreading her skirt.

"What do you want?" asked Mrs. Miller.

"Sit down," said Miriam. "It makes me nervous to see people stand."

Mrs. Miller sank to a hassock. "What do you want?" she repeated.

"You know, I don't think you're glad I came."

For a second time Mrs. Miller was without an answer; her hand motioned vaguely. Miriam giggled and pressed back on a mound of chintz pillows. Mrs. Miller observed that the girl was less pale than she remembered; her cheeks were flushed.

"How did you know where I lived?"

Miriam frowned. "That's no question at all. What's your name? What's mine?"

"But I'm not listed in the phone book."

"Oh, let's talk about something else."

Mrs. Miller said, "Your mother must be insane to let a child like you wander around at all hours of the night—and in such ridiculous clothes. She must be out of her mind."

Miriam got up and moved to a corner where a covered bird cage hung from a ceiling chain. She peeked beneath the cover.

"It's a canary," she said. "Would you mind if I woke him? I'd like to hear him sing."

"Leave Tommy alone," said Mrs. Miller, anxiously. "Don't you dare wake him."

"Certainly," said Miriam. "But I don't see why I can't hear him sing." And then, "Have you anything to eat? I'm starving! Even milk and a jam sandwich would be fine."

"Look," said Mrs. Miller, arising from the hassock, "look—if I make some nice sandwiches will you be a good child and run along home? It's past midnight, I'm sure."

"It's snowing," reproached Miriam. "And cold and dark."

"Well, you shouldn't have come here to begin with," said Mrs. Miller, struggling to control her voice. "I can't help the weather. If you want anything to eat you'll have to promise to leave."

Miriam brushed a braid against her cheek. Her eyes were thoughtful, as if weighing the proposition. She turned toward the bird cage. "Very well," she said, "I promise."

How old is she? Ten? Eleven? Mrs. Miller, in the kitchen, unsealed a jar of strawberry preserves and cut four slices of bread. She poured a glass of milk and paused to light a cigarette. *And why has she come?* Her hand shook as she held the match, fascinated, till it burned her finger. The canary was singing; singing as he did in the morning and at no other time. "Miriam," she called, "Miriam, I told you not to disturb Tommy." There was no answer. She called again; all she heard was the canary. She inhaled the cigarette and discovered she had lighted the cork-tip end and—oh, really, she mustn't lose her temper.

She carried the food in on a tray and set it on the coffee table. She saw first that the bird cage still wore its night cover. And Tommy was singing. It gave her a queer sensation. And no one was in the room. Mrs. Miller went through an alcove leading to her bedroom; at the door she caught her breath.

"What are you doing?" she asked.

Miriam glanced up and in her eyes there was a look that was not ordinary. She was standing by the bureau, a jewel case opened before her. For a minute she studied Mrs. Miller, forcing their eyes to meet, and she smiled. "There's nothing good here," she said. "But I like this." Her hand held a cameo brooch. "It's charming."

"Suppose—perhaps you'd better put it back," said Mrs. Miller, feeling suddenly the need of some support. She leaned against the door frame; her head was unbearably heavy; a pressure weighted the rhythm of her heartbeat. The light seemed to flutter defectively. "Please, child—a gift from my husband . . ."

"But it's beautiful and I want it," said Miriam. "*Give it to me.*"

As she stood, striving to shape a sentence which would somehow save the brooch, it came to Mrs. Miller there was no one to whom she might turn; she was alone; a fact that had not been among her thoughts for a long time. Its sheer emphasis was stunning. But here in her own room in the hushed snow-city were evidences she could not ignore or, she knew with startling clarity, resist.

Miriam ate ravenously, and when the sandwiches and milk were gone, her fingers made cobweb movements over the plate, gathering crumbs. The cameo gleamed on her blouse, the blonde profile like a trick reflection of its wearer. "That was very nice," she sighed, "though now an almond cake or a cherry would be ideal. Sweets are lovely, don't you think?"

Mrs. Miller was perched precariously on the hassock, smoking a cigarette. Her hair net had slipped lopsided and loose strands straggled down her face. Her eyes were stupidly concentrated on nothing and her cheeks were mottled in red patches, as though a fierce slap had left permanent marks.

"Is there a candy—a cake?"

Mrs. Miller tapped ash on the rug. Her head swayed slightly as she tried to focus her eyes. "You promised to leave if I made the sandwiches," she said.

"Dear me, did I?"

"It was a promise and I'm tired and I don't feel well at all."

"Mustn't fret," said Miriam. "I'm only teasing."

She picked up her coat, slung it over her arm, and arranged her beret in front of a mirror. Presently she bent close to Mrs. Miller and whispered, "Kiss me good night."

"Please—I'd rather not," said Mrs. Miller.

Miriam lifted a shoulder, arched an eyebrow. "As you like," she said, and went directly to the coffee table, seized the vase containing the paper roses, carried it to where the hard surface

of the floor lay bare, and hurled it downward. Glass sprayed in
all directions and she stamped her foot on the bouquet.

Then slowly she walked to the door, but before closing it she
looked back at Mrs. Miller with a slyly innocent curiosity.

Mrs. Miller spent the next day in bed, rising once to feed
the canary and drink a cup of tea; she took her temperature
and had none, yet her dreams were feverishly agitated; their
unbalanced mood lingered even as she lay staring wide-eyed at
the ceiling. One dream threaded through the others like an
elusively mysterious theme in a complicated symphony, and
the scenes it depicted sharply outlined, as though sketched by
a hand of gifted intensity: a small girl, wearing a bridal gown
and a wreath of leaves, led a gray procession down a mountain
path, and among them there was unusual silence till a woman
at the rear asked, "Where is she taking us?" "No one knows,"
said an old man marching in front. "But isn't she pretty?"
volunteered a third voice. "Isn't she like a frost flower . . . so
shining and white?"

Tuesday morning she woke up feeling better; harsh slats of
sunlight, slanting through Venetian blinds, shed a disrupting
light on her unwholesome fancies. She opened the window to
discover a thawed, mild-as-spring day; a sweep of clean new
clouds crumpled against a vastly blue, out-of-season sky; and
across the low line of rooftops she could see the river and
smoke curving from tugboat stacks in a warm wind. A great
silver truck plowed the snow-banked street, its machine sound
humming on the air.

After straightening the apartment, she went to the grocer's,
cashed a check and continued to Schrafft's where she ate breakfast and chatted happily with the waitress. Oh, it was a wonderful day—more like a holiday—and it would be so foolish to
go home.

She boarded a Lexington Avenue bus and rode up to Eighty-
sixth Street; it was here that she had decided to do a little
shopping.

She had no idea what she wanted or needed, but she idled
along, intent only upon the passers-by, brisk and preoccupied,
who gave her a disturbing sense of separateness.

It was while waiting at the corner of Third Avenue that she
saw the man: an old man, bowlegged and stooped under an

armload of bulging packages; he wore a shabby brown coat and a checkered cap. Suddenly she realized they were exchanging a smile: there was nothing friendly about this smile, it was merely two cold flickers of recognition. But she was certain she had never seen him before.

He was standing next to an El pillar, and as she crossed the street he turned and followed. He kept quite close; from the corner of her eye she watched his reflection wavering on the shopwindows.

Then in the middle of the block she stopped and faced him. He stopped also and cocked his head, grinning. But what could she say? Do? Here, in broad daylight, on Eighty-sixth Street? It was useless and, despising her own helplessness, she quickened her steps.

Now Second Avenue is a dismal street, made from scraps and ends; part cobblestone, part asphalt, part cement; and its atmosphere of desertion is permanent. Mrs. Miller walked five blocks without meeting anyone, and all the while the steady crunch of his footfalls in the snow stayed near. And when she came to a florist's shop, the sound was still with her. She hurried inside and watched through the glass door as the old man passed; he kept his eyes straight ahead and didn't slow his pace, but he did one strange, telling thing: he tipped his cap.

"Six white ones, did you say?" asked the florist. "Yes," she told him, "white roses." From there she went to a glassware store and selected a vase, presumably a replacement for the one Miriam had broken, though the price was intolerable and the vase itself (she thought) grotesquely vulgar. But a series of unaccountable purchases had begun, as if by prearranged plan: a plan of which she had not the least knowledge or control.

She bought a bag of glazed cherries, and at a place called the Knickerbocker Bakery she paid forty cents for six almond cakes.

Within the last hour the weather had turned cold again; like blurred lenses, winter clouds cast a shade over the sun, and the skeleton of an early dusk colored the sky; a damp mist mixed with the wind and the voices of a few children who romped high on mountains of gutter snow seemed lonely and cheerless. Soon the first flake fell, and when Mrs. Miller reached the brownstone house, snow was falling in a swift screen and foot tracks vanished as they were printed.

*   *   *

The white roses were arranged decoratively in the vase. The glazed cherries shone on a ceramic plate. The almond cakes, dusted with sugar, awaited a hand. The canary fluttered on its swing and picked at a bar of seed.

At precisely five the doorbell rang. Mrs. Miller *knew* who it was. The hem of her housecoat trailed as she crossed the floor. "Is that you?" she called.

"Naturally," said Miriam, the word resounding shrilly from the hall. "Open this door."

"Go away," said Mrs. Miller.

"Please hurry . . . I have a heavy package."

"Go away," said Mrs. Miller. She returned to the living room, lighted a cigarette, sat down and calmly listened to the buzzer; on and on and on. "You might as well leave. I have no intention of letting you in."

Shortly the bell stopped. For possibly ten minutes Mrs. Miller did not move. Then, hearing no sound, she concluded Miriam had gone. She tiptoed to the door and opened it a sliver; Miriam was half-reclining atop a cardboard box with a beautiful French doll cradled in her arms.

"Really, I thought you were never coming," she said peevishly. "Here, help me get this in, it's awfully heavy."

It was not spell-like compulsion that Mrs. Miller felt, but rather a curious passivity; she brought in the box, Miriam the doll. Miriam curled up on the sofa, not troubling to remove her coat or beret, and watched disinterestedly as Mrs. Miller dropped the box and stood trembling, trying to catch her breath.

"Thank you," she said. In the daylight she looked pinched and drawn, her hair less luminous. The French doll she was loving wore an exquisite powdered wig and its idiot glass eyes sought solace in Miriam's. "I have a surprise," she continued. "Look into my box."

Kneeling, Mrs. Miller parted the flaps and lifted out another doll; then a blue dress which she recalled as the one Miriam had worn that first night at the theater; and of the remainder she said, "It's all clothes. Why?"

"Because I've come to live with you," said Miriam, twisting a cherry stem. "Wasn't it nice of you to buy me the cherries . . . ?"

"But you can't! For God's sake go away—go away and leave me alone!"

". . . and the roses and the almond cakes? How really wonderfully generous. You know, these cherries are delicious. The last place I lived was with an old man; he was terribly poor and we never had good things to eat. But I think I'll be happy here." She paused to snuggle her doll closer. "Now, if you'll just show me where to put my things . . ."

Mrs. Miller's face dissolved into a mask of ugly red lines; she began to cry, and it was an unnatural, tearless sort of weeping, as though, not having wept for a long time, she had forgotten how. Carefully she edged backward till she touched the door.

She fumbled through the hall and down the stairs to a landing below. She pounded frantically on the door of the first apartment she came to; a short, redheaded man answered and she pushed past him. "Say, what the hell is this?" he said. "Anything wrong, lover?" asked a young woman who appeared from the kitchen, drying her hands. And it was to her that Mrs. Miller turned.

"Listen," she cried, "I'm ashamed behaving this way but— well, I'm Mrs. H. T. Miller and I live upstairs and . . ." She pressed her hands over her face. "It sounds so absurd. . . ."

The woman guided her to a chair, while the man excitedly rattled pocket change. "Yeah?"

"I live upstairs and there's a little girl visiting me, and I suppose that I'm afraid of her. She won't leave and I can't make her and—she's going to do something terrible. She's already stolen my cameo, but she's about to do something worse— something terrible!"

The man asked, "Is she a relative, huh?"

Mrs. Miller shook her head. "I don't know who she is. Her name's Miriam, but I don't know for certain who she is."

"You gotta calm down, honey," said the woman, stroking Mrs. Miller's arm. "Harry here'll tend to this kid. Go on, lover." And Mrs. Miller said, "The door's open—5A."

After the man left, the woman brought a towel and bathed Mrs. Miller's face. "You're very kind," Mrs. Miller said. "I'm sorry to act like such a fool, only this wicked child. . . ."

"Sure, honey," consoled the woman. "Now, you better take it easy."

Mrs. Miller rested her head in the crook of her arm; she was quiet enough to be asleep. The woman turned a radio dial; a piano and a husky voice filled the silence and the woman, tapping her foot, kept excellent time. "Maybe we oughta go up too," she said.

"I don't want to see her again. I don't want to be anywhere near her."

"Uh huh, but what you shoulda done, you shoulda called a cop."

Presently they heard the man on the stairs. He strode into the room frowning and scratching the back of his neck. "Nobody there," he said, honestly embarrassed. "She musta beat it."

"Harry, you're a jerk," announced the woman. "We been sitting here the whole time and we woulda seen . . ." she stopped abruptly, for the man's glance was sharp.

"I looked all over," he said, "and there just ain't nobody there. Nobody, understand?"

"Tell me," said Mrs. Miller, rising, "tell me, did you see a large box? Or a doll?"

"No, ma'am, I didn't."

And the woman, as if delivering a verdict, said, "Well, for cryinoutloud. . . ."

Mrs. Miller entered her apartment softly; she walked to the center of the room and stood quite still. No, in a sense it had not changed: the roses, the cakes, and the cherries were in place. But this was an empty room, emptier than if the furnishings and familiars were not present, lifeless and petrified as a funeral parlor. The sofa loomed before her with a new strangeness: its vacancy had a meaning that would have been less penetrating and terrible had Miriam been curled on it. She gazed fixedly at the space where she remembered setting the box and, for a moment, the hassock spun desperately. And she looked through the window; surely the river was real, surely snow was falling—but then, one could not be certain witness to anything: Miriam, so vividly *there*—and yet, where was she? Where, where?

As though moving in a dream, she sank to a chair. The room was losing shape; it was dark and getting darker and there was nothing to be done about it; she could not lift her hand to light a lamp.

Suddenly, closing her eyes, she felt an upward surge, like a diver emerging from some deeper, greener depth. In times of terror or immense distress, there are moments when the mind waits, as though for a revelation, while a skein of calm is woven over thought; it is like a sleep, or a supernatural trance; and during this lull one is aware of a force of quiet reasoning: well, what if she had never really known a girl named Miriam? that she had been foolishly frightened on the street? In the end, like everything else, it was of no importance. For the only thing she had lost to Miriam was her identity, but now she knew she had found again the person who lived in this room, who cooked her own meals, who owned a canary, who was someone she could trust and believe in: Mrs. H. T. Miller.

Listening in contentment, she became aware of a double sound: a bureau drawer opening and closing; she seemed to hear it long after completion—opening and closing. Then gradually, the harshness of it was replaced by the murmur of a silk dress and this, delicately faint, was moving nearer and swelling in intensity till the walls trembled with the vibration and the room was caving under a wave of whispers. Mrs. Miller stiffened and opened her eyes to a dull, direct stare.

"Hello," said Miriam.

NOTES ON THE AUTHORS

GERTRUDE ATHERTON (1957–1948) was an American novelist who wrote chiefly of life in California. Her best books include *The Californians* (1898), *Rezanov* (1906), *Black Oxen* (1923), *The Jealous Gods* (1928), and *The Sophisticates* (1931). Her 1902 novel, *The Conqueror*, was a biographical novel of Alexander Hamilton. Gertrude Atherton was an early Feminist and her works reflect her strong belief in the independence of women.

LOUIS AUCHINCLOSS (b. 1917), in addition to writing thirty-one works of fiction and eleven of non-fiction, led a distinguished career with a Wall Street law firm for forty-five years. He is also President of the Museum of the City of New York, and a member of the National Institute of Arts and Letters. Some of his best short fiction is collected in *Tales of Manhattan* and *Skinny Island: More Tales of Manhattan*. His novel *The Rector of Justin* is a multi-faceted study of the founding headmaster of an Episcopalian boys' school in New England and is perhaps his masterpiece.

ELIZABETH BOWEN (1899–1973) was the only child of Protestant Anglo-Irish parents. She grew up in Dublin and in Cork, and at the age of seven was taken to England for schooling. She began to write when she was twenty and had her first volume of stories, *Encounters*, published in 1923. During a writing career that lasted another fifty years, she produced more volumes of short stories and many novels, including the modern classics *The House in Paris* (1935) and *The Death of the Heart* (1938). While fantasy played no part in her nine novels, it is an important element in many of her best stories.

367

GEORGE MACKAY BROWN was born in the Orkney Islands, a region of mixed Norse and Gaelic tradition, in 1921. All his books—fiction and poetry alike—have a mythic, even an eddic, dimension. He was at Newbattle Abbey College when Edwin Muir was Warden. He read English at Edinburgh University and afterwards did postgraduate work on Gerard Manley Hopkins. His works include three novels, *Greenvoe, Magnus,* and *Time in a Red Coat;* five collections of short stories; and five collections of poems. He lives and works in Orkney.

TRUMAN CAPOTE (1924–1984) was a native of New Orleans. His first novel, *Other Voices, Other Rooms* (1948), was an international literary success. He twice won the O. Henry Memorial Short Story Prize, and was a member of the National Institute of Arts and Letters. His other books included the "non-fiction novel" *In Cold Blood,* the travel books *Local Color* and *The Muses Are Heard,* two plays, *The Grass Harp* and *House of Flowers,* and two screenplays, *The Innocents* and *Beat the Devil.*

WALTER DE LA MARE (1873–1956) was a noted poet, novelist, short story writer, and anthologist. His 1922 novel, *Memoirs of a Midget,* is as fresh and alive today as the year it was penned. De la Mare also wrote a number of superb ghost stories, among them *Miss Duveen, The Three Friends,* and *The Green World.* G. K. Chesterton compared the suffocating vividness of *Seaton's Aunt* with that of *The Turn of the Screw.*

Edward Morgan FORSTER, better known as E. M. Forster, was born in 1879 of mixed English and Welsh ancestry. He was educated at Tonbridge School and King's College, Cambridge, of which he was for a time a Fellow. His best-known books are his novels *A Room with a View, The Longest Journey, Where Angels Fear to Tread, Howard's End,* and *A Passage to India.* His stories were published in two volumes, *The Celestial Omnibus* and *The Eternal Moment.* A *Collected Tales,* gathering both books, appeared in 1946. In 1953 he was awarded membership in the Order of Companions of Honour by Queen Elizabeth II. On his ninetieth birthday, in 1969, he received the Order of Merit. He died in Coventry, England, in 1970.

MAVIS GALLANT (b. 1922) is a Canadian novelist and short story writer. Her books include *The Other Paris; Green Water, Green Sky; My Heart Is Broken;* and *From the Fifteenth District.* She has said that most writers emerge from a "solitary childhood" ridden with the "shocks of violent change". She lives in Paris, and her work appears frequently in *The New Yorker*.

CHARLOTTE PERKINS GILMAN (1860–1935) produced one authentic literary masterpiece, *The Yellow Wallpaper*, which she published in 1892 in *The New England Magazine*. Most of her energy was devoted to Feminist endeavors. She produced a body of works on the social and economic situation of women, particularly *Women and Economics* (1898). Much of her work, including novels, stories, and poems, is of interest to anyone studying the development of Feminism in America.

WILLIAM GOYEN (1915–1983) burst upon the literary scene with *The House of Breath* (1950), which received the MacMurray Award for the best first novel by a Texan and was nominated for the first National Book Award in Fiction. Subsequently he published four more novels and four story collections, a non-fiction life of Jesus, a book of poems, and had five plays produced. His fiction, blending the colloquial cadences of the Southwest with uniquely refined lyricism, is also full of spirits and ghosts.

GRAHAM GREENE (b. 1904) is known both as an English novelist of suspense (*This Gun for Hire*, 1936; *Brighton Rock*, 1938) and as a chronicler of good and evil, of faith and its enemies (*The Heart of the Matter*, 1948; *A Burnt-Out Case*, 1960). He was born in Berkhampstead, Hertfordshire, and received his education at Berkhampstead School and Balliol College, Oxford. For years he was an editorial associate of the Bodley Head, London. His name frequently is raised as a contender for the Nobel Prize in Literature—an honor which has so far eluded him.

SHIRLEY JACKSON (1919–1965) was born in San Francisco and spent the early part of her life in California. She attended Syracuse University where she met the literary critic Stanley Edgar Hyman, whom she married. They lived most of their lives in North Bennington, Vermont. Jackson achieved fame in 1948 with the publication of the intellectual horror story, *The Lottery*, in the pages of *The New Yorker*. It became an American classic. She produced six novels, two collections of short stories, a children's book, a non-fiction study of witchcraft, and two non-fiction books about her family.

HENRY JAMES (1843–1916), the American novelist, is called "The Master" by many for his contributions to the history of the novel form. His works are celebrated for their psychological penetration and detailed analysis, their subtlety and intricacy of style, and their authorial detachment. Throughout his long career, James frequently used the supernatural for purposes of psychological symbolism, as in *The Turn of the Screw* (1898). Among his greatest achievements are *The Portrait of a Lady* (1881), *The Aspern Papers* (1888), *The Wings of the Dove* (1902), *The Ambassadors* (1903), and *The Golden Bowl* (1904). In 1915 he naturalized as a British citizen. In 1988 a commemorative stone was placed in Poets' Corner of the Cathedral of St. John the Divine, in New York.

BARRY N. MALZBERG was born in New York and graduated from Syracuse University. He is the author of more than fifty novels and two hundred short stories. Surrounded by controversy from the outset of his career, he published between 1969 and 1975 more than any science fiction writer had in an equivalent period of time since the American inception of the genre. He was awarded the John W. Campbell Memorial Prize for his novel *Beyond Apollo*. He lives in Teaneck, New Jersey.

JOYCE CAROL OATES (b. 1938) is a graduate of Syracuse University and lives in Princeton, New Jersey, where she is on the faculty of Princeton University. Her works include four collections of essays, a non-fiction study of boxing, nineteen novels, thirteen collections of short stories, six collections of poems, three plays, and a children's book. She also has written screenplays from her own novels. She received the National Book Award for the novel, *Them*. She is a member of the American Institute of Arts and Letters.

JEAN RHYS (1894–1979) was born in the Windward Islands, the daughter of a Welsh doctor and a Creole mother. She moved to England at the age of sixteen, and spent the First World War there. Her first book a volume of short stories, *The Left Bank*, was published in 1927. It was followed by four novels, which enjoyed a modest audience. It was not until 1966, with publication of her novel *Wide Sargasso Sea*, that she achieved critical and popular acclaim. Her early books have since been "rediscovered."

HOWARD LEWIS RUSSELL (b. 1962) is a graduate of the University of Alabama, where he majored in English. He is the author of two exhuberant novels, *Rush to Nowhere* (1988) and *Iced Tea and Ignorance* (1989). He works in the creative department of a prominant New York City advertising agency and lives in Manhattan. *The Wedding Cake Couple* is previously unpublished.

LYNNE SHARON SCHWARTZ (b. 1939) is one of the rising stars of American fiction. She is the author of five novels and two collections of stories, *Acquainted with the Night* (1984) and *The Melting Pot and Other Subversive Stories* (1987). Most of her short fiction is about relatively normal, civilized people, each of whose shielded life is suddenly pierced—often by what they most secretly fear. She lives in Manhattan.

MURIEL SPARK has published eighteen novels, including *A Far Cry from Kensington* (1988). She is also author of a play, three volumes of criticism and biography, three volumes of poetry, a book for children, and five collections of short stories. She was elected an honorary member of the American Academy and Institute of Arts and Letters in 1978. She lives in Rome.

ELIZABETH SPENCER (b. 1921) is a recognized master of the short story form. Her stories have received O. Henry Prizes, a Pushcart Prize, and the Award of Merit for the Short Story, given by the American Academy of Arts and Letters. Her other prizes include the Rosenthal award, a Guggenheim Fellowship, and a Senior Fellowship from the National Endowment of the Arts. She is a member of the American Institute of Arts and Letters. Perhaps her best-known work is the novel, *The Light in the Piazza*. Elizabeth Spencer lives in Chapel Hill, North Carolina.

PETER TAYLOR (b. 1912) was born in Trenton, Tennessee, and has spent most of his life in the South and the Middle West. His fellowships and awards include a Fulbright Grant, first prize in the 1959 O. Henry Memorial Awards (for *Venus, Cupid, Folly and Time*), and a Pulitzer Prize. He is the author of nine collections of stories, two novels (*A Woman of Means* and *A Summon to Memphis*), and a volume of seven "dramatic pieces," *Presences* (1973) which is full of fantasies and dreams. Joyce Carol Oates called his *Collected Stories* "one of the major works of our literature."

DYLAN THOMAS (1914–1953), the English lyric poet born in Wales, was so celebrated for his poetry that his very distinctive prose has been overlooked. Written in a highly "poetic" style, and combining surrealism with elements of traditional Celtic fantasy, his short stories conjure up bizarre and unforgettable experiences. His prose works include *Adventures in the Skin Trade and Other Stories, Portrait of the Artist as a Young Dog,* and *Quite Early One Morning.* In 1984 *The Collected Stories* was met with critical acclaim and brisk sales.

JOHN UPDIKE was born in Shillington, Pennsylvania, in 1932, and graduated from Harvard University in 1954. While best known for his novels *Rabbit, Run; Rabbit Redux;* and *Rabbit is Rich,* Mr. Updike has published ten collections of short stories of the highest distinction, the most recent of which is *Trust Me* (1987). Of that work, the New York *Times* cited his "dazzling variety of perception to which his restless and inquisitive imagination transports him, as well as his uncanny ability to make a reader . . . feel as if his mind has been read and his own experience intuited."

DENTON WELCH was born to English parents in Shanghai in 1915 and educated in England. He intended to become a painter, but a collision between his bicycle and an automobile caused spinal injuries from which he never recovered. He instead began to write, and was one of the most gifted writers to emerge in post-World War II Britain. His oeuvre includes four novels, two collections of stories, a book of poems, and his *Journals. The Stories of Denton Welch* were published in one volume in this country in 1985. He died in 1948 at the age of 33.

EDITH WHARTON (1862–1937) is best remembered for her studies of the tragedies and ironies in the lives of members of the middle and upper-class New York society in the 19th-century. Like the work of Henry James and Gustave Flaubert, her novels are characterized by deep psychological characterization, a preoccupation with moral dilemmas and strict adherence to artistic form. Her best-known works are *The House of Mirth* (1905), *Ethan Frome* (1911), *The Custom of the Country* (1913), and *The Age of Innocence* (1920), for which she was awarded the 1921 Pulitzer Prize.

TENNESSEE WILLIAMS (1911–1983) has exerted a strong continued influence on the growth of American drama since the first production of *The Glass Menagerie* in 1944. He produced more than two-dozen full-length plays. His poetry and prose are less known, though he published two volumes of poems, five volumes of stories, two novels and a prose autobiography. He made his home in New York and Key West.

VIRGINIA WOOLF (1882–1941) with the publication of *Jacob's Room* in 1922, became accepted as an avant garde novelist of extraordinary gifts. Her essays, collected in the two *Common Readers* and *The Death of the Moth,* as well as in subsequent collected editions, reveal her erudition and critical prowess.

Her short stories are less well known. *Monday or Tuesday* (1921) was the only book of stories which appeared in her lifetime. After her death in 1941, her husband, Leonard Woolf edited and published *A Haunted House and Other Short Stories*, which made available her shorter works of fiction. *The Complete Shorter Fiction of Virginia Woolf* was published in this country in 1985.

A NOTE ON THE EDITOR

ROBERT PHILLIPS (b. 1938) is an American poet, fiction writer, critic, biographer, and anthologist. His awards include a CAPS Grant, a Pushcart Prize, fellowships from Yaddo, the Djerassi Foundation, and the MacDowell Colony, the Arents Pioneer Medal from Syracuse University, and an Award in Literature from the American Academy and Institute of Arts and Letters. He lives in Katonah, Westchester County, New York, with his wife and son.